THE LOST MUMMY

PEGGY GARDNER

ISBNs:
Paperback: 978-1-64184-855-8
Ebook: 978-1-64184-856-5

DEDICATION

The stories of Johab, a young half-American and half-Egyptian boy, whose playground is the tomb of an ancient queen, provided hours of entertainment for my nephews, John Walter Cox and Darren William Cox. As they were growing up in Hong Kong and Singapore, the Johab stories became our special connection.

This book is dedicated to them, my children, my nieces and nephews, and all children and grownups who love stories that transport them to other lands and other cultures, especially those thousands of years in the past that remain right over our heads in the night sky and with the rising of the sun.

CHAPTER 1

DECEMBER 6, 1972

Where is Ahemait, the crocodile god, when you need him?

—Johab Bennett, age 11

The great Egyptian Goddess Nut arched across the night sky in Cairo with her hands on the one side of the planet and her feet on the other. At dusk, she had just swallowed the sun and moon, and the stars were twinkling in her belly overhead.

From his forbidden perch on the balcony rail, three stories high, Johab Bennett waved a little nightly salute to Nut, hearing his mother's voice in his head: "That's nonsense, Johab. The earth orbits the sun; the moon orbits the earth, as the Lord decreed." Then she'd turn a pleading face to his father: "John, you are filling Johab's head full of those old Egyptian myths. He's confused. My priest will sort him."

Not likely. Those Bible stories in his mother's Coptic Christian church didn't hold a candle to his father's stories. As the lead Egyptologist for the New Kingdom Project, Johab's American father left their old priest in the dust when it came to telling stories about ancient times. You wouldn't find old mummies of Abraham or King Solomon lying around. Those ancient people didn't know squat about how to preserve a body. The Egyptians were masters at it.

Just as a smug expression appeared on his face, so did streams of tears. His father didn't trust him anymore; he had to hide out here on their apartment's balcony to blubber like a baby or check out the ghosts.

Tonight, the ghosts of Cairo tucked their spidery webs about themselves, shifting in and out of the thick smoke of charcoal fires that smothered the city with no *khamsin* in December, these south-westerly winds that blew the ghosts away in the spring. Johab blew his nose on his sleeve and then did it again just to irritate someone. Somewhere—too far away to be imagined—the old crocodile god Ahemait sat just inside the gate of the underworld, the *Duat,* waiting to eat human hearts.

Just the bad ones. The people who didn't do what they were sup-posed to do in this world. Maybe use a handkerchief for a snotty nose instead of a sleeve. Johab shivered with a kind of delicious dread as he imagined the gods of Egypt making their nightly journey through blood drinkers and evil spirits that guarded the gates so they could be reborn with the sun.

In the distance, Cairo's night lights twinkled like Christmas, less than three weeks away. Johab fought back tears again. Not being trusted was one thing, but just this afternoon, his father had threat-ened to send him, his sister Jasmine, and his mother to his grandpar-ents in Michigan where they celebrate only one Christmas—not two.

How could his funny, kind father, his very best friend, send his family to America at Christmas? Johab scowled into the night, thinking about how strange his father had acted this afternoon on the trip back from Queen Hatshepsut's temple in the Valley of the Kings. His father never made threats or rash decisions. Today, he had done both.

Just before they reached the outskirts of Cairo at dusk, his father yanked the jeep to the side of the highway, pulled a small leather pouch out of his jacket pocket, and dangled it as though it were full of desert scorpions. "What's in here is dangerous, Johab. I can't tell you anything. You, your sister, and mother must go to a safe place. I've decided. You'll be spending Christmas with your grandparents. Not another word. I'll talk to your mother later."

From the grim expression on his father's face, Johab didn't dare ask any questions, so he did what his father called "pulling a face," and pouted the rest of the way home. Swinging open the front door, he brushed past his little sister Jasmine and stomped outside to sulk on the balcony. Maybe he'd fall and break his leg so his father would be sorry.

Johab swung a leg down from the ornamental rail and kicked at an aging hunk of concrete. Just one more nudge would send it crashing down to the sidewalk below. Barely hanging on with one hand, Johab leaned so far over the rail that his mother would scream in fright. If he timed it just as Rati, the grouchy old doorman, moved under the ledge to light another cigarette, that block of concrete would squash him like a piece of flatbread.

Johab cautiously eased his foot back, imagining a chalk outline of Rati's body, his yellowed fingers holding onto that last, hand-rolled cigarette. The police could trace the crime easily. All they had to do was look up and dust the balcony for his fingerprints and footprints. Then, the police might cut off Johab's head, or put him in a sack and throw him in the Nile River. That's what the ancient people used to do. Even though he was a normal sized eleven-year-old, Johab was small enough to fit nicely into a grain sack.

To get himself into the not-thinking-about Christmas mood, Johab turned his mind to his favorite things—Egyptian mummies. His father had told him everything about the ancient Egyptians, even gory things like scooping out organs from the dead, slurping out their brains through their nostrils, and pickling their bodies so that they lasted forever.

Actually, it was his cousin Mohammed who said "scooping, slurping, pickling." Johab's father spent most of his waking hours three thousand years in the past and would never speak disrespectfully of the embalming practices of an ancient people he admired.

Johab frowned down at the spark of a cigarette that meant Rati was just three stories down, at the edge of the balcony. He edged his toe against the concrete chunk, pushing it firmly against the wall. "Fraidy cat," Johab whispered to himself, glad that his cousin wasn't here to push the block over and blame it on him. Self-righteousness replaced the pout on Johab's face.

Cousin Mohammed was jealous of him for three reasons: Johab had gone with his father on field trips and to his office in the Egyptian Museum for as long as he could remember; Mohammed's father, Tarek, worked as a guard at the Museum, wore a gun, and rarely paid attention to Mohammed except with his belt; and, there was the Christmas thing.

As an American, Johab's father celebrated on December 25th and Johab's mother, a Coptic Christian, celebrated on January 7th. Two Christmases. Two rounds of gifts. Even though Mohammed's family was always included, it wasn't the same for his cousin.

It might not be the same for Johab if his father carried out his threat to send them to a cold place like Michigan. Johab shivered in the night air as though those ghosts had slipped through the balcony rails. He sucked in his stomach and pushed out his chest. Johab was named after the great general and pharaoh Horemheb. He should be braver, even with a nickname, one he chose for himself.

His mother loved repeating the story. "You weren't even two years old when you banged on the dinner table with a very red face and shouted: "I be Johab! Don't say other name!" Half of the boys in his class were called Mohammed or Youssef. Johab liked the nickname he had chosen, and Horemheb, the important real name of a famous ancient Egyptian that his father had given him.

Johab's father told him that long-ago Egyptians carved their names on stones or pieces of gold that they wore so that when they died, their spirit, their "ka," could find them. So, on almost every trip to the desert, Johab and his father sat around the campfire, carving their names into a soft stone—side by side **Johab -- John.**

Johab dug at his eyes, forcing back tears. His father shared everything with him. That's why he called Johab his "ka," his double, a kind of soul, more than just his son and a partner in his work. The hieroglyph, the written symbol for *ka* was a set of shoulders with two raised arms, just like the referees use for a touchdown in American football. Those raised arms were his and his father's secret sign for good things.

Johab wiped his face with dirty hands to disguise those icky tears streaming down his cheeks. Nothing good was happening now. Christmas wouldn't be Christmas in the state of Michigan, even though he was half American. Even worse, his father had treated him like a child today, a child who couldn't be trusted with a secret in some dumb little pouch.

A blast of sand out of the desert whipped along the street below, stirring a dark bag of trash, moving it slowly into life, the way that Ahemait the crocodile god creeps from the Nile to wait for the judgment of human hearts, hungry for the evil ones. The weak streetlights below made spooks out of garbage bags.

Johab squinted down at the pile of trash, fighting the fear that had tugged at the edge of his consciousness. That fear didn't begin when his father showed him that pouch. It was on his father's face this morning when he perched on the bay of cliffs to sketch Queen Hatshepsut's Temple from a different angle. "She's not there. Never was. Different place. He hid the map. That's it. Her sarcophagus was a ruse."

His father flushed as though he hadn't meant to be overheard. He shoved his sketchbook into his battered leather case. "Out of here, Johab. Sorry. We need to get back. I have to work on a problem."

Johab's father had promised a two-night campout in the desert and a dig in the ancient village of the tomb workers. They had arrived late the evening before, too late for hot dogs on an open fire. They had eaten the pita bread, humus and olives packed by Johab's mother—her idea of a picnic. Now they were going home. It wasn't even noon. It was time to whine.

"You promised we would stay another night. You said we'd dig around in that old village. You never break a promise, Dad. Never."

Whining didn't work. Johab's father, who always told him everything about his work, was silent during those miles back to Cairo until they reached the outer city at sunset.

That's when his father pulled over on the verge, jabbed his hand into the lining of his field jacket, and dangled that small pouch in front of Johab. The expression on his father's face so frightened him that Johab could still repeat every word: "I'm telling you about this *thing* with the understanding that you never, ever speak of it to anyone except Ian Parks."

Johab nodded, wide-eyed, feeling a bit comforted because his father had mentioned his best friend, an archaeologist at the British Museum, who was Johab's own godfather. The pouch had swung between his father's thumb and forefinger like a tiny pendulum, Edgar Allen Poe's pendulum, but smaller. *Just as deadly* thought Johab as he scooted against the passenger door. His father's face had remained unreadable.

"This pouch will be hidden in the lining of my field jacket. If anything should happen." He dropped his face in his hands with a stifled cry. "Good God. What am I saying? I just need to need to get you, your mother and Jasmine away before . . ." His voice trailed off as he slammed the truck into gear.

"Before what? Before what?" Johab's voice sounded squeaky, like that of a small child, not his father's partner.

"No more questions, Johab. I need to think. Ian is the only person I can trust." That abrupt statement caused Johab's heart to hurt. He remembered that the ancient priests who embalmed the dead put the lungs, liver, stomach and intestines in sealed Canopic jars. The heart, where the soul lived, was left in the body to be weighed against the goddess Maat's feather. If Johab didn't have a trustworthy heart, Ahemait's big crocodile teeth would be waiting for it.

Johab flinched as an arm shot out to snatch him away from the balcony railing.

"You're jumpy tonight. I didn't mean to scare you this afternoon, son." John Bennett looped his arm around Johab, pulling him close and gazing out over the city. "I know that I hurt your feelings and made you angry. I never want to do that."

Johab's eyes widened with pleasure as he tucked himself against his tall lean father. His father always seemed to know what he was thinking.

"There are . . . difficulties . . . on the Project." His father's voice had a pained undertone. "I need to talk to Ian, but he's somewhere out in the field. I'll have to find him. You, your mother and Jasmine will be safe at your grandparents in Michigan."

"But I don't want to go at Christmas." Johab sniffled in the cool night breeze then flashed his most forgiving smile up toward his father's face. "If you could just tell me about that secret pouch thing. What you said you wouldn't. Because I could help. If you would tell me." Johab felt himself lapsing into a stutter as he remembered the sharp tone of his father's voice earlier, telling him never to mention the pouch.

The sudden stiffness of his father's body belied his gentle voice. "You are not easily diverted, Johab. I guess staying on track is the mark of a promising scientist." He ruffled Johab's hair. "Dinner is ready. I haven't mentioned Michigan yet. Your mother made honey cakes tonight. If we don't show some interest in her moussaka, we can kiss the cakes goodbye."

CHAPTER 2

Without daring to mention the word Christmas, Johab watched his father plough through a serving of moussaka and hold out his plate for a second. Johab fidgeted, pushing food from one side of his plate to the other, hoping that travel would shrink that great gob before his mother noticed that he wasn't eating.

His father was strangely silent, but his mother went on and on about her sister Rayya. The stork would be bringing them a new cousin soon. Mohammed's mother was "expecting a little stranger." Johab rolled his eyes and was just about to enlighten his mother with a biology lesson when his four-year-old sister Jasmine had one of her famous sinking spells.

Two little feet in shiny black patent leather shoes flung themselves skyward, flipped the edge of her plate, and drummed against the side of the table as she shouted: "Nasty potatoes. You put beady little meat things all over them!" Mashed potatoes and diced lamb plopped onto the tablecloth.

Johab's jaw dropped. Jasmine would get it this time. He eyed little hunks of greasy meat leaking into his mother's white damask tablecloth. Jasmine rarely got so much as a "no," but this time, she'd pushed the limit. She might get whacked. She didn't. Jasmine's sharp protests of "too early for bed" and his mother's soft murmurs of reassurance echoed down the hall like a two-part song, strangely harmonious.

Johab glanced across the table at his father's bemused smile and felt a sense of relief that he didn't have Uncle Tarek for a father—his wide leather belt permanently creased in the center where it was folded for a double whammy. Johab's parents didn't believe in hitting children. Ever. Even Cousin Mohammed who usually deserved a swat.

He could hear his mother's soft murmurs coming from Jasmine's bedroom. Trying to reason with Jasmine would drive a saint to violence. His mother was a saint. Johab knew exactly how to reward her. Clean plate club. He braced himself, the way he did when his mother got on her cod liver oil kick, opened his mouth, and spooned in enough moussaka to choke an elephant. The cinnamon made him gag, but his mother would feel better if one of her children showed an interest in her cooking.

She did, and dessert was his reward, three cakes, dripping with honey and extra walnuts. A small cup of Turkish coffee slid across the table toward Johab before she could snatch it away.

"John, you know that Johab isn't allowed . . ." A sharp rap at the front door interrupted her. In a flash, she was across the room, twisting the lock, exclaiming, "Who could be calling this late? Rayya's baby isn't due for a month, but she might . . ."

At almost the same instant, as he shoved himself back from the table, his father's chair squealed against the floor like a wounded creature. "Wait! Don't open the . . ." his words stopped in midair.

The lock splintered with a loud crack. Two men charged into the room, their hooded galabeyas hiding faces of thieves in the night. A third man, a tall specter in a black robe, blocked the door, leaned almost casually toward Johab's mother and cracked his fist into her questioning face. She dropped into a silent heap on the floor.

The screech of his father's chair against the wooden floor and dishes crashing off the table were the only sounds in the room. Trapped in his chair by his father's sudden, backward thrust against the table, an image flashed into Johab's mind. He was pinned, like one of those hapless insects on a board, its wings stilled forever. The next image was of how brightly the small line of blood trickled from his mother's mouth across her pale and silent face.

Keeping the table as a barrier between him and two of the men, Johab's father flung his chair toward them, edging his way to the far side of the table toward the china cabinet.

The gun. On top of the tall cabinet, out of the reach of Johab and Jasmine. Johab, frozen for a moment, watched his father shift his weight quickly and shove the table with all his strength against the two men His father was trying to buy time to reach his .38.

Time stopped. Their robes flaring like wings of raptors, the two men slammed against Johab's father, knocking him face down on the floor, wrenching his arms painfully upward behind his back. His legs drummed against the floor, urgent as a hammer drill.

"Where is it?" A cold, calm voice cut through the noise of the scuffling, the words carefully spaced, in the tone of a man who never repeats himself. The hooded man remained on the far side of the room, unmoving, as though he were aloof from the chaos taking place, watching impassively as the thick-set man kneeling on the back of Johab's father twisted his arms slowly and painfully upward as though testing their breaking point.

"Tell me what you found if you want to live." The man nudged the silent, crumpled form of Johab's mother with the toe of his shoe and added cryptically, "If you want your family to live."

A trapped rabbit. Johab knew exactly how it would feel. He couldn't shift so much as an inch in his chair as long as those men had his father anchored against the table leg. His eyes darted from the still outline of his mother to the frantic pumping motions of his father.

Johab stared at the man by the door. The hood of his robe hid his hair and wrapped around the lower part of his face. Under his eyes, his nose jutted out, beaked as the hawked-nose god Horus. His eyes glittered, black as obsidian, reflecting only his prey.

"Hold him still, you fools." The words were Arabic but the accent was not Egyptian. "You, John Bennett, have no time in which to be stupid. One kick and your wife's skull will crack like an egg."

He motioned toward Johab. "My men will throw your son over the balcony like a piece of trash. Give me the information I want. The amulet . . . that fool at the museum should have . . ." The rush of his angry words halted as Johab's father bucked fiercely against the man who seemed intent on pulling his arms from their sockets.

The other man, with a chokehold on his neck, ground the face of Johab's father into the floor as he struggled to speak.

"Release his neck." The tall man's order was reluctantly obeyed by the burly man who rolled to his knees, his hands poised like a hammer ready to fall on the head of Johab's father.

Twisting his face toward the man by the door, Johab's father coughed out a telling word. "You!"

The word meant nothing to Johab. The next words did. "I should have known . . . you don't think I would bring anything valuable to my home. My work stays at the Museum."

The silence that met his father's response provided an opportunity. Johab went slack, his backbone skittering like a disconnected domino train against the hard wooden slats of the chair. Slithering down from the chair and wiggling under the table, he had to act quickly. No way could he reach the gun on top of the china cabinet. *He could reach the thing this man might want.* The pouch was in the lining of his father's field jacket in the hall closet, just across from where his mother was lying as still as a corpse. If he could just reach the closet, grab the jacket, and give them the leather pouch, the men would leave.

"Only tell Ian Parks. Don't tell anyone else about it." The words of his father had been very clear. The pouch contained something "dangerous." Not more dangerous than what was happening to his father. And had already happened to his mother.

Noiselessly, Johab inched toward the hall closet.

Not noiselessly enough.

"You, boy! Stop!" The man kneeling on his father's back shouted in a guttural voice.

Painfully, Johab's father rotated his head toward Johab and gazed directly at his son, narrowing his eyes. Johab had seen that look once before when a cobra slid into their campsite in the Valley of the Kings. Johab froze, just as he had then.

His father struggled to lift his head. "If you'll get these goons off me, I'll go with you to my office. My conditions are that you leave my family alone and get this scum out of my home."

The hawk-nose man ignored Johab's father, stepped toward the hallway table, and yanked the phone cord out of the wall. He looked directly at Johab. "I set the conditions. Boy, you stay here with your mother. Don't leave this apartment. I have people watching it. Don't contact anyone, not the police, not a neighbor. You do that, and you will ensure your father's very painful death. Then, we'll get you and your mother. Stay here. Don't move. You hear me?" It was a question that didn't require a response.

Then, they were gone. There was nothing but the sharp bang of the door and the insatiable noise of horns punctuating the drone of Cairo traffic.

Johab scooted across the floor to his mother, turning her over, and dabbing at the blood on her mouth with his shirttail. She stirred and moaned softly. Her eyes didn't seem to be focusing on him, but her first words did. "Johab, I heard that wicked man's threats." Flat on her back, she peered distractedly around the room. "Where have they gone with John?" She clutched at Johab's arm as though it might be the only lifeline left to her.

"I don't know, Mother. I think to the Museum." He eased his mother into a sitting position. Her mouth was swelling and still bleeding from the blow, but she was struggling to her feet.

"We must call the police! We need help, now . . ." Her voice trailed off into a whimper as she stared at the frazzled wires of the phone dangling from the wall socket.

"No, Mother," Johab whispered. "That man said they would be watching. He said if we call the police, he . . ." Johab sucked in the unspoken words as though saying "kill" and "father" would choke him.

"Let's get out of here. Now!" The shrillness of his voice startled him. All of Johab's survival instincts were focused on getting out of this place as he tugged on his mother's arms.

"We'll go to Rayya's. My sister will know what to do. Your Uncle Tarek can go to the Museum. " Pushing herself to her feet, his mother seemed to be back in control. Except, she wandered aimlessly around the table, picking up shards of broken china.

Aunt Rayya lived twenty minutes away, but Johab was uneasy about going there. She was a "take charge" lady. She'd call the police immediately if she thought her only sister's family were in danger.

His Cousin Mohammed was a worse threat. He would poke his nose into everything. Pry and pry until he got some information that would lead him to more. He couldn't find out about the pouch—that last look from Johab's father had been a grim warning.

"Aunt Rayya can't call the police. We can say that some men came to the apartment, and Dad went with them to the Museum but hasn't come back." Johab looked hopefully up at his mother, crossed the room, opened the closet door and pulled out his father's field jacket.

"How do we explain this?" His mother touched her damaged lip.

"Explain what?" Jasmine's sleepy eyes took in the damage around the room. "Did Johab break the dishes?" A rather hopeful expression appeared in her eyes until she saw her mother's face and burst into tears. "Hurt, hurt, band-aid!"

Jasmine's wails prompted his mother to act. Holding Jasmine with one arm, she grabbed her emergency money from a vase on the china cabinet and stuffed it into her purse. At the same time, Johab pulled on his father's jacket, righted an overturned chair, stood on it, and groped for the gun in the recessed top of the cabinet.

"Johab! What are you doing? Your father never lets you touch his gun. Get down this instant!" Johab's mother was having a hard time sorting her priorities, but Johab knew that the old rule of "don't touch the gun" had just gone out the door with the men who took his father. "Why in the world are you wearing your father's old field jacket?"

Johab plunged his hand into the oversized pocket. A reassuring lump was there. "I think Dad would want me to wear this tonight."

"If it makes you feel better. Come on. Your Uncle Tarek will help sort things out." Johab's mother was clearly not herself. Her brother-in-law's quick temper did not make him a "sorting out" kind of person.

Johab sighed with relief. His diversion with the field jacket had worked. He had slipped the gun unnoticed into the jacket pocket.

The front door was not an option. Someone could be watching from the street. "New game. Be as quiet as a mouse, Jasmine. I'll get you something special if you don't make a single sound until we see Aunt Rayya." Johab led his mother and sister through the kitchen, out the back service entrance, and tiptoed down the creaking stairs of a narrow, steep passageway used mainly for deliveries.

Stepping into the still, black night, Johab took in his first deep breath. The heavy, sweet odor of flowering jasmine mingled with the stench of uncollected garbage, comforting Johab. He knew Cairo alleys. They were familiar places.

CHAPTER 3

Holding up his hand as a silent warning, Johab motioned his mother and Jasmine into the grim space of the alley. Nothing lit this passageway. Piles of garbage lined the narrow lane between rows of apartment complexes. This was the underbelly of Cairo that scavengers knew. Johab and Cousin Mohammed knew it, too. Alleys were more interesting than streets. This was his territory.

"We'll be safer going the back way. This is the way Mohammed and I always go. I don't need a light," Johab whispered to his mother as he boosted a pouting but silent Jasmine up on her back.

Stepping into the pitch-black warmth of the alley, Johab had the strangest sensation of sinking into a vat of molasses, thick, black treacle that his father loved on toast. He shivered, put on a brave face and picked the pace. At this moment, nothing felt safe about these alleys at night. Every twist and turn seemed less and less familiar. Then, like the flattened prow of a beached boat, Aunt Rayya's apartment building reared up beside them.

Before he could stop her, his mother raced around the corner and dashed up two flights of stairs with no concern about being seen from the street. Under the dim entry light, with her elbows jutted out and a sleepy Jasmine bobbing on her back, his mother looked like the white vulture goddess Nekhbet, known as the protector of mothers and children. Johab could almost see her robe of vulture feathers lifting her up one flight and then the next. Her feet seemed to fly. Then one of them kicked the door loudly enough to wake everyone in the complex.

The door swung wide, and Aunt Rayya's very large stomach appeared before she did. That "little stranger" cousin-to-be would soon outweigh Aunt Rayya. "What in the world!" Rayya reached up, twisted her sister's face toward the entryway light, and shouted for all the world hear: "I knew that soft-spoken husband of yours would let you have it one of these days."

Johab's mother shoved his Aunt Rayya aside, set Jasmine down, and pulled Johab tightly against her. "Never! John would never hit me. We've been robbed!"

Johab gasped. Their story had just taken a new turn with his mother's outburst.

"Tarek! Tarek! Get in here now! Call the police!" Rayya was simultaneously clutching Johab's mother, trying to close the door, and struggling to reach the phone.

Rayya shouted orders down the hall at her scowling, sleepy husband as he came out of the bedroom. Johab's Uncle Tarek readjusted his baggy pajama bottoms, hit the wall switch, and blinked as he ambled into the living room. "What the devil is going on here?" His eyes settled on Johab. "You causing trouble, boy?"

Squeezing uncomfortably between his aunt's swollen stomach and the entryway table, Johab smacked his hand down on the phone, holding it firmly in the cradle. "No police, Aunt Rayya. The robbers took Dad to his office. They warned us not to call the police, or they would do something terrible to him."

"Terrible?" Johab's cousin, Mohammed, strolled into the living room, rubbing his eyes and smiling as though he had just been awoken in the middle of an interesting dream. "You have all the luck, Johab. This sounds exciting." Mohammed grinned expectantly at Johab.

"Mohammed, this is not one of your games." Johab's mother spoke sternly to her nephew. "This is a life and death matter. They've taken John!" She burst into sobs.

Startled from his sleepiness by his sister-in-law's outburst, Tarek rammed an arm down the sleeve of his guard's jacket, fumbling with the buttons as he stretched unforgiving fabric across his stomach.

"All of you stay here," he barked. "I'm going to John's office at the Museum. I'll check with the night guard. This is probably a misunderstanding. You know how those archeologists are—all jealous of each other, wanting to be the first to find crappy old stuff."

A sly grin crept across Tarek's face. His audience was not receptive. He glowered down at his son. "Mohammed, make yourself useful. Get your Aunt Soya some tea." The door banged behind him.

Mohammed crooked a finger at Johab, beckoning him toward the kitchen. "I know something else is going on here. I saw Aunt Soya's face. Someone punched her. Tell me what happened. The truth."

Johab couldn't bear to look at Mohammed directly. Mohammed loved to pry, to twist things to his own advantage, to tell the truth only when it was a matter of the truth or his father's belt. Mohammed's wheedling tone grated on Johab's nerves, already raw with fear.

"What did the robbers look like? Did they have guns? What's going on? Why did your father leave you and go with them? We're best friends. Best friends don't keep secrets." Mohammed was fishing for information, always fishing.

Johab stared at Mohammed's moon-shaped face, puffy from sleep. His mouth was skewed into the curved sickle of a sneer, like a waning moon. Johab remained silent.

Aunt Rayya burst through the swinging door. "Mohammed, your aunt needs that tea, now!" She turned on the burner under the kettle. "Go find something for your cousin to wear to bed." She whirled toward Johab and began peeling his father's field jacket off his shoulders as Johab struggled to keep it on. "OK, keep that old thing. It's smelly and dirty, but you need to get to bed. Boys your age should be asleep at this hour."

Pushing both boys out the kitchen door ahead of her, Aunt Rayya's voice echoed down the hall. "Mohammed, if I hear one more sound out of you, you will answer to your father when he returns. Now, get to bed and be quiet."

Johab scrunched to the far side of the bed with Mohammed's questions continuing to hammer against his skull as he tried to hear the low voices of his aunt and mother in the living room. Soon the soft rasp of Mohammed's breathing was the only sound.

Wide-awake, Johab listened for his uncle to return. He crept to the bedroom door and peered through the crack just as Tarek hustled officiously through the front door.

"Not a sign of John at the Museum. The night guard was nowhere to be found. Probably took off early. Not supposed to. I'll have to report him. No light in John's office. Door locked. I checked. A black car was parked across the street, but it sped off when I drove up. We should call the police."

Johab pushed aside the bedroom door and rushed toward his uncle. "Please don't call the police! Wait until morning. Let's do what those men said. Maybe they just want something Dad found. When they get it, they'll bring him back." Johab almost convinced himself.

"Johab's right," acknowledged his aunt. "We all need to go to bed. Soya, you and Jasmine can sleep on the couch. Johab, go back to Mohammed's room. Things will look different in the morning."

Johab waited for what seemed an endless time to be sure that everyone in the house was asleep. Then, holding his shoes, he tiptoed into the living room. His mother was sitting upright, staring straight ahead with Jasmine's head in her lap. "Mother," Johab whispered, "we need to get out of here. They'll find us. They must know that Uncle Tarek was at the Museum tonight. If he saw their car, they saw him."

His mother remained stiff as a statue, as though she didn't want to listen. "You know what those men were like," Johab said. "They'll come here. We may not have much time. We need to go." Johab turned a pleading face to his mother—it was the best facsimile of Mohammed he could produce—but this time it was real. Then he added the zinger. "We're putting Aunt Rayya's family at risk."

The threat to her sister struck home. "I know," his mother acknowledged. "We shouldn't have come here. Rayya's little unborn baby and Mohammed—if those terrible men came . . ." Her voice trailed off, tears coursing silently down her cheeks, a cluster of dried blood like a small rosette on her upper lip. "Where can we go?" Her voice quavered at the word "go." Johab had never seen his mother helpless.

Desperate to reassure her, remembering the dark and quiet alleys, Johab said: "Let's go the same way we came. We can leave Aunt Rayya a note telling her we've gone to a safe place. We can look for a taxi." Johab had no notion of where they might go, but he knew that he would be a good guide through the labyrinths of alleys in this part of Cairo.

After scribbling a note on the telephone pad, his mother scooped up her sleeping daughter, and followed Johab out the door. Clutching his mother's sleeve, Johab paced in unison with her down two flights of steps and thought of wooden stairs leading up to a guillotine and stone stairs leading down to a dungeon. The ghosts of the night that he had watched earlier on the balcony were swirling about his head and whispering something in his ear. "The dead. The dead. The dead."

Smacking the side of his head to shut out that ghostly refrain, Johab paused at the last step. "Wait here. I'll check for that black car Uncle Tarek saw before we circle around to the alley. It could be on that cross street." Johab squinted into the darkness and moved into the adjacent alley. He wished he had one of those sniperscopes or snooperscopes that the U.S. Army used in World War II. Infrared. They could see anything moving at night.

Just as they rounded the corner into the alley, a stifled screech split the night silence as his mother's leg brushed a pile of garbage. "Something touched me! There, Johab."

He clutched her hand, tighter than usual. "Just a rat, Mother. You can see his tail moving on that pile. They make tunnels all through the garbage. The Zabbaleen, the garbage people, crack them up beside the head with a stick. Rats don't scare them."

With her voice still trembling, she shifted Jasmine to her shoulder and grabbed Johab's arm. "How do you know these alleys so well, Johab? Have you and Mohammed been playing in these places after we told you not to go there again?"

Johab didn't answer. It was better not to lie. The night was only partially over. There would be time for more lies. In the deathly stillness of these tunnels through the sleeping city, it had come to him. The voices of those ghosts had whispered it into his ear. There was a place where they might hide, a place where those men would never think of looking for them.

CHAPTER 4

Far down the alley in the glimmer of a faint street light, an old taxi belched its fumes into the night smog. "Quick, Mother. I have an idea. Let's catch that taxi. We have a long way to go."

The sneer on the grizzled face of the taxi driver turned to skepticism as Johab waved him over—a woman and two children appearing out of a dark alley at this time of night could be a problem. He stared at Johab's mother, taking in her Western dress and bloody lip with a knowing sneer. "Trouble at home?" He pushed the back door open.

Johab dug through his mother's purse and showed two bills to the driver, not answering his question. "Qarafa. The Northern Cemetery." Johab spoke quietly but with more authority than he was feeling. His mother gasped, staring wide-eyed but speechless as Johab pushed her and Jasmine into the back seat.

"You mean the City of the Dead—at this hour?" The taxi driver turned a quizzical face toward Johab.

"Yes," Johab replied, "the City of the Dead, the Northern Cemetery. We have relatives there who are expecting us." That was partially the truth. His mother's parents were buried in the Northern Cemetery. He remembered taking flowers to their tomb.

"OK. You pay. I'll take you. You like *al-musiqa al-diniyha*?" He leered across the seat at Johab's mother as he shoved a cassette into the slot above the radio, his teeth yellow as from an unearthed skull.

"My mother likes folk music. My Dad and I like Django Reinhart. Sometimes we listen to Chuck Berry." Johab had the unsettled sense that he was talking too much, dropping clues.

He glanced at his mother's face. Her lips were pursed, her expression grim, her eyes dry. His mother did not like visiting cemeteries. She especially disliked the idea of going into the tombs of pharaohs and always sent his father off on his field trips with a reminder: "It's bad luck to disturb the dead."

Sadness as thick as tar swept over Johab as the taxi sped along the highway, out toward the Moquattam Hills. Johab's father would know how to tease his mother out of her dark mood by telling her stories about conversations he had with the ghosts in the tombs, funny ghosts who told jokes about the tourists.

His father would have no interest in the City of the Dead. In chronological time, the dead there couldn't compare to the New Kingdom dead. If any mummies were in the City of the Dead, they would have been stolen from the mummy pits at Sakkarek.

The abrupt screech of brakes startled Johab. They were at the perimeter road near the City of the Dead. Beyond the road, a few pale oil lamps flickered in windows. The driver stretched out his hand: "No farther. I go no farther. Those people don't like being disturbed, especially at night." The driver's reference to "those people" was not to the dead but to the poor and homeless who had turned the tombs of the dead into their own homes.

Johab shoved money into the driver's hand, swung the door open, and pulled the sleeping Jasmine out of the taxi. "It will be OK, Mother. We'll be safe here. I know a place." His voice rang with more confidence than he felt. He did know a place. He remembered a vacant mausoleum, its pale ochre color setting it apart from the more usual earth-colored structures around it.

Boosting Jasmine up into her arms, he led his mother down a dirt road through a maze of tombs, leaning headstones, and small, mud brick structures stacked against two-story buildings with crumbling cornices.

It looked different at night, but he had to find the place. In the summer, he and Mohammed had taken a bus to the City of the Dead and spent the day prowling through the Northern Cemetery. Giggling and thumping each other with the sheer pleasure of being in a place where they were not allowed to go without their parents, they had peered inside of mausoleums that were occupied and were surprised to see cooking pits glowing with charcoal and make-shift furniture filling the room.

An old woman had come up silently behind them, whacking Mohammed with her stick broom and shouting: "Out of here, you nosy boys!" They had dashed along worn pathways, stumbling against each other. Finally, out of breath, they had slumped against the side of an ochre-colored mausoleum that appeared to be empty.

The wooden door hung at an angle. A pile of dried flowers rested on a slightly elevated stone slab in one corner. Spider webs glistened in the sunlight coming through a small window.

"Let's get out of here. Somebody's dead under that slab. It's creepy," Mohammed had urged. Johab had felt strangely comforted in the place, as though the dried flowers had been left lovingly for the dead, but he wanted Mohammed out. This place was his private find, something he didn't want to share with his cousin.

Now, Johab peered down a dark alleyway, searching for a familiar landmark, two large domes by two smaller ones, popping up like mushrooms above hundreds of lower, flat-roofed structures. He and Mohammed had been in the Cemetery in July. Now it was December. Without paid tomb watchers, someone might have moved into the mausoleum. His mother, holding Jasmine tightly, followed him into the darkness.

A glimmer from the moon pierced through a patch of clouds splashing a nearby hut with gold. It was his mausoleum, the door still hanging ajar. Johab rummaged in his father's field jacket for the small flashlight that was always there and aimed the beam through the door into the corners of the room. The dried flowers were still there, almost like a small offering of welcome.

"We can sleep here, Mother. We'll be safe. Jasmine can lie on Dad's jacket." Johab's mother, who hadn't spoken a word since they hailed the taxi, sank to the gound, curled against Jasmine, and closed her eyes.

Johab pushed the angled door back on its one, rusty hinge, propped himself against it, and fell into a dreamless sleep.

Chapter 5

Sunlight filtered through spider webs that draped the tiny window of the hut like lacy curtains. Johab's eyes popped open before he dared move another muscle. The first muscle to move lifted the corner of his mouth into a faint grin. He had just awakened in the City of the Dead. Even Mohammed might see the humor. He'd save that little joke for when he was in better spirits.

Johab wasn't the only one awake. The City of the Dead had come to life. Roosters crowed. Women called to each other as they strung their morning's laundry between the gravesites. Johab's mother sat up and looked around in confusion, last night's cloudy expression in her eyes replaced by wide-eyed shock. "Johab, where are we? This is a hovel."

"Mother, we're in Qarafa. We're safe for now. We can't go home or to Aunt Rayya's. We must be very careful until I can find Dad." His mother flinched as she trailed her fingers across her bruised face to the swollen lump on her lip.

"I remember now. Those men took John. Then we left Rayya's and got in a taxi." The cloudy expression returned. "I can't sort it all out. My head doesn't feel right. There's a big bump on my forehead." She groped across Jasmine's sleeping form and grabbed her purse. "I have money. We can go to a hotel. We can't stay in a place like this."

"No! Those men will be looking for us. They will check the hotels. I'm sure they know where Aunt Rayya lives." Johab's mother gave him a puzzled look, as though someone with an authoritative tone of voice had taken over her polite son.

Johab cocked his ear toward the small window, listening to the sounds outside. "We must be very careful around the people here, Mother. They can't know who we are. We will not speak English. We must be careful that Jasmine doesn't say anything in English." He looked over skeptically at his sleeping sister. She rarely followed his advice.

"I need to go the Museum today to try to find out about Dad." Johab's mother was silent. It was a good sign. "Jasmine will be hungry when she wakes up. I'll go outside and look for food." Johab eased Jasmine off his father's field jacket, jammed his arms in the sleeves, and shoved the broken door open.

Odors of charcoal smoke and grilled meat energized Johab. Children raced down the alleys; laundry dried in the sun; women made patterns in the dirt with twig brooms. There were no concrete streets and no obvious storefronts—otherwise, the City of the Dead resembled any city, with structures of different shapes and sizes angling in all directions. Second and third stories had been added to some of the original mausoleums to provide living space for extended families.

A seller of *ful medames*, fulbeans, stood by a large copper pot hanging over a bed of coals. Fulbeans were the favorite breakfast of his mother and many Egyptians. Johab despised the mushy beans, especially when his mother tried to disguise them with a runny fried egg on top.

Hunger ruled. Johab dug for coins in the pocket of his father's jacket. His fingers grazed something in the lining behind the pocket. The pouch. He had almost forgotten it. He yanked out his hand. Even if it didn't hold scorpions, the pouch was deadly. It had brought Johab's family to this poor place. He pinched the pouch through the lining—whatever was in it felt soft, no jewels or gold, nothing valuable.

"What do you want, boy? You're blocking my view. Buy or move on!" The bean seller's hands were grimy and his face sullen, but his pot simmered invitingly.

"A bowl of fulbeans, please," Johab said, holding out a few coins.

"Where's your bowl? Or do you want them in your hands," the man sniggered loudly, giving his pot a stir.

"I don't have a bowl. Can I borrow one? I'll bring it back."

"No you can't, but I'll sell you one—cheap. This coin and this coin and this coin will do." He pawed through the small pile of coins in Johab's outstretched hand, choosing the larger ones. Picking up a cheap tin bowl, he thumped dirt out of it against his leg, and wiped it inside with the sleeve of his soiled robe. "There you go, boy. Here's your big bowl of beans, and you own the bowl."

Holding the warm bowl in cupped hands, Johab kept his eyes lowered as he saw passersby glancing quickly at him, and then looking away. He didn't want to know his neighbors in this place or let them know anything about him or his family. He shoved open the door to the hut with one foot and handed his mother the bowl.

The beans were cooked to a mushy softness. Johab's mother eyed the bowl scornfully. "Overcooked and no flavoring." But, she ate them, sharing a small flat piece of wood as a spoon with Johab and Jasmine, who looked disgruntled at Johab's idea of a "picnic."

"Mother, why don't you rest here today with Jasmine. Stay close to this place. Don't talk to the neighbors." With a rueful expression, Johab added. "If someone asks, tell them you are hiding from your husband because he beat you, and you are afraid. They'll leave you alone. They don't want trouble here."

"Your father would never. . . ."

Johab stopped his mother's statement in mid-sentence. "I know, Mother, but the people living around here don't know that. We need a story that they can believe. They will believe this one—just look at some of the women here."

His mother started to respond, but Johab had already broken the rule about never interrupting grown-ups. He might as well compound his offense. "Don't tell them anything about us, not our names. Nothing." Johab spoke sternly, a tone he had never used with his mother before. But things were not as before. Things were very bad. "I need a little money from your emergency fund. I'll be back in a few hours. Stay here. Please," he added when he noticed the frown forming between his mother's eyes.

As soon as he reached the main highway outside the City of the Dead, Johab hitched a ride on the back of a donkey cart heading toward the center of Cairo. The driver gave him an odd look, but motioned him onto the cart. Johab looked down at his feet. English leather shoes, knee-high socks, and shorts. They were dirty, caked with the dusty clay of Cairo alleys—not the clothing of a native boy hiking from the Northern Cemetery. That was one of the first things he needed to do—find different clothes for them. His family needed to "blend in." That was the only way they could be safe.

In the distance, Johab could see the rooftops and tents of the great Khan el-Kalili market. He would circle around by Al Azhar Street near the cotton and cloth markets. He hopped off the cart, waved his thanks to the driver and headed at a fast clip to the Khan.

Anything could be found at the Khan markets at any price—from stuffed rabbits smoking pipes to semi-automatic rifles. Johab headed toward the row of shops where the cheapest goods could be found—cookware, food supplies, and clothing.

He ducked under the awning of the nearest tent. "Three galabeyas—a woman's, a small girl's, and one for me." A man rose from behind a mountain of fabric and selected a blue robe with glittering threads. "A nice one for your mother? Very pretty, no?" The man smiled, showing jagged, nicotine-stained teeth.

"No. Plain ones. Everyday. Cheap." Johab responded firmly in Arabic.

"Huh," grunted the man, seeing his profit from the boy that he thought was an English schoolboy disappearing fast. He tossed three robes at Johab. They were coarsely woven, an ugly off-white color, but sturdy. They would do.

Johab pulled coins from his pocket and handed them to the man. "More than enough, right?" Johab had watched his mother barter in the markets for years. He knew the right words.

Irritated at being outmaneuvered by a boy, the shopkeeper hissed at him, "Stingy English boy. Get out of here. Take them. Go!"

Johab rolled his mother's and Jasmine's robes into a wad, shook out his own, and pulled it over his head. Now, he would be in disguise, just like his favorite detective Sherlock Holmes. Johab was just another Egyptian boy of the streets, with no one questioning why he wasn't in school. He headed in the direction of the Egyptian Museum.

The building loomed ahead, huge and hostile. It was not the place of happy hours with his father, but it was still early. The front doors were locked. No tourist buses were in sight. Johab knew he had to be very careful. A boy dressed like him might be planning to pick the pockets of tourists. The guards would be watching. Uncle Tarek might be on duty this morning and recognize him.

Johab sprinted past the front of the building, glancing up at the Goddess Hathor with her cow's horns above the entrance. The receiver of the dead, Hathor smiled down on Johab. Queen Hatshepsut loved this goddess. Johab stopped short.

That's when it all started. He and his father were at Queen Hatshepsut's Temple when his father turned grumpy—or maybe just worried with good reason. Johab gave Hathor a curt nod and hurried to the back of the Museum. Two guards talked excitedly near the back entrance.

Johab ducked behind a low barrier of shrubs. Tunneling into a thick bank of bushes that shielded several large garbage bins, he tried to get close enough to hear the guards' conversation. One of them was waving his hands and pointing to the door.

Creeping closer, Johab crawled into a patch of prickly bushes and closed his eyes to protect them from thorns. A soft barrier blocked him. "What in the name of . . .?" His father's favorite oath started to pop out of Johab's mouth, but he gasped in horror. The "soft" barrier was a man in a guard's uniform tucked neatly under the shrubbery. His cap was on his chest. His eyes were open, his mouth ajar. Except for a second, dark-red smile that spread along his throat from ear to ear, he looked quite peaceful.

CHAPTER 6

Johab rolled away, unmindful of thorny bushes tearing his skin, desperate to scream and attract help. But, he clamped his fist over his mouth. No screaming now. No place for that. He glanced at the guard's face one more time. *Not Uncle Tarek.* It was the night guard, Mr. Razek. Johab backed away from the corpse, careful not to touch him, straining to hear what the guards, not a dozen feet away, were saying.

"Well, I don't know where he could have gone," muttered the short, beefy one. "I told Mr. El-Hasiim that everything looked fine, and no one had tampered with the lock. The staff probably forgot to reset the alarm and left the door open. We get blamed for everything," he said peevishly. He flicked his cigarette stub into the shrubbery. "Razek probably went home early. That's what I'd like to do."

Johab closed his eyes. Mr. Razek had gone home. He thought briefly of the ceremony of death conducted by the gods Anubis and Maat. He could almost feel the black jackal's paws against his back. Anubis would weigh the heart of the dead against the goddess Maat's feather to determine its final resting place—a safe port or into the jaws of the crocodile god. He hoped that Mr. Razek had a feather-light heart and that he was safe in some other world. This world had passed him by.

Beneath the bushes, the sun blazed unmercifully through rags of clouds. Under the course fabric of Johab's robe, his father's jacket was unbearably hot. He scooted along the border of the hedge, keeping the guards in sight, leaving the stiffening guard behind him. In this heat, the corpse would soon reveal itself.

Johab felt an overwhelming need to get back to his mother and Jasmine. It was too dangerous to be near the Museum during the day with dead bodies under the bushes. Which of his father's colleagues might be working in the Museum right now? Who could he trust?

"Difficulties on the Project," that's what his father had said on the balcony, just before they went inside for dinner. The faces and names of people who worked with his father on the New Kingdom Project blurred into a group that could talk nonstop about excavating a lower terrace without ever noticing a tired boy tugging on his father's sleeve. Bad manners weren't illegal. What about envy? Uncle Tarek said the archeologists were jealous of each other. Could one of his father's coworkers be behind his kidnapping? Who was trustworthy?

The answer came from his father's words—Ian Parks, his father's friend. Finding him was the problem. His father said he was somewhere in the field near Syria. The desert was vast there. Johab glared up into the mid-day sun. There was no wiggle room in the instructions of his father about the dangerous pouch: "Tell only Ian."

He needed help from the best. What was it that Sherlock Holmes said about having all the evidence before you theorize? The only evidence that Johab had was a missing father, a mysterious pouch, and the discovery of a dead guard.

Sherlock prized logic. So, first things first. That was logical. His mother and Jasmine needed their disguises now so they could go outside the mausoleum in the City of the Dead. He had to find a way to make their new home more livable. Then, he could look for clues about where those men had taken his father. He had one advantage. He had seen their faces—now he was disguised.

Johab kicked out the bottom of his robe and strode confidently away from the Museum down a wide street lined with shops. The increasing noise of morning traffic was a familiar song, loud yet comforting. Not for long.

"Clumsy boy! Watch where you go! You almost tripped me!" Johab sprawled at the feet of a large woman, only the slits of her eyes visible atop billowing waves of black fabric. Ducking his head and apologizing, Johab scooted into the foyer of a nearby shop to inspect his scraped knee.

He groped under his robe, searching the lining of the jacket. The shopkeeper wagged a finger at him, gesturing him away. Cairo was not the friendly city he knew—maybe his clothes made a difference. He grinned. He needed to look different.

Johab's fingers touched the small pouch in the jacket lining. It was secure. He was sure it was what those men wanted. As long as the pouch remained safe, his father would not be harmed.

Johab knew that he needed to open it, find out why its contents were such a big secret, and then hide it. He scowled. His father said to give it *only* to Ian Parks. He didn't say: "Don't look." The priest in his mother's church talked about sins of "commission" and sins of "omission." If he did look, that might be a sin of commission. If he didn't, it would surely be a sin of omission. He would opt for "commission."

Hunger, fatigue, a huge blister on his right toe, and a bad mood were Johab's traveling companions back to the Cemetery. As he turned into the pathway leading to the tomb, he could see a faint stream of smoke wafting upward from an odd pipe angled out of the window.

Inside, a charcoal brazier glowed in the corner atop freshly stacked bricks of clay formed in the shape of a small oven. A chicken split into quarters sizzled on the grill beside a small, battered pan, steaming with rice and lentils.

Four crudely made wooden chairs with colorful pillows angled around a makeshift table supported by bricks on top of the tomb slab. Reed sleeping mats were rolled up against the wall. Their new home had been transformed. "Johab, come meet our neighbor, Mrs. Zadi." The voice of Johab's mother had a familiar, lilting quality to it—not the dull, strange monotone of this morning.

Swags of black and white speckled cloth festooned the squat woman sitting as comfortably as a hen on its nest. Her beady, bird eyes took in everything. Her mouth puckered in and out, then opened with a gold-toothed smile. "What a fine son you have. Where have you been all day, leaving your mother to do all the work?"

"Out." Johab was required to be civil, not conversational.

"Mrs. Zadi helped me find some things we need. There are shops all over the Cemetery. It's like a city. We do need to have our dinner now." She helped Mrs. Zadi out of the chair and ushered her out the door.

"Mrs. Zadi seems helpful, but she gossips, says dreadful things about our neighbor across the street, Mr. Feisel."

Johab didn't want to discuss the neighbors and maintained a sullen expression. He should praise his mother for her shopping—his father always did. But, he was alarmed that she had spent time with this Mrs. Zadi. She might be a spy. He didn't like her question with its implied criticism of him. She was a bad influence on his mother.

His mother's smile, even with her swollen lip, made life seem as though it might be normal again—at any moment his father would come bursting into the room, recounting his narrow escape and how he had outwitted his captors. Johab's mother seemed too light-hearted for someone living in a borrowed tomb.

Johab shivered, remembering Mr. Razik, the dead guard. He would not tell his mother. So far, she had asked no questions about his trip into Cairo. The new robes might divert her. He shoved the wad of robes across the table.

Jasmine looked at the small one with distain. "I'm not wearing that stiff thing. I'm wearing my pink top."

Johab's mother rubbed the cloth between her fingers, wrinkling her nose. "Our street cleaner's galabeya is of better fabric that this." Noting the glum expression on Johab's face, she continued with artificial gaiety: "This is a game, Jasmine. We're going to pretend to be someone else."

Jasmine smiled. She liked games. Johab had brought her the robe as a present. It was ugly, but it was a present.

Dusk and the greasy film of modern-day Cairo stretched like low-lying fog along the Moquattum Hills into this city loud with ghosts. The living in the City of the Dead went to bed early. A few mausoleums had electric lights, powered by generators from nearby mosques, but most of the Cemetery darkened when the sun went down.

Groggy from too much chicken and those tasteless lentils, Johab fought sleep as he watched the shadowy forms of his mother and Jasmine settling onto their mats. He reached carefully into the pocket of his father's jacket, felt behind the lining and pulled out the leather pouch.

"Dangerous," his father had warned. It was about five inches long and knotted with a leather thong. A poisonous baby snake, an Asp, like the one that killed Cleopatra might be nestled inside. Turning his back to his sleeping sister and mother, he positioned the flashlight on the pouch. No movement. Johab worked the knots apart and dumped the contents onto his mat.

Nothing valuable. No gold rings, no rare seals. Just a few folded pages from the little notebook that his father always carried and fragments of papyrus, a ancient paper made of reeds. He recognized his father's writing on the notebook pages. Mostly, the pages were covered with precisely drawn hieroglyphs, the pictorial writing of ancient Egypt, with notes in English below. That kind of work was always on his father's desk. There was nothing new here.

He unfolded the sheets, careful not to further damage the crumbling edges. It was very old. One sheet was covered with what appeared to be a map. Johab recognized the shape of the river stretching through Kemet as it was called in the old world. There were tiny marks for the ancient cities from north to south, but no names.

Johab sighed with frustration. He knew that map well, even the names of the old cities—Hwt-ka-Ptah and Yunu squaring off across the river.

Dozens of these maps could be found in the bazaars at the Khan, fakes made from banana stalks for the tourists. The two remaining pages were more puzzling. He sniffed them. His father had trained him well. The chemical treatments used on papyrus for the tourist "rare finds" could not duplicate the feel and smell of decaying papyrus.

Johab stretched the pages carefully, shielding the beam of his flashlight. A few of the hieroglyphs looked familiar.

Why would his father describe these pages as dangerous? What could be hidden in these ancient symbols that posed such a threat to their family? And, to poor Mr. Razek, the guard who was past experiencing threats? The knife that pared his throat open had been brutally efficient.

Johab touched his own throat cautiously. He remembered that Mr. Razek's uniform had only a few, dark traces of blood. He must have been left to bleed face down on the ground and hidden in the hedge later. There had been no signs of a scuffle where the body lay. Positioning Mr. Razek under the shrubbery with his hat placed squarely on his chest seemed a particularly cruel touch—as though the killer had "laid out" his victim.

Johab shuddered. Again, he thought about the Goddess Maat's feather of justice. The ancient world that he saw through his father's eyes now seemed unconnected to this one. Mummies, tablets on tombs commemorating the dead—those dead seemed harmless, at peace. Johab did not fear ancient bodies. He did imagine Mr. Razek hanging around like a lost soul, not belonging to this world and not departed for the next.

Johab touched the ancient pages. Maybe the hieroglyphs here were words from the *Book of the Dead*. Johab carefully re-folded the sheets and his father's notes, stuffing them back into the leather pouch, and tightly knotting the cord.

He swept the beam of the flashlight around the room. Where could he hide the pouch? He shouldn't carry it with him. It had to be in a place where his mother would never clean and Jasmine wouldn't think of looking.

A ray of moonlight struck the old wooden ledge of the window. A section under the lower part had originally been coated with clay, but with the wood partially rotted, the clay fragments had fallen away. Johab tiptoed past his sleeping sister and probed the fragile wood under the sill. There was just enough space in which to stuff the pouch. Now, he simply had to replace the clay coating.

He felt a quick sense of gratitude to Mrs. Zadi, in spite of her nosiness. She had left a tin can half-full of damp clay used to fill the space around the chimney pipe to keep out mice. Johab dipped his fingers into the clay and sealed the pouch away from curious eyes until he could find a safer place or locate Ian Parks.

The moon radiated through the blemished glass window of the hut, casting a silver patina across Johab's mother and sister at sleep in a cemetery. Johab tucked his knees against his chest, rolled into a tight ball, squeezed his eyes shut and prayed that his sleep would be short and temporary.

CHAPTER 7

By noon the next day, Johab's search took on an air of aimlessness as he walked up and down familiar streets in Cairo. Sherlock would have a plan based on clues left at the scene of the crime. Clues might be in the pouch, but Johab couldn't decipher them.

He caught a reflection of himself in the window of a passing car. Clues in the pouch might stump him, but he could do disguises as well as Sherlock. His face smeared with dirt and axle grease resembled that of any ordinary boy from the streets of Cairo—an invisible boy in an expensive neighborhood, hoping no one would question him. He must get inside their apartment. The kidnappers might have left clues. At any rate, he needed to find his father's address book with Mr. Parks's phone number.

Johab squinted down the street, searching the sidewalk ahead for any sign of Rati and his twig broom. The old caretaker might recognize him, and he probably bore a grudge for the practical jokes he and Mohammed had played on him. A cheap robe and dirty face might not do the trick. It was a risk he had to take—the apartment first, and then, his father's office at the Museum.

He spotted the headline of a morning newspaper in a kiosk along the street and stopped in his tracks. "Museum Guard's Body Found" blazed across the front page. Johab stuffed a coin in the rack and grabbed a paper. Four hungry dogs had sniffed out Mr. Razik's body. A busload of tourists posing for photographs on the steps of the Museum screamed as the dogs dragged the guard's body past them.

Johab spotted a familiar name and read on. "The slain guard may be connected to the disappearance of a well-known Egyptologist and his family, according to Tarek Elsaid, brother-in-law of the missing scientist." Johab read his Uncle Tarek's interview with increasing dread. "A late night visit from my sister-in-law and her children leads me to believe that there is more to this business than meets the eye. They ran away from my house in the middle of the night. I don't know where they went, but John Bennett isn't letting them contact us. My wife is sick with worry about her sister."

Johab's eyes filled with tears of fury. *John Bennett isn't letting them contact us.* This was the thanks his father got for helping Uncle Tarek keep his job. Now, the police might be looking for his father to connect him to the murder of Mr. Razik. Johab dared not show the newspaper to his mother. She would march to Aunt Rayya's house and let Uncle Tarek know how she really felt about him. His mother's disapproval of her brother-in-law was thinly disguised, but she was civil for the sake of her sister. Johab could not expect any help from his uncle now. What would his father do?

Johab's face lit up. He would "think outside the box." His father had explained to him that scientists are trained to think linearly, one step at a time, and, at times, the path is too narrow. He could almost hear his father's voice. "People in ancient Egypt had other ways of thinking. Their gods had human forms with the head of a frog, a cobra, an ape, a lion. That meant their gods had the skills and cunning of different kinds of animals."

"Skills and cunning" were exactly what Johab needed at this moment. Old Rati was marching down the street waving his twig broom at someone who did not belong in this neighborhood.

"Out of here, boy!" he shouted, flailing the air with his broom. Johab smiled slyly as he ducked into the back alley. His disguise had worked, and he was comforted by his father's jacket underneath his robe. The next step would be trickier—getting inside without being seen. Only delivery people used the rickety back entrance.

It was almost too easy. The pile of garbage was so high that it made a perfect observation hideout. Not a soul was in sight. Johab crept up the stairwell, clutching the key in his father's jacket. Yellow police tape looped the door. He lifted the tape carefully, inserted the key into the lock, pushed the door open, and gasped.

A cyclone had hit the place. Obviously, those men had come back to look for the thing Johab's father didn't have. Stuffing from the slashed couch fluttered around Johab's feet like dirty cotton candy. Desk drawers stood on end. Flies clustered on the ruins of his family's last dinner together.

Johab pushed the door open to his father's study. The notebooks were gone from his desktop. The address book was nowhere to be found.

Johab knew exactly how the ancient kings must have felt, watching robbers violate their tombs. Johab's home had been torn apart by the same kind of men. It felt like a hostile place. He needed to get out.

As he crept back down the hall, he glanced into Jasmine's room and remembered her tear-streaked face when she realized that her favorite doll had been left behind. He pulled the blankets off her bed, searching for her doll. The front door lock rattled. He froze.

Aunt Rayya's voice thundered outside the door. "I tell you I won't have the police pawing over my sister's things! Tarek told me they have her photograph albums at the police station. *Our* family photographs. Disgusting." Her voice soared with indignation. "I'm taking her personal things home with me, police or no police."

Johab hunkered down behind Jasmine's bed and listened with a sense of comfort that some things never changed. His aunt's family was missing. The police might even now be linking his father to a murder (thanks to Uncle Tarek). Yet, here stood Aunt Rayya yelling at Rati about family photographs.

The noise at the front door increased with Rati's protests: "The police told me nobody is to come in. I am to call them immediately if anyone tries."

Aunt Rayya's haughty voice overrode his protests: "This is family, Rati, family. Doesn't that mean more than the police?" Aunt Rayya was rarely logical, but she was effective. The door swung inward. Her shriek of anguish over the state of the living room could have woken the dead.

Johab seized the opportunity, shot through the kitchen, into the utility room, and out the back door, not daring to lock the door behind him. The blind eyes of Jasmine's doll—long ago knocked into the empty space of her head—rattled softly in Johab's hand as he sped down the back stairs. At least one thing was accomplished. Jasmine would be happy tonight.

Johab craned his neck around the corner of the building by the cross street. No suspicious car. No police. And, no address book with Ian Parks's phone number. No clues. Police tape hung like limp flags along the upper balcony. A wasted trip but . . . clues didn't mean anything unless they were analyzed. He needed to think like Sherlock.

Those bad men had returned to look for something in the apartment because they couldn't find it in his father's office. That meant his father had not given away the secret in the pouch. Johab took a deep breath and headed in the direction of the Museum at a half-trot. At the least, he might find Ian Parks's phone number in his father's office.

The sun hung at half-mast in the dirty sky over Cairo as Johab sped down cluttered alleys between apartment buildings. Working his way down alleys toward the Museum would take more time, but he needed to get there after closing. It might be possible to slip in the back entrance then. The guards were always wandering in and out to smoke and talk.

The great, granite statues of the gods at the Museum entrance seemed strangely alert, oblivious to the tourists flocking around, as though they were remaining on guard just as they had for thousands of years at the temples and tombs to protect the fallen kings.

Johab remembered the greeting he always gave them—silently in his head so that only the statues could hear and people around him wouldn't think that he was crazy. It was a little chant his father had taught him from *The Doctrine of Eternal Life*: "Thou shalt exist for millions of years, a period of millions of years." He was sure that the statues were comforted by those words.

Shadows of the evening and a thick smog worked in unison to create a hostile atmosphere around the Museum. Johab crept alongside the shrubbery, keeping a wide berth because of what might lie beneath a bush. He stared suspiciously at every nearby car. He ducked as a flash of headlights lit up the row of shrubs. It felt weird being an outsider in a place that used to feel like another home.

He was no longer just John Bennett's son, free to roam about the Museum while his father worked. He was the son of a man identified as "missing," a man who might be connected to the death of a guard.

Two guards stood, nervously lighting cigarette after cigarette, at the back door marked "Staff Entrance," their voices unnaturally loud. Getting past them wouldn't be easy. Gripping the ring of keys in the pocket of his father's jacket, Johab eyed the men with frustration. They were on edge tonight, the memory of the murdered guard as close as every shadow.

Johab spotted a delivery truck, stranded adjacent to the back entrance with its left rear wheel splayed at an angle. He eased along a low hedge, crept over behind the truck, and waited.

Two scrawny, feral cats—two of those thousands of unclaimed cats that feed on the mice and rats tunneling through Cairo's rubbish—were stalking something in the garbage heap. It was another cat, a large, tawny female who preferred solitude. Her yowl of protest split the silence of the evening.

"What the hell!" shouted the shorter guard who, two days earlier, had dismissed the dead guard as having "gone home early." He clutched at his holster, struggling to jerk out his pistol. The second guard, convulsed with laughter, followed him to the edge of the garbage bins, and thumped him on the back. "Cats. Nothing but cats. Calm down before you shoot one of us."

The cats created the perfect opportunity for Johab. Moving swiftly around the truck and up a few stairs, Johab eased through the door and into the dimly lit halls of the working section of the Museum. He offered a brief prayer to the goddess Bastet who protects cats. His mother would be furious if she knew that he was sending small prayers to the old gods — but his father would understand. It was time to pray to any gods who might be willing to help.

Johab edged quietly down the hall toward his father's office. A bare light bulb dangled from the ceiling at the end of the hall, casting odd patterns along the wall. A dozen more steps, then he would be there.

At that instant, a short figure burst from the adjacent hallway, the click of steel-capped heels echoing like castanets against the granite floor. Under the wavering shadows of the light bulb, the legs of the person blocking his way were as sturdy as the columns on a tomb. Johab held his breath, fear stopping any movement. He was trapped.

CHAPTER 8

The fox knows many things,
but the hedgehog knows one great thing.

—Archilochus

A collision couldn't have been nosier. Miss Wenkle threw up her hands, her armload of folders flying everywhere, her first scream resounding down the hall.

"Shush." Louder than a cobra, Johab's hiss stopped the second scream. "Please. Be quiet, Miss Wenkle. It's me, Johab. Don't give me away." Johab grabbed her arm and pulled her against the door of his father's office. It was not locked. Flooded with relief, Johab pushed inside.

The apparition in the hallway was *only* Miss Wenkle who did research for his father and several other scientists on the New Kingdom Project. To Jasmine, Miss Wenkle was "Mrs. Tiggy-Winkle" despite his mother's efforts to correct her: "That's a little hedgehog lady in your book. She's not real. This lady is our friend, Miss Wenkle."

Never had Johab been happier to see anyone, especially this plump, short woman who toddled about her work on impossibly high heels, her ankles flowing over the edges of her too-tight shoes like pudding from an over-filled pan.

Sinking back against his father's desk, Johab eyed the speechless Miss Wenkle, bracing herself in the open door, gasping for breath. Why hadn't he thought of her sooner? She was the person his father most trusted at the Museum, the one he invited to their home to share every holiday, and a person Johab hardly ever noticed.

Johab eyed the silent woman with new respect, remembering his father's comments about Miss Wenkle's value to the Project: "Miss Wenkle can find anything I need, anytime. Her filing system is incredible."

Her files were now scattered across the floor. A bright light blazed at the end of the corridor. They could hear a guard thundering down the hall, waving his flashlight in one hand and, probably, his gun in the other.

Like a bristly hedgehog on alert, she pulled the door to the office closed behind her and blocked it with her body as she waved the guard away. "It's just me, Miss Wenkle!" she shouted in a somewhat theatrical tone of embarrassment. "These silly heels of mine slipped on the floor. I thought I was going down when I dropped my files."

The guard aimed his flashlight down the far corridor that reflected only empty space ahead of the beam. He fit his gun back into the holster and bent to gather up the files.

"You're . . . sure you're OK, Miss Wenkle? You didn't hurt yourself? I could hear your scream. I thought something terrible must have happened. You shouldn't be working this late after all the things that are going on around here. You worked for Dr. Bennett, didn't you?"

"I work for several of the scientists in this wing," she responded vaguely. The guard obviously wanted to check the door, but Miss Wenkle's ample body blocked any chance of that. "I'll be leaving soon. I just need to sort all those files. How stupid of me to wear these shoes on this slick floor. Thank you for checking on me." Her tone was dismissive.

The guard walked away, pointing his flashlight at the floor and toward the ceiling, smiling as he went. He'd have a funny story to tell the other guards. The fact that Miss Wenkle could even balance on those heels, considering her generous figure, was a constant source of amusement. Her near-miss with the floor would entertain the other guards. They needed a good laugh.

Miss Wenkle busied herself picking up the last few sheets of paper from the floor until the guard had turned down the far corridor; then, she pushed the office door open. "Johab," she whispered. "what in the world are you doing here? What has happened to John? I went to your apartment looking for all of you. Police were all over the place—someone had trashed the apartment." She paused, breathless. "You need to tell me everything."

Johab exhaled a breath that he had held too long. Could he trust her? His father trusted her, but that was before those pieces of papyrus in the pouch had changed their lives. Miss Wenkle waited for his response, looking determined.

Johab had no option. He would tell her some things but not the main thing, not anything about the pouch. "Three men broke into our apartment and took Dad away. We don't know where. They hit Mother. They threatened us and told us not to contact the police. So, we've been hiding. I can't tell you where, but we are safe."

"Johab, *you're* not safe. Look at you. I hardly recognized you in that dirty robe." Miss Wenkle had that "I'd like to scrub you" expression that his mother often wore.

"That's the point, Miss Wenkle. I can't be recognized. Those men who took Dad know who I am. If they find Mother or Jasmine or me, Dad won't stand a chance. He'll have to give them the information they want."

"What information? What could be so important as to put you at risk? I know your father's work. There is nothing so important that he would risk his family." She shook her head, her expression grim. "We have to get you to the police station and sort this out."

Johab shrank back against his father's desk. He needed the wiles of Cousin Mohammed more than ever. He had to convince Miss Wenkle to help him no matter how far-fetched his plan might seem, and he needed her silence.

"Miss Wenkle, my father thinks you are smart." A look of pride, very fleeting, lit her eyes. Johab knew that would be the key. "There is no one else who can help us or help my father. Those men are holding him somewhere, and I have to find him. The police are . . ." his voice trailed off, his opinion of the police undecided. "Just look how long it took them to find the guard—and a pack of dogs actually found him."

"Mr. Razik? You know what happened to him?"

"I found him yesterday, before the dogs did," Johab muttered glumly, ashamed that he had allowed the dead to be defiled. "I think the same men that took my father killed Mr. Razik that night."

Miss Wenkle propped herself against the desk. This was just too much for a woman who prided herself on order. Her life was tidy; everything fit into folders, and every folder had a label that was cross-referenced with other folders.

Johab reached out and clasped the plump fingers busily shuffling and reshuffling files. "You're the only one who can help me, Miss Wenkle. You know my father's work. You can help me find answers as to why this has happened."

Finding answers. Well, that was a different matter altogether. Miss Wenkle had been a librarian in the British Museum, before taking the position with the New Kingdom Project in Cairo. Finding answers was a logical and analytical activity, requiring the same careful work as creating a cross-referenced filing system.

"All right." Her voice trembled with anxiety, but her back was ramrod stiff. "I'll help. The guard may return if I don't leave soon. We can't let him find you here. The police have already been here asking lots of questions about your father. Everyone working here is on edge."

Johab knew Miss Wenkle was right. He couldn't be seen here with her. But where could a dirty boy of the streets not be noticed with a middle-aged British woman? It came in a flash. The Khan el-Kahlili, the largest market in Cairo. All the tourists went there. No one would notice an Egyptian boy showing an English tourist around—such boys were often alongside the tourists, hoping to find one gullible enough to overpay them as guides.

"Can you meet at the Khan at noon tomorrow? Two shops past the main entrance, left side." Miss Wenkle nodded.

She clutched his arm. "I can't let you wander around the city at night. I will drive you to wherever Soya and Jasmine are. I won't tell anyone."

Johab's head moved from side to side as mechanically as a metronome. Words were not necessary. Miss Wenkle caught on quickly.

She opened the office door cautiously. "The guard isn't in sight. I need to get my purse and lock my office. You stay here. Hide under the desk. I'll tap twice on the door when I'm ready to leave. I'll think of some way to divert the guards if they're at the back entrance."

Diverting the guards is just what Miss Wenkle did with a masterful performance. Johab crept behind her down the hall toward the exit. She clomped along as loudly as possible, as if to hide the tread of Johab's sandals. Shoving the back door open, she hissed: "Now!"

It happened so quickly that if Johab had not been alerted in advance, he would have leapt to aid Miss Wenkle. She hit the top step, threw her purse with a resounding thump against the back of one of the two guards, and screeched at the top of her lungs as she staggered down the steps, flinging herself against the second guard.

"Oh dear," she twittered, still clutching one guard while the second one scooped up the contents of her open purse lying on the ground. "These dreadful shoes—that makes twice tonight that I've slipped. Whatever will people think of me? I'm so clumsy. I hope I didn't hurt you when I fell against you," she smiled apologetically up at the guard, who staggered against her sudden weight. She was making no attempt to right herself.

Johab made his dash for the shadows of the shrubbery, unnoticed by all but Miss Wenkle. When he reached the bushes, he crouched, panting to catch his breath. He was suddenly ashamed as he watched Miss Wenkle hobbling toward her little Volkswagen. How could he have ever laughed when Jasmine called her "Mrs. Tiggy-Winkle"? Tonight, she had exhibited nerves of steel.

The moon passing overhead beamed down on Johab's smiling face as he headed toward the outskirts of Cairo and back to the City of the Dead. Wouldn't his father laugh about how Miss Wenkle tricked the guards? She might look like a hedgehog lady, but she had both spikes and brains.

CHAPTER 9

No one keeps a secret so well as a child.

—Victor Hugo

The moon provided scant light to guide Johab back to the City of the Dead where he hoped to find his mother and Jasmine fast asleep. He was wrong. They were both sitting upright, fearful and silent. Johab didn't want to tell them anything—not about Aunt Rayya at the apartment or Miss Wenkle agreeing to help him. It would be better that way. His mother or Jasmine might accidentally let something slip.

People who lived in the City of the Dead thought of themselves as a community apart with special concerns for the welfare of each other. Most of them were poor. So poor that some of them could be bribed. It would be better if his mother and sister knew nothing.

Johab pulled the eyeless doll from his robe and tossed it to Jasmine. She smiled, clutched it to her, burrowed underneath the blanket on her mat, and fell instantly asleep.

"The apartment. Any sign of . . ." His mother dared not say his father's name. He had to say it for her.

"There is no sign that Dad has been back, but those men returned after we left for Aunt Rayya's. Dad's papers are gone. The police have put yellow tape on the doors." Johab patted his mother's arm, happy that she had not seen the state of their apartment. "We're lucky that we left. They can't find us here."

Johab's mother seemed comforted by his assurance. As he looked around the small room, Johab realized that "luck" had little to do with their present circumstances. The rotten, wooden door of the hut had a space underneath large enough for rats to move in and out freely. The few pieces of crude furniture, the curtains, and a small fire were his mother's attempts to create a home. Their old apartment was off limits. This was their life now. It would be their life until Johab could find answers.

Unable to sleep, he sat with his back against the wall, trying to remember anything his father had said that might be a clue. Something he had mentioned in an offhand way on the trip to Queen Hatshepsut's temple was nagging Johab.

"The Abbott Papyrus—you remember it, Johab? Ian showed it to us in the British Museum last summer. It has very old information about grave robberies that occurred in the 20th Dynasty. Maybe . . ." his voice had trailed off.

"Maybe what?" Johab had responded, impatiently. The Abbott Papyrus that so excited his father and Mr. Parks bored him. It described a tomb robbery trial that Rameses IX conducted after he discovered that highly placed people in the government, including the necropolis police, were involved.

"Rameses discovered that tomb robbing involved respectable people, people in his government. He put them on trial. Remember those objects from the police raid last week? Mr. El-Hassim asked me to document them as New Kingdom items, but only one of them is on display, and I don't . . ." He stopped abruptly. "Let's talk about something else. You haven't been spending much time with your cousin lately. Why don't we take Mohammed to the Camel Market this weekend?"

Johab wasn't spending time with his cousin, because Mohammed was becoming such a bully, teasing little kids, poking holes in their bicycle tires, putting camel dung on swing sets in the playground. He had been so frustrated thinking about Mohammed that he didn't listen closely to his father on the trip to the desert that day.

He tried to think about his father's comment now. Why did a story about important people robbing tombs thousands of years ago cause his father to act so out of sorts that day? It couldn't relate to the papyrus in the British Museum—that trial Rameses conducted happened over 3,000 years ago.

Johab was thinking so hard that his head hurt more than the blisters on his feet. The tire-soled sandals that he had bought for almost nothing as part of his disguise rubbed his feet unmercifully. He lay back with a hopeless feeling on his mat. His sleep was shallow, his dreams fragmented and filled with giant, empty tombs which opened into bottomless pits with nothing to break his fall.

Johab awoke to the sound of pots clanging, wondering what excuse he could find to go into the city. Miss Wenkle had promised to meet him at the Khan at noon. His mother supplied the answer.

She looked up from a giant copper pot balanced on the small brazier and smiled brightly at Johab. "I have an idea for making a little money, just enough to get by until we . . ." She stopped and swished something in the pot. "I'm soaking some beans. The ones that the man down the street sells are nasty. My grandmother taught me how to make them with garlic, chili, and cumin. If you go into Cairo today, you might get some supplies for me at the Khan. They'll be cheaper there."

Johab stared at her, still clinging to the edge of his dream— something that his father had said about passageways in tombs. No, maybe it was something in his dream, just before he was falling into a pit and awoke.

His mother chattered away, certain that Johab shared her excitement about her new *Ful Medames* project, fulbeans. He beamed back at her. She hadn't considered that their neighbor who sold nasty beans might not appreciate the competition. She had seemed so lifeless during the past few days—not at all like the woman his father described as "a modern Nefertiti," the ancient queen whose name meant: "the beautiful woman has come."

Calling her "modern" was his father's idea of a joke. Johab's mother and her sister, Rayya, were the only children of traditional Coptic Christian parents. The sisters had worked as receptionists at the Egyptian Museum, a respectable occupation for young, unmarried women.

His mother's only "non-traditional" act of her life was in marrying his father, an American Egyptologist. Her sister's marriage to Tarek Elsaid, a handsome man who changed jobs often, caused the first friction between the sisters. Rayya asserted: "He was baptized as a Christian. He'll settle down. He makes me happy."

Johab had overheard his mother telling his father: "Back then, when he was younger, Tarek could charm the birds out of the trees. Then . . ." she would pause, looking disconsolate, "he would shoot all of them in flight."

His Aunt Rayya put on a brave front at being happy. Johab's father got Uncle Tarek a better-paying job as a guard at the Museum and continued to intervene on his behalf when Uncle Tarek's temper ran amuck. Families look after each other even when they don't much like some of the relatives. That might have been an Eleventh Commandment, according his mother.

Johab loved hearing about his parents' romance. "Your father's reputation preceded him. He was making his mark in the field before he moved to Cairo." She would look affectionately at her husband through dark and slanting eyes.

"He tried speaking Arabic to everyone—from the floor sweepers to the boys bringing sweet tea to his office. No one could understand him. Back then, he could read Arabic fluently, even the ancient dialects, but speaking was another matter. I took pity on him. I had to help him." Pity didn't bring his parents together. Johab knew that his mother had chosen John Bennett as her safe haven, and his father wanted no other woman.

"That old cart can be used for hauling the fulbeans." Johab stopped daydreaming about his parents when his mother spoke. "Our neighbor, Mr. Feisel, found it."

What else had Mr. Feisel found? Johab had seen the old Bedouin across the street. He never spoke to anyone but Johab's mother. Why was he so chummy with her? Giving her a cart? Johab remembered seeing native boys selling fulbeans along the streets of Cairo, some pulling carts, some with donkeys pulling carts. He had never even looked into their faces. They were boys his age. They didn't go to school. They didn't have their own rooms full of clothes and books and toys. They were lucky to have sandals with rubber tire soles and a place to lay their heads at night.

Now, he would be one of them. Johab's face lit up with delight. A seller of fulbeans would be a perfect disguise. He could roam the streets of Cairo, get close to the Museum, the police station, and no one would see him as anyone but a seller of fulbeans. It was perfect. His mother's objective to earn money was a minor goal. His was much more important. He would be free to head to Cairo every day, no questions asked.

"I just put in the beans to soak; they need to cook all night to be ready in the morning. Mrs. Zadi said that beans cooked the old way sell easily. I haven't cooked them in years. Your father doesn't like . . ." She stopped with a vacant-eyed expression.

"Yours will be the best beans in Cairo," Johab reassured her, trying to divert her thoughts from his father. "We'll make enough money to buy food—chicken sometimes." Johab felt edgy. The sun was high above the horizon. Time was creeping up on him. He had arranged to meet Miss Wenkle at the market and had overslept.

"Mother, I'll get your spices from that place you like in the Khan." Johab felt a tinge of regret. He was taking advantage of his mother's new fulbean project as a way to escape her daily supervision. He had no option. Cousin Mohammed wasn't the only manipulator in the family.

CHAPTER 10

With his mother's supply list in hand, Johab scanned the road outside the cemetery for a lift into Cairo. Nothing was in sight. It would be a long walk. Johab kicked up his pace. Thinking about the busy marketplace brightened his spirits. The Khan el-Khalili must be the grandest market in the world. Hundreds of shops filled the massive bazaar with temporary awnings, tents, lean-tos, and the walled-in structures of the gold-sellers.

The Khan had everything that anyone might need—toys, old camouflage military jackets, deadly curved knives, fresh corn on the cob roasting over open braziers, and baskets heaped high with candies. It was a noisy, colorful, exciting place.

Johab hitched up his robe and broke into a trot alongside the highway. Both he and Mohammed knew the Khan well. With a few tricks, they could make their coins last all day. Unexpectedly, at that moment, Johab felt a different kind of loss when thinking of Mohammed. He and his cousin had played together all of their lives, but Johab knew that their friendship had been changing for months.

Throwing rocks at rats, turning over garbage bins, and figuring out ways to torment the doorman, wasn't as much fun as it used to be. The lies of Mohammed were becoming more convoluted.

Johab could understand lying to avoid Uncle Tarek's belt, but Mohammed lied for the sake of lying. Even though he feared his father, Mohammed seemed more and more like him, his games taking on a mean edge. No one should tease small children. Mohammed found the tears of children amusing. Johab did not.

Now that he couldn't contact Mohammed, he missed exploring alleys with him. He didn't miss going to the Museum with him. Mohammed only wanted to see mummies. The blackened, shrunken face of Thutmose IV in his orange linen wrappings on display in a glass case was a source of continual amusement to Mohammed.

Johab could hardly bear to look at Thutmose, his open mouth a grimace of despair. Thutmose had been an inventive king. He convinced his subjects that the Great Sphinx had called him his son—and that his efforts to excavate the Sphinx from the walls of sand around him were ordered by the Sphinx himself. Thutmose should be hidden in a fine, gold-leafed coffin, not placed under glass for curious tourists and the jokes of Mohammed.

Johab paused for a deep breath as he spotted the Khan in the distance; he looked forward to seeing Miss Wenkle. She knew his father's work better than anyone. She also knew all the people on his father's project. She even knew Ian Parks from her work at the British Museum in London where she had lived all of her life before coming to Cairo two years ago.

Johab circled past the madrassa, an old clinic, so that he could enter from the other side of the Khan, still thinking about Miss Wenkle. She was his parents' friend, not really his. She had no family, so Johab's parents had made her as much a part of their family life as possible. She had shared the last two Christmas celebrations, as well as other holidays.

Last Christmas, Miss Wenkle brought Johab house shoes that were too small and wooden blocks for Jasmine that she never took out of the box. This past summer though, after visiting London, she had returned with an elegant doll for Jasmine and an entire set of Hardy Boys mysteries for Johab. Miss Wenkle's stock had risen considerably.

She seemed so cautious, law-abiding to an extreme, so suited to her job of documenting and filing information. Johab remembered his father chuckling when he described how she backed her small Volkswagen repeatedly in and out between the marked stalls in the employee lot until she was exactly equidistant from both white stripes.

In Johab's world, order had been turned upside down. How could someone so cautious in parking a car help him find criminals?

A white-gloved hand darted out from a close-packed crowd of tourists trailing behind the flag of their guide and clutched his arm. Johab instinctively yanked away, but the hand gripped him firmly, dragged him into a tent, and pulled the flap closed. "It's OK, Johab. It's just me." Miss Wenkle peered out from under an enormous straw hat, her sunglasses so large that only her cheeks and chin were visible. "We're safe here. I know the owner. He's gone to lunch. We can talk until he returns."

From her large purse, she pulled out some fresh dates, a small carton of *baba ganoush*, and a package of English crackers and spread them on a small table, pointing to a chair. "Sit. Eat. You look starved."

Johab scooped up the mashed eggplant, relishing its familiar, tangy taste and eyed the dates. "Can I keep those for Jasmine?" He asked.

Miss Wenkle carefully removed her hat and glasses and stared at him with a puzzled expression. "No. Eat them." She tapped her big purse. "I brought more for you to take to Jasmine and your mother. Now, I want to know everything you know about what happened to your father and where you are hiding."

Johab opened his mouth, and then crammed it full of dates. He could tell partial truths, like Mohammed used to do, or he could tell outright lies as his cousin did now. Miss Wenkle locked her eyes into his eyes, staring so hard that Johab knew that she would discover any lie he dared to invent. He had to trust her. He had no other option. That scurrying, breathless, plump hedgehog lady was decked out like a typical tourist so she could blend in with scores of British and Americans piling out of buses into the Khan. She had even switched her trademark high heels for sturdy walking shoes to complete her disguise.

"I told you about the men who took my father away. I didn't tell you what happened earlier." Johab paused. He was breaking a promise that he had made to his father about the pouch. He would need to be very careful about how he revealed that information.

"Something was bothering Father that morning when we were at Queen Hatshepsut's Temple." Johab felt suddenly guilty that he had been so oblivious to his father's worries.

"Father told me that he had found some information that was very dangerous, and he needed to talk with Ian Parks. Dad said that he was going to send Mother, Jasmine, and me to my grandparents in Michigan immediately. He said we weren't safe in Cairo."

Miss Wenkle's eyes widened slightly, but she didn't appear surprised. "There was something your father told me a week ago, and I've been thinking about it after he disappeared. We were talking about a recent discovery of ancient artifacts. It was in all the newspapers. The police broke up a trafficking ring which sold two small statues and an amulet to an undercover policeman."

She gripped Johab's arm. "Your father said that everyone was excited about these items because they were very unusual and from the New Kingdom period. He spent some time looking at the amulet. I saw him making a Polaroid photograph of it. He speculated that these things might have come from an undiscovered tomb—they were very unusual objects. I know that your father asked Mr. El-Hasiim, the director of the Project, lots of questions."

Miss Wenkle paused. "I don't think your father trusts Mr. El-Hasiim. He told me that he started to tell Mr. El-Hasiim something about the amulet, but he changed his mind." She shook her head, as though mystified. "Your father said something else very curious, Johab, almost under his breath. I don't think he realized that I heard, but my hearing is *very* good. He said: 'They think Thutmose moved her mummy. The woman in Amenhotep's tomb was not our lady.'"

Johab stared at her, puzzled and waiting.

"That's all he said, Johab." She polished her sunglasses. "But your father told me that he was taking you for a couple of days to Hatshepsut's Temple so that he could think about some things. And now *this* terrible *thing* has happened to him." Her voice trailed into a whisper as though "this thing" was too painful to be named.

Miss Wenkle clenched her hands. "Mr. El-Hasiim had the audacity to suggest that your father has probably just gone into the field on a wild goose chase. That's what he said to staff when the police came to interview everyone on the Project—after Tarek reported that your family had not returned to your apartment."

She unclenched her hands and rubbed them vigorously together as though ridding them of something untouchable. "I don't trust Mr. El-Hasiim. I don't much trust your Uncle Tarek either. John saved his job more than once, and Tarek made disparaging remarks about him to a reporter. He's puffed up with self-importance." She shook her head with disgust and reached for Johab's hand. "What can we do, Johab? Where are your mother and Jasmine?"

Johab felt a tinge of guilt that he had not told Miss Wenkle about the pouch with the papyrus pages and notes. He remembered now that one of his father's notes included a pencil sketch of the back of an amulet, which he thought was odd. Usually, it is the front of an amulet that is interesting—not the back. He dared not tell Miss Wenkle about the pouch. That information could make her vulnerable. Johab needed Miss Wenkle's help, but he couldn't put her at risk.

He would answer her first question to throw her off track. He wouldn't tell her where they were hiding. "We need to try to find out the names of the men who took Dad. I think the only way we can do that is to find out what information my father thought was so dangerous that he wanted his family to leave the country."

Johab frowned, trying to connect what seemed to be a series of disconnected events. "We had been at Deir el-Bahari that morning—before the men broke into our apartment at night. Dad kept drawing and re-drawing the terraces of Hatshepsut's Temple. Then, he just jumped up and said we were going home. At the edge of the city, he stopped the jeep and told me he had dangerous information and needed to find Mr. Parks out in the field."

"Dangerous information?" queried Miss Wenkle. She had been listening intently to every word. Johab knew he needed to choose his words prudently, so that he didn't reveal any information about the pouch.

He stared at her, wide-eyed. "It's all very confusing to me, Miss Wenkle. I don't know what could be dangerous about Dad's work.

Cousin Mohammed thinks he has a boring job compared to Uncle Tarek who gets to carry a gun."

"Your Uncle Tarek. *Humph*." The sound was far from lady-like as Miss Wenkle sputtered her disapproval. "Mr. El-Hasiim told him in no uncertain terms not to discuss any of the Museum's business with journalists. Now what information do you think your father might have that could be dangerous?"

Miss Wenkle's erect neck and severe stare reminded Johab of the cobras in baskets he had seen in the Khan. Their eyes could freeze a mouse in its tracks, and he was the mouse.

"I think the information might have something to do with Queen Hatshepsut. When we were at her temple, Dad thought of something important. He didn't tell me what it was," Johab said regretfully. "He did say something about the police catching robbers and bringing New Kingdom artifacts to the museum. Then, he started talking about the Abbott Papyrus that described tomb robbers 3,000 years ago. I didn't get the connection. Fact is, I was getting bored."

The increased noise of shoppers at the Khan made Johab realize that they were in a public place discussing very private information. "I need to know how to contact Mr. Parks. Dad told me he's in the desert near Syria." Trying to make it appear as an afterthought, he added: "If you have any information about the amulet the police found or just *anything* about his work that was worrying him . . ." Johab's voice trailed off as the noise of shoppers outside the tent increased.

Miss Wenkle stood, clamped her huge hat on her head, picked up her purse and drew out a wad of bills. "Here. You didn't tell me where your mother and Jasmine are, but you probably need some money. I'm assuming that you don't want to risk telling me for fear that those men who took your father could pry information out of me."

She pulled on her white gloves and said in a matter-of-fact tone. "Well, they might. I'm not brave enough to tolerate much pain. As for your father's work, someone took the current files off his desk."

Then, she turned and gave Johab a coy smile, "But what they didn't know is that I keep duplicates of every important file in my office. John was always afraid of losing papers in the field and insisted that I keep copies. I will go through everything that he has given me during the past month to see what I can find related to Hatshepsut, her temple, or that amulet."

She looked thoughtful. "I just remembered something. The Polaroid photographs of the amulet would usually be kept in a special box, not in his office files. I'll look for them. The shopkeeper will be back any minute. You probably shouldn't be seen here with me. We don't know who might be spying on us. We can meet here in two days. I'll go through your father's work, nose around a bit."

Miss Wenkle lifted the tent flap and prepared to blend in with the tourists. "Your mother and Jasmine, Johab? Are you certain they're safe?"

"With relatives," he assured her. The graves of his grandparents were in the City of the Dead, so he wasn't telling a lie.

CHAPTER 11

*It should be noted that children at play are not
playing about; their games should be seen
as their most serious-minded activity.*

—Montaigne

The angry scab on the hipbone of the little gray donkey, Sekina,
attracted an ugly knot of blow-flies. Johab knew that a female blow-fly
could lay up to 200 eggs per batch. He uncurled his fist slowly and
smacked a clutch of flies, thinking of that old fairy tale, "The Brave
Little Tailor," that his father used to read him. "Seven at one blow,"
the little tailor boasted, never realizing that swatting a few flies could
bring him fame.

Turning his palm up, Johab scraped off two squashed flies on
the sleeve of his robe and touched the curling edges of his donkey's
burned flesh, inching the belly strap away from the wound. Fairy
tales belonged to a time when he was a child with no worries about
the future, no responsibilities. Not only did he have to worry about
his family, he was now a not-so-proud owner of a scruffy donkey.

Johab scowled, thinking back to the afternoon two days ago. It all
started with that buttinski neighbor, Mr. Feisal's gift of a cart. After
a perfectly stellar meeting with Miss Wenkle at the Khan, Johab had
returned to the City of the Dead very full of himself for lining up
considerable detective work for Miss Winkle—and not giving her
so much as a clue about where he had hidden his mother and sister.

Strutting down the hard-packed dirt path to the tomb that was now their home, Johab stopped short. "What the?" The wreck of a donkey cart blocked the door. Two wheels splayed out from a rusty, metal frame with mismatched wooden planks forming the bed of the cart. His mother beamed through the door at him as though Santa Claus had paid an early visit. "Our neighbor, Mr. Feisel, thought we might want to take our fulbeans business away from this neighborhood. He says the bean seller here is testy about competition. Mr. Feisel found this cart for you. Very nice of him."

Johab kicked a half-rotted wheel. Just what he'd expect from a man who boiled mummies for oil, according to that nosy parker Mrs. Zadi. He stepped over one of the wooden shafts, stood between them and tried to pull the contraption away from the door.

"Get yourself a donkey, boy! Or you're the donkey!"

Johab glared across the road at Mr. Feisel, who seemed unduly amused by his efforts to move the cart.

"The donkey hospital close to Moquattam. The do-good Brits fix up the injured ones and give them away for free."

The donkey hospital was nothing more than some makeshift pens and a lean-to where volunteers worked on severely burned donkeys that had been cast aside by their owners as useless. On these hills outside of Cairo, thousands of donkeys were used by the more than thirty thousand Zabballeen, the garbage people who sorted and recycled trash, jobs that had become their birthright, their enterprise. And, in the midst of the filth and stench of burning rags, rotting carcasses and vegetables too rancid for the hogs to eat, the donkeys were less valuable than the hogs.

At the animal hospital, Johab immediately spotted a small, gray donkey in a pen by herself, her head hanging at half-mast, her eyes glazed with pain. The charred skin, stretching along her entire left side, had separated over her hipbone. Flies swarmed around the festering wound plastered with salve.

Two young foreign women wearing men's clothes were struggling with a donkey that had just been led into the lean-to. It was crazed with pain, thrashing about, kicking slats from the flimsy fence, and baring its yellow teeth.

Red-faced with frustration, one of women seemed somewhat taken aback by Johab's question about getting a donkey. He had spoken to her in English, American English. "That one over there," she pointed to the small donkey with the cast-down head. "We call her Sekina. She's not as bad off as she appears. Food and water will do wonders for her." The woman looked skeptically down into Johab's dirty face. "Where did you learn to speak English like that?" she blurted out.

Johab whirled away toward Sekina, grabbed her rough rope halter and pulled her out of the pen. "Thank you. Thank you," Johab waved his hand. "I'll take good care of Sekina. That one's about to bite you!" he shouted in his best street Arabic, hoping that the flashing yellow teeth of a donkey with laid-back ears would divert the woman's curiosity. He had been careless, but she returned to her struggle with the donkey without a backward look.

A pile of dried grass hand-fed by Jasmine did wonders for Sekina's spirit. Johab's mother put on more salve and pronounced that the wound was "drying." Sekina could earn her keep immediately. So, just as the sun god Ra was reborn at dawn after a night of fighting the Lord of Chaos, Johab lifted his mother's pot of fulbeans into the cart, adjusted a make-shift rope harness on Sekina, and struck out for the city.

Johab and his donkey picked their way carefully in and out of the noisy streams of traffic along the Cairo streets. The burn on Sekina's back might heal quicker with mummy paste. Johab had heard that it had miraculous qualities.

Mrs. Busy-Body Zadi had whispered to his mother in her raspy did-I-say-that-loud-enough-to-be-overheard voice: "Mr. Feisel keeps old black human bones and mummified animals from the tombs in his hut. He boils them to make paste and oil. The nasty stuff is worth as much as gold on the black market." Mrs. Zadi spat out the words through an eye-catching set of gold-capped teeth, smiling conspiratorially.

If an ounce of mummy paste costs the same as an ounce of gold, it must have great curative powers, for donkeys or even boys, Johab reflected. The seeping blister on his toe caused him to shift his weight to his heels. The ill-fitting sandals required by his disguise were cheap. Comfort wasn't part of the equation in disguises.

Johab urged Sekina forward, ducking his head when a black car passed, terrified that the man with the eyes of a vulture might be in that car, looking for him. Johab thumped the donkey's rump to hurry her through the crowded intersection. Fear must not force him into alleyways. He had beans to sell and things to do.

He led the donkey along streets where the morning's laundry flapped like anchored kites overhead, streets where people would exchange a few coins for a warm breakfast.

"Fulbeans, cooked the old-fashioned way. Exotic!" Johab shouted, his voice as loud as a carnival barker, hoping that the hint of red pepper in the beans would give him an edge in sales. Copper pots clanked down toward Johab from balcony after balcony along with shouts of "one scoop, two scoops" until his pot was empty.

Johab knew his mother would praise him when he returned with coins. "You are just like your father. You can do anything." Then her face would darken with emotion, the way it did these days.

Johab glared at the crushing stream of traffic that forced him and Sekina to walk along the gutter. He wasn't going to be "just like his father." He wasn't going to be an archaeologist preserving the treasures of Egypt. A boy who sold fulbeans to help feed his family wasn't going to find the secrets of kings under desert sands. Someone who could read clues among the hieroglyphs would find those treasures.

Tears suddenly flushed his eyes. He gritted his teeth and squinted, hoping that passersby would blame the bright sun for his red eyes. "You sissy. You cry baby. You ignoramus," he whispered fiercely against Sekina's neck, burying his face against her prickly mane, trying to remember a time when he didn't feel so alone, so desperate.

Why hadn't he paid more attention when his father tried to teach him how to read hieroglyphs? Then he could translate the symbols on those papyrus sheets in the secret pouch to unlock this scary mystery that had become his life.

Johab swiped his runny nose with the coarse sleeve of his robe. His old life was lost. It had begun to disappear that day on the highway just outside of Cairo when his father raised his voice and warned him *never* to tell anyone but Ian Parks about the pouch. That should have been his first clue that something was seriously wrong. Uncle Tarek shouted. His father *never* did.

Two hours later, the world had turned into a terrible place. Johab struggled to keep the images of that night at bay. But, the ugly sounds stayed in his head. The splintering wood from the door being kicked open. The frantic thumps of his father against the floor as the men held him down. The stillness of his mother's crumpled form. And, the worst sound of all, a helpless silence from himself, trapped against the table, thinking that he could hear the rustling of scorpions in that hidden pouch, recognizing at that moment that evil has many sounds.

Johab scowled at the cars whizzing by too close, as though he and his donkey were invisible. His expression brightened. A good disguise meant being undetectable. Who could imagine that he would have taken his mother and sister to hide in a cemetery? A faint grin lifted one corner of his mouth. His father might not have thought of such a place. Tombs were a major part of his life, ancient tombs, not like those found in the City of the Dead.

A horn blasted next to Sekina's ear. Johab lifted his hand for the favorite Egyptian sign of supreme irritation, but Sekina acted first, braying loudly in the window of the offending car. Better the donkey than him. His mother wouldn't approve of the gestures he had recently added to his store of signals. A sly expression crept across his tear-stained face. Cairo streets were ripe places for learning useful things. Things his mother didn't need to know.

CHAPTER 12

The fulbean pot was empty; today, he had enough buyers within two short streets. Tomorrow, the beans would be sold quickly, and he would have hours for important business. "Come home early, Johab. Just a snack to tide you over." His mother had pressed a small packet of roasted hazelnuts into his hand. Before he could explain that he might be late, she added: "Don't exhaust the donkey."

As Sekina paused to snatch up a clump of grass, Johab prodded the donkey, jumping sideways to avoid her nip. Sekina nuzzled him, her brief show of temper forgotten. The brevity of a donkey's memory would be a blessing, Johab reflected. Remembering his old life was a pastime that he could ill afford. Only three things were important: keeping his mother and sister safe; not being recognized; and, finding his father.

Johab caught a glimpse of his reflection in the window of a passing car. The men who took his father would be searching for a boy who looked like Johab did that night—Western clothes and leather shoes—not a boy in a dirty galabeya trailing a scabby donkey through the streets of Cairo. Johab tugged Sekina's halter, urging her into a fast trot. Those men could be looking for him at this very moment. If they couldn't get information from his father, he would be a bargaining chip. Johab looked around the busy streets nervously. He would be safer doing his thinking and planning in his hiding place with the dead.

The noonday sun shimmered against the distant domes of mosques in the Northern Cemetery. As he reached the edge of city, the rhythmic clicking of Sekina's hooves assured Johab that the donkey was confidently heading home. "I will find him. I will find him. I will. I will." Johab chanted softly to the rhythm of the donkey's hooves on the road.

He almost dreaded looking into his mother's face when he returned. She would never ask if he had learned anything about his father. Like a bird with a damaged wing that knows it has lost the sky forever, his mother had become mechanical in her responses. She smiled as an afterthought. She sang Jasmine to sleep in a tired voice. She dusted the hut, endlessly. The only light in her eyes reflected pain, too deep to discuss.

He would think of a good story to tell his mother, one that might cheer her up—one about hiding. That would please Jasmine. She loved playing hide and seek. He would tell one of his father's favorite stories, about how the goddess Isis hid with her son Horus on the island of Chemmis. Johab frowned up at the overhead sun. A mother and her son hiding might be too close to home. He'd have to leave out the best parts. His mother didn't like to hear about family members murdering each other—even the ancient gods—chopping up their siblings thousands of years in the past.

Johab could hear his father's voice, reminding him that the past was always just around the corner in Egypt. The great pyramids of Giza soared upwards in the distance. Johab couldn't see them from this road, but he knew they were there, great, solitary citadels, keeping watch over him.

He arched his stiff back against the blazing afternoon sun, feeling the warmth of reassurance that his father was out there somewhere, hidden in an unknown place, but safe. How could it be otherwise? His father was a time traveler, not in some futuristic, intergalactic capsule off to a fictional new world. His father was a fact-finding, scientist of an ancient world. That was the power of his father's work in Egypt—making history live. History wasn't in old books. It was all around in Egypt, with pyramids touching the sky and tombs just waiting to be discovered far underground in the Valley of the Kings.

Johab could feel his chest swell under his dirty galabeya. His father often took him across that invisible barrier into an ancient and magical world that anyone with imagination could see. Cousin Mohammed wouldn't know where to look for it. The past was a bore to him. Staying in the present and just on the edge of trouble made his cousin happy.

For a moment, the rusted old heaps of cars chugging past Johab and his donkey might have been golden-wheeled chariots—flashing across the desert sands into an ancient world where kings never died. The kings spent their vast fortunes to ensure an everlasting life with their gods, constructing temples, and making sure that their tombs were filled with the things they would need in the afterworld.

Good idea. Johab tucked his unopened bag of hazelnuts into his pocket. He had already made of list of things he might need: a prized pocket knife that his mother refused to let him carry, his Sherlock Holmes mysteries, sets of Crazy Eight and Authors in case people in the afterworld liked card games. He would add other items later. He dared not tell his mother the purpose of the list. She had very decided views on the afterlife. In his mother's world, burial practices were not negotiable, as she had reminded his father frequently.

"Those poor ancient people were pagans, ignorant of the true faith. John, you must quit filling Johab's head full of those stories about pharaohs traveling with the moon and sun after death. He's confused." Johab's mother considered the priest at her Coptic Christian church as an authority on the afterlife. But, Johab planned to keep his list for the afterworld, just in case.

Sekina planted her feet, stopped in her tracks, and brayed loudly. The harness had shifted and was rubbing against her old wound. Given a chance, Sekina would bite him for staring into space, not paying attention to her comfort. Her loud bray was just a warning of worse things to come.

Johab moved her harness and stared distractedly over her ears, thinking of the tombs in the Valley of the Kings. To avoid robbers, the kings carved out their tombs in the sides of cliffs in a remote valley, hiding their bodies and their treasures.

For centuries, robbers had plundered the tombs that Johab and his father visited. These days, the tombs reeked of bat dung and held only fragments of clay pots and slivers of coffins, useless to thieves once the gold had been peeled away. No mummies. No gold. Nothing interesting until Johab's father made the musty, dark tombs shimmer with life. "These old stones tell wonderful stories, Johab. See the holes where the old stelae with sacred hieroglyphs were hung? Their cats, their birds, even apes were mummified. The kings wanted their families, their pets, and their treasures around them forever."

A memory returned to Johab in a flash. His father had been out of sorts on the way to Queen Hatshepsut's temple. No jokes. No good stories. He had talked about Queen Hatshepsut's architect Senenmut. "Her temple is one of the wonders of the world. The temple *grows* out of the natural landscape. It belongs here. It's a part of this world, yet it seems to conquer the world. I think that is what Senenmut is telling us about Queen Hatshepsut. Even in death, she would remain part of this world, just like her temple."

As Sekina neared the turnoff to home, Johab was overcome with remorse. On that last day in the desert, he had fidgeted, tossed stones in the air, and complained about the heat as his father sketched the temple over and over. Then his father had stood, cocked his head, and said: "Listen. You can almost hear Queen Hatshepsut whispering when the wind blows along these terraces. What do you think she's saying?"

"I'm hungry. I'm tired. I'm hot. I'm bored. I wish the tourists would leave me in peace. That's what she's saying." Johab flinched with shame now. A short time later, his father had rushed him to the jeep and headed silently back to Cairo.

Johab's memory was now painfully clear. They had crossed by ferry, stopped briefly for gas and sped by the posters of President Sadat along the highway. Usually, the posters would prompt his father to talk about what the potential war might mean in terms of protecting the archaeological sites. But this time, his father was quiet—until he stopped the jeep, showed Johab that leather pouch and told him that Christmas would be in Michigan.

Now, as Sekina brayed to announce their arrival at the City of the Dead, Johab stared ruefully at the clusters of mud-brick mauseleums, the dun-colored, packed path ahead leading off toward a distant mosque. Except for a few chickens scratching near a rotting post, nothing moved in the heat of the sun. No one was thinking of Christmas.

CHAPTER 13

. . . but he was a very fine cat, a very fine cat indeed."

—Samuel Johnson

The mangy, ill-favored, yellow tomcat staked out the new family in his hut as his personal property. He eyed them from a safe perch under the eave of the roof, carefully determining his strategy of ownership. First, he had to ensure that no other cats got within yards of his place. He managed that feat with only the loss of a quarter of his ear. The territory was his, won by tooth and claw. The black tomcat, who owned the family next door, slunk down the alleyway with his front paw laid open to a hungry swarm of flies.

Gifts. Those would endear the yellow tomcat to his newly claimed family, especially the ragged boy who moved so confidently along the alleyways of the City of the Dead. The first gift was a large, sodden rat, tenderized by the sharp teeth of the cat. He laid it carefully in the middle of the entry way so that it would easily be seen.

The woman shrieked in horror. The little girl laughed. The boy picked it up by the tail and threw it on a pile of garbage. Clearly, they didn't appreciate large gifts. The next presents were three mice, laid carefully end-to-end at the door stoop.

The boy had seen him leave this gift and laughed out loud. "He's bringing us mice, Mother. That yellow cat is bringing us his food."

The boy moved closer and held out his hand. The tomcat would not make friends in an obvious way. Centuries of aloofness had been bred into the Goddess Bastet's children. He lifted his tail, shook it at the boy, and moved on down the alley. He would watch the boy and his home. This was his family now, and he would protect them from the snakes and small mammals that seemed to bother these human creatures. And, he would find a gift that was acceptable.

By mid-morning of his second day of selling beans from the clumsy cart, Johab had pocketed a few coins and could look forward having the rest of the day following leads that would help him find his father in a city of millions. He hung around the local police station, checking out posters of criminals. None of the men who broke into their apartment resembled the flat faces of the "wanted" on the black and white posters.

Aunt Rayya's apartment was only a couple of blocks away. She must be trying to do something about her sister's disappearance. She was *family*. A personal insult or injury to one member was considered a kick in the teeth to all the family. Johab could imagine the furor in the police station if Aunt Rayya thought they weren't doing enough to recover her family. From the street, Johab could see the front door of her apartment, welcoming and comforting. He almost cried out with shock.

Like a shark trolling for prey, a sleek, dark car cruised along the street just ahead of him. Johab jerked Sekina to a halt, squatted down, hid his face against her withers, and pretended to be working on the cart's wheel.

Uncle Tarek stood in the doorway, hitched up his pants, clapped on his guard's hat, and sauntered toward the car that was quietly idling beside the curb. Through the spokes of the wheel, Johab could clearly see the driver's side of the car. Uncle Tarek moved next to the window.

The darkened glass slid down partway. The conversation was muffled; Johab could hear nothing but the background noise of traffic. Uncle Tarek's hand moved across the open glass and back into his pocket. As his uncle turned away, Johab caught a glimpse of the driver. The clothes were different, a black jacket and a tie; beneath a well-groomed thatch of silver hair jutted a large, beaked nose. Johab forgot to breathe. The darkened glass of the window slid slowly up; the car eased forward, turned the corner, and disappeared.

Uncle Tarek stood by the curb for a moment, and, then, glanced across the street. Johab could almost hear his uncle thinking that the little beggar with a broken-down cart looked vaguely familiar. He watched Tarek fingering the wad of cash in his pocket, lifting his head higher, almost strutting back toward his apartment. Betrayal energized his uncle.

The evening shadows disguised the City of the Dead as Johab and Sekina returned at dusk. The rounded humps of tombs and mosques, convoluted alleyways, women sitting in the doorways at the end of the day, and children laughing and playing—it could have been any neighborhood in Cairo. But it wasn't. It was a place of last resort. Johab thought that the dead must be happy to share their space with so many poor people. The thought was a small comfort.

Johab needed comforting. He dared not tell his mother about Uncle Tarek taking money from the man who had stolen his father. She would find a taxi immediately. Her anger would make her careless in the face of danger. Johab couldn't even imagine what she would say to Uncle Tarek. Whatever she said or did would be justified. The Goddess Maat's scales of justice hung askew when uncles betrayed their families. Another secret would have to be kept from his mother.

As he eased the cart next to the place that was becoming as familiar as home, a streak of yellow shot out of the doorway of the hut where that old Bedouin, Mr. Feisel, lived. The tomcat had something in its mouth. The cat moved swiftly, only a trace of rippling yellow fur disturbed the dust in the alley connecting the tombs. Just in front of Johab's feet, the cat dropped his donation and puffed up his tail to affirm that this gift was rare.

It was rare. A blackened fragment of a hand with pieces of linen wrap still clinging to it decorated the doorstep. As he bent over the cat's newest gift, Johab noted that it was amazingly well preserved. Touching the blackened fingertip of the hand, he felt a surface smooth as a polished stone, hardened with resin. His father had described the process of mummification in detail.

When Johab tried to explain how the ancient Egyptians were preserved for eternity, his cousin Mohammed had shrieked: "Morbid! Nasty! Gross!" Then, he had begged for more details.

It wasn't gross. Long before the Egyptian kings invented elaborate rituals to preserve their bodies, people in Egypt had wrapped their dead in reed mats or animal hides and buried them with food, pottery, and a few treasures made of bone and ivory. Johab could remember his father showing him objects from some of the oldest graves. "They look like poor things compared to the gold and jewels in the great pharaohs' tombs. But they are beautiful in their own way." His father's voice had been tender, as though he might have been one of the mourners at those old gravesites.

Johab suddenly felt squeamish as he looked at the blackened hand curled by his foot, not behind glass in the museum. He had to admit that mummification was a bit bizarre. Johab remembered begging his father to tell him exactly how mummies were preserved. "It is a bit grisly—too much information for a boy your age," his father had said dismissively.

"I like grisly things," Johab remembered protesting. "When I asked about mummies in school, our teacher told me not to talk about such gruesome things. I told her mummies weren't gruesome. They were the kings of Egypt. She made me sit in out in the hall for an hour. Wasn't she wrong?"

His father had ignored his question. Teachers were not supposed to be wrong. He simply sat Johab down and detailed every step of the process that kept 3,000-year-old corpses looking somewhat human.

Johab remembered most of it: the priests pushed small hooks through the nostrils into the ethnoid bone of the nose, wiggling them to clear out the bone, so they could remove the brain through the nose; the mortuary priest worked from the left side of the body to remove the liver, the lungs and other organs to place in Canopic jars.

Johab had seen many of those jars at the museum. His cousin said those jars, topped by statues of animals representing guardians of the dead, were full of "innards." Johab frowned. His cousin didn't know squat about sacred vessels.

When Mohammed popped off, Johab had felt a bit nauseous, remembering trays of animal brains and stomachs at the butcher's. Then his father had reminded him softly, just away from Mohammed's hearing that "the heart was special. It stayed in the body. The priests were careful not to damage the heart."

His father had paused for a moment. "Your mother always talks about hearts, Johab. She says your Aunt Rayya has a 'good' heart and her priest at the church has a 'kind' heart. I don't think we're too far removed from those ancient priests who cared about hearts."

At this instant, Johab's heart ached unbearably with the memories of his father. He let his hand drift down to the tomcat's back. The yellow cat yowled softly, pleased that the boy was so transfixed by his gift of the mummy's hand. Johab glared down at the disrespectful cat that had interrupted good memories of his father.

He stiffened, startled by a different thought. The black market trade in mummies disgusted his father. Johab couldn't imagine that people still believed that mummy powder could make warts fall off.

Johab scowled at the cat. Clearly, the cat had snitched the blackened, shriveled hand from somewhere inside of Mr. Feisel's hut. What Mrs. Zadi told his mother must be true. Mr. Feisel boiled mummies and dabbled in black magic. Mrs. Zadi told his mother that he was "an ill-tempered grouch who lived like a hermit." Someone to avoid at all costs.

Still, theft was theft, and Johab did not intend to be a party to the cat's thievery. With his thumb and forefinger, Johab picked up the fragment of the mummy's hand. It was light as a piece of driftwood sapped by the sea. He could see traces of blackened nails—even the grooves of the knuckles remained. This hand was part of what had been a human being, a person with a beating heart.

Johab felt overwhelmed with disgust. Earlier today, the discovery of Uncle Tarek's disloyalty had angered and saddened him, but he could do nothing about it. *He could do something about this.*

Johab marched across the alley, not at all fearful of the ominous shadows cast by the disappearing sun. Cradling the ancient, blackened fingers in his own small hand, he hit the door sharply with his fist.

"Don't break my door!" The shout from inside the hut was loud, followed by the noise of an overturned chair and a curse. The door swung open. Mr. Feisel, the grease of his evening meal still on his fingers, glared down at Johab.

"What do you want, boy?" His breath was ragged, as though the effort to get across the room had taxed him. He clutched the frame of the door. "What's that in your hand? What do you mean bringing me something like that?" He backed away, clearly startled by the sight of mummy fingers.

"The cat . . . I saw the cat bring this out of your house," Johab blurted out. "It belongs to you."

"I don't have a cat. I wouldn't keep that thing in my house if you held a gun on me. Whatever gave you that notion?" He exploded in a series of coughs and sneezes. "Has that old biddy, Mrs. Zadi, been telling tales again?" He grimaced, his mouth clenched in a phantom smile that disappeared instantly.

Johab hung his head. It was clear that Mr. Feisel was shocked by the return of the cat's find. He nodded. Mrs. Zadi had been the tale-bearer.

"I thought so. I see how some people look at me around here after she's made her rounds. I don't deal in mummies. Tell your Mrs. Zadi that." He pushed the door shut in Johab's face.

Johab felt the flush creeping from his gut right up to his ears. Mr. Feisel nailed it. He had listened to Mrs. Zadi whispering to his mother: "He dabbles in the magic. He's not a Christian, like us," proud of a faith she didn't practice. "Tell your children never to go near his house. He cooks evil things and sells the mummy oil."

Johab stood in front of the closed door for only a second. Mr. Feisel had the look of a man indignant with surprise, with irritation, not one caught in an illegal act. Johab paused, took in a great swoop of air and tapped lightly on the door again. It swung open.

"What now? I'd call the police on you for disturbing a man's evening meal, but I don't like the police any better than I like Mrs. Zadi." He dusted his hands together, as though clearing the air of the police, Mrs. Zadi *and* Johab.

"I made a mistake, sir. I saw the cat come past here over to our house, and I thought he stole this mummy hand from you, especially after what Mrs. . . . after what Mrs. . . ."

Johab stuttered, hard-pressed to put a name to the neighborhood gossip.

Mr. Feisel looked hard at Johab. "It's good to admit when you're wrong. Just remember the old saying about never judging a book by its cover. Mrs. Zadi is very friendly to newcomers around here. Your mother needs to be careful."

Johab stood without moving, subdued by advice that he knew was kindly meant. "What can I do with this?" he asked, extending his hand with the mummy fingers dangling over the side like the claw of a friendly bird.

"I'd take it to one of the graves here, dig a little hole, deep enough so the cat won't find it, and let it rest with the dead." Mr. Feisel walked over to move a pot off the bright coals of his brazier. "Come on boy. I'll go with you. I know just the place."

Johab followed Mr. Feisel as he moved quickly down the dusty alley. He walked stiffly but purposefully as though determined to appear vigorous. After a quarter of a mile, he turned into a small section where the graves were covered by plain slabs of concrete.

"Here. Dig under the edge of this one. The poor won't mind sharing their graves. Who knows, this hand might have belonged to a king," he chuckled. Johab grabbed a nearby stick and dug at the clay-packed ground under the edge of the tomb slab. The last rain had washed a small gulley where the concrete met the ground. He tucked the blackened fingers carefully into the crack and covered them with dirt.

Johab would have said a prayer, but he wasn't sure which of the gods look after fingers in the afterworld, so he stepped back and followed Mr. Feisel. At the end of the alley, he could see his mother looking anxiously in all directions. She had seen his cart by the front door.

"Your mother will have your hide for not telling her that you were home, and rightly so." Mr. Feisel seemed amused.

"Boy. Just a minute." Mr. Feisel grabbed the sleeve of Johab's robe. "I don't know what you're doing here. Your mother seems like a nice lady. I heard her talking in English to your sister. She switched to Arabic the minute she saw me watching them."

Johab had a sinking feeling. He knew that his mother and Jasmine would forget "the game." Again and again, he had warned them not to speak English.

Mr. Feisel watched the fear play across Johab's face. He clapped him on the back and said, "Don't worry, boy. I keep my own counsel, and I'll keep an eye on your mother and sister when you're gone. I know what it's like to have someone after you—and *you* have someone after you."

Johab nodded toward Mr. Feisel and headed in the direction of his mother who might have been waving him into a safe port.

CHAPTER 14

O Villany! Ho! Let the door be lock'd
Treachery! Seek it out.

—Shakespeare

Over the desert, humped and tawny as a great, sleeping lion, the sky arched robin's egg blue. It was a fine December morning for travel. Sekina's eyes were bright, her head erect. She would have brayed with happiness and brought down the wrath of the neighbors if Johab had not held her nose. She must sense that they were heading for an adventure, not just selling fulbeans.

A new leather and rope harness had *magically* appeared on the cart this morning. Johab saluted the open door of Mr. Feisel's hut. That kind of magic had nothing to do with the occult, but with the kindness of strangers—a magic residing in their hearts.

His entire body reverberated with anticipation. Today, Miss Wenkle was to meet him at the Khan. Three long days had passed since he had talked to her at the market. By now, she would surely have some information. Johab urged Sekina into a trot, heading toward a crowded street not far from the Museum. If he sold the fulbeans quickly, he would have time to swing by the back entrance to the Museum before going to the market.

He might catch a glimpse of Uncle Tarek and check out the guards who seemed most friendly to his uncle. Johab needed to put his friends on one side, his enemies on another, and those that he was unsure about in the middle. That would be Sherlock's approach:

line up the evidence and discard what didn't contribute to solving a problem.

A dejected expression crossed Johab's face. Human relationships were messy, not like pictorial hieroglyphs on tombs in which a snake looked just like a snake. Tarek was his uncle. His betrayal was painful to think about. Maybe he was missing something. Could it be that Uncle Tarek was doing his own investigation? No. The cash transaction through the window of the black car stacked the evidence against Uncle Tarek. There was no mistaking the driver of that car.

Flinging back his head in frustration, Johab shouted up toward balconies lining the street: "Fulbeans with the three secret ingredients of ancient Egypt: cumin, cardamom, and coriander. Spices of the kings!"

Within minutes, Johab had scraped the bottom of the pot clean. Maybe Miss Wenkle would bring lunch to the Khan, something better than yukky beans. With an empty stomach and a hopeful twinkle in his eyes, he turned the donkey and cart toward the Museum.

"Move over, you stupid boy. Get that donkey out of my way!" A portly woman, wedged into a small car, her generous jowls quivering with anger, shouted at him, waving her fist. Screaming and honking were prerequisites for using Cairo streets. A small donkey and a skinny boy traveled at their own peril.

Not responding, Johab slipped back into his disguise and guided Sekina with gentle thumps on her rump. He looked dirty and poor, but he was an expert with a donkey and a superb seller of fulbeans. Best of all, no one working at the Museum could possibly recognize him as John Bennett's son.

As he neared the back of the building, he clutched the donkey's halter. Her eyes rolled with ecstasy as she spotted a night-blooming jasmine in a pot near the walkway.

A few employees, some Johab recognized, stood near the back door. One of the guards eyed him suspiciously and moved in his direction. Johab gripped Sekina's halter, ready to move quickly.

"You boy! You!" The guard shouted from the back driveway. "Don't let that donkey eat the plants. Keep that beast in the street."

Johab nodded, jerking Sekina's halter as she stretched for clump of shiny green jasmine leaves. Donkeys' necks were long as a giraffe's when they spotted something green. When Johab turned back towards the Museum, his mouth went slack.

Miss Wenkle was smiling, almost preening, as she walked down the back steps with a tall, well-dressed, silver-haired man who waved to her like an old friend as he moved toward a black car taking up two parking spaces.

Johab ducked his face into Sekina's neck. He had not recognized the car less than ten feet away from him. How could he be so blind to the danger right under his nose? The man tossed his briefcase in the passenger's seat, backed expertly into a narrow space and sped out of the parking lot, going in the wrong direction. So much for the rules that Miss Wenkle followed; apparently, they were meaningless to her friend.

Her friend. A wave of bitterness swept over Johab. Uncle Tarek's betrayal paled in the face of Miss Wenkle's treachery. She had been the only hope. Now, she had gone over to the dark side. That silver-haired man laughing so casually with her was the very same man who had hit his mother in the face and snatched away his father. He was the same man who had slipped money to Uncle Tarek. And, he was using the "Staff" entrance, as though he belonged there.

Johab yanked Sekina's head around and headed toward the Khan. The small donkey looked soulfully at the shrubbery. It would have been a well-deserved feast after she had obliging pulled the cart with a driver who wasn't as expert as he thought he was. Sekina had to work twice as hard on the turns just to keep the fulbean pot from tipping over. The boy didn't notice that extra effort. Now, he was jerking her harness sharply, angry about something. Sekina was a good donkey with a good heart. Otherwise, she would have nipped him to teach him a little lesson about the care and tending of donkeys.

Johab's first impulse was to rush back to the City of the Dead and find a new place for his mother and Jasmine. With relief, he remembered how he had avoided telling Miss Wenkle about their hiding place. They were still safe, and Mr. Feisel would watch out for his mother and Jasmine. In spite of Mrs. Zadi's gossip, Johab sensed that the old man who sat whittling a block of wood on his front step was a safe port.

He couldn't rely on Miss Wenkle anymore. She had been a friend of their family, someone who shared special holidays with them. That made him doubly angry. He would go right now and confront her in the market. It would be safer in a crowd. His lips formed into a small pout. She could have those stupid house slippers back. He would like to keep the Hardy Boys mysteries.

Outside the busy Khan, Johab scanned the streets for a place to leave Sekina. Donkeys weren't allowed in the Khan where Miss Wenkle said she'd meet him. Just at the edge of the street, a small, dirty boy, who appeared to be no older than Jasmine, sorted through a pile of trash by one of the front stalls. His begging bowl rested on the ground by his foot.

Johab beckoned to him. "I'll give you these coins if you hold my donkey right here. Pay attention, because she likes to break away if she sees something to eat." Johab frowned. If the boy disappeared with his donkey and his cart, he'd be selling fulbeans on foot. It was time for a Cousin Mohammed lie.

"Don't move from this spot. I'll be watching you from under the flap of that tent over there." Johab gestured toward a large, striped tent that had just been invaded by a gaggle of tourists. "You move, and you won't get any money. And, my donkey will bite you." Worse than Mohammed who *teased* children, Johab had just *threatened* one. Hard times required hard measures. He'd give the boy an extra coin.

Sneaking alongside the tent, Johab knew he couldn't let Miss Wenkle see him before he saw her. He had to be prepared for a trap. The tall man might appear without warning. He could even be holding hands with Miss Wenkle. Every tent flap held danger behind it.

Circling around the backside of the tent where they had met three days before, Johab looked both ways to be sure no one was watching,. Then, he dropped to his knees, poked his head under the tent like the proverbial camel, and slid on his belly behind a pile of "genuine antique" Persian rugs.

Within seconds, the embalmment process was underway. Three thousand years later and nothing beside him for the afterlife, but Johab couldn't fight the tears or the sneezing. Formaldehyde, benzene and styrene wafted up from the dyes on those rugs.

Just as Johab struggled for what might be his last breath, the tent flap opened and a hot, dry desert wind swirled the odors of chemicals up and away, right into the smiling face of Miss Wenkle. Wearing the same disguise—a big hat, over-sized sunglasses and her trademark white gloves—she appeared totally at ease as she settled into a chair near the tent flap, whipped off her hat and fanned her guilty face.

"I'm here, but I'm hiding," Johab hissed at her from behind the pyramid of rugs.

"Come out where I can see you, Johab. Aren't you being a little paranoid? I checked all around the area. No one saw me come in," she said calmly.

"Maybe not, but I saw you," Johab said between clenched teeth. "I saw you with *him*, just an hour ago. You were laughing with the man who took my father."

"The man who what?" Miss Wenkle's exclamation split the air as she sprang from her chair with surprising ease for a person so plump. "I don't know what you're talking about. Come here this instant so I can see you. I can't talk to a pile of rugs."

Johab inched forward, edging around the stack of carpets but keeping his foot hooked under the flap of the tent for a quick escape. He glared at her. "I saw you with him this morning. You were laughing at the back door of the Museum. *I think you know where my father is.*" Johab spat out the words slowly and emphatically, syllable by syllable.

Miss Wenkle dropped back into the chair, her legs splayed at an awkward angle, and clutched her purse against her chest like a shield to deflect the bullets of Johab's accusation.

"I never . . . I wouldn't . . . I don't . . . " she paused as the torrent of negative phrases passed automatically through her lips. "Good heavens," she whispered in a stunned voice. "Do you mean Mr. Barzoni?"

"I don't know his name," muttered Johab. "I just know that I will never forget his face or his nose or his voice. You were holding his hand and laughing. I don't trust you anymore," Johab sniffed, holding back tears of frustration. He had been too gullible, trusting her in the first place. That's what trust does. Makes people careless. He was done trusting anyone but his parents—and maybe Aunt Rayya.

CHAPTER 15

Johab watched Miss Wenkle as she shifted forward, holding her big hat in one hand next to her head. Like Wadget, the Egyptian goddess with two cobra heads; neither head moved. Only her purse, clasped against her chest, rose faintly up and down. She might be having a stroke or a heart attack. Johab shuddered with anger. He wouldn't call a doctor. Let that old rug seller who owned this tent find her. Before long, the formaldehyde in these new rugs would embalm her.

"Johab," her voice had a tinge of sadness that he had never heard before. "I think of you and your family as my family. Surely you know that." Johab clenched his jaw, staring past her, unwilling to meet her eyes.

"You saw me giving Mr. Barzoni the proof of one of your father's manuscripts that had already been returned to a journal for publication. Mr. El-Hasiim told me to give Mr. Barzoni a copy, because it will be published next month. Mr. Barzoni is a wealthy and influential man. Your father knows him well. He has contributed generously to the New Kingdom Project. We surely can't be talking about the same man." She seemed distracted, trying to pull her thoughts together.

"Dad knew the man who broke into our apartment. He threatened to kill us. I'd recognize him anywhere." Johab's voice cracked with emotion.

Miss Wenkle sat up straight, clutching her purse as though it had become a life preserver in seas too wild to be imagined. "Now, I'm paranoid. I don't know whom to trust anymore. Mr. Barzoni is a patron of the Museum. Mr. El-Hasiim, allows him access to information about the New Kingdom Project." She paused as though rethinking her comments. "Your father never allowed Mr. Barzoni to see his work before publication, but Mr. El-Hasiim insisted I make a copy for Mr. Barzoni."

A bright flush spread from her neck to the roots of her blond hair. "I think I may have been stupid, Johab. Mr. Barzoni is a persuasive man. I thought his questions were asked out of concern for John." Her voice trailed off.

"What questions?" Johab demanded, rising to his feet but remaining close to the rugs, near his escape hatch.

"Mr. Barzoni said that he was worried about your father and family, because the police didn't seem to have any answers. He said he knew that I was a friend of your family and asked me to contact him immediately if I heard from any of you. He said he had connections that could help in ways that the police might not be able to do."

She paused, as though struck by a sudden insight. "Other than getting a copy of that article, Mr. Barzoni didn't ask me about your father's work. Come to think of it, he was grilling me about your mother's family here in Cairo and your father's family in Michigan. I might have . . ." Loud voices outside the tent startled her.

"That's my friend who owns this shop. Some men out there are giving him trouble. You've got to get out of here, Johab." She pushed him toward the back of the tent. "Your mother's church near your old neighborhood. Meet me tomorrow around five. I sometimes go to the services there. It won't seem suspicious. Now, go!" She raised the bottom of the tent, and shoved Johab into the back alley.

Johab crouched beside a pile of trash behind the tent. He needed to know if someone had followed him to the Khan. If so, his cover was blown. Maybe, Barzoni had followed Miss Wenkle. She was somewhat of an amateur.

Creeping alongside the tent, Johab peered around the flap. The two men talking angrily to the shopkeeper seemed vaguely familiar, especially the one with legs like stumps. Johab could hear snatches of their demands. " . . . English woman . . . someone saw her . . . three days ago."

Johab's eyes widened in shock jaw as Miss Wenkle burst from the tent smack into the middle of the three men and flipped her thumb toward the pile of rugs.

In an officious voice, she growled: "I told you that I wanted to see the next shipment of *real* Persian rugs, not those cheap, machine-made things." She pointed scornfully to the pile of new rugs in the tent. "The wool has to be hand-rolled and dyed with native plants. Do not call me again until you have the rugs I want to see." She flounced around and headed toward the entrance of the Khan but not before she had turned her back on the two men and winked slyly at the shopkeeper.

Johab's faith in Miss Wenkle was restored. She might have let her guard down with Mr. Barzoni. He was obviously a man of influence and had been given free rein within the Museum. Someone like Barzoni might easily sweet-talk a middle-aged, single woman.

Johab stopped that train of thought in its tracks. Miss Wenkle had risen to the occasion. She popped out right between two men who were tracking her and turned the tables on them by providing a perfect excuse for being in the tent. Then, she topped off the trick by winking at her friend as she breezed down the alleyway. She was someone who could think and act quickly, someone that Johab needed as an ally.

The little beggar stood on stork-like legs, continuously rubbing Sekina's neck as though determined to earn his payment. Johab felt a twinge of remorse. That boy couldn't be much older than Jasmine. In Cairo, many young boys worked from sun up to sun down to make a few coins for their families. He knew about those boys but didn't like thinking about them. Now, he was one of them.

Johab glowered into the mob of shoppers. *Parading* as one of those boys was not the same thing as *sharing* their misery. If he could reverse the past few days, he'd have a future. These boys had no future. Johab knew that he could never look at them in quite the same way again. He handed over more coins than he had intended to give the boy.

As soon as he reached Salah Salem Street, a wave of tiredness swept over Johab. He hopped on the back of the cart and clucked to Sekina when she slowed down to nibble grass. That donkey ate at every opportunity. Johab hadn't eaten all day. She could carry him home. The bumpy cart and the hot, late afternoon sun lulled him into a state of relaxation so he could think about important things.

Like the pouch. Could his father's notes explain the hieroglyphs on the old papyrus? He knew that the earliest hieroglyphs were chiseled into stone. By Queen Hatshepsut's time, reed pens were being used on papyrus. Johab remembered being bored when his father tried to teach him about hieroglyphs and show him how they changed to be more "hieratic."

"Remember when you learned to print your name, Johab? First, you learned block capital letters. By the time you were in the second grade, you were writing your name in cursive, linking letter to letter. It is much faster. By the time of the New Kingdom, the scribes were using hieratic script as a kind of cursive writing on papyrus."

Why hadn't he listened? If there was a dangerous message on the papyrus in the pouch, he could have interpreted it immediately. He was mostly interested in his father's work because he loved being with his father—not because he liked looking at hieroglyphic squiggles.

As he looked back toward the skyline of Cairo, Johab perked up and announced to Sekina: "It will be different. I'll be different. I'll study everything about the ancient Egyptians. I'll start tomorrow. I'll go to the library and . . ."

He couldn't go to the library. He couldn't be seen with a book. He was a street boy, a seller of fulbeans. Dropping his disguise meant danger. He would have to play the game until he could get information about his father. A sly grin spread across his face. He now had his first real piece of information. The kidnapper had a name—Mr. Barzoni.

CHAPTER 16

Appearances are often deceiving.

—Aesop

Jasmine's beaming face met Johab as he unhitched Sekina from the cart. "Johab! Johab!" She shrieked. "Look what Mr. Feisel made my doll." She held out a small bed, its posts lashed together with strips of rawhide, its headboard expertly carved with hieroglyphs from the chapel of Queen Hatshepsut. Ankhs, little crosses with loops at the top, lined the edges. A striding prince—the Queen herself disguised as a man—held the flail of authority. A tiny bull completed the design.

Mr. Feisel was full of surprises. So was Johab's mother. "We need a few things from our apartment. Do you think I can go there by taxi after dark when I can't be seen?" She examined the coins that Johab dropped in her hand from the sale of fulbeans. "We don't have enough money to buy everything we need," she complained, her frustration obvious.

Johab remained silent. They were reversing roles. His mother was asking him for permission. And he stood, stony faced, knowing he had to refuse her. It was too risky. The men who followed Miss Wenkle to the Khan must be working for Mr. Barzoni. Someone would be keeping a close watch on their apartment. Johab was a wizard at getting in the back way. His mother did not frequent alleys. Going there was too risky.

The pained expression on his mother's face demanded a compromise. "You make out a list, Mother. I'll do it. We can't trust taxis. There is an important man . . ."

"What man?" she interrupted, her radar on alert. "Does he know John? Can he help us?"

"He can hurt us." Johab might as well be blunt. Fear would make her careful, and all of them needed to be very careful. "I can't tell you his name. You have to trust me. I will get the things you need."

His mother hesitated. Johab was her only son, and by the old custom, he was entitled to make decisions when his father wasn't available. But this was the Twentieth Century. Mothers did not allow their young sons to take risks. If that man came to their neighborhood again, what would keep him from taking Johab?

Johab could almost read her mind and grabbed his mother's hand. "I look like a street boy. You look like a woman who should be shopping for gold at the Khan. I can get into our apartment. I can be as invisible as a ghost," he affirmed with more confidence than he felt. Now he had a reason to stay in Cairo after the fulbeans were sold tomorrow. He could meet Miss Wenkle at his mother's church with no questions asked.

Dinner that night was only bread, but delicious. His mother had commandeered a large, metal tray called a "*safeeh*" and put it directly over the hot coals of the brazier. The warm, sweet odor of freshly baking bread permeated the room. At the end of their meal, she prodded the charcoal and slapped another slab of dough on the *safeeh*. "For Mr. Feisel," she said. "He's been nice to Jasmine, and he brought us a bucket of water from the well up the hill," she pointed toward the larger mausoleums.

"He wheezes a lot. I'm going to offer him my special salve for his chest. It worked on Sekina's burn." His mother folded the slab of warm bread onto a tin plate. "Take it to Mr. Feisel while it's hot."

Johab tapped gently at Mr. Feisel's door. It swung open immediately. Mr. Feisel stared at the bread, drooping over the edge of the plate, as though it might be something poisonous, something as objectionable as a mummy hand, an unwelcome gift. Johab stepped inside, uninvited, and plopped the tin pan down on his table. "It's burning my hand," he protested. "Mother made it for you. It's what we ate tonight."

"Oh." Mr. Feisel grunted and dropped into one of the two chairs by the table. He tore off a piece of the bread and shoved it in his mouth. "Sit, boy. What is your name? I heard your sister call you 'Johab.' What kind of name is that?"

Johab was sensitive about his name. At school, there were several Mohammeds, a few Yusefs, a couple of Maleks, one Ali but no one named for a long-dead Egyptian king. "I'm named for Horemheb. He was an ancient king and a great warrior. I'm called Johab for short." Johab tried to put his nickname in the best light. He didn't dare reveal his first name as "John." Mr. Feisel had probably guessed by now that his mother was someone clearly out of place in the City of the Dead.

My m . . . m . . . mother," he stammered, "likes history, the old things."

Mr. Feisel gave him a sharp look. "Your mother's not the only one who likes old things. Do you think I don't read the newspapers, Johab? I suspect that I might know who you are, but I don't know why you're here."

Johab needed a really good Mohammed lie to explain to Mr. Feisel why they were camping out in a ramshackle hut in the City of the Dead. It came to him in a flash. Their next-door neighbor at the apartment had been evicted earlier in the year. He remembered peeking through curtains, embarrassed at the sight of Mr. Otto's weeping wife and children with their possessions on the street. The painters arrived the next day. All traces of the Otto family disappeared within twenty-four hours.

Johab perked up and shot Mr. Feisel a sad smile. "We were evicted. That's why we're here. We didn't have any other place to go." Mr. Feisel seemed interested. Johab decided to elaborate on his story. "We don't know why the landlord did that. We were paying our rent. But he just threw us out with no warning. My father . . . ." Whoops. He had forgotten about his missing father.

In his best Mohammed style, Johab came up with another twist to his tale. "My father works out of the country. We're trying to get word to him." That was a good twist. A number of his classmates had fathers who worked out of the country. "We think he is in Saudi right now," he added lamely.

Mr. Feisel chomped on the remaining crust of bread, pushed back his chair and eyed Johab skeptically. "Which turnip wagon do you think I fell off, boy?" he asked caustically. Mr. Feisel used the idiom in English. "You've been telling me this story in English. It might be a believable story, but boys selling fulbeans for a living don't speak English fluently. You do."

Johab gulped. Caught up in his underwear—that's how his father would have described his predicament. That's exactly what happened to Mohammed when he began to elaborate on what could have been a simple and straightforward lie. Of course, there was nothing straightforward about lying.

Johab twitched nervously. His father despised lies, but then his father wasn't facing a hostile, old man with skin scorched as dark as a Nubian, staring down at him in disbelief.

Mr. Feisel lifted both hands openly, as if to save Johab from a trap of his own making. "I have something to show you." He walked over to a small cabinet with intricately carved doors, pulled out a box, and turned toward Johab with something cupped in his hand.

"What do you think of this object?"

Johab stared. "I know what it is. I've seen them at the Museum. It's a piece of an ancient cylinder seal made of blue faience."

Afraid to say any more, Johab's first thought was that Mr. Feisel had an illegal piece of an Egyptian treasure. He didn't know much about cylindrical seals but could see that the ankhs on this one were beautifully drawn. It had been broken, but what was left was very fine.

A smile lifted the weather-beaten cheeks of Mr. Feisel, and he bent toward Johab as if to reveal a very important secret. "It was given to me by Mr. Howard Carter on the very day that he opened King Tutankhamen's burial chamber."

CHAPTER 17

Johab gasped in disbelief. This old man was lying or delusional. Johab eased a step back toward the door. Howard Carter was a legend, the best-known Egyptologist in the world because of his discovery of King Tutankhamen's tomb in 1922. That find had caught the public's attention in ways that no other tomb discovery ever had and turned Egypt into a tourist destination.

King Tut was only a minor king. Yet, Carter's find was the first tomb of a pharaoh to be photographed and documented 3,000 years after it had been sealed. In the past, robbers had pillaged all the ancient burial chambers almost as soon as they were sealed. Although there was evidence that tomb robbers had broken into King Tut's main tomb, the burial chamber was untouched.

The discovery of Tutankhamen's tomb made headlines all over the world. Johab's father had read to him parts of Howard Carter's diaries, old newspapers, and magazine accounts from the period trying to recreate for Johab that sense of excitement the world shared.

He remembered his father telling him how carefully Carter tried to photograph and document everything. But, the king's body in its red quartzite sarcophagus was saved for the "grand opening event," with many photographers, including some from Hollywood left waiting.

Johab could almost feel his heart thumping in his chest as he remembered how the resin used to preserve the body had glued King Tut to his gold coffin. Carter and his helpers literally hacked the mummy away from the coffin, separating King Tut's head and his limbs from his body.

Johab recalled that his father had defended Mr. Carter. "He was desperate to remove the mummy and get the coffin to safety before thieves could tear it apart to get the gold. He reassembled the mummy, put it in a small wooden box, and left him in the tomb."

Not all of him. Johab's father told him that later x-rays of the body showed some ribs and a breastbone missing.

Mr. Feisel's throat-clearing "harrumph" brought Johab back from thinking about King Tut's mummy to the incredible statement that Mr. Feisel had just made—that he was there when Howard Carter opened King Tut's burial chamber.

"You look skeptical, Johab. I could tell you unbelievable stories about what I saw." Mr. Feisel's eyes seemed to focus on something far away and long ago. "It was like a carnival show. Howard Carter opened the tomb to newspaper people and visiting royalty. They brought camels loaded with gunnysacks full of ice for the visiting dignitaries' drinks."

A sad expression crossed Mr. Feisel's face. "Carter's number one funder, Lord Carnarvon, died that next spring. That's when all the rumors about the curse of the mummy began."

Johab nodded. He knew about the *Mummy's Curse.* He and Mohammed had watched Lon Chaney staggering about shedding linen strips as he terrorized the living. His father thought most stories and movies about mummies were either misguided or silly. But, he told Johab: "Without public interest, we won't have the funding that we need to study the past."

That was it! He suddenly remembered what has father had said the day they drove to Luxor. He had begun explaining about the need for scientists and the Egyptian people to work together to protect the tombs and treasures.

Then, his father's face had darkened with anger. "Trading in rare Egyptian art is a crime this country simply cannot allow. We must stop illegal antiquity trade." His father's voice had risen to an angry pitch. Illegal tomb robberies from the ancient time to the present were an awful crime, a subject that Johab's father sometimes gave public speeches about. But he didn't turn red and get into a snit. His father's bad mood had lasted for the rest of the trip.

Fake "treasures" didn't bother his father. Johab remembered laughing with him about the "rare" blue faience beetles that tourists bought by the thousands as "tomb finds" at the Khan.

"The tourists go home happy, thinking they've found an ancient treasure. The shopkeeper is happy with his sale. Everyone wins—TTT has been a bonanza for tourism in Egypt." Johab's father referred to the King Tut exhibit as TTT, "tut trap for tourists," because busloads dashed over to the King Tut exhibit for an hour and missed the incredible collection in the rest of the Museum.

Johab felt a special kinship with King Tutankhamen. His name was shortened to a nickname—Tut. Johab admired the gentle face of this young king captured in his gold mask. He was very sorry that his mummy got whacked into pieces. Maybe his bones could frolic in the afterworld, in the Fields of Yalu, without a head attached to his body.

Dismemberment of mummies made Johab uneasy. So did Mr. Feisel standing close to him and holding that ancient seal from King Tut's tomb. It would not be a good idea to accuse this old man of stealing tomb treasures. The confrontation they had over the yellow tomcat and the piece of a mummy's hand had made Johab more judicious. Mr. Feisel did not take kindly to rash accusations.

As though reading Johab's thoughts, Mr. Feisel pointed to a chair and said, "Sit. We need to talk about our fathers."

Johab slumped into the chair across from Mr. Feisel. He was not prepared to talk about his father. According to the "eviction" story, he had told Mr. Feisel, Johab had stranded his father somewhere in Saudi Arabia.

Mr. Feisel reached across the table and brushed his hand across Johab's cheek. "I can see the disbelief on your face, but I was there at the tomb. I was twelve years old and doing the work of a grown man, hauling buckets of dirt and stone away from the sides of the tomb. I don't believe Mr. Carter had any idea what he would find."

"It's been fifty years since that day, and it will stay with me as long as I live." The pupils of his eyes darkened as though he might be staring into that tomb. "I think that you and I have a connection, Johab, through our fathers." Johab responded with a blank expression.

"My father knew Mr. Carter when he was a very young man working with Mr. Petrie, a real pioneer in Egyptology. The Museum had just been moved to its present location near Tahrir Square. My father was head groundskeeper but spent more time in the Museum doing special jobs. He fell in love with the history of his country. He read everything he could find about the ancient people. He longed to go into the field with Mr. Carter, but he couldn't afford to leave his job. In the field, he wouldn't be paid any more than five piastres for digging and hauling. He had to support a large family and needed the six English pounds he got a month. So he sent me. He had a premonition that Howard Carter was going to find something wonderful."

The room became so quiet that Johab dared not breathe. Mr. Feisel's face was transformed, like someone who had just witnessed a miracle, too rare to be discussed.

"Only a few of the field workers were allowed inside of the chamber before Mr. Carter and his staff closed it under guard so they could catalog everything just as it had been originally left. I don't know why I was so lucky—maybe because I was just a boy, and Mr. Carter could see how excited I was. Earlier that morning, I had brought him this piece of a cylinder seal—I found it when I was sifting through a bucket of debris around the front of the tomb. He told me that it was a good-luck sign—not of any value, too damaged, and I could keep it."

Mr. Feisel rubbed the seal with his thumb. "I gave it to my father. You'd have thought I had brought him a king's ransom. He always kept it with him."

"Our fathers, Johab. That's our special connection. Mine loved the ancient history of this country. I know that your father must have loved it too."

Johab was stunned at that statement and glared across the table at Mr. Feisel. Mr. Carter discovered Tutankhamen's tomb in 1922. If Mr. Feisel had been twelve years old then, that meant he was in his sixties now. Mr. Feisel's father could not possibly be alive. He was talking about his own father in past tense, and he was talking about Johab's in the same way.

"My father isn't dead!" Johab blurted out, tears welling into his eyes. "You don't have any right to talk about him like that."

"Oh, no, no, no. . . ." Mr. Feisel's protest trailed off as he reached across the table and patted Johab's arm. "I didn't mean that. I just meant. . . ."

He stopped, staring at Johab as though re-evaluating him. "As I told you the day you came pounding on my door, accusing me of feeding that tomcat a piece of mummy. . . ." Johab started to interrupt. That's not exactly what he had said to Mr. Feisel that day when the tomcat brought him the gift of a mummy's hand.

Mr. Feisel stared Johab into silence and continued. "As I told you that day, I keep my own counsel. That's the way that I keep busybodies out of my affairs. I was once very foolish and talked to someone at a newspaper about being with Mr. Carter on that dig. I think I may be the only person still alive today who was there."

He nodded toward Johab in a conspiratorial fashion. "There are people out there who believe that I might know something about Mr. Carter's other discoveries. And there are all those old tales about the 'mummy's curse' against all those people who died after the tomb was opened."

Mr. Feisel whacked the table with his fist. "That's utter nonsense. People died every day in Egypt with typhoid and malaria. No antibiotics. I was of interest to newspapers because I was there, and I didn't die. People I didn't know were coming to my house, even when my father was on his deathbed. After he died, I had to disappear. I know about disappearing."

He looked directly into Johab's eyes. "I won't ask you any questions, but I'll tell you what I think. You can decide if you want to trust me."

He held up his hand, the knuckles puffy with arthritis, and popped his thumb and fingers up one by one.

"One: I'm my father's son. I'm interested in anything that relates to ancient Egypt—that means believing in the old mysteries and helping in any way that I can to preserve our history for our future."

"Two: I find it very interesting that a ring of thieves has been caught trying to sell antiquities that are rumored to be very rare, yet no further information has come out about these things—and only one of them is on display at the Museum."

"Three: Shortly after some thieves were caught, a well-known American specialist in Egyptology goes missing, along with his family."

"Four: A mother and her two children wearing Western clothes arrive at an abandoned tomb in The City of the Dead during the middle of that same night."

"Five: The boy in the family, who can spot an ancient cylinder seal across the room, spends long days in the city even though he probably sells his fulbeans before noon."

"My conclusion," Mr. Feisel popped his hand open, reinforcing his five points, and looked directly at Johab, "is that part of this family is missing, that the mother and the son are terrified of being found, and that the son may be trying to do something to locate his father."

Johab felt himself working up a strong protest, even if it meant another series of lies. "No," said Mr. Feisel, putting up his hand to stop Johab. "I don't want any answers now. They might include stories about how your father is getting along in Saudi Arabia. We've already gone down that road." Johab looked down, shame-faced.

"You just think about the things I told you tonight about myself. I haven't shared that information with anyone for years. I think fate brought you here. It was a kind of omen that directed you to my door carrying a mummy's hand."

Johab would dispute the word "fate" as being responsible for his family's situation. The word "evil" worked better. And as for the mummy hand being some kind of omen, that cat continued to leave gifts of dead mice at their door, hardly omens.

It was late. His mother would be wondering why he hadn't returned from Mr. Feisel's, but his head was too full to think clearly. This old man living in the City of the Dead might be the only person still alive who had seen the rarest of things—a burial chamber of a pharaoh untouched for thousands of years. Now that same old man was claiming that he and Johab had a "connection."

Even more disturbing, Mr. Feisel had put some clues together. He had guessed the identities of Johab and his family. He suspected that the disappearance of Johab's father was linked to the black market in stolen treasures—even Johab had not made that connection though it seemed ridiculous.

Mr. Feisel knew that Johab and his mother were afraid. That would have been easy to guess, but it troubled Johab.

As Johab backed out of the hut, Mr. Feisel muttered softly: "Remember the words of Hathor, lady of the sacred land. She speaks of 'a resting place for him who has done right within the boat of the blessed.' I like to think that she is always reminding me to be one of those who has done right. I think she wants me to help you, Johab."

Those last words kept Johab awake half the night as Hathor, the Egyptian goddess, with her cow's horns visited his dreams.

CHAPTER 18

A snake lurks in the grass.

—Virgil

The sun pierced the small window of the hut, casting slivers of light that danced across the hard clay walls of the converted mausoleum. Johab awoke with a start. It was late. The brazier was cold. Jasmine huddled under her blanket. There was no sign of his mother. Usually, she was up stirring beans for his trip into the city. He rolled to his feet and crept to the door, pushing it ajar.

His mother's laughter stirred memories that Johab had not dared to think about for days. There she was in her ill-fitting galabeya, perched on the front stoop of Mr. Feisel's hut, the two of them laughing like old friends.

The easy familiarity of his mother and Mr. Feisel set Johab's teeth on edge. He had lain awake half the night thinking about that preposterous claim that Mr. Feisel had been with Mr. Carter when King Tut's tomb was opened.

Mr. Feisel had seen right through the lies and made it clear that he knew some of the secrets that Johab had tried so hard to hide, especially about his family's identity.

Mr. Feisel might have pieced together some information, but he could not possibly know what was hidden under the window ledge—only Johab and whatever gods might be watching knew that secret place. It would take the aid of a god or an Egyptologist to help him interpret the meaning of the hieroglyphs on those old papyrus sheets inside the pouch.

Johab looked daggers at the two of them laughing together. Mr. Feisel knew too much or had *guessed* too much. Seeing his mother so friendly with Mr. Feisel, Johab had a sinking feeling that his mother had been tricked into telling their neighbor much more than she should have—that's probably how he learned who they might be.

"Mother!" Johab's nervousness shot his voice into a strained, high pitch. Startled, his mother looked at him quizzically.

"Jasmine needs breakfast. She needs it now!"

Mr. Feisel winked broadly at Johab. "Your boy seems a little out of sorts this morning. Late nights will do that."

Johab's mother stood up, dusted off the back of her robe and stalked over, grabbing him by the arm and pushing him inside their hut.

"What do you mean shouting like that at me, young man?" Clearly, his mother was back in the catbird's seat. He had just stepped over the boundary of what was allowed—even though he thought he was in control.

"I couldn't find you when I woke up," he stammered. "The fulbeans weren't cooking, and I thought something had happened to you. I saw you laughing with Mr. Feisel. You don't know about him . . . about what he. . . ."

Johab didn't dare reveal Mr. Feisel's secret or what Johab now believed was a pack of lies about King Tut's tomb. Peaceful co-existence with this neighbor might be necessary. After all, Mr. Feisel had offered to look after Jasmine and his mother when Johab was in the city. That offer brought some peace of mind.

"He is a very kind neighbor. He warned me not to speak English to Jasmine, just as you are always warning me, Johab," she said, clearly irritated.

"You were talking and laughing like old friends. I don't think we can *totally* trust Mr. Feisel. I don't think we can totally trust anyone," Johab muttered.

"The donkey woke me up," his mother responded sharply. "Sekina was about to wake everyone in the neighborhood until Mr. Feisel found her some hay. He thanked me for the bread you took to him last night. Then, we started talking about recent news releases about the move of the Temple of Isis at Philae to the island of Agilkia. Some of the old structures and statues are already under water, but I know your father . . ."

Johab interrupted, in a fearful tone. "You haven't told him anything?"

"I don't talk about personal things with the neighbors, Johab. Not Mrs. Zadi, not Mr. Feisel. Mr. Feisel is too much of a gentleman to pry. On the other hand, Mrs. Zadi does nothing but pry," his mother responded acidly.

She reached over and pushed his sleep-tufted hair into some semblance of order. "I thought you needed a break from selling beans this morning, Johab. I've been thinking that I might let you go into the city this afternoon to get some of our things from the apartment if you are very careful."

And meet Miss Wenkle at your church. Johab kept a very open face. When his mother mentioned a "break" from work, it usually meant a different kind of work.

"You and Jasmine and I will visit your grandparents' graves this morning. They are way over on the other side of the cemetery, but it will be a nice walk. I haven't been there for years."

Johab thought about the evening ahead of him. Getting things for his mother from the apartment was a convenient excuse for going into Cairo. He needed to scout out the church before Miss Wenkle arrived so that he could find a good lookout point to be sure that she wasn't being followed. Miss Wenkle might have information about his father—or about Barzoni, the man who had taken his father.

Johab scowled. Now, his mother was planning a trip to his grandparents' tomb, way on the other side of a dusty cemetery, as though she might be anticipating a picnic on a fine day at an oasis in the desert.

At this minute, Johab's world seemed to be even more out of kilter. He had only a few options. Miss Wenkle had earned his trust again when she outwitted those men who followed her to the Khan. He was not so sure about Mr. Feisel. Getting his mother to talk about the project for the temples at Aswan Dam might be a clever way to get information about his father. Mr. Feisel could be on Mr. Barzoni's payroll—just like Uncle Tarek.

You are too suspicious, Johab thought with disgust. Mr. Feisel had lived in the City of the Dead for years, according to Mrs. Zadi, who made certain that the neighbors suspected him of dealing in black magic. There were no resin-darkened arms and legs, no linen-wrapped cats and birds stacked in Mr. Feisel's hut. There was only a simple brazier, a cot, a table and chairs, and that fine, carved cabinet in the corner. *And, a rare cylinder seal.* But, from what tomb? Some things about Mr. Feisel just didn't ring true.

"A trip to my grandparents' graves would be a fine way to start the day." Johab flashed a smile at his mother. He wasn't prepared to tell her how he planned to end the day by meeting Miss Wenkle at their old neighborhood church. That was a lie of omission. He was getting much better at those kinds of lies.

Johab, Jasmine, and his mother set off, their robes flapping around their ankles in a cool, early morning breeze blowing up from the south. They had walked for half an hour, winding in and out of small, cordoned-off family plots when Jasmine began to drag her feet and whine. They were at least ten minutes away from his grandparents' graves.

"Jasmine, I'll tell you the story of Khufu and the magicians." Johab needed to distract his sister from the heat and dust. Like his father did for him, he would teach her about the ancient world.

"Did Khufu own a big, black car?" Jasmine's calm observation sent a frisson of fear down his spine, stopping him in his tracks.

He swept up Jasmine and hissed between his teeth. "We're playing the quiet game, Jasmine." He ducked behind a tomb and beckoned his mother toward him. "Put up your hood, Mother. Pretend to be pulling weeds away from graves. Don't let the men in that car see your face."

Hesitating for only a moment, his mother flipped up the hood on her galabeya as though she were shielding her face from the early-day sun, knelt by the side of a stranger's tomb, and began pulling weeds and stacking them in piles.

Johab clutched a squirming Jasmine. He had to divert her. "You remember how I told you about Bastet, the goddess who protects cats? That old yellow tomcat is one of her cats. Would you like to put out a bowl of milk for him to see if he'll let us pet him?"

The cat was mangy and ill-tempered, but Jasmine had shown an interest in him. It was Johab who chased him with his offerings of mice away from the hut. Jasmine stopped wiggling. They watched the car fishtail at the fork in the road as it headed toward the section of the cemetery near his grandparents' graves.

Johab spoke softly, hoping that his voice wouldn't carry across the blocks of tombs to the car that had come to a standstill. "The men in that car took Dad. They must be looking for your parents' tombs. We can't be seen together. I'll carry Jasmine and keep her quiet. We'll circle far away from the main road."

Johab's whisper had taken on a frantic tone. "Wait until we're out of sight, Mother. Gather up the weeds and walk very slowly back toward the secondary road. Don't use the main road. Walk slowly. Keep your face hidden."

His mother nodded without speaking. He watched her twist the stalks of weeds into bundles for the donkey as she wandered among the graves, stopping at times to examine a tomb. Her disguise was masterful, just an ordinary woman, poor by the style of her galabeya, spending a quiet morning among the dead.

CHAPTER 19

Johab and Jasmine walked hand in hand along the alleys of the cemetery, gathering odd bits of trash, examining them for value, children of the City of the Dead scavenging for their livelihood. Johab and his mother reached home by two separate routes at the same time. Her expression was tense, not the *almost* carefree woman she had tried to be earlier that morning. "Who was in that car?" she demanded, staring directly into his eyes.

Johab's mother was returning to her old self by degrees. She was more like the mother he remembered during these past two days than she had been since the frightening night of his father's disappearance.

He shifted from foot to foot uneasily. Telling her too much might put her and Jasmine in more danger. He didn't want to frighten his mother, but she wanted information. "The men in that car were the ones who broke into our house. The car's owner is a friend of Mr. El-Hasiim." His mother's face brightened.

"That's a relief. We'll go this very minute to let Mr. El-Hasiim know that this man who pretends to be his friend must be reported. The police will be able to find your father."

Just as Johab feared, his mother had absolute faith in the order of things. If something was against the law, a report should be made to the police, and things would be set right. Important people such as Mr. El-Hasiim were honorable because their positions declared that they should be.

Police corruption was a fact of life in Cairo. It had been in the headlines recently. Two crooked policemen were snagged as part of the ring of thieves selling antiquities that Mr. Feisel had mentioned.

Johab stared into his mother's hopeful face. They could not go to the police. Mr. Barzoni had told Miss Wenkle that he had police "connections." As for Mr. El-Hasiim, Johab knew that his father did not trust him. How could Johab convince a mother who trusted almost everyone?

Simple honesty. Well, not all that simple. Parts and pieces of honesty. That might work. Johab felt a moment of regret that lately he seemed to be more like his Cousin Mohammed than himself. He had been trapped by his own lies in front of Mr. Feisel. His mother was well acquainted with the wiles of her nephew Mohammed. Too much twisting of the truth would not be a good idea.

"I was scouting around the outside of the Museum, trying to find out things." His mother nodded encouragingly. "I recognized the man who came out of the back entrance and got into that car as the man in our house—the one who hit you. He's friendly with Mr. El-Hasiim. Mr. El-Hasiim told a newspaper reporter that Dad probably ran off on a field trip without telling anyone. He's trying to cast doubt on Dad."

"Just wait until I see Mr. El-Hasiim. John manages the project. That man's just a . . . a *figurehead*." She spat out the word. "I just feel so helpless, staying in this place day after day, watching you leave and wondering if you'll come back." Her voice trailed into a thin thread of frustration.

Johab spotted an opportunity. "This evening, Mother, I'm meeting a friend, someone I can trust who may have information that will help. I will need to stay in the city late."

Her motherly instincts came out full force. "And, just who is this friend? This someone you can trust?" she asked acidly, as though she resented being left out of some kind of inner circle.

"It's a person who worked with Dad. If I say the name then I might be putting that person at risk. We probably put Aunt Rayya and Mohammed at risk by going to their house that night those men took Dad."

Johab tactfully omitted Uncle Tarek's name, but his mother nodded, probably aware of the omission but not really caring about a risk to Tarek. "I need time, Mother. Some time to sort things out."

"Just a few more days, Johab," his mother said very decisively. "Then, I'm going to ask Mr. Feisel for his advice. We need someone to help us, and I trust Mr. Feisel."

It was time to head into Cairo and scout out a good place to watch the street in both directions in front of the church. Johab half-heartedly lifted his hand in a greeting to Mr. Feisel who was sitting on his stoop in the mid-day sun. He wished that he could trust that old man the way that his mother seemed to trust him.

Johab made slow progress into the city along a hot highway as the mid-afternoon sun scorched his head.

"*Salam!*" The friendly shout rang out from a rusty, dented pickup, its bed encircled by a makeshift board and rope structure. In the back of the pickup were three camels, packed as tightly as sausages in a can, two outer camels facing in one direction and the middle camel facing in the other. None of the camels appeared to be in a good mood. "Climb on," the men shouted. "We'll take you to the edge of the city."

A free ride was a free ride, especially in this heat, but Johab knew not to trifle with an unhappy camel. He swung up to the back bumper, clutched one of the rails, and waved the driver ahead. The camels groaned and pushed against each other, daring Johab to get one inch closer. The ropes binding their knees restricted any movement without the absolute cooperation of the others. With camels, that kind of cooperation wouldn't happen. Like it or not, they were squashed into the pickup bed, but they could spit and did.

Johab hung off the back of the pickup with camel saliva coating his hands, staying as far from their pouting mouths as possible. The breeze created by the speed of the pickup was refreshing. At the first intersection near the city, the pickup slowed, and he hopped off the back, waving his thanks, wiping gummy hands on the sleeve of his robe. Traveling with camels had its downside.

With a sigh of relief, Johab spotted the dual towers of his mother's church, the Christian crosses on its domes marking it as an alien among half a dozen mosques with similar domes and no crosses. Johab always thought of the church as the place he *had* to go every week with his mother whether he wanted to or not. Now, he was checking it out from a different perspective. It was no longer a sanctuary with wide, welcoming doors and boring sermons. Mr. Barzoni might be lurking in that cool interior.

If he could watch the streets way up high in one of the towers, no one would be able to see him. He and Mohammed had tried to climb the winding stairs to the towers once, but the caretaker caught them. Those were the days when they explored everything off limits. Today was serious business.

Johab could not afford to be recognized by the priest or any member of the congregation. His family had disappeared. They needed to remain lost.

Johab darted up an alley near the church. Three large trash bins angled outward, giving him a clear view of the street in front of the church. The odors were rank, but the view of the church was good. A cab stopped at the corner. Johab could see a leg with a high-heeled shoe stretching out the door. Then, it whipped back. A door slammed. The cab sped away. The long, black car moved in a deadly, sure way after the noisy, careening cab.

Johab shrunk back against the garbage bins. Was that Miss Wenkle in the cab? The high heel of the shoe was certainly her trademark. If so, Mr. Barzoni must be tracking every move she made, hoping she would lead him to Johab's family.

Mr. Barzoni must want them very badly. Looking for graves of his mother's relatives seemed far-fetched. But, undeniably, that was Mr. Barzoni's car at the cemetery this morning. Did Mr. Barzoni know that Johab had the pouch? What had that man forced his father to tell him.

Johab knew that he needed to study those sheets of papyrus until they made sense.

Perspiration trickled down the back of Johab's neck as he waited and waited, his only company a fat rat sniffing the garbage.

CHAPTER 20

A young Egyptian woman swaggered down the sidewalk wearing an over-sized hat that looked familiar. Instead of the usual flat-footed walk that swayed a robe gracefully, she clomped along on impossibly high heels. A block behind her, a matronly figure, her head swathed in a scarf, flapped along the street in ill-fitting sandals. She turned up the alley and headed toward the trash bins where Johab was hiding.

Her voice rang out with false assurance. "I knew you'd be in the alley, Johab." It was Miss Wenkle with a large scarf concealing her head and the top of her suit. Her feet looked uncomfortable in Bedouin sandals.

She squatted down by Johab, giving him a quick hug. "Just as I was getting out of the taxi, I saw Mr. Barzoni's car. I paid the driver a mint to get him to drive away fast. Most taxi drivers here drive like maniacs without extra pay." Her uneasy smile was meant to be reassuring. It wasn't.

"That girl was on her way home. She was happy to trade shoes and give me her scarf as part of the bargain. I thought she'd throw them off the track if they came this way looking for me again."

She lifted Johab to his feet. "This garbage is nauseating. We can sit in that little enclosed garden at the back of the church. I look like an Egyptian woman in this scarf. You look like . . . What is that nasty stuff on your hands?" She wrinkled her nose.

"Camel spit." Johab led her to a corner of the enclosure with a clear view of the street. "Any news? Of my father?" His face was expectant with hope.

Miss Wenkle sat motionless, then said softly: "I don't know where he is, but I think you'll feel some relief at what I overheard."

"What? What?" Johab's shrill voice startled a flock of nearby pigeons.

Miss Wenkle looked cautiously about. "Let me tell you just as it happened, exactly what I did and what I heard. Then, you can draw your own conclusions." The look Johab gave her did not bode well for her narrative style.

"Yesterday morning, Mr. Barzoni arrived early. He appeared to be agitated and demanded to see Mr. El-Hasiim immediately, even though he was in a staff meeting. So, I went to get him."

She smiled slyly at Johab. "That was a perfect opportunity for me to listen outside Mr. El-Hasiim's office, because everyone else was in the meeting. I put my ear right against the crack of the door. It's hard to hear, because those old doors are very thick. I had to watch for anyone coming down the hall, but I heard some things."

"What things? What things?" Johab couldn't contain himself. Any news would be better than this vacuum of silence since his father had been taken.

"Mr. Barzoni accused Mr. El-Hasiim of holding out on him. He mentioned a small statue on the black market. This part I heard clearly, because Mr. Barzoni was angry. 'It's New Kingdom. I want to know where it was found and who found it.' I couldn't exactly make out Mr. El-Hasiim's answer, but he denied that he had information about the statue." She pulled Johab tightly against her.

"This might be the most important, and I could barely make out the words. Mr. Barzoni said that John Bennett had been 'on to something,' that he had 'probably discovered another entrance.'"

She shook her head in frustration. "If John had made some kind of new tomb discovery, he would have shared it. He would never have kept something that important from his colleagues."

Johab looked down at his dirty feet in sandals that were beginning to shape themselves into a comfortable fit. He thought about the pouch with the papyrus sheets and his father's small pages of notes. Mr. Barzoni had appeared to be talking about something that happened in the past. The present was more terrifying. "Did he say anything else about Dad?"

"Yes. That frightens me. Mr. El-Hasiim asked him about John. Mr. Barzoni said 'John Bennett won't talk until I hold the final card—his family. I will find them.'" Miss Wenkle crammed her knuckles against her mouth, but the tears in her eyes betrayed her terror. "He is an evil man. I went back to my office because people were coming down the hall. A few minutes later, Mr. Barzoni came into my office, smiling like he always does, asking questions about your family."

She brushed tears of frustration away from her eyes. "I can't believe that I ever thought that man was charming. Charming like a scorpion. He's got John somewhere, Johab. How will we ever find him?" Her voice trailed into a fine thread of unspoken misery.

Johab blinked back tears. This was no time to give into his emotions.

He needed to think logically, just like a scientist conducting an experiment. But this "experiment" involved the lives of his father, his mother, his sister, his own and probably that of Miss Wenkle. The experiment would be their deathtrap if any mistake were made.

"Did you find anything in Dad's papers, Miss Wenkle?"

She reached into her bag and dug around, pulling out two small sheets of lined paper that had been torn from a small, spiral notebook, the kind that his father always kept in the pocket of his shirt. "All the papers that were on the top of your father's desk are gone. But, as I told you before, I typed information for him at the end of every day, and I have copies. I looked through John's desk. These pages were tucked behind one of the top drawers. They didn't fall out of a file. I think he intentionally hid them."

Agitated, she shifted around to face Johab. "That night those men took your father to his office—the night they killed the guard—I think they made your father take all the files from his desk. At that time, he may have managed to stick these pages behind the drawer."

Johab eased the creases from the small wrinkled pages and felt a flush of confidence. "These are drawings of the locations of tombs in the Valley, Miss Wenkle. See the small circles with numbers by them? Those are used to identify sites of tombs. See that squiggle. Those are the hills south of Deir el-Bahri. Dad sometimes drew maps just like that when we were out in the field. He said it gave him a new perspective."

"What are these little pictures along the edge? A top hat, some kind of animal and a man's jacket." Miss Wenkle looked puzzled. "Those don't look like hieroglyphs."

Johab smiled. "Everyone going to an English school here would recognize that—it's a hat, a sheep, and a suit. *Hat-shep-sut*. That's the way that we learned to pronounce Queen Hatshepsut's name like English and Americans do. My father was making this note clear for someone like me."

He looked slightly disappointed. "I guess he didn't think I would recognize the hills of Deir el-Bahri, but I did," he said with more self-assurance than he felt.

"This next page," Johab looked puzzled. "I've never seen this before—it's the inside of a tomb with rooms leading toward a main burial chamber. But, look at this."

Johab pointed to a sketch of a shaft at the edge of the drawing. "The drawing is tiny, but you can see that it is a shaft. He's even drawn some rubble inside of it. And, here in the corner, he has marked the coordinates."

Johab rubbed his head, trying to recollect something. "This looks familiar." It came to him in a flash. The pouch. The same sketch was on one of the notes in the pouch.

Miss Wenkle sat, tense and expectant, as though Johab would reveal something important. He disappointed her. "We need more information about Queen Hatshepsut's temple and tomb. Can you get it?"

"Anyone can. It's public information. I don't see how that would be helpful. Restoration work on her tomb went on for years—the tomb was never finished. It's closed now. The floods washed too much rubble into it."

She glanced at Johab's hopeful face. "You know that your father's interest was in the villages around the tombs—not the tombs. Those are past exploring. The robbers pillaged and destroyed them centuries ago—sometimes immediately after the kings were buried."

Her voice was indignant. "No sooner had a royal mummy been placed in the tomb than the thieves began drugging and bribing the guards. I know that the people were poor and the tombs held a fortune in gold and jewels. But these were their gods being buried. They didn't even think of kings and queens as human beings. I don't understand that kind of disrespect."

In a law-abiding world like that of Miss Wenkle, people did not disrupt the sleep of the dead or fling their mummies out of a golden coffin, then chop it into pieces for the gold fused to the wood. What appealed most to Miss Wenkle was the perfect order in the ancient world of the Egyptians. It was a world where the actions of people are stored in their hearts and weighed by the god Anubis at the time of their deaths. The weighing of hearts seemed to her a sane system of justice.

Miss Wenkle's move to Cairo did not appear *sane* to some of her colleagues at the British Museum where she had worked for twenty years. To the people who knew her, Miss Wenkle was a forty-two-year-old spinster, doomed to ride the same bus to the same job every day of her life. They didn't know the other side of Hetty Wenkle.

Almost every day during her lunch hour, she went upstairs to the British Museum's Egyptian Galleries and fell in love. The placid and self-contained faces of rulers carved in stone, the funerary statues with colors bright as the day they were painted captured her imagination in ways that nothing else had ever done.

At the end of each day, her mother, a bitter and bossy woman, greeted her with the same words: "Why are you so late? Why aren't you more considerate of your mother?" It didn't matter if she were early, on time or late—which she never was. The stifling world in her mother's small, London row house never varied until quarreling cats turned that world around.

There had been another relative, one that Miss Winkle loved as dearly as her father. Her uncle was an officer in the British army. He had been posted in Egypt during the war; afterward, he returned with his wife Alice, to work at the British Embassy in Cairo.

At their annual London visits, Uncle Cyril and Aunt Alice regaled their niece Hetty with the wonders to be seen in Egypt. As precious as the yearly visits were to her, the wonderful letters her uncle wrote almost every week brought a rare and exotic world even more alive to her.

That world ended when her Aunt Alice became ill, and her uncle brought her home to London to die within a month. Uncle Cyril only lived a few more months. On the way to his funeral, her mother said that Hetty's uncle "didn't have the courage to face life alone."

Miss Wenkle thought her uncle's death was the end he would have chosen for himself, a fitting conclusion to a fine love story, but her mother wouldn't have understood that kind of affection, so Miss Wenkle remained silent. Her solace was in her uncle's letters from Egypt, a constant reminder of another country, sunlit and full of ancient treasures.

Her mother died, quite suddenly, on a foggy afternoon, complaining about the neighbor's noisy cats. The death happened so quickly that her mother's words disappeared with no more fuss than the closing of a door.

Miss Wenkle's close friends, Sarah and Ella Hemstead, sisters who worked with her at the British Museum, encouraged their friend Hetty Wenkle to "think about options." She had stared blankly at them. She never considered that she had any options.

The day after her mother's funeral, the best friend of Johab's father, Ian Parks, brought her another option. A position with the New Kingdom Project was open in Cairo. She applied by telegram and was accepted immediately. Giving her supervisor a month's notice, she leased her mother's house, packed a few bags, and boarded a ship for Cairo.

She had never regretted the decision. The kindest person on the Project was Johab's father, who had shared as much of his home life as he could, knowing well that Miss Wenkle had none.

When she first met his son, she wondered if his name for a warrior king—Horemheb—might present problems for a boy growing up. His odd nickname, "Johab," seemed to suit him. Whenever she could pry him away from his pesky cousin Mohammed for a brief chat, Johab never failed to surprise her with how much he knew about the history of ancient Egypt.

Miss Wenkle's face fell in the midst of those memories. This small dirty boy perched beside her on a garden wall of a church he couldn't enter for fear of being recognized watched her helplessly.

He was too young to be facing the terrible thing that had happened to his family. And, she was too inexperienced to help him. She stood up abruptly. The two of them had no option but to be stronger and braver than they were supposed to be.

She grabbed Johab's hand, pulling him to his feet. "We can't stay here. Barzoni's men might drive by at any time. They seem to be tracking me everywhere. I will lead them a merry chase. And, I intend to turn the tables on *Mr. Barzoni*." His name rolled off her tongue as though she were getting rid of a bad taste in her mouth.

"He's too obvious with his questions. He must think I'm very stupid not to realize what he's doing, so I intend to play right into his hands. I'm going to try to help him," she said, a small smile settling in the corners of her mouth.

"You're going to what?" Johab exclaimed, dumbfounded that she had announced defection to the enemy.

"It's what the British did in World War II; the Americans did too. They sent spies into the enemy camps. Those spies may have had as much to do with winning the war as thousands of troops. Intelligence is everything. That's what we need now.

We need to know what Barzoni and El-Hasiim know and what they are trying to find. And I'm just the simple, busybody, helper bee that they can turn to for information."

She beamed. "I'll convince them that I think your father might have known a secret, something he didn't want to reveal. Since I did all his typing and filing related to the Project, I have total access to his work."

Pushing herself up, Hetty dusted her hands. "More than that, I'll make trips to the Khan daily and trips to your old neighborhood. I'll be seen everywhere, and they won't have the foggiest notion of where I'm going or why. It's what they call in detective fiction 'a red herring.'"

She touched Johab's cheek. "I'll get copies to you of everything your dad worked on this past month. With two of us looking at his files, we're sure to find something. Let's meet in two days, same time, same garbage pile?" Her question sailed into the wind as she strode toward a busy intersection, her hand aloft to hail a taxi.

CHAPTER 21

Thou shinest in the horizon,
thou sendest forth the light into the darkness.

—The Legend of Osiris, Papyrus of Ani

There was no "camel taxi" on the road back to the City of the Dead that night. Johab trudged along, wagging a heavy pillowcase with things his mother had wanted from the apartment. He took side roads, avoiding the cars with bright lights on the main highway. The moon was at midpoint on the horizon by the time he reached his new home.

Smoke wafted up from hundreds of charcoal braziers, adding to the smog but strangely comforting to Johab, as though life continued in a normal way even though that life was taking place in the middle of a cemetery.

In some ways, living here was like camping in the desert on hard sleeping mats, food on a charcoal brazier, and cold nights. His father wasn't around to build a campfire under the enormous canopy of stars or to tell stories about the god Osiris. Johab could not look at the moon, hanging low in the sky, without thinking about how the ancient pharaohs expected to rise from the dead like Osiris to reclaim their lives in another world.

As Johab pushed open the door and dropped the pillowcase full of things from their apartment in Cairo, his mother whirled around and dropped the large wooden paddle she used to stir the fulbeans. "I was worried about you. I can't sleep until you're home."

Johab felt that his mother's fear was greater than his. She was confined every day with Jasmine. He was free to roam Cairo. His mother needed good news.

"I met my friend, you know, the one I told you would be helping us." Johab was careful not to say "she," or his mother was guess instantly that it was Miss Wenkle. He had to keep her identity secret, especially now that she was going under cover to infiltrate the enemy, just like a World War II spy.

"This person," Johab pronounced "person" carefully. "This person is going to get me information about something that Dad was studying before those men came. We think that Mr. Barzoni believes Dad has information about a tomb and won't give it to him."

"He's alive." His mother's face beamed with more joy than Johab had seen since that terrible night in their apartment.

"He's alive. We're sure," Johab affirmed with a sense of confidence that he hadn't felt in a week. Miss Wenkle's eavesdropping had given him hope that Mr. Barzoni would keep his father safe until he got what he wanted. As long as he, Jasmine, and his mother could stay out of the clutches of Mr. Barzoni, his father wouldn't talk.

His mother attacked the bean pot with new vigor. "Well, then. We need to find *someone else* we can trust and get that person to contact the police." She put great emphasis on the words "someone else" as though Johab's secretiveness about his friend was annoying her.

Johab flinched as though she had struck him. "Mother!" his voice rose to a near screech, causing her to drop her wooden paddle again. He needed to convince her that if she did anything to reveal their hiding place, she might cause the death of his father. He had to tell her something that would preoccupy her, make her even more fearful, and would cause her to be more careful, more secretive.

Uncle Tarek. That information would keep her stewing for days. Like his Aunt Rayya, his mother believed that family loyalty was more important than personal feelings. That's why she tolerated Uncle Tarek's bad manners, his foul temper, and his mistreatment of Mohammed. Her beloved sister Rayya had chosen Tarek as her husband. That meant he was family.

Learning about Uncle Tarek taking money from Mr. Barzoni would galvanize his mother in a way that Johab wasn't sure he could handle diplomatically. This going to the police business had to be stopped. Now. He tried to soften the blow. "Mother, you aren't going to like what I'm about to tell you." She stopped stirring the beans and waited.

"It's Uncle Tarek. I saw him on the street outside of his apartment talking to Mr. Barzoni."

"You what?" she exclaimed, her voice soaring to a screech as her face flushed.

"You what?" She shouted again, her voice soaring to a higher register. Johab didn't know if she was experiencing shock or anger.

It was denial. "Your Uncle Tarek would never do anything to hurt your father. His job *depends* on your father. Tarek is family. Johab, you must have seen him with someone else." Her mouth pursed into that thin line that Johab recognized when she confronted him for not being exactly truthful.

Johab shook his head sadly, keeping his eyes cast down at the floor. He couldn't bear to see what he knew would be pain and disbelief in his mother's eyes. "It was *him*, Mother, with Uncle Tarek. I was there on the street with Sekina after I delivered the beans. I thought for a minute he might have recognized me, but he didn't. I watched Mr. Barzoni give him something. I think it was a wad of money. Uncle Tarek had a guilty look on his face."

Johab's mother turned and walked over to the sleeping mat where she hid her purse during the day, snatched it up, and moved toward the door.

Johab blocked the door. "Where are you going, Mother?" he demanded.

"I'm going to tell Tarek what I think about him. Then, I'm going to help Rayya kick him out of the house. That's where I'm going," she said through gritted teeth.

Johab grabbed her arm and pulled her back. "Mother, I knew it would upset you if I told you about Uncle Tarek. That's why I've kept it a secret for days. If you let Uncle Tarek know where we are hiding, everything will be lost. Mr. Barzoni will find us. Then Dad will tell him everything he wants to know." Johab's voice had reached a high crescendo. "If you do that, Dad will die."

The word "die" hung for what seemed an interminable time in the stillness of the small tomb. His mother dropped her purse, walked over to the brazier, and began stirring the beans again.

Her voice was tense. "I am so angry, Johab, not with you, but with that brother-in-law of mine. When I think of how much your father has done for him. I know that he doesn't hit Rayya. She would have told me. But his punishment of Mohammed has made Rayya talk about leaving him for years. Now she has this new baby on the way and . . ." her voice trailed off sadly.

"I won't do anything now, Johab. I agreed to let you have time to find out what you can in the way that you need to do. I think that's what your father would want. He considers you the most responsible little boy he could imagine. You always looked after Jasmine, keeping her from falling when she was learning to walk."

His mother looked solemnly into his eyes. "You continue to look after her, after us. I saw how clever you were this morning to get us safely away from that black car in the cemetery."

She smoothed down Johab's cowlick. "I believe you now. This morning, I thought that you might be imagining things, because people often come in cars to visit their family tombs. That car had two men in it. They weren't bringing flowers to the dead." Her voice sounded tired—but accepting of the reality she was facing. Her family, with Uncle Tarek as part of it, had just evaporated as a cohesive unit.

She added a few more chunks of charcoal to the fire, put the lid on the beans, and stretched out on her mat. Within minutes, her soft breathing comforted Johab. She had moved into a safe and dreamless world of sleep.

Chapter 22

Sleep could wait. Johab knew that he needed to study the old papyrus sheets and his father's notes again and again until they made sense. The clay under the windowsill had dried, leaving no trace of the hidden pouch. A helpful spider had stretched his web under the ledge to keep the secret. Johab would leave it some tasty flies on the window ledge.

After digging out the pouch and unfolding the papyrus sheets, Johab realized he recognized some of the symbols. There was the lion goddess Pakhet, one of Queen Hatshepsut's favorite goddesses, and a falcon with arched wings representing Horus.

A shiver moved down his spine. The eyes of the hawk-god Horus stared off the page at him. Horus represented both the sun and the moon, light and the dark, good and evil. Once, when Johab and his father were in the desert, a small fennec fox had wandered by, its over-sized ears alert to danger. A hawk with outstretched talons dropped from the sky with no warning. The scream of the fox stopped almost as quickly as it had begun.

Johab remembered how his father had tried to console him by explaining why the Egyptians had chosen the fast and fierce hawk to represent their great god Horus. Johab was not comforted. That little fox had looked at him with a sense of curiosity, not fear. He should have protected it.

The first time he saw Mr. Barzoni's beak-like nose, Johab thought he was looking at a reincarnated Horus. *That was disrespectful to Horus. His father wouldn't approve.* Horus was the god of joy. The shape of Mr. Barzoni's nose didn't make him at all like Horus. The black-suited Mr. Barzoni was a vulture, scavenging on carrion, living off the dead. That's what tomb robbers were—vultures stealing the past from the Egyptian people.

Now that Horus rested favorably in Johab's mind, he offered up a short prayer to to the hawk-god to watch out for his family with those sharp eyes that see the smallest mouse as he soars above the earth.

Johab angled his flashlight on the papyrus and noticed the impression of a three-inch oval as though some object had been wrapped in papyrus. Something else struck him as curious. The hawk's eye of Horus had been separated into six parts with the flat, circular center of the eye iris repeated twice. Not that strange. The ancient priests sometimes used the symbol of Horus' eye to show measurements for their medicinal compounds.

Flipping to the next page, he squinted at a tiny drawing that he had missed earlier. It was almost identical to the carving on the wall of a chapel at Karnak. A tiny figure of Queen Hatshepsut wearing the bulbous crown of Upper Egypt stood by two pillars, the *djed*. At the side of the pillars were numbers.

Johab recognized the symbol for one thousand, three symbols for one hundred, and four symbols for ten. The number was 1,340. But what could that mean?

Johab frowned into the shadows cast by his flashlight, trying to remember everything he could about Queen Hatshepsut. He knew that she invented her own ancestry so no one could question her right to rule. The carving on her temples told the story.

As the daughter of King Tuthmosis I, she should have inherited his kingdom, but, as a woman, she knew her legitimacy to rule would be questioned. So, she simply replaced her earthly father with a heavenly one—the great god Amun—and invented her own miraculous conception.

Johab grinned in the darkness of the room, knowing that his mother wouldn't like what he was thinking. Every Christmas, she told him the story of the angel coming to visit the Virgin Mary and bingo, she was having a baby. It seemed to Johab that the great god Amun and the Christian god had something in common—these "visitations" created an amazing son, Jesus, and a powerful daughter, Hatshepsut. When Johab tried to discuss this idea with his mother, she sent him to his bedroom.

He remembered hearing his mother's angry voice through the thin apartment walls. Later, when his dad tucked him into bed, he said sheepishly, "If you have ideas about theology, about the gods, that are different from what you hear in church, it's probably best that you discuss them with me, Johab. Your mother has very fixed ideas about who rules heaven." He had reached out, pushed Johab's hair back, smiled and said, "Scientists like us have to be open to all possibilities, right?"

After his father had closed the door that night, Johab remembered lying awake, thinking about the supreme god of the ancient Egyptians visiting Hatsheput's mother and telling her that her baby daughter would be named "She Whom Amun Embraces," that is, Hatshepsut.

Something about this story bothered Johab. It seemed to him that Hatshepsut had demoted her father Tuthmosis I to the role of a kindly uncle, someone who wasn't much more important than Joseph as a member of the Holy Family.

His father had tried to explain the difficulty of being a queen in a world that preferred kings. "If Hatshepsut had accepted her destiny as Tuthmosis' daughter, she would have waited for a male heir. That wasn't our Hatshepsut."

"Our Hatshepsut." That's what his dad called the queen, a ruler he admired for her ingenuity and her inventiveness. "She just needed an opportunity to show her people that she could be a great pharaoh. She would make the Nile flood regularly; she would protect her people from their enemies; she would create prosperity. She did all these things. And, she left a magnificent temple to remind her people that she would always be with them."

But where? Robbers had ransacked her tomb. Her mummy had never been found. But that last day in the field when he was sketching her temple, his dad had blurted out something odd. "Her architect Senenmut outwitted those thieves!" Johab wrinkled his forehead, trying to remember. That was just before his dad had ordered him into the jeep and taken off for Cairo.

When Jasmine cried out, Johab turned off the flashlight, moved across the darkness of the hut, and patted his sister's head until she fell asleep. He needed to hide the pouch again, but make a copy of the papyrus pages first. He fumbled through the pockets of his father's jacket for a notebook and dug in the front pocket for the pen that his father always kept there, a real fountain pen with a gold tip so flexible that he could push it into broad or narrow strokes to copy hieroglyphs.

Johab copied the symbols as carefully as he could manage. He could remember the numerals—no need to copy those. His father's note said: "Numbers? Calculations from the first shaft or days before she could be moved—less likely."

A scuffle of footsteps sounded outside. Johab clicked off the flashlight. Silence settled around him. He held his breath. The footsteps moved down the alley. Johab crept over to the window and peered out. A tall figure circled from the end of the alley toward their hut, looked around, and then entered Mr. Feisel's hut.

Johab breathed a sigh of relief. It was only Mr. Feisel taking his evening constitutional. He had told Johab's mother that he often had trouble sleeping and would take short walks. When the oil lamp in Mr. Feisel's hut no longer gleamed through the window, Johab returned to his work.

An idea struck him. What if he transcribed everything in reverse order and went from the bottom of the page to the top? That might confuse anyone who saw his copies. He finished within an hour, then copied the sketch that Miss Wenkle had found hidden in his father's desk. It appeared to be the layout of a tomb with metrical measurements of 112M and 70M marked on a line diagonal to the layout.

Johab rammed the pouch back under the ledge, smeared damp clay under the sill, and looked around for a hiding place for his copies. Across the room, the eyes of the yellow tomcat followed him from its post at the foot of Jasmine's sleeping mat.

Jasmine had christened the yellow tomcat "Bastet," because Johab told her that Bastet was the guardian goddess of cats. "It's a boy cat, Jasmine. You can't give it the name of a girl," Johab had argued.

"It likes being called Bastet. It doesn't listen when I call it that silly name 'Howard Carter' that you gave it." Jasmine had lifted her chin defiantly, looking a great deal like their mother. "It knows that its name is Bastet. That's what we will all call it." Bastet it was.

The cat curled up every night at the foot of Jasmine's mat. It drank the goat milk that Johab's mother poured into a pottery shard. It sat on the stoop watching for Johab to return at the end of the day. But, it would tolerate no affection from anyone but Jasmine.

When they had returned from their interrupted trip to her parents' graves, Johab's mother put her foot down. "We never keep animals in the house."

"I promised Jasmine she could keep the cat if she would be quiet while we were hiding from the men in the black car. A promise is a promise, Mother."

Muttering about "fleas and mange" when the cat first moved inside, his mother soon became Bastet's strongest ally. If Jasmine wandered more than a few yards away, the cat yowled.

"That cat is better than a watchdog. I never worry about Jasmine wandering off. Bastet simply won't allow it," his mother said as she poured an extra measure of goat's milk for the cat. Johab despised goat milk. It tasted like every bad weed that grew alongside the road. Rank. That was its taste. Bastet was welcome to his share.

Where could he hide these copies he had just made? A large burlap bag of dried beans stood in the corner. It would be perfect. His mother wouldn't reach the bottom of the sack for two weeks. Johab dropped to his mat, exhausted, and fell into a dream-filled sleep of tomb shafts, mummified cats, and his father's voice trying to tell him something.

CHAPTER 23

Let me eat my food under the sycamore tree of my lady,
the goddess Hathor, and let my times be among the divine
beings who have alighted thereon.

—Budge Translation, Papyrus of Ani

His father's voice was hanging on the edge of his dream when Johab awoke. They had been climbing down the cliff at Wadi Sikker Taqa el-Zeid, following the same route as Howard Carter when he found the limestone sarcophagus in the cliff tomb and claimed that it might have been intended as the burial site for Hatshepsut.

His father was saying over and over: "Carter was wrong. He knew he was wrong. This was just another way to. . . ." The dream ended. The noise of his mother stirring fulbeans was the only sound in his head.

"Wake up, sleepy head." She smiled down at him. "I've fed Sekina, and the beans are ready to be loaded. You need to eat before you leave."

Johab vowed that if they ever returned to a normal life that he would never eat fulbeans again. Goat milk was out of the question. Maybe he could run some errands or translate for the tourists and pick up extra money for better food. He'd have to be very careful. The hotel guards kept a sharp eye out for boys who found tourists an easy mark. Those large handbags were often hanging open and tempting. The Khan might be a likely place to earn extra money.

Car horns blared in the early morning like noisy, metal mon-sters forcing Johab and Sekina to the gutter of the street. Morning laundry, strung across balconies, flapped in the breeze. This morning was like hundreds of other mornings in Cairo. Johab was struck by how normal life seemed in this neighborhood where he could sell his beans in half an hour and no one suspected how desperate he was.

As Johab scooped out beans into pots dangling from balconies, he thought about how quickly the days were passing. It would be Christmas soon. The non-Coptic Christmas would be celebrated on December 25. The Coptics would wait until January 7 when the Gregorian calendar, the "true calendar" according to his mother, named the date of Jesus' birth.

Johab ladled generous servings into the pots, thinking how lucky he was to have two Christmases. He thought of his cousin. When Mohammed was old enough to know that Johab got two holidays, he puffed out his lower lip and glared jealously at all the presents piled under Johab's tree.

Johab's father had been watching Mohammed slam his old pull-toy against the floor. He had swept Mohammed up in his arms, pointing to the Christmas tree, showing him the "American" side and the "Egyptian" side with their different ornaments.

The pout stayed on Mohammed's face. "There is one, two, three, four presents—all for Mohammed. Your mother said that you can spend the night here on December 24 and have an American Christmas with us." Mohammed's laugh was as guttural as Uncle Tarek's. His face had beamed as Johab's father set him down. Johab knew that look. It was the look of "belonging."

Johab came to an abrupt halt. Sekina's braying echoed down the street as the cart shifted uncomfortably against her back leg. All this thinking about Christmas made Johab remember that his grandparents in Michigan would be sending Christmas presents, but no one would be at the apartment to receive them.

Had anyone told his grandparents that their son and his family had disappeared? Maybe the police or someone at the Embassy had contacted them. He knew his grandparents' phone number. They would be frantic with worry. He must get a message to Miss Wenkle immediately.

By noon, Johab reached the Museum and circled with Sekina toward the back of the building. The donkey moved willingly, remembering the forbidden shrubbery. Getting her teeth into those plants would be paradise.

The shrubbery, so tempting to Sekina, unnerved Johab. The memory of crawling against the corpse of Mr. Razik the week before still gave him nightmares. Mummies were one thing. Unwrapped, their faces appeared to be carved from dark wood, the skin stretched back from the teeth in a pained smile, as though they had mixed emotions about who might be watching them.

The body of Mr. Razik was quite another thing. It was soft and shifted like a bag of sand when he bumped against it. The eyes of Mr. Razik were fixed, staring upward at nothing.

Remembering the wound on his throat, Johab gasped for air. He needed to think of something else. He said a quick prayer to Maat, the goddess of truth and justice. Surely Mr. Razik's heart had been weighed and found worthy.

Johab glanced over at the cars in the back lot. Miss Wenkle's blue Volkswagen was parked exactly between the white stripes, the left front window open a couple of inches to keep the hot sun from cracking the windows.

Johab could slip a note to her by pushing it through the crack in the window. If he angled it just so, it would land on the car seat. He dug through the slit in the side of his robe, reaching for the pocket of his shorts where he kept a notebook and pencil stub. No one was hanging around the back door. He needed to be quick. A boy loitering near parked cars would arouse suspicion.

Anyone seeing a note on the seat could open the car with a coat hanger. He needed to disguise his message as something else. He printed in large letters, "My Market List." He listed some items: "fulbeans" (Miss Wenkle knew about his disguise); "rugs at Khan" (she had told the shop keeper in front of Barzoni's men to call her if new rugs arrived); and, "soap" (she had commented about Johab's dirty face).

Surely that would be enough clues for her to guess that Johab was at the Khan near her friend's shop, waiting for her. He had no idea when she might leave work, so he'd simply hang out around the Khan, hoping she understood his clues.

The crowd of shoppers at the market created a perfect environment for a boy who wanted to be invisible. Johab spotted the little beggar who had held Sekina for him earlier in the week. The boy's face lit up like a Christmas tree when he saw Johab and the donkey rounding the corner where he wheedled coins from passersby.

Johab tossed him the donkey's rope and faded into the crowd of shoppers. A large group of German tourists, their faces reddened by the sun, pushed down the street toward the jewelry shops, shoving him aside in their eagerness. He was not offended. He was invisible.

Many tourists—their wallets and purses fat with traveler's checks and cash—made a beeline for the jewelry shops to get their names set in hieroglyphs on little gold rectangles. Johab looked at them skeptically. Money was there for the taking—a foot out to trip someone, a quick slight of hand as he rushed to help lift the fallen tourist, and around the corner with a purse before anyone noticed. Mohammed had described the scenario often, daring Johab to try it.

Even now, on a diet of fulbeans and goat's milk, Johab could not stoop to crime. His mother would rather starve and his father would be speechless at the thought.

CHAPTER 24

The cow's horns on the goddess Hathor pointed at Johab as though she were disappointed that he would even think about robbing a tourist. The statue, in one of the poorer shops, was about a foot high, carved from balsa wood, but painted crudely, the stars lopsided on her belly.

Cornering two British women tourists, the shopkeeper in his best English was telling them that his "grandfather had been part of the crew that discovered King Tut's tomb" and had left him this statue as "his inheritance." The man was leering hopefully at the women as they examined the statue of Hathor.

"The paint doesn't look very old for something that is supposed to have been in a tomb for three thousand years," the taller woman pointed out to her companion.

"Desert is very dry. Paint stays new," the shopkeeper assured them.

"I can't believe that anyone could buy a treasure from King Tut's tomb for a hundred pounds." The tall woman spoke out again, clearly wanting to leave the shop as the owner barred their exit.

Johab sensed the frustration of the woman. The set of her jaw resembled his aunt in Michigan. What if someone tried to take advantage of her? His father wouldn't like that. Johab didn't either.

Speaking English quietly so as not to be overheard by other shoppers, Johab tapped the woman's arm, and said, "If you'll come with me, I will show you a shop that won't cheat you. I can guarantee that you will *not* find a treasure from King Tut's tomb in this market. You can find very nice copies that are cheaper than the copies in the museum shop."

The shopkeeper savagely shoved Johab aside and pushed himself between the two women, determined to make a sale to the shorter woman. The tall woman thrust her bag between the shopkeeper, herself, and Johab. "Here!" Her voice was sharp and authoritative. "You don't push small boys around in front of me. Come on, Ella, we are leaving this rude man's shop." Her icy voice froze the man in his tracks.

Johab skittered around the corner, feeling the glare of the shop-keeper on his back. He intersected the women at the next corner.

The woman called Ella motioned to him. "Here's the boy who was trying to help us, Sarah." Johab checked around. No one resembling Barzoni's men were in sight. He needed to do a good deed to make up for his shameful thought about tourists as an easy mark.

"If you come with me, I'll show you a shop that has good copies of the ancient gods and goddesses. That was a poorly made statue of Hathor. The stars were wrong. Her horns were crooked."

"Listen to this little fellow, Sarah," chimed the woman called Ella. "His diction and vocabulary are excellent for a native child, though the accent is a bit like an American."

Johab had an immediate sinking feeling. What if these women had read a local paper? The story of the murdered guard and the missing Bennett family had made headlines. It was time to put a Mohammed slant on things. "I *learn* English from Americans at the factory where copies of treasures are made," he beamed up at them as though proud of his fluency.

"Well, you learned it very well," affirmed the woman named Sarah. "If you would direct us to a better shop, we would be grateful. That man back there was most irritating."

Within minutes, they had arrived at a reputable shop. Johab, keeping his head low, whispered, "Bargain for the statue. Never pay the marked price. You shouldn't pay more than ten British pounds for any of those medium-sized statues. I'll wait for you outside in case you have any trouble."

He watched them enter the shop and peered through the glass window while they picked up several statues. They lined up half a dozen, then settled for Hathor with her cow's horns, Maat with her feathered wings, and sleek Anubis with his head of a jackal. With their treasures wrapped in rough paper, they burst out of the door of the shop beaming, looking both ways for Johab.

"We bought three beautiful copies for a total of thirty pounds—they had been forty pounds each, but we did just what you said. We bargained." Ella smiled as though they had found original treasures at a bargain-basement price. She reached her closed hand out toward Johab. "For you, young man, for helping us."

Another day in another time, Johab would have refused. His parents would have expected him to help tourists without any thought of payment. But today was not that day. Johab thanked them profusely, clutching the bill, thinking that to examine the amount in front of them might appear to be rude, but the British note would be more money than he could make in days of selling beans.

When he was a safe distance from the shop whose owner might recognize him, he opened his hand. His "tip" was a twenty-pound British note. That was a fortune. He could buy white flour, a bag of sugar, a jar of honey, fresh dates, good olive oil, and new robes for Jasmine and his mother. His old one suited him well enough. The more worn and dirty it became, the better it served as a disguise.

He squinted at the sun. It must be close to two o'clock. Miss Wenkle might have gone to her car and found the "Market List." He would hang around the back of her friend's rug shop. He had never seen the face of her friend, but it would be better not to take any chances. He squatted at the back of the tent and peered under the edge.

The sound of Miss Wenkle's voice erupted from the tent, talking above her normal range, telling someone that she would only "deal with his brother" and when might she expect him back?

"In the country with relatives. Don't want trouble here." The response was brusque.

Miss Wenkle seemed taken aback by his response but quickly regained her composure. "I'll come next week to see if he has the rug I want." She flounced out of the tent.

Johab followed her serpentine pathway—she had probably read enough spy novels to know that a good undercover agent never moves in a straight line. She paused to handle the brightly patterned scarves heaped on tables outside of tents.

In a flash, she ducked into a dark alley. Within seconds, Johab found her hiding place inside a half-splintered crate, her scent of rose geranium masking the garbage. She pulled him inside, her cornflower blue eyes wide with unease.

"Johab, did you hear my friend's brother? I think that Barzoni's men frightened him. I hope they didn't do anything worse. Things may be getting out of control, Johab." She paused and was silent for a moment.

"I was able to convince Mr. El-Hasiim that I could help Mr. Barzoni if I could review John's recent work that was no longer on his desk." Miss Wenkle smiled grimly. "His files appeared magically. My *review* meant hours at the copy machine." She showed Johab a bundle of papers, cleverly wrapped in a checkered native headdress.

"I know they are becoming suspicious of me. My apartment was ransacked while I was at work yesterday." Johab grabbed her arm.

"Don't worry. Nothing was taken. I reported the break-in to the police. They looked around and told me that 'foreigners' were easy targets for thieves, and that it would probably happen again. Can you imagine that kind of complacent attitude by police." Her question was an indignant statement, as she remembered the conscientious English policeman, armed only with a stick, patrolling her old neighborhood in London.

She refocused on Johab. "When I mentioned the break-in to Mr. El-Hasiim and Mr. Barzoni this morning, they both told me a ring of thieves had been working in my neighborhood, so I shouldn't keep cash or jewelry in my apartment."

In an arch tone, she added, "How would Mr. El-Hasiim and Mr. Barzoni know anything about thieves in my neighborhood when I've never told either of them where I live? The so-called ring of thieves was looking for information. Every drawer had been dumped on the floor. Nothing was taken, not even the cash in the spare sugar bowl. My mother always kept her valuables in the false bottom of her garbage pail. So do I!" She blurted out with a self-satisfied grin.

She shifted her weight from one knee to the other. It was cramped and hot inside the crate. "These are copies of papers your father has been working on this past month."

Johab felt the slightest tinge of relief that Miss Wenkle said "has been working on" as though his father had been momentarily interrupted and would return to his work soon.

"I didn't find anything related to a new tomb." She looked soberly at Johab. "We both know that the recent antiquities bust must somehow be connected to this business with your father. When I think back over the week before he was taken, I know that he was worried about something that made him secretive."

She frowned. "I can't find any connection to a new tomb. The government controls excavations. Archeological teams from other countries are carefully monitored. There are no new sites. But, the desert is a very large space. That's why the kings and queens chose places far away from the cities for their burial sites."

Her frown darkened. "All that space along the wadi at the head of the Valley of the Kings—and those cliffs—makes guarding those sites almost impossible. Anyone can get in or out without being seen."

She shook her head in frustration. "There must be something I'm missing."

"But if you can't find anything, Miss Wenkle, how can I?" Johab interrupted, trying not to appear as disappointed as he felt.

"A child's eyes can sometimes see things that an adult can't."

Johab flinched at the term "child." He didn't have the luxury of feeling like a child these days.

Miss Wenkle brushed a smudge of dirt off his cheek. "I meant to say a 'boy,' Johab. But that isn't right either. You're doing a man's job. We are partners. We need to be on an equal footing. From now on, you are to call me 'Hetty.'" Johab glanced up with a surprised expression.

"I use my nickname just as you do. My given name is Hildegarde. She was a 12th Century saint. My father's hobby was reading about medieval saints. I was born when he was going through the saints whose names begin with 'H.' It could have been worse," she said ruefully. "He could have been down the list as far as St. Humilitas. That would have been a worse joke. Humility has never been my strong suit."

Peering around the edge of the crate, she glanced both ways down the alley. "We need to get out of here. Tell your mother that I called your grandparents in Michigan. I only told them that you, your mother, and Jasmine are safe, and we're sure that John is alive. They wanted to book a flight to Cairo, but I convinced them to wait for now—that it wouldn't be safe for you to meet them. I don't think anyone followed me to the market this afternoon, but a car often seems to be trailing my VW."

She shoved the bundle of papers into Johab's hands. "I put another disguise in this package. It's the cover of an old textbook on ancient Egypt. The papers will fit inside that cover. Anyone seeing you reading will think you are studying an old textbook. I have identical copies and will keep studying them."

"You went with your dad into the field, Johab. I never did," she mused, regretfully. "People like me who only see information on paper or a piece of pottery after it has been cleaned can't possibly have the sense of place that the archeologists experience. You've been lucky to be with your dad out there in the Valley." She gestured south toward the desert.

"But, Miss Wen . . . I mean, Hetty," Johab blurted out, knowing that if his mother heard him calling Miss Wenkle by her first name, she would give him her "showing respect" lecture. "Dad wasn't looking for tombs. He dug in the villages where the people who did the work lived. The layers of mud brick houses preserved things such as pottery and old tools. Dad was interested in the people who built the tombs. He said the tombs are just tourist attractions."

Miss Wenkle's plump chin nodded in agreement.

"That's just it, Johab. Sometimes when people aren't looking for something, it finds them," she exclaimed, as though the puzzle had been solved.

"But how? What?" Johab's question hung in the close confinement of the wooden crate, the noise of the marketplace, a backdrop.

"In some of his written notes, he underlined Hatshepsut's name. In his notes on KV20, which was supposed to have been Hatshepsut's tomb in the cliffs, he wrote 'soft bedrock?' with a question mark. We know that tomb was never completed because of the poor quality of the limestone."

Miss Wenkle swatted at a swarm of flies in the smelly crate and leaned toward Johab, whispering as though someone might be listening. "He also underlined words that are on Hatshepsut's mortuary temple. Something about her directing the people in every sphere and living eternally. Your dad's note said that the queen would not let her body be found by thieves. She was too clever. Then he wrote the word "shaft" with a question mark. I put a paper clip for you on that page of his papers."

She patted the bundle of papers in his hands. "These other papers are just typed materials with sketches of the corridors of tombs, KV20, KV60 and KV19—nothing related to his recent work. I don't know why he had them on his desk. Nothing about those sketches is unusual. I compared them against other sketches of these tombs in our archives. Same old stuff."

She scooted outside of the wooden crate and stood nervously watching the alley. "You may see something that I didn't. Maybe Mr. Barzoni found something when he took your father back to his office that night. Or, maybe your father left something that none of us have seen."

Johab flushed. Miss Wenkle, that is, Hetty, was probably a good mind reader. *He was not ready to reveal the secret of the pouch.* He clutched the cloth-wrapped papers to his chest. "I'll study these. Maybe I'll remember something else from that day at Hatshepsut's temple. My father said something when we were getting into the jeep. I just can't remember what it was. I keep having this dream about it . . . I can hear his voice, but the words don't make sense."

"Don't try so hard, Johab. That can keep you from remembering. It will come to you," she assured him blithely. "Let's meet here day after tomorrow. Same time, same dirty alley."

She smiled as though to reassure him. "We'll find something. The two of us, working together, will sort this out, partner." She lifted her hand in a half salute and, in a flash, had turned the corner and disappeared into a noisy tour group following a woman waving a yellow flag.

CHAPTER 25

Johab sank back on his haunches inside the wooden crate thinking about his new "partnership" with Miss Wenkle. He remembered how she had often tried to talk to him when she visited and how he dismissed her presence to Mohammed as "just a lady from Dad's office." Now, she was his partner. She might be as old as his mother, but she was not just a lady from his father's office. She could fade into a group of tourists like an undercover spy.

She was Hetty. He rolled her name carefully as though savoring something a bit strange for the first time and liking the taste. A good idea struck him. He would convince his father to take her on a field trip. He could imagine them sitting at the campfire under the canopy of stars while his father explained why his study of the workers of ancient Egypt was so important. Hetty would get that. There is much to be discovered in ancient Egypt that doesn't wear a golden mask.

The rustling of mice in the trash near where Johab squatted startled him out of his daydream. The noise of the Khan, the steady drone of routine shoppers, had decreased in volume. By mid-afternoon, the tourists would seek their air-conditioned hotels.

Johab had been comforting himself by imagining being with Hetty on a field trip, watching her find an old pottery shard for the first time. Thinking about field trips with Hetty provided a kind of balance, helped him push back the "real" business of this partnership. Hetty was invaluable for one reason—she was the only person who could get close enough to Mr. El-Hasiim and Mr. Barzoni to spy from inside the Museum.

He felt a nudge of guilt. He hadn't told Hetty about the pouch. She was being watched and followed. Someone had broken into her apartment. Mr. Barzoni might suspect she knew where Johab was hiding. There would be no other reason for trailing her. It was best to keep the pouch secret from her.

Johab stuck his hand in his pocket and brought out the British note those ladies had given him at the market. He remembered the store his mother liked best. But, the shopkeeper knew him. That little beggar holding Sekina would need to make the purchases.

As Johab approached, he saw the little boy curled in a tight knot, dozing in the hot sun, ignoring Sekina's mouth nuzzling his neck. Johab stood over him, hands on his hips and said dryly, "Some guard. The donkey could have been miles from here."

"No, no." The boy leapt up and unwound a length of harness from around his midriff. "I promised to wait right here with Sekina. I tied her to me. She couldn't run away. You can trust me."

Johab assumed a stern expression and whispered. "I'm going to *trust* you with a great deal of money, because I want you to buy some things for me. If anyone asks you why you are spending English pounds, you tell them that your father carries bags at a hotel, and this was his tip. The owner of the shop where I'm sending you shouldn't be suspicious. He deals in English pounds every day."

Johab reached into the pocket of his shorts, digging for his pencil and notepad. "I'll make you a list." Johab began writing on the pad of paper.

The boy shook his head. "What's the matter? I'll pay you extra." Johab was annoyed. He needed things purchased and loaded in the cart so he could be on his way to the City of the Dead.

"It's not that. I . . ." The small boy drew a circle in the dust with his bare toe, his downcast eyes fixated on his circle, then blurted out, "I can't read!"

The boy was younger than Johab but older than Jasmine. She had already learned to read and print some words, both in Arabic and English.

Johab looked away, not wanting to embarrass the boy. He was embarrassed *for* the boy and *for* the country that Johab considered his home, even though he held an American passport. What kind of country does not help all its children learn to read? What kind of country lets its children be invisible?

Johab sized up the boy. He was using him to watch Sekina and now to run errands. It would be a courtesy to know his name. "What's your name?"

"Cyril." The whisper was so low that it was almost inaudible.

Johab could not believe his ears. He expected to hear "Yusef" or "Ahmed." "What did you say?"

"Cyril. Before my father died, his friend was a British officer named Cyril. My father named me for that man." The boy stood erect. Johab had the feeling that a salute might be appropriate.

"That's a nice name, Cyril. Why don't I tell you what I need? Then you can repeat back the list, and we'll see what you remember." Johab sighed. It would probably require repeated trips to the shop. Johab named the foods, the amounts, the description of the sheaves of golden wheat on the sack of flour his mother always purchased, and held his arms up to show the length of the robes he wanted for his mother and Jasmine.

"The shop is near the far corner, over there." He pointed. "I'll wait for you here with Sekina. I know just about what everything should cost and how much change I should get back. I expect to have every penny of it."

Johab felt a tinge of shame that he was so suspicious of this young beggar. He had grown up ignoring the beggars of Cairo. His father always dropped coins in their cups. His mother said that they were part of the Cairo "mafia" and begging on streets was a "disgrace."

Johab had a different perspective now that he was invisible. No one passing by looked into his face. Rude drivers honked their horns at him and his donkey. Shopkeepers eyed him suspiciously. But, he had *chosen* to hide behind a disguise that made him invisible. He couldn't imagine Cyril's actual invisible life.

Cyril flinched under Johab's stare. Cyril's galabeya would take the prize for a disguise. It had almost as many holes as fabric. Instead of cheap sandals, his feet were bare, splayed out at the toes as though they had never been confined by footwear. A layer of dust glazed his dark hair. But his eyes were bright with anticipation as he named the items, one by one, with the descriptions and amounts. He rattled off the list quickly.

Johab was amazed. "You didn't miss a thing, Cyril. What a memory!" Cyril beamed as though compliments were as rare as an eclipse of the sun.

"This is a twenty-pound note. The shopkeeper is honest, but you need to be careful—someone might be working for him who is not so honest. If you see a big, black car anywhere near, meet me over there. I can't be seen. " Johab pointed to the farthermost edge of the Khan toward a broad street and watched the small beggar clutching a twenty-pound note disappear.

CHAPTER 26

Standing by the busy Al Azhar Street, Johab waited restlessly for Cyril to return with his purchases. He would be more generous to Cyril today. He was ashamed that he hadn't even asked the boy's name when he hired him to guard the donkey.

With one large sack slung over his shoulder and another almost dragging the ground, Cyril came beaming around the corner. "I got all the good things you told me to get, Master of Sekina."

Johab flinched. "Master of Sekina." That sounded like something out of an Arabian Nights tale. This boy named Cyril, who didn't read newspapers, could not know his name. His name would be safe. "I'm Johab. But that's just between us. You can't tell anyone. I'm on this kind of . . . secret mission . . . I'm in disguise."

Cyril's eyes widened. Knowing someone on a secret mission, running errands for him—that was very special. Begging was a boring job. The only interesting part was dodging the police. They told him that beggars were a "bad image" for the tourists and to take his bowl someplace where there were no tourists. No one gave him coins but the tourists—so he had to take the risk that the police would appear and chase him away.

Now, here was this older boy named Johab who had a fine donkey, was on a secret mission, and paid him generously. What good fortune.

Cyril helped put the food and robes in the cart, lingering over the placement longer than was needed.

"Hurry up, Cyril. I need to be going." Johab held out a fist full of coins to Cyril. "For your trouble today. Be here day after tomorrow. Same time, same place."

Cyril put his hands behind his back. "I can't take that much money."

"What do you mean, you can't take it? You earned it. You watched Sekina; you did my shopping. It's yours, Cyril." Johab pushed the coins toward the boy.

Cyril studied his bare feet, shaking his head. "He will take it all from me. He always does. This is more than begging money. I need to save it for Alice."

"Who will take it? Who's Alice?" Johab could see Cyril's hands trembling as he tried to conceal them by readjusting Sekina's harness. Cyril didn't answer. Johab took his small, trembling hand and held it firmly.

A torrent of words fell on Johab and Sekina. They were full of emotion, but softly uttered as though to muffle the pain of the words. "That man, that Mustafa. He makes me call him uncle, but he's not my uncle. He lives with my aunt. She was married to my father's brother, my real uncle, but he died. My aunt took Alice and me to live with her after my father and real uncle died. The other Alice, the British officer's Alice left money for a doctor for my mother when Alice was being born. The doctor could only save Alice, not my mother." The words came out in a jumble, as though they had been saved for the ears of someone who would immediately know all the people involved.

"Wait . . . wait, Cyril. I don't understand. You live with your aunt and an uncle who isn't really your uncle. You and someone named Alice live with them? And he takes your money?"

Cyril squatted down, dropping his head between his knees. He had said too much. This boy who gave him money would not want to know about his life. No one did. Mustafa would beat him when he returned with only a few coins to show for a day of begging. He could expect that—as certain as the sun going down each day.

Despite his beatings, Cyril thought of himself as lucky. Mustafa never beat Alice. He said that Alice would be a "class act as a beggar" and when she was older she would be "very valuable." Cyril wasn't sure what that meant, but he knew that it would be bad for Alice.

They would have to leave his aunt's house before Alice got much older. But to where?

The next thing Cyril felt was Johab's arm around him, the two of them, squatting by Sekina's hooves, shoulder-to-shoulder, just like good friends. Cyril had never had a friend, except for Alice. She was only three. A little sister didn't count as a real friend.

Johab's voice was quiet and steady. "Tell me about where you live and what happened to your family. I may not be able to help you, but I can listen, Cyril." Johab could almost hear his own father's voice counseling him when something had gone wrong at school or when he had an argument with Mohammed. He always said, "I can listen."

Cyril was sniffling, tears cascading down his cheeks. Sympathy was harder to deal with than the beatings. He hadn't experienced kindness in years. Maybe the glances of the tourists when they slipped coins into his bowl could be interpreted as sympathy, but he thought they were simply looks of pity. He did not want to be pitied.

He muttered between sniffs, wiping his nose on the sleeve of his robe: "My father worked for a British officer named Cyril and his wife Alice when I was very young. I don't remember them. The officer had to go back to England because his wife was ill. My mother was expecting Alice and having some problems, so before they left Cairo, the officer's wife hired a doctor to look after her. That sick English lady cared about my mother."

Cyril paused as though continuing had become too painful. Johab patted his arm to reassure him that he was still listening.

"Something went wrong when Alice was born. My mother wasn't strong. She died right there in our house. My father was there, but I was at my aunt's house. She was married to my father's brother then. My real uncle was a good man." Cyril added, reflectively.

"My father and uncle worked on the cruise boats, those that go to Luxor. They spoke some English and studied about the ancient kings and queens so they could become tour guides. That job paid more. But then . . ." Cyril's voice trailed off. "They both caught typhoid. My father had such high fevers and chills. I still remember how blankets on the bed would be soaked, but I couldn't do anything to help him."

Cyril pulled his shoulders back, as though he were repeating a script he had memorized but found difficult to recite aloud. "They died—my father and then my uncle. They were in the big hospital, but I was not allowed to see them. My aunt told me what happened when she came to get Alice and me. That's when we went to live with her."

Cyril paused as though he wanted to stay at that moment in time. "Living with my aunt was OK when Alice was a baby. I took care of her while my aunt worked at the hotel laundry during the day. At night, my aunt would hold her. She didn't pay much attention to me, but she was kind. That's before Mustafa moved in." Cyril's voice took on a sharp edge.

"He's the one who sends me out begging. He even tore extra holes in my galabeya so that I would 'look the part' as he says." Cyril pulled up the sleeve of his robe, now wet with snot and tears from wiping his nose and eyes. "See the holes. They weren't there when my aunt bought it."

Cyril stared at his bare feet. "If I don't have a good day of begging, he beats me. He beats me sometimes when I do have a good day of begging." Cyril's voice was even and controlled.

"My aunt hates Mustafa, but she is afraid of him. Sometimes she says that Alice and I are not her 'blood' relatives, and she should not have to be responsible for us." Cyril's small back arched, as though he were expecting the lash of a strap at any moment.

"Tell me about Alice. I have a sister too, a little sister. I know about sisters." Johab's voice was soft and intentionally soothing.

"Alice," Cyril pronounced her name "Al—*eece*" with the accent on the second syllable so that it didn't sound at all like an English name. "Alice is three years old. She is very beautiful with the biggest brown eyes you can imagine and lashes as long as . . ." He looked around smiling, "as long as Sekina's, but much more handsome."

The smile faded quickly. "Mustafa holds her on his knee. Sometimes he puts kohl under her eyes. One day, he took red stuff out of my aunt's rouge pot and put it on her cheeks. My aunt said he made her look like a baby harlot. My father would have killed him for that." Cyril muttered through clenched teeth.

Cyril turned toward Johab, clutching his arm. "That's why I can't keep the money. I need for you to keep it for me. Please. If I can earn enough money, I can take Alice and leave my aunt's house. It's just a hut in a bad place. Alice can't grow up there. She can't stay around Mustafa."

Despite Cyril's pleading face, Johab knew that he couldn't take on someone else's troubles. He had his own sister to protect—and a mother. A wave of guilt swept over him. He had a mother and a father, though temporarily missing, who loved him. And, his Aunt Rayya would never willingly let anything happen to him or Jasmine. He had grandparents in Michigan that were a phone call away. He had a family.

Sometimes the family wasn't perfect. There was Uncle Tarek who had recently fallen further from grace. Uncle Tarek was always flawed as an uncle for hitting Cousin Mohammed. On the other hand, Uncle Tarek sent Mohammed to the same English school where Johab went. He never hit Aunt Rayya. Johab smiled to himself. He wouldn't dare. The fact is, Johab had an almost perfect family. Cyril had almost nothing.

The noise level had increased with late afternoon shoppers leaving the market. Johab needed to get back to the City of the Dead while it was still daylight to review the papers that Hetty had brought him. This little boy with the odd name of Cyril, at least odd for an Egyptian, was a problem. Because Johab had listened to his story, he could no longer distance himself from Cyril's problems. He needed to think. He needed time.

Johab stood up, grabbed Sekina's harness, and said, "I'll keep your money for now, Cyril. It's right here in my pocket. This is Cyril's money in the Johab Bank of Egypt, safe as deposited." Johab knew that he sounded too light-hearted, too frivolous in the face of the sadness that was Cyril's life, but being glum wouldn't help Cyril now.

"In two days, we'll meet here again. You can watch Sekina for me, and I'll try to figure out how I can help you. It's just that . . ." Johab paused. Cyril was a stranger, a boy sent out to beg by people who didn't even want him around. Johab didn't know how much he could share with him. There was only Hetty at this time, so maybe he could confide in Cyril, but he would do it carefully.

"That secret mission I mentioned? Well, I'm working under-cover—just me and a British lady. You may have seen her in the Khan, large hat, big sunglasses?" Cyril nodded affirmatively. That description fit dozens of tourists that he saw every day in the Khan. He must have seen her.

"We are hiding from a man who drives a long, black car. He and his men are looking for me. I can't tell you why. It's too secret. But, if you can be another set of eyes for me when I'm at the Khan, I'll pay you to be my lieutenant."

Cyril's face lit up. "Lieutenant" sounded almost as impressive as "major." "I'll do it, Johab. I'll do anything you ask. I'm very good at remembering things." He was still basking in the glow of Johab's praise for remembering every item on the shopping list.

"I know that you are, Cyril. But you also must be very good at *forgetting things.*" Johab emphasized the last two words and noted the confusion on Cyril's face. "In spy terms, that means you never give out anyone's name. You never tell anyone but me what you see. You never, even under torture, repeat anything that I tell you. Is that clear?" Johab put on his best stern face. This was official business.

Digging in the pocket of his shorts, Johab pulled out a few coins. "Here, Cyril, use these for the man who is not your uncle, that Mustafa. Maybe this will satisfy him for the begging money. I hope that he doesn't hit you tonight. I don't want to think about that."

As he turned Sekina toward the street, looking back over his shoulder, he could see Cyril, no more than a shadow against the brightly striped tents of the Khan, almost invisible. Maybe that invisibility could be put to good use. Perhaps Cyril could help him and he could help Cyril. It was difficult to think of how, but the possibility gave Johab comfort as he headed home.

CHAPTER 27

*Maat is the goddess of order and harmony on earth and in
the sky. She weighs the hearts of the just and the unjust.
She determines the balance. She will look after the Cyrils of
this world.*

—Johab Bennett

When Sekina pulled the wobbly cart into the small space in front of
their tomb, it was just like an early Christmas. Jasmine burst from
the door and flung her arms around Johab's legs shouting, "What
have you brought me? What have you brought me?"

His mother was more restrained, but the pleasure on her face
cheered Johab. "A large jar of honey, this good flour. I will make
your favorite sweet cake for tomorrow. We must wait for the dough
to rise tonight, but Mr. Feisel gave me some wild yeast that he keeps
fermenting."

She paused. "I had almost forgotten that old method of making
yeast. I always use those little packages from the store. The old-style
yeast tastes better. And, then . . ." She stopped and looked sternly at
Johab. "Where did you get all these things? Selling fulbeans couldn't
pay for this."

He could afford to be truthful this time. "I did a favor for some
nice British ladies at the Khan. They were being cheated by one of
those men who sell poorly made copies of the gods. You can't imagine
what that man was going to charge them, Mother."

"So," she looked directly into his eyes, "how does helping a couple of ladies result in you buying all these things? Helping them should have been something you would do out of courtesy."

"I know, Mother." Johab's answer was dismissive. There were times when his mother seemed to be living in their former life and didn't understand that the rules had changed. "They *insisted* that I take money for helping them. They gave me a twenty-pound note, but I probably saved them more than a hundred pounds. They were grateful." Johab reassured her, knowing that she wouldn't agree.

"We just don't take money for helping tourists, Johab. Your father wouldn't like it," she said definitively.

There was no room for a Mohammed twist on things now. Johab needed to be brutally honest. They weren't just camping out, playing at being poor. "Mother, I earned this money. Dad isn't here to tell me what he would and wouldn't like. I have to do the best I can to get things we need."

His mother flinched when he mentioned his father, but she nodded her head. "You are doing much more than any boy your age could be expected to do, Johab. You are being the man of this family." Her statement almost echoed the one that Hetty had made earlier when they were hiding in the wooden crate, the statement about a "man's job."

His mother turned toward the cart, rummaging around. "What's this, Johab?" She picked up the stack of his father's papers that Miss Wenkle had wrapped in the old, checkered headdress.

Johab snatched them. "Just an old textbook on Egypt. Someone gave it to me. It's not worth anything—I just want to read about the things my father studied."

The lie brought a smile to the face of his mother. "That will make your father happy. Next to his family, his work was the most important thing to him. Why don't you stay home tomorrow? We'll have a feast with all these good things you brought. You need a rest."

That was exactly what Johab needed, time to study his father's papers.

His mother pulled the robes out of a small, cloth bag. "The fabric in these is soft, so much nicer than the other ones you bought us earlier."

Johab looked chagrined. It seemed that Cyril was better at bargaining. But then, Johab had sent him to an honest shop in the Khan. His lieutenant might be a good find after all.

The City of the Dead woke early. Johab heard crowing roosters, the clatter of carts on clay-packed streets, and an occasional shout as someone chased a hungry dog away from a chicken coop. Johab moved around the sleeping forms of Jasmine and his mother and eased the door open. The sun was barely edging its way above the horizon, casting soft shadows across the tops of the mosques. It was the time of day he liked best.

He remembered how the early-morning sun against the limestone terraces of Queen Hatshepsut's temple could take his breath away. He gasped now. He just remembered the thing he couldn't remember before. *Why hadn't he remembered something so important?*

That last day in the field, he and his father had just crawled out of their sleeping bags to watch the sun lighting the far-off cliffs. "She's still here. That mummy with the very pronounced jaw in the basement of the Museum is not Hatshepsut," Johab's father had muttered.

"How do you know?" Johab knew enough about the excitement of finding a long-lost mummy of a king or queen. It would make the front pages of newspapers around the world.

Johab's father had turned away, as though he had said too much. "I always have this feeling, Johab, when we come to visit her temple that Hatshepsut is welcoming us."

"Yeah," responded Johab, "but she would think of us as 'infidels' wouldn't she? She wouldn't want us nosing around her temple."

"She wouldn't even recognize this world," his father had responded, "unless she's been looking down on it since she left it. That's what she believed, that she would live forever in the land of the gods. I think that she would have welcomed us, because we appreciate what she left. Time to fix breakfast, Johab. I need to finish my sketches." His father had closed the door on the mummy discussion.

Johab grimaced in frustration. With all of the things that had happened since that morning at Queen Hatshepsut's temple, he had forgotten important things. He needed to ask Hetty if she could help him contact Ian Parks. Mr. Parks might not know that Johab's father was missing if he were out in the field in a remote place.

Johab tiptoed back inside to get his father's papers, settled onto the mud-brick step of the hut, and carefully inserted the pages into the cover of a book called: *Everything to Know about Ancient Egypt.* Johab grinned sarcastically. What kind of writer would claim that "everything" about ancient Egypt could fit between the covers of one book? Johab angled his back against the wall, held the covers upright, and positioned himself to take advantage of the early morning light in a place where no one would bother him.

CHAPTER 28

A dark shadow fell across the page. Johab slammed the covers closed. Mr. Feisel stood over him with slightly bleary eyes, smiling as though he had a great secret that he would never divulge.

"A little casual reading, Johab?"

"I . . . just an old textbook I found at the Khan."

Mr. Feisel settled himself, uninvited, on the stoop next to Johab. "Just a word to the wise, Johab. Many boys living here don't know how to read at all. And, those who do certainly wouldn't be reading a textbook in English on ancient Egypt." He paused and smiled quizzically. "Might get in the way of your disguise, don't you think?"

Johab could ignore him or involve him. Johab was still suspicious of that story about him working with Howard Carter when the tomb of King Tut was opened.

Mr. Feisel interrupted his thought processes. "You know that I might be able to help you, Johab."

Johab glanced up into the weather-beaten face of this old man whose breath smelled like garlic and who attracted rumors about dealing in black magic.

"I know a few things about antiquities. I can read hieroglyphs. The hieratic script is harder, but I can read a bit of that, too."

Johab was stunned. Mr. Feisel never failed to amaze him. His robe looked dirty. His face was covered with a half-stubble of beard. He was gruff. Yet, he made a lovely doll's bed for Jasmine. He had helped bury the mummy hand. He carried water for Johab's mother. And, his advice to Johab had been sound.

Johab could not be careless in this place. It was a neighborhood of strangers.

Suspicion had to be his watchword. His family and now Hetty depended on his ability to decide who might harm them.

The corners of Mr. Feisel's eyes crinkled with his half-smile. "Try me, Johab. Draw me a hieroglyph that you know."

Johab hesitated, then licked the tip of his pencil and carefully drew a cartouche with Queen Hatshepsut's name on it, using the symbols his father had taught him.

"That old girl!" Mr. Feisel laughed. "You might have given me something a little more difficult than Hatshepsut."

Johab looked chagrined. Actually, the hieroglyphs in Hatshepsut's name were among the few that he could interpret. He knew the "a" sound for the bird with the tail and the "w" sound for the bird without the tail. The upside-down bowl for "t" was easy, and the snake for "d" and snail for "f" were simple. But when the consonants were doubled, such as "bb" or "nb" or even tripled as in "nhm," Johab had quickly become frustrated.

"I have to learn English and Arabic, Dad," he would protest to his father. "Mohammed doesn't have to learn ancient scripts. You can translate for me."

His father's response had been terse. "If you just want to be just a visitor, a tourist looking at odd pictures and marks on the walls of tombs, you don't need to learn anything else. But, if you want to understand Egypt's past, you must know the language."

Johab had tried, but not very hard. He wondered now if Mr. Feisel had tried harder. "If I brought you some hieroglyphs . . . I . . . uh . . . don't have them with me right now. Could you translate them?"

"I could try. Where did these hieroglyphs come from? What site? What source?"

"I don't know." Johab could honestly say that. All he knew is that the papyrus sheets were in the pouch, and, from the shape of them, at one time they had been squeezed into a tight, oval space. That's why the folds were sharp and crumbling at the edges.

What did he dare to share with Mr. Feisel? No one in the neighborhood seemed particularly fond of him. He never sat out on stoops with other men at night, smoking cigarettes or water pipes. Maybe that was a good thing. He had told Johab that he "kept his own counsel." Johab liked the sound of those words. They sounded like something he had heard his mother's priest say at church.

He had no option. He couldn't consult his father's colleagues. His missing father had come under suspicion, thanks to the comments to the press made by Mr. El-Hasiim and Uncle Tarek. There was no one else.

Mr. Feisel pulled himself up, patted Johab on the head and said, "Let me know if I can help," then crossed the alley.

After looking in two directions, Johab returned to the study of his father's papers Maybe anyone seeing him with the textbook would think that he was just looking at pictures. He worked from the most recent papers backward. Some of the typing had been done on his dad's old Royal typewriter. The text was full of corrections. Other pages, typed by Hetty from his notes, were neater.

Halfway through the stack was a hand-written page with a paper clip that piqued his interest, because it listed tombs with their official numbers. KV20 was the original burial place of Hatshepsut's father Thutmosis I—and intended for Queen Hatshepsut.

His father's notes were fragmented: "KV20 recorded by Belzoni—then Carter. Double tomb and circling tunnels? KV42 more interesting. Why unfinished? Purposefully unfinished? His father had underlined *purposefully*. "Note the burial chamber on the papyrus" was in small, block letters.

Johab reread the section. These must be clues for a single reason. His father didn't work on old tombs now. They were open for tourists or closed as dangerous to tourists—but rarely of interest to Egyptologists. Something had sparked his father's interest, something connected to the papyrus in the pouch.

Tonight, he would copy some of the hieroglyphs and hieratic script from the copies he had made—a copy of a copy to show Mr. Feisel. That should keep him a safe distance from what was in the pouch. Mr. Feisel was always awake early. He'd give it to him in the morning, because he was meeting Hetty at the Khan tomorrow. Tomorrow might be a very good day if both Mr. Feisel and Hetty helped.

The fragrant odor of cinnamon wafted out the door as his mother announced, "Johab, the sweet bread I promised you is ready. Mr. Feisel gave me two old clay pots for bread-baking, the kind they used in olden days." She smiled sadly. "I think your father would like it."

The shape of the bread was odd, cone-shaped at the top, but the crust was thick and chewy, the soft interior rich with honey and cinnamon. "It's better than anything you've ever made, Mother," exclaimed Johab. "The old way is really the best." His praise made his mother as happy as he had made Cyril yesterday. Can't underestimate praise.

This might be an ideal time to bring up the problem of Cyril and Alice, but only as a theoretical problem—not a real one. Johab simply couldn't take on Cyril's problems. He had enough of his own. He just wanted his mother's opinion. But, he would need to add a Mohammed flavor to the story he was going to tell his mother. She couldn't know that the story involved anyone he actually knew.

"I overheard something when I was standing by some of the workers in the Khan this week. It sounded like a very sad story. I just wondered what thoughts you might have about this kind of thing," Johab blurted out.

"What kind of thing, Johab?"

"Well, they were saying that this little boy in their neighborhood—they thought he might be six or seven, but he was so thin, they weren't sure. He and his little sister are living with their aunt. She isn't a real aunt like Aunt Rayya but was married to the little boy's uncle who died." Johab's mother listened, her face expressionless.

"Anyhow, this bad man moved in with the aunt. Now, this man makes the boy go out to beg. And, he tells the aunt that the little girl will be worth a great deal of money. Oh yes, he beats the boy—almost every day," Johab added casually, as though he thought of it as another interesting point. He watched her closely, gauging her response.

Johab's mother's eyes widened and her mouth became a thin, tight line. "These *workers*, Johab, who were telling this story . . ." Her emphasis on "workers" suggested that they were the lowest of the low. "Why haven't they gone to the police? Why aren't they doing something about the man beating that child? That kind of thing disgusts me. We have people in the police department trained to deal with that kind of situation. As for what a little girl might be worth in terms of money, I wouldn't dream of talking about such a thing with you. Nice people don't talk about things like that. Those kinds of things get turned over to the authorities."

From the firm set of her mouth, Johab decided that his mother did not want to have a "theoretical" discussion. She didn't like the topic.

Night fell early in the City of the Dead, the darkness interrupted by an occasional candle or oil lamp flickering in a window. Johab stretched out on his mat, waiting for his mother and Jasmine to fall asleep so that he make a copy of his copy for Mr. Feisel.

"Johab?" His mother sat up in the far corner of the dark room. The coals under the simmering pot of beans reflected pinpoints of light in the eyes of Bastet, curled at the foot of Jasmine's mat.

"I've been thinking about what I said this morning when you told me the sad story about that little boy and girl. I began thinking about our priest's sermon last Christmas. He talked about the gift of the child Jesus and how that gift had changed the world."

She paused to ensure that Johab was listening. "Then he said something else that I just remembered tonight. Your story made me think of it. He said that God's gift of his child should remind us every day that many children in our country live in terrible conditions, and we must remember that as God's children they are all members of our family."

She paused for a moment. "Even though those children's blood uncle is dead, his widow, that aunt, has obligations to them. She is their family." His mother made a small, sniffling sound, then added sharply. "She's a bad woman to allow them to be mistreated by that man. She's very much at fault. Johab?"

"I'm still awake. I hear you."

"I just wanted you to know that I spoke too hastily this morning. The story you heard from those men has troubled me all day. The police should probably be notified, but they could make things worse—as in our case." His mother's voice drifted off. Johab hoped that she was in a dreamless sleep, free from the daily worry about his father and about children in a harsh world.

He snapped on the flashlight. Digging into the bag of beans, Johab found his dirty sock stuffed with his drawings of the hieroglyphs from the old papyri. Propped against the wall, he began copying the symbols and rearranging them on the page. Getting Mr. Feisel to translate the hieroglyphs without understanding their importance would be a challenge. He could just imagine Mr. Feisel's knowing eyes answering his own question: "Who do you think you're fooling?"

CHAPTER 29

Consider the little mouse, how sagacious an animal
it is which never entrusts its life to one hole only.

—Plautus

Johab awoke to the sound of his mother's humming as she stirred
the beans. The thing he loved most about his mother was her ability
to start each day with anticipation. Her sister Rayya said that she
woke up like a goose in a new world, but she meant it in a kind way.
Johab's mother never carried anger into the next day. Grudges were
simply left behind.

Even her fury with Uncle Tarek for making a deal with Mr. Barzoni
had been shoved onto some back burner of her memory. After that
first, furious outburst when Johab had told her about Uncle Tarek
taking money from Mr. Barzoni, she had not spoken ill of him since.
She had not spoken of him at all.

His mother smiled with misty eyes. "I've been thinking about
your Aunt Rayya and Mohammed. You must be missing your cousin
as much as I miss my sister."

Johab tried to pull on a glum face, but he wasn't really missing
Mohammed. His cousin's bullying and lies bothered Johab more than
he dared to say. Mohammed was a blood relative. That counted with
his mother. So did schedules.

"Time to load the beans, Johab. I let you sleep late. I saw you
studying with the flashlight—your father did that sometimes when
we camped in the desert." She smiled at Johab, her face bright and

open—not a trace of suspicion about Johab's shady business with the flashlight last night.

He hadn't exactly been studying. He was trying to determine how he could trick Mr. Feisel. Johab needed help without telling him why the help was needed or what the hieroglyphs might reveal.

Hetty sprang to mind with just a flash of affection. She understood intrigue. She showed no guilt for trying to trick her boss Mr. El-Hasiim. Being a partner with someone like Hetty, who loved the Hardy Boys and the Sherlock Holmes mysteries, created a strong bond. For his last birthday, she had surprised him with a collection of Edgar Allen Poe stories. Hetty would understand his need to use Mr. Feisel while keeping him in the dark—she knew the wiles of detectives.

Within minutes, Johab had a half-eaten slice of cinnamon bread in his hand and was tapping lightly on Mr. Feisel's door. The door swung open with sinister silence. A sharp, glittering blade flashed in Mr. Feisel's hand inches away from Johab's throat. The boy gasped and jumped backwards.

"Just a chisel, Johab," Mr. Feisel laughed. "We don't cut throats with chisels. We don't even carve up mummies with them—the resin would dull the blade," he chortled.

Getting accustomed to Mr. Feisel's sense of humor was taking some adjustment. Johab's mother had always insisted that he be absolutely respectful to his elders. Laughing at them was unforgivable. Laughing with them rarely happened. Children were sent out to play when adult conversations became interesting.

"You have something for me?"

Johab held out several pieces of notebook paper with carefully penciled hieroglyphs scattered across the pages.

"The order of these hieroglyphs looks peculiar. It would help if I knew the source."

Johab changed the subject. "I'm off to sell my beans. Do you think you can translate these today?"

"We'll see. I promised your mother that I'd try to find a bale of good hay for Sekina. That donkey is happy with weeds, but she's working too hard for that as a steady diet. You know, Johab, I could be of much more help to you and your family if you would trust me." Mr. Feisel's stare was alert with curiosity.

"It's not that I . . . I just. . . ." Johab stared down at his rough sandals.

"I know. Boys like their secrets. Get along with you. Your customers are waiting for their beans." The door closed with Johab standing there feeling mixed emotions—guilt for not being open with Mr. Feisel and fear that too much openness could put his family at greater risk.

He hurried to hook Sekina to the cart. Being busy helped him think less about his little lies. He should have left an hour ago. In the neighborhood of his best customers, the same pots dangled, but the voices were irritated. "You're late, boy. Next time I won't wait. I'll buy from that old man who comes early."

"You will if you like the taste of camel dung. That old man never washes his beans," shouted another neighbor. Laughter rang out. The neighborhood was astir. Johab remembered his old neighborhood with an unexpected longing and smacked Sekina's rump. He would be late to meet Hetty.

The busy corner outside the Khan where Cyril always squatted with his bowl was deserted. Drat that boy. He depended on Cyril. Without being seen, Johab needed to slip down the back alley behind the shop of Hetty's friend. He couldn't do that with a donkey and cart.

A small hand slipped into his. Cyril had crept up behind him, the hood on his robe pulled across the lower part of his face. "I'm here, Johab. I didn't forget. But I'm—how did you say?—under cover."

Johab grabbed Cyril's arm to hand over Sekina's lead rope. Cyril flinched. "I'm in a hurry. Take Sekina over there and wait."

Cyril nodded, only his eyes visible.

Strange little boy, Johab thought. Why would anyone keep his hood up in this kind of heat? He would talk to Cyril later, after he met Hetty. At the least, he would ask if Mustafa had beaten Cyril or if the coins had been enough to ward off the beating.

Johab trotted down the back alley of the Khan, keeping close watch over the shoppers and the streets leading into the market. No black car was within sight. If her friend weren't in his shop, Hetty might be waiting in the crate behind the tent.

She wasn't. The wooden crate was empty. Johab lifted the back flap of the tent and peered inside again. She wasn't in the shop. He looked both ways down the alley. No giant hat. No oversized sunglasses. No Hetty. Frustration swept over him. He had overslept, irritated his fulbean customers, and now, missed Hetty. She must have given up on him and gone back to the Museum. He would take Cyril to watch Sekina while he slipped another "Market List" into Hetty's car. This was not turning into a good day.

Cyril was leaning against Sekina. From his perspective, Johab could have sworn that the donkey was propping up the small boy, instead of Cyril keeping the donkey from straying. They looked like one of those tomb statues carved from granite in which the man and the child are inseparable. This statue was a donkey and child, eerie in its stillness.

An uneasy feeling came over Johab as he hurried toward them. "Cyril? Cyril?" Johab repeated his name. Cyril turned sad, dark eyes toward Johab, keeping his hood up even under the shade of a tent's awning.

With a flash of his hand, Johab pushed the hood back and gasped. A large, purple bruise blazed across Cyril's face from ear to chin. His mouth puffed out on each side of the angry, blood-encrusted split of his lower lip. Cyril leaned against Sekina as though she had become his only lifeline.

Johab eased Cyril down to the ground and squatted beside him, gingerly touching his cheek. "Mustafa did this, didn't he?"

Cyril nodded, even that small motion causing obvious pain.

A wave of anger that he hadn't felt since that night that Mr. Barzoni hit his mother swept over Johab. He wanted to find this Mustafa, confront him, tell his neighbors, and make someone do something to protect this small boy.

"I bit him." Cyril's whisper was so soft that Johab could barely hear him over the steady hum of shoppers in the market.

Cyril moved his shoulders back, gave Johab a lop-sided smile with his split lip, and repeated, "I bit him."

"Why in the world would you. . . .?" Johab burst out, stopped by Cyril's next statement.

"It was the mouse. I wouldn't swallow the mouse. Even though he had skinned it and claimed it would make me well, I wouldn't swallow it." Johab stared at Cyril in shock, speechless.

"I gave him the coins last night. The ones you gave me. He said it was enough for a day of begging." Cyril paused. "I thought it would be OK, but my aunt said he'd been drinking all day, and I should stay away from him."

Cyril fingered his lip. "It was later when he came. I was asleep. He kicked me in the side to wake me and told me that he had some 'medicine' that the ancient people used. He said it would help me work harder, that I must be sick or I would bring home more money."

Cyril halted, his voice breaking with soft sobs. "He knocked down my aunt. She tried to stop him. He sat on top of me, dangling this bloody, skinless mouse by its tail over my face."

His sobs increased. "It was a nasty little thing with gray fur still on its ears and head. Its beady eyes were staring at me, but I think it was dead." In unison, both Cyril and Johab shuddered.

"Mustafa screamed, 'Swallow! Swallow!' and called me bad names."

Cyril's sobbing stopped as he gasped out: "I saw his big, fat thumb, and just clamped on."

Cyril paused as though overwhelmed by his indiscretion. "He screamed and screamed, Johab. Then he socked me in the face. My aunt ran for a rag to tie around his thumb. There was blood everywhere. He was jumping around, holding his hand. I ran. I ran away. I've been hiding all night."

Cyril's sobs renewed. "I left Alice, Johab. I left Alice with that terrible Mustafa."

Somehow, not finding Hetty in the market seemed like a minor problem compared to what Cyril was experiencing. "Don't cry, Cyril.

It won't do any good. People are looking this way. We need to think of something together. I'll help you." Johab patted Cyril awkwardly on the shoulder, concerned that they were attracting attention.

Things like this didn't happen these days. Johab knew that the ancient doctors sometimes prescribed the swallowing of mice for children who were very ill, hoping that the liveliness of these small rodents would restore the child to health. Mummies of children with a mouse inside told a different story. Johab had read about this practice, and his father had tried to explain it as an ancient remedy for ill children. Johab thought it was disgusting. He remembered his father telling him that desperate parents would risk any treatment to save their ill child. That bad man Mustafa was not a worried parent.

First things first. Johab had to get a message to Hetty. Then, he needed to decide what to do about Cyril. "Do you feel like walking, Cyril? You can ride in the cart if you want." Johab questioned the small boy who propped himself against Sekina.

"My ribs hurt. I think bouncing in the cart would make them hurt more. Can I just walk with you, Johab? I'll be quiet. I'm good at being undercover," he assured Johab. "I don't know what I will do without you," he added plaintively. Johab had the sinking feeling that his day was spiraling out of control.

CHAPTER 30

They wound in and out of traffic, heading to the Museum. "I know that place," Cyril beamed. "I used to beg there often. Those buses of tourists are the best targets for good begging. But now, the guards chase me away."

"Good begging?" That was something Johab needed to think about. Clearly, Cyril's moral compass was slightly askew. And, if the guards had been watching more carefully, instead of chasing away children, that poor guard, Mr. Razek, wouldn't be rising and setting with the sun in some other world.

Johab watched Cyril's thin, bird-like legs moving quickly, his small hands grasping Sekina's neck occasionally as though the act of moving alone hurt too much. He didn't complain.

This boy, Cyril, was someone special, thought Johab. He might look like a small, dirty, illiterate beggar. Looks, as Johab had lately discovered, were very deceiving. A small boy had done battle with evil. That man, Mustafa, was evil, and Cyril had bested him, at least for the moment, by biting his thumb.

They moved to the back of the Museum. Hetty's VW was there, but the windows were rolled all the way up and the locks were down. Johab couldn't get a note into the car. "Cyril, I know your ribs hurt even though you are being brave. I have to do some things that can't wait, my undercover work. I need you to help me. Remember me telling you about someone who was my partner?"

Cyril nodded. "That lady. One of those English ones with a big hat." Cyril wouldn't recognize Hetty as an individual, but he knew her as a class, one of those noisy, sometimes generous tourists who left the Khan carrying more packages than he could imagine any one person needing.

"She was supposed to meet me at the market at noon, but she wasn't there. I was late, but I don't think she would have gone back to work without leaving me a message. I'm worried." Johab stared at the back entrance, a germ of uneasiness making him more anxious. No black car. Only a single guard, smoking at the back door. Things were too quiet.

"I need you to scout for me, Cyril. Do you know what that means?"

"Yes," beamed Cyril. "It means that I'm your lieutenant, and I do everything you tell me and report back to you. It means that I don't tell anybody anything unless you say it's OK."

Cyril never seemed to forget a thing that Johab had told him. Amazing. Maybe he did need Cyril as much as Cyril needed him.

"I want you to go over to that guard, the one smoking. I'll move Sekina and the cart so he can't see us. Just ask him if he's seen Miss Wenkle today. Tell him that she asked you to run an errand for her, and you need to talk to her."

Cyril marched toward the guard, confident as though he had been given orders at the highest level of military command. Johab could see the guard gesturing, then pointing in another direction. Cyril walked swiftly back toward Johab.

"She's been hurt, Johab. She's in that hospital not too far from here. That guard said she fell down the stairs. No one saw it happen. A man, a Mr. Barzoni, found her unconscious at the bottom of the stairwell." Cyril provided the information carefully and precisely, just as the guard had related it to him.

Johab felt the dull throb of helplessness, as though his feet were mired in deep sand, and he had to force a reaction. "Let's go, Cyril. I know a shortcut to the hospital through these back streets. If we hurry, we can get there in half an hour. We need to check on Hetty, I mean, Miss Wenkle."

Sekina balked. Two extra trips through Cairo in one day were more than allowed. No water. No grass. Not even a carrot for a treat. The boy was neglecting her. She would repay him with stubbornness.

"Stupid donkey!" shouted Johab when Sekina blocked traffic in an intersection for the second time.

"Let me," said Cyril softly. He moved close to Sekina and whispered in her ear. She lifted her head, picked up her feet, and trotted amicably alongside the two boys, the cart clattering behind.

"How did you do that?" Johab asked. "She never does what I tell her to do."

"It's secret donkey language," Cyril said slyly.

"Oh, yeah. As if I'm going to believe that," Johab retorted, but Cyril's value meter raised another notch. Anyone who could make Sekina move when she had made up her mind to stay must be some kind of magician.

As they approached the hospital, Johab began looking for the staff entrance. He knew he would have a hard time getting by the reception area in the front. He had been here with his mother once when she visited a woman from her church. The receptionist at the front desk had aimed a blood-red fingernail at a sign on the wall: "No children allowed" and begun applying a second coat of polish. The odors of Lysol and illness had been so thick in the air that Johab felt nauseous as he waited on a hard bench for his mother.

A third-floor window facing the alley at the back of the hospital flung open. A young woman wearing a white cap dumped a pail of oily gray water out the window. She watched as it streamed down the side of the building. The same odors of disinfectant and illness that Johab remembered wafted past him and Cyril.

"That door, Cyril. See those people coming out. That's where I need to get inside. I can't go through the front door wearing this old robe. I need to know Miss Wenkle's room number, so I can sneak past anyone who might be watching her. Here, I'll write a message on this, and you take it to the woman at the front desk. Tell her that the florist is going to bring flowers and needs the room number." Johab whipped out his stub of a pencil and printed a message with Miss Wenkle's name and request for the room number.

Within minutes, Cyril was back, waving the slip of paper. "It's on the third floor, 3067. That woman wanted to know why the florist didn't bring the flowers to the front desk. She said he had no reason to be suspicious of the help taking them. She told me to leave immediately. Then, just as I headed toward the door, she said that the florist owner ought to buy his help better clothes."

Cyril grinned self-consciously. "I got the information. I guess that's what matters."

"We'll find you a better galabeya, Cyril. Wait here with Sekina. Don't move unless someone chases you away. If that happens, head toward that next apartment block. I'll find you there."

Johab sidled up to the back entrance. White-capped nurses, a couple of men with stethoscopes around their necks, and two work-men clustered at the back entrance. A cloud of smoke hung like fog around the entrance. His mother hated cigarettes, and his father had given up his pipe to please her.

Sometimes Johab liked the odors drifting from *shiisha* pipes in the sidewalk cafes where the local men drank sweet tea and talked endlessly. But cigarettes had a sharp, dry odor of grass burning. He edged nearer to the door, his eyes already stinging from the smoke.

A truck chugged down the alley and screeched to a halt at the back door. Four men jumped off the back and shouted: "Hold the door." They bumped a stack of large boxes up the steps. Opportunity presented itself. Johab held the door open for them.

Within seconds, he was inside and speeding up the nearest stair-case two steps at a time. Half a dozen paces down the hall, a room with 3067 painted in black letters faced him. He pressed his ear against it. No voices. He carefully pushed it open. The body in the bed did not look like Hetty. A giant, white wrapping of gauze made an unseemly turban bearing a close resemblance to a *hedjet*, the white war helmet of Upper Egypt.

Blue-black half-circles below her eyes were the only mark of color on her pale face. A splinted finger jutted upward like a warning gesture. The late afternoon sun filtered through the window, casting strange, net-like shadows across the room.

Johab shuddered. The shadows and light resembled a giant spi-der web. Hetty was at the center, bound and helpless. He was at the edge. One tiny move in the wrong direction would tug one of the fibers of the net. He had no doubt that the large and deadly spider in hiding was Mr. Barzoni.

He shook his head to clear it. It was only a plain, hospital room with a bed, a floral fabric privacy screen, and a bedside table on wheels. "Miss Wen . . . Hetty," he corrected himself. "It's me, Johab."

Her eyes fluttered open. They were bright and alert inside those dark circles. "Johab, you shouldn't be here. Mr. Barzoni just left. He brought those awful, smelly lilies. They are overpowering." She reached for Johab's hand. "I've got to get out of here. I need to get back to my own apartment. Mr. Barzoni says that I must stay in the hospital. I heard him talking to the doctor outside. I think he bribed him to keep me here." She hissed the words in a torrent under her breath.

"But how did this happen, Hetty?" Johab patted the hand without the splint awkwardly. People in hospital beds made him uncomfortable. Hetty looked vulnerable with her large, misshapen turban.

"I was hurrying down the hall from the room with the copy machine and paused to assemble my papers. When I came to, I was lying at the bottom of the stairwell—remember those stairs just past Mr. El-Hasiim's office? There were people bending over me. Mr. Barzoni was there, and then the ambulance came." She struggled to sit up.

"I have a headache and a broken finger." She waggled the splinted finger. "They say I must have tripped because of my high heels. I think I had a concussion, but it wasn't bad, because I remember everything that happened in the ambulance and everything that has happened in this hospital—including those pills that I won't take."

She looked grimly at Johab and pointed to the bottle on the bed stand.

Drawing herself up against the metal headboard, she whispered sharply: "I also remember the palm of a hand on my back just before I fell and the distinct odor of that nasty spice cologne that Mr. Barzoni wears. I didn't mention that to anyone. I didn't tell them why I was hurrying from the copy machine."

Her voice was animated; she pulled Johab close to the side of her bed. "I found another sketch of a tomb, Johab. It wasn't in the regular file. It was clipped to the back of that photograph that your father had taken of the amulet—that one with an oval shape and a carved carnelian on top. That amulet was part of the things the police returned when they caught those thieves. Your father kept Polaroid photos in an archival box in the copy room. I just remembered it when I went to make some copies of his papers from my duplicate files."

She frowned. "Someone took all my files. They were on the floor beside me when I fell, but no one seems to know what happened to them after the ambulance came."

She gestured toward a small door in the corner of the room. "Get my jacket there in that small closet. I put the photo and the sketch in that inside pocket before I left the workroom and started down the stairs. I hope they are still there."

Johab pulled the jacket off the hook to check. A photograph, clipped to a sheet of paper, was inside the pocket.

"You keep them, Johab. I think the photo and your dad's notes about it are very interesting."

She paused a moment. "I hate to ask you to do anything for me. I shouldn't have gotten myself into this fix, but Mr. Barzoni has no right to tell my doctor when I can leave. I believe he shoved me down the stairs for a reason. I must be getting close to information that he doesn't want me to have."

"I can help you, Hetty. Just tell me how." Johab reached for her good hand. "I'd take you with me but you wouldn't like the place where we're hiding. Mother would want to take care of you, but the place isn't nice."

"No, you need to keep your hiding place a secret." She patted his arm, the splinted finger clicking against the bed rail. "Mr. Barzoni would track me to find you. I have friends, two British ladies who are visiting from London. They are staying at the old Semiramis Hotel on the Nile. I need to write them a little note and have you take it to their hotel. They'll get me out of here."

Johab handed her his pencil stub and a page from his notebook. She wrote a brief note, holding the paper awkwardly with her splinted finger, folded it in half and addressed it to "The Misses Sarah and Ella Hemstead."

"I'm asking my friends to come get me and stay for the rest of their vacation at my apartment. You can shove notes under the door of my apartment, but you'd better be very careful. Be sure to leave messages in code, just like the Market List you made. I'm sure Barzoni's men have been watching my apartment, wondering what they should do about me."

She shook her head, her lips tightly pursed. "Now, they have another problem. The stairs didn't do the job." She held his hand tightly. "I'll be out of here by tomorrow, Johab. My two friends will make Mr. Barzoni wish he'd never confronted an English woman if he tries to stop them. Get me a message at home. Put a meeting place in code. You're clever. You can outwit Mr. Barzoni. I'll be up and around in a couple of days. Be very careful." She angled her undamaged hand over her eye, and gave Johab a quick, flick of a salute.

Actually, the gauze turban looked exactly like a *hedjet*, the white war helmet of a pharaoh, and Hetty appeared as regal as an ancient queen. The spider web of shadows in the room had disappeared.

CHAPTER 31

Johab moved swiftly down the hall and sped down the stairs, two at a time. From the back door, he spotted Cyril and Sekina and hurried over to them. "We have one more errand, Cyril, then, we'll think about how to help your little sister, Alice," Johab promised with more assurance than he was feeling.

"We need to go to that old hotel on the Nile, you know the one that the tourists think is like 'Old Cairo' back before World War II. My dad told me they have a piano player with slicked down hair playing Hoagy Carmichael songs, and they charge too much for cocktails, but the tourists love it."

Cyril nodded in agreement as though Hoagy Carmichael might be his favorite pianist and cocktails as common a drink as well water.

The traffic was worse late in the day. Sekina balked often in protest, but Cyril talked softly to her, and she clattered briskly along. They followed the wide street along the Nile, ignoring the car horns of bad-tempered drivers.

The Semiramis Hotel rose up in front of them, all of its outside rooms featuring small balconies with a view of the Nile. The front sidewalk had erupted with a broken sewage line, but a temporary fence cordoned it off from the flow of tourists who filed up the few short steps, loaded with packages, eager to escape the heat.

Two of the women moving along the sidewalk caught Johab's eye. He couldn't be this lucky. They were the same women he had helped in the Khan when the shop owner was trying to cheat them. It didn't ring a bell when Hetty gave him the note with their names on it. Now, he remembered. The tall Sarah, and the shorter one, Ella, were making a wide detour around the bubbling sewage but heading at a fast clip toward the hotel.

It was worth a try to intercept them before they reached the door. With their ragged robes, he and Cyril might not get inside an expensive hotel, even with a note for guests from Hetty.

"Hold Sekina here, Cyril. Don't budge." Johab eased past the white-gloved doorman and stepped in front of the women just as they reached the doorway. The tall one glanced at him with annoyance.

"Is your name Hemstead? Is Hetty Wenkle your friend?" At those questions, the tall woman's mouth dropped ajar.

"It's that boy, that little Egyptian boy who speaks English with an American accent, Ella."

The doorman moved toward them, shoving Johab aside and shouting: "Get away, boy. Get off this property. Don't bother our ladies!"

Sarah flung a protective arm around Johab's shoulders. Her voice would drop the temperature by degrees: "This young man is a friend of ours. I assume that we can talk to our friends on the steps of our hotel." The doorman glared at Johab, backed away, but was close enough to eavesdrop.

"I can't stay here, but Miss Wenkle gave me this note for you. I was supposed to leave it at the desk, but when I saw you, I remembered your first names and thought that couldn't be a coincidence. You had to be her friends from England. Miss Wenkle needs your help. Sorry, I can't stay. I must. . . ." Johab backed down the steps, ignored their pleas to wait, and fled down the sidewalk.

There were too many people nearby who would wonder why a tourist in an expensive hotel was having such an intense conversation with a poor, native boy. He needed to get away as soon as possible.

Cyril had already pressed Sekina back into the busy evening traffic around the Semiramis Hotel, heading the donkey away from the commercial area of the city.

Streetlights were coming on. Charcoal soot and the residue of gasoline engines formed a dense blanket over the city and transformed it at night to a magical place—if you didn't look too closely.

Shadows hid piles of garbage. Only the odors remained. Cats, dogs, rats, and mice burrowed into the garbage, eager to take their share before the Copts arrived with their carts and donkeys to claim the lion's share.

"Wait up, Cyril." Johab yelled as he dodged between lanes of cars stalled at an intersection. "Where are you heading?"

"I've got to see if Alice is all right, Johab. I don't know what Mustafa might do to her. He was so angry with me. All that blood on his thumb. He was screaming and waving his hand when I ran away." As the darkness settled in, Johab knew that Cyril had been revisiting the scene of his crime. Utter hopelessness blanketed that little boy with his slumped shoulders as surely as the smog settled on Cairo.

"Wait a minute, Cyril. Pull Sekina over there, out of the traffic. I need to know where you live and who might be around. We must have a plan." Johab spoke with a sense of authority that he wasn't feeling.

Cyril bobbed his head in agreement. That's why Johab was the major and he was only the lieutenant. A plan. Those words had a comforting sound as though order might be imposed over the chaos that had become his life. "I live on the edge of the city, in one of those little houses in that direction, about half a kilometer." Cyril waved across several lanes of traffic.

"We need to think this through, Cyril. Will your aunt be at home? What about Mustafa? Won't he be there?"

Cyril thought quietly, forcing himself to hide his agitation from Johab. "Usually, my aunt works at the hotel laundry on the evening shift. Mustafa goes down the street to drink with his friends. I don't know how much I hurt his thumb." Cyril gazed up at Johab with a proud expression. "I think I felt the bone with my teeth. He has a very fat thumb. I may have hurt him badly. Maybe he has the police waiting for me," Cyril added, a new fear creeping into his voice.

"He wouldn't dream of going to the police, Cyril. Just look at you. One look at your face, and they'd throw him in jail. That's where he belongs," Johab added for Cyril's benefit.

Someone should have stopped Mustafa from hitting Cyril a long time ago. It should never have started. Johab's confidence in law and order was faltering every day. Little boys shouldn't be beaten by non-uncles. Nice ladies like Hetty shouldn't be pushed down stairs. The world where his father did important work and his mother was almost always happy had been an orderly world. Now, it was spinning more and more out of control.

Johab straightened his shoulders and thumped Sekina on the rear. He would now have to control as best he could those things within his control. He looked at the small boy with the bruised face and split lip and thought about Cyril's little sister whose "eyelashes were longer than Sekina's." Those two little children were surely within the sphere of his control. If he didn't help them, who would?

Within half an hour, they had bounced across the rough, clay streets, furrowed with the wheels of carts and entered a grim, patched-together cluster of hovels and shops. Johab thought to himself that he preferred the City of the Dead. The alleys were wider and the air cleaner.

"It's there," hissed Cyril, pointing to a small hut of mud bricks with an old corrugated tin roof. Not a light shone in the window. Maybe no one was at home.

"Cyril. You'd better hide here. Crouch down behind Sekina. No one will recognize the donkey, but they might see you. I'll just walk over that way and casually glance into the window. Where does Alice sleep?"

"It's only two rooms. The front one is the kitchen. That's where Alice and I sleep. My aunt and Mustafa sleep in the other room." Cyril sketched the shapes of the rooms on Sekina's back. She arched against him as though the tickling pleased her. "Johab, Alice won't come with you. You'll be a stranger to her."

"I know, Cyril. We're just on a scouting trip. We need to have a plan before we do anything." Johab drifted along, seemingly without purpose, angling past one small hut towards Cyril's hut. Half a block away, he could hear loud music and see the lights of a shop where a few men hung about, smoking and laughing. He flattened himself against the wall and peered into the open window.

It was deathly quiet. An uneasy feeling swept over Johab. What if Mustafa had left and taken Alice? What if he intended to sell her? Cyril said he told their aunt she was "valuable." She could be gone forever. Johab had heard his mother and Aunt Rayya talking about the underground slave market. They didn't think he listened, but he and Mohammed made a special effort to listen when their mothers talked in hushed tones. That meant they were discussing something really interesting.

He jumped when something bumped against him. "I tied Sekina to the lamp post. The light's been out for years. No one can see her there." Cyril trembled against Johab.

"Mustafa is down there, on that porch with those other men. He has a very big bandage on his hand and is telling those men to watch out for me. I could hear him telling them that I bit him out of spite and if he gets his hands on me he will ship me off to other relatives."

Cyril was shaking so badly that Johab drew in the boy closely to steady him. "I don't have any relatives, Johab. He's going to kill me. I know he is. He told me that he killed a man once, tied rocks to him, threw him in the Nile, and he never came to the surface." Cyril gazed in the direction of the Nile, Egypt's main source of prosperity, and saw it only as a vast, brown, unforgiving graveyard.

"Did you see your aunt, Cyril? Is she there with Mustafa?"

Cyril shook his head. "She says that's a bad place. Only men and a few bad women go there. Mustafa sometimes tries to make her go with him, but she won't. I don't know where she is. She doesn't go to sleep this early. She may be at work. Alice could be there by herself. She goes to bed early."

"OK, Cyril. We have to move quickly. I've been pushing against this door. It seems to be locked. I'll boost you through this window. You need to be very quiet in case your aunt is in there. If Alice is there, put your hand over her mouth so that she can't talk or cry. We must be totally silent," Johab whispered in a muffled voice.

He bent down and cupped his fingers to boost Cyril up to the window ledge. Cyril was as light as Maat's feather. Within seconds he was inside, creeping across the room. Johab could see his shadow as he paused by the open door of the second room.

The silence from the hut was eerie. Johab had the sense that time had stopped. Loud bursts of laughter and the scratchy noise of an old record coming from down the alley formed a bizarre backdrop to the silence in the hut.

"Here," hissed Cyril. "Take her. She won't make a sound."

A warm, damp, soft bundle was pushed through the window. Johab clutched it and moved away. Cyril's small shape filled the window and dropped quietly to the hard-packed clay below. He grabbed Johab's shoulder and pushed him around the side of the house. "Quick, Johab, take her to Sekina. Get into the cart with her. I'll lead Sekina. She'll go faster for me."

It seemed to Johab that the lieutenant had assumed the command, but the soft bundle was beginning to make a few noises, almost cat-like sounds. He cradled the bundle carefully. Blankets were wrapped tightly around Alice. He couldn't distinguish her head from her feet, but hoped he was holding her upright.

The rough boards of the cart felt strange against his bottom. He had rarely ridden in it. The empty fulbean pot rolled noisily. He angled his back against it, pushing it against the sideboard of the cart. They could not risk so much as a rattle.

Sekina's hard little hooves made a tapping sound that seemed almost ear splitting in the silence of the night. Any minute, Johab expected to see a huge man with a white bandage on his hand blocking their passage from this seedy neighborhood. Cyril must be working magic on Sekina. She was trotting briskly along the street, not balking, not turning sideways to cause the cart to skid out of control as she always did when Johab drove her.

A small voice came from within the bundle of blankets. "Are you Cyril's friend? Are you the one saving us?"

Johab rocked her gently. "The one saving us." Alice's whispered words had a magical ring, like something that one of the pharaohs might have said to a god, might have inscribed on the sides of his temple for people in the future to read.

They were a safe distance from Cyril's neighborhood. He stopped Sekina and turned to Johab, his hands palms up in the "What do we do now?" gesture.

Johab spoke as definitely as though his words might also be incised on the limestone wall of a tomb. "Go toward the City of the Dead."

Only a few cars passed them on the road. Several pickup trucks rattled by with cages of chickens and a couple of goats in the back. The lights of Cairo twinkled behind them like a blanket of early Christmas lights spread out to the edge of the desert.

Alice had fallen asleep. Johab pulled back the blankets from her face and could feel her sweet child's breath on his neck. He thought of Jasmine and how soft and innocent she was when she slept. Awake, she was developing her own personality and could be loud and demanding. Bastet and Mr. Feisel had become the targets of her demands lately. Johab was too busy to pay much attention to his sister.

He clutched Alice against him. He needed to find time for Jasmine. It was his job to tell her the stories about the ancient gods and the kings and queens. He had to take the place of their father for now. That meant teaching Jasmine.

Even in the darkness, the road felt familiar. "Ahead, Cyril. Sharp right turn. The yellowish tomb on the left. Just lead Sekina into that small enclosure at the front door."

Sekina came to a halt, happy to be back in familiar surroundings, and let loose a loud bray.

Johab boosted Alice to his shoulder, wrapped his arm protectively around Cyril's small shoulders and pushed the door open with his foot. His mind raced with ideas about how he could explain two orphans who were not blood kin that he had just brought through the door.

Waiting for him with a low, flickering lamp, his mother shoved her chair back from the table and stood with an astonished look on her face. Jasmine sat bolt upright on her mat.

"I've brought cousins!" announced Johab. "New cousins for our family!"

CHAPTER 32

Nourish thy children, O thou good nurse, stablish their feet.

—Esdras, *The Bible*

Johab's mother had never failed him in a critical moment. She rose to the occasion. She reached for his bundle, unfurled the sleeping Alice from the wad of blankets, and placed her gently on the mat by Jasmine, who began stroking Alice's hair and telling her cat to move over.

His mother put her hands on Cyril's shoulders and eased him into one of the chairs. The oil lamp, flickering on the table, cast a wicked glare across his damaged face. She gasped loudly and looked across the table at Johab. "This is the boy? This is the girl?" Johab nodded. His theoretical story, the one that he told his mother he heard from workmen in the Khan, was now being examined in the light of a small oil lamp. He could not read his mother's expression. At this tense moment, he didn't want to know what she was thinking.

Within minutes, Cyril was asleep on a blanket next to Johab's mat with a cool, damp cloth against his face. Johab's mother reached for him, pulled him tightly against her, and pointed toward his mat. "You go to sleep now, Johab. It is very late. I'll take care of Sekina."

Johab could hear the mumbled sounds of conversation outside, his mother and Mr. Feisel talking softly, water being poured into Sekina's tub, and then silence.

A rooster's crow woke Johab early. The sun had barely skimmed the edge of the horizon. Most of The City of the Dead slept, its live citizens almost as quiet as those lying in their tombs. Johab eased himself upright.

Cyril was curled into a knot on his blanket, the side of his bruised face dark purple in the morning light. Jasmine and Alice were a tangle of arms and legs. Bastet blinked his green eyes at Johab, daring him to disturb the little girls.

Creeping past the sleeping children, Johab pushed the door open. His mother was sitting on the doorstep, staring at the faint glow of the morning sunrise. She patted the stoop beside her. "Do you ever think about those lists that were sometimes painted in the tombs? I think they were called 'declarations of innocence' or sometimes a 'negative confession.'"

Johab nodded. He had seen those lists of things people said they had *not* done in their lives. Bad things. They were lists meant to assure the gods in the afterlife that the person entombed had lived a good life.

"I guess they wanted those lists in case Maat's feather wasn't enough insurance when Anubis weighed their hearts," Johab said lightly.

"No, Johab. I'm serious. I don't believe those old stories of the kings and queens living with gods and goddesses in some afterworld. I was brought up as a Christian, just as you are." She looked piercingly into Johab's eyes as though daring him to dispute her assertion.

He wouldn't dare this morning. After his sudden introduction of two new "cousins," he knew he was on very thin ice.

His mother continued. "I do remember thinking about those declarations of innocence that the ancient Egyptians put on their tomb walls, such as I have done no wrong; I have not been neglectful," she mused, staring into the brightening sky. "Those lists include sins of commission and sins of omission. Our priest said sins of omission, such as not caring, not acting, might be worse than sins of commission. I couldn't sleep last night, so I talked to Mr. Feisel about the children. He knew I was up waiting and worrying last night because you were so late. He won't talk. We'll have to think of some story for Mrs. Zadi. She *will* talk."

Johab breathed a deep sigh of relief. All the way from the outskirts of Cairo to The City of the Dead, watching Cyril's bony little arm patting Sekina while he clutched the soft bundle that was Alice, Johab knew he had made a decision that could not be reversed.

These children were his responsibility until he could find a better option for them. Being orphans on the streets in Cairo without Mustafa and their negligent aunt wasn't necessarily a better option. Johab had expected to wake up to a disagreement with his mother.

She never failed to surprise him. "Let's go feed those children breakfast, give them a bath, and decide from what branch of the family these cousins have come." She gave Johab a wink and pushed past him into their hut.

Cyril hunched against the wall as though to make his body as small and inconspicuous as possible; his eyes held fear. When he saw Johab, a lop-sided smile lit up his face, half of it purple and indigo.

Johab gently pulled Cyril to his feet. "Mother, I think that his ribs might be broken. He walks sort of bent over, and his mouth probably needed stitches."

His mother steered Cyril to a chair and watched him easing himself down. "There's not much that can be done about broken ribs. I'll wrap his chest to make him more comfortable. Let me see your lip." She swabbed at the crusted blood. "It's a nasty cut, but it doesn't appear infected. You'll have a very impressive scar, little boy." She patted him on his shoulder.

Cyril's face was upturned, open, expectant, reminding Johab suddenly of a baby bird, hoping that an obliging parent would drop something tasty in its mouth.

It did. "Johab, don't you think introductions of your cousins are in order?"

"This is Cyril and that is Alice," Johab pointed toward the little girl sleeping peacefully with Jasmine. "Their father worked for an English major, and they are named for him and his wife. The wife was ill, and they had to go back to England."

An idea flashed into Johab's mind. After they had solved the problem of finding his father, he would ask Hetty to try to find the major who was Cyril's namesake. Maybe he could help Cyril and Alice.

With the speed of one of those filmstrips flipping through a reel, Johab flashed on everything that had happened the previous day, sorting what he could tell his mother. Cyril knew things that even Johab's mother didn't know.

Miss Wenkle was his partner. That wicked Mr. Barzoni had pushed her down stairs. Now, she was in a hospital bed. It wouldn't do for his mother to find out things from Cyril. Separating who knew what from who *should* know what was becoming a problem.

Johab decided that he should tell his mother about Miss Wenkle helping him and about the so-called accident that put her in the hospital. The pouch must remain a secret. His mother might insist he turn it over to Mr. Barzoni, hoping that he would free her husband.

Johab stared at the far wall. It was clear to both him and Hetty that Mr. Barzoni was dealing in stolen Egyptian treasures. He might even be the mastermind behind the theft that the police had discovered. Something had gone wrong with that scam or the police would not have found the few valuable treasures that they did.

Mr. Barzoni had not found what he wanted or he would have disappeared. Johab frowned. Pushing Miss Wenkle down the stairs in the middle of the day when anyone might have seen him was a desperate act. Risky. There were more clever ways to get rid of a foreign woman and make it look like an accident. Maybe Mr. Barzoni figured out where Johab was hiding and no longer needed Miss Wenkle.

Johab shook his head slowly. No. That black car cruising through the cemetery near his grandparents' tomb was on a fishing expedition, looking for any connection to Johab's family.

Mr. Barzoni had told Miss Wenkle that he had contacts. For all Johab knew, half the police force could be working for him. Mr. El-Hasiim certainly was—and Uncle Tarek.

"Mother, we need to talk." Johab's voice cut across the clatter of his mother's bread making.

She flipped a large round of bread off the grill, pulled off a section, dribbled it with honey, and set it on the table in front of Cyril. "Let's walk toward the well for water, Johab. Cyril, keep Alice in the house when she wakes. Don't let anyone see either of you yet. Johab and I will be back soon."

Mr. Feisel sat on his stoop, hammering his chisel against a plank of wood. He nodded. Johab was eager to talk with him about the hieroglyphs he had given him the previous day. Mr. Feisel was intent on his woodworking. They might have been strangers. Johab and his mother walked to an open section of the cemetery. No one was around.

"Talk, Johab. What are we to do with these children?" His mother's voice was on edge as though the enormity of taking someone else's children had just hit her.

"They can't go back, Mother. They can't *ever* go back. When Mustafa—that's the man who lives with Cyril's aunt—tried to feed him a mouse, Cyril bit his thumb. Now that man will kill Cyril if he finds him."

"What . . . ?" His mother's question sounded like a wail. Johab clutched her arm to reassure her that some things were still normal. Her son was there beside her.

"You remember that Dad and I talked about the ancient practice of feeding mice to children who were very ill, making them swallow a mouse whole?" His mother nodded, her face a mask of disgust.

"Well, Mustafa tried to make Cyril swallow one because he didn't make enough money begging." Johab's face contorted. "That's when Cyril bit him. He had already kicked Cyril. Then, he hit him in the face. Cyril ran away and hid. We went to his aunt's house last night and took Alice. Who knows what bad things Mustafa might do to her?"

Johab added the last part to suggest something even worse than swallowing mice and breaking ribs. He wasn't sure what that might be, but it worked. The expression on his mother's face was just the same as when he had told her about Uncle Tarek taking a bribe from Mr. Barzoni. *Unfathomable anger.*

"You did exactly right, Johab. You and Cyril are brave boys. I would never have been so brave. We need to disguise these children as part of our family."

Johab beamed. His mother was getting into the spirit of things. "Disguise" was Johab's favorite word now. Jasmine was not likely to slip carelessly into English now that she had Alice, who couldn't speak English, as a playmate.

With Cyril driving Sekina, they could sell the fulbeans twice as fast with more time to search out clues. The disguise would be even better. Mr. Barzoni would be looking for one boy, not two.

"No fulbeans today, Johab. Cyril needs to rest. So do you. You have big, worry circles under your eyes." She pinched his cheek. "That's not all, is it? Your father . . ." her voice dropped to a fearful whisper.

"No, Mother. I need to tell you about my partner, the person who has been helping me." His mother glanced at him sharply.

"It's Hetty, our friend Hetty."

"Our friend, what?" His mother's disapproval of him using her first name outweighed her curiosity. "You don't mean Miss Wenkle?"

"She's been helping me by going through Dad's files, looking for clues that . . ."

"But, she can't . . . I mean . . ." his mother's interruption faltered. "She's a nice English lady and fond of our family, but she wouldn't want to be involved in this kind of thing. What can someone like Miss Wenkle do to help?" she added as an afterthought.

"You wouldn't believe me if I told you what a good spy she is, Mother." Johab's voice was firm. No one, not even his mother, could question Hetty's skills. "They took her to the hospital yesterday because Mr. Barzoni shoved her down stairs at the Museum. Her friends will get her out today, because . . ."

Johab's words were a frustrating tumble of sounds for his mother. She was still trying to envision Miss Wenkle as a master of intrigue. She thought of Hetty Wenkle tottering on high heels, bustling about the office to be sure that everything was in the right file. The image of master spy didn't fit. A startled expression crossed her face. "You mean the man who took your father attacked Miss Wenkle? At the Museum?"

Johab grabbed his mother's hand. "She's OK, just a bump on the head and a broken finger. You can't imagine how much Miss Wenkle is doing to help find Dad. She told me that our family is the only family she has," Johab added proudly, assessing his mother's reaction to that bit of information.

"I sneaked into the hospital yesterday to see her. Cyril helped me find her." Johab was determined to put Cyril in the best possible light.

"Hetty . . . I mean Miss Wenkle told me that Mr. Barzoni pushed her down the stairs. She didn't see him, but she smelled his cologne. She thinks he's worried about what she might find." Just at that moment, Johab thought of that amulet, an ancient Egyptian treasure that the police found when they busted that ring of thieves. He needed to examine the photograph that Hetty had given him immediately. He steered his mother back toward their hut.

"Why don't we just say that Cyril and Alice are cousins from Alexandria who are staying with us because their relatives can't afford to keep them? Mrs. Zadi would accept that story, especially when she sees how skinny Cyril is. We'll have him keep his face hidden until the bruise isn't so bad."

His mother nodded. It sounded like a good story, cousins from Alexandria. She had never told Mrs. Zadi about her sister Rayya, so she could invent a sister or brother in Alexandria. It would be nice to have another close relative, even a fictional one. With the dirt scrubbed off them, Cyril and Alice would be handsome children; she would be happy to claim them as a niece and nephew.

Angling back to the hut, Johab winced as his mother's fingers dug into his shoulder; it was not a friendly pinch. "Just a minute, young man, what is this Hetty business? What do you mean calling a grownup woman by her first name?"

CHAPTER 33

Two trips for bath water. One trip to get a bale of hay for Sekina. And, fifteen minutes to listen to his mother question the state of Cyril's robe. "No one in our family would dream of letting their children be seen in a thing like this." The day was moving on, and Johab had not looked at the photograph of the amulet or been to see Mr. Feisel. Keeping his mother in a receptive mood meant following her orders.

Finally, Cyril, Alice, and Jasmine settled down for an afternoon nap. Johab protested, "I haven't taken a nap since I was four years old." His mother didn't disagree.

Sitting outside, Johab looked at the photograph. Actually, there were two, both taken with a Polaroid camera, and slightly stuck together. One photo had been taken at close range with a ruler alongside the piece of jewelry to show its size, about a four-inch oval.

Even with the fuzzy Polaroid shot, Johab could see that the craftsmanship was amazing. The cabochon-cut carnelian stone stood half an inch above a broad band of encircling gold. Johab's father rarely used a Polaroid camera because of the poor film quality. He must have needed a quick copy before turning over the amulet to Mr. El-Hasiim. Johab studied the second photograph. It was the back of the amulet with a plate of gold held by a tiny hinge standing ajar, exposing the cavity within.

The ruler showed a three-inch, oval-shaped hollow within the amulet. Johab gasped. *Just the size of the odd, oval marks on the old papyrus sheets!* Ideas were flashing through Johab's mind faster than he could control them. This was the amulet from the recent police bust of the antiquities ring. His father had been the first one to examine it. The hinge on the back was so cleverly flattened into the design that no one but an expert would have noticed it.

The papyrus must have been hidden in the amulet. His father had removed the sheets, made notes, and hidden them in a pouch he called "dangerous." Had he begun to suspect Mr. El-Hasiim? Why did he not say Mr. Barzoni's name that night when he was taken? His father said "you," so he surely recognized his captor. Earlier that day, when his father told Johab that the information in the pouch was dangerous, the tone of his voice was the same as when that cobra had slithered into their camp.

Within seconds, Johab trotted over and tapped on Mr. Feisel's door. The face before him was a rich, deep brown—a Bedouin face with a thin, grizzled mustache on the upper lip and eyes deeply set below a forehead of heavily furrowed lines.

"I was expecting you," Mr. Feisel growled. "The hieroglyphs you drew for me don't make much sense. I'd like to see the originals."

Johab sucked in his breath. A lie probably wasn't going to work here. "I can't. I promised."

Mr. Feisel nodded. "Promises are important, Johab. I would never ask anyone to break a promise, but it seems to me that you are getting yourself into a tricky situation."

Johab gulped. "Tricky" was a mild description of the situation he was "getting himself into."

"Suit yourself. I'll tell you what I deciphered." Mr. Feisel pulled out the first sheet of hieroglyphs that Johab had drawn for him. "See this set here?" He pointed to the top line of symbols that Johab had rearranged from the bottom to the top of the page. "They read like something out of the *Amduat*, like one of those funerary texts. They seem to be an explanation of the path to the underworld, but backwards, as though the passage goes the wrong way, up instead of down."

Johab sat focused, completely attentive. His reversal of the hieroglyphs was working. They should have been going up instead of down if he had managed to reverse them correctly.

"These on next page are easy to read. These say that 'she will not be in the hall of waiting.' That seems clear enough. This next . . ." he pointed to the middle of the second page of Johab's drawings, "is not so clear—it could be that you didn't trace these exactly. I think it says that 'she rests in the house of gold or it could say in the house of the sun.' You see here," he pointed with a thick forefinger, "a couple of small symbols on the side here. One appears to be a *djad* pillar—that is an old symbol for Osiris—but this other one puzzles me. It appears to be a sketch of a small tunnel. See how it bends here?"

Johab pinched his own leg, hard. He should have recognized that little symbol was not a hieroglyph on the papyrus. *It was the same sketch that his father had made in his notes.* It was the sketch of a tunnel in a bent tomb.

He had seen drawings somewhat like that before on diagrams of tomb layouts. The sketch on the papyrus was odd because it had two little boxes attached, and an angular line from one box to the center of the last bend before it branched. *He should not have copied that for Mr. Feisel.*

"This section at the top of the page would be something I'd expect to see at the end of a text, although I had to rearrange the hieroglyphs for it to make sense." He gave Johab a hard stare. "It appears to be some kind of threat or chant to prevent someone from disturbing a burial site—telling about the Lake of Fire in the secret cavern of Sokar where such evil people go."

Mr. Feisel pointed toward the symbols. "It is a very boastful claim if I'm reading it correctly. It says the house of gold holds someone who will never be an equal to anyone on earth and will live forever as a god. Humph." Mr. Feisel made a grunting sound. "Not too boastful for our old pharaohs—they *all* would have believed that."

Pushing Johab's sketches toward him, Mr. Feisel said: "I can help your mother. I have no idea about those children you dragged home in the middle of the night, but your mother seems to think they need help. I trust her instincts. She's a kind lady."

Mr. Feisel gave Johab a stern look. "You, my boy, are harder to help. I think you have information that might be *very* important to someone. I also think that person is dangerous and involved in your father's disappearance."

Johab squirmed.

"Getting too close, am I?" Mr. Feisel's lips twitched in that almost-but-not-quite smile. "You may be forgetting something, Johab. I have a long history of working in the digs around the old tombs. I told you about working with Mr. Carter when I was just a boy when we discovered Tutankhamen's tomb."

Johab noted that the tomb discoverers had now become "we," but it seemed imprudent to make that point at this time.

"I spent much of my life in the field working with the archeologists from other countries, the French, the Polish, the Italians. I'd be working with one of those councils for antiquity preservation today if I were younger." A look of discontent clouded Mr. Feisel's expression. "I know more about the subsidiary valleys, the cracks in the cliffs, and the old paths that lead into those excavations than any of those so-called Egyptologists know."

He glanced sheepishly at Johab. "I don't mean your father. My old friends tell me that your father isn't in this for the glory. He really wants to preserve the sites, especially the workers' villages. That's valuable work. The ancient people who built the tombs and made such treasures were the workers, the painters, the makers of jewelry, and the carvers. The kings and queens simply ordered them made." He flexed his arthritic hands.

Unexpectedly, Johab felt close to Mr. Feisel. Dad would like this man who carved lovely things. He really could read hieroglyphs; maybe, just maybe, he *had* been there with Howard Carter. Johab could hardly wait to introduce his father to Mr. Feisel.

His face fell. He wouldn't be introducing his father to anyone until he got to the bottom of this puzzle. For now, he would take Mr. Feisel's translations, rearrange them to match the original symbols, and see if the writing on the papyrus made any sense.

Johab remembered his manners. He thrust his hand out and tentatively touched Mr. Feisel's large, brown knuckles. "Thank you for helping me, Mr. Feisel. I really do need your help." He paused.

"I can't tell you the source of the hieroglyphs. I made a promise. I have to keep it."

When Johab left Mr. Feisel's hut, he saw Cyril sitting on the step, his hood pulled up around his face, watching Jasmine and Alice playing in the alley with a small wooden duck. When they pulled it by the string, the mouth opened. It must have been one of Mr. Feisel's creations. Their peals of laughter echoed down the alley, and suddenly The City of the Dead was just another neighborhood with children playing in the street.

"She's in there, that nosy woman asking all kinds of questions." Cyril aimed his thumb at the door behind him.

Mrs. Zadi, of course. Scurrying along the street like a purposeful fat rat, she arrived daily with a small packet of tea or advice about cooking or shopping. Her real purpose was too obvious. She transported information faster than a carrier pigeon.

Many in the neighborhood seemed wary of her, but Johab's mother was a stranger here. She had been grateful for advice in the beginning, but now her lips were tight and her eyes troubled as Mrs. Zadi pried for information.

Johab burst into the room. "Ah! Here's my fine, little fellow," Mrs. Zadi gushed in an obsequious voice. Johab bristled, but Mrs. Zadi was a guest. He needed to control his irritation.

"As I was telling your mother, Johab, those little children, your *cousins*," she stressed the word as though she didn't find it quite credible, "don't resemble you and Jasmine at all. That robe the little boy is wearing must be a hundred years old. I've never seen anything so shabby." She smiled fatuously.

"He likes comfortable clothes," Johab responded, returning the same inane smile. "Mother, didn't you promise to take a walk with us before dinner? The children want to pull weeds for Sekina."

Mrs. Zadi waited a moment for Johab's mother to remind him that she had a guest. That's what his mother would have done in the past and later she would have chastised Johab for interrupting. Instead, she sprang to her feet and smiled apologetically. "I did promise them, Mrs. Zadi. I hope you don't mind." His mother was acquiring some Mohammed skills.

Mrs. Zadi gathered up her large cloth sack, scooped the extra packages of tea off the table into it, and flounced out the door.

Johab's mother shrugged her shoulders, smiled, and said, "Let's go get the children and find some weeds for Sekina."

The day was ending on a fine note. Johab watched Jasmine and Alice running along the perimeter road, their laughter a comforting backdrop against a brilliant sunset. His mother was talking quietly to Cyril who clung to her hand tightly.

Johab didn't feel so much as a frisson of jealousy. If Cyril's aunt had ever felt any affection for him, she would not have let Mustafa abuse him. Cyril needed a mother; Johab was willing to share for a moment.

CHAPTER 34

Friendships begin with liking or
gratitude—roots that can be pulled up.

—George Eliot

Spicy odors of cumin and coriander filled the room as Johab awoke to his mother's voice: "You told me last night that you wanted to sell fulbeans today and get a galabeya for Cyril. I don't know if he is fit to travel. His ribs are still sore. I could hear him groaning in his sleep last night."

"I'm well. I'm well." Cyril chirped from his blanket on the floor. "I have to go with Johab. I'm his lieutenant."

"Neither of you is going anywhere until you have a nice poached egg for breakfast." Johab's mother pointed to a bowl on the table piled with brown eggs. "I traded my silk scarf this morning to that neighbor down the street who keeps chickens."

Johab gulped. It was her Hermes scarf, the one his father had bought her when he went to a meeting in Paris. His father had told him what it cost. She should have been able to buy all the chickens, the coops, and the eggs, with change left over. But, the market for Hermes scarves in the City of the Dead was limited.

Johab smiled. "That was clever of you, Mother." Parting with a gift from his father must have been sad for her. "Those poached eggs sound good." Johab flinched with that lie. It wasn't even close to being a white lie. He *despised* poached eggs, nasty soft yellow globes, surrounded by icky white gelatinous circles. He called them monster eyes. His mother had long ago given up the battle to make Johab eat eggs. Now, she had assumed the general's post; the major and his lieutenant were going to eat poached eggs before they went out to do battle.

Cyril gulped his egg down in two bites, mopping the bowl with a square of bread. Johab felt near to projectile vomiting as he pushed his egg around in the bowl.

His mother turned to give a final stir to the beans. When he was certain that her back was turned, he quickly switched his poached egg with Cyril's empty bowl and gestured to Cyril to eat it. Cyril obliged. Cyril was good for something else that Johab couldn't have imagined. He was a human garbage disposal. No one could enjoy poached eggs, but Cyril ate everything on his plate.

They were off with Sekina and the cart just as the sun angled up from the horizon and the ancient gods were freed from the underworld to travel the sky with Osiris. Johab inhaled the dry, early morning desert air and felt a sense of well being that he hadn't experienced for days.

He had an aide. More importantly, Cyril paid attention to everything he said. He waved his hand in the general direction of the great pyramids of Giza, and announced: "As my lieutenant, Cyril, you must be educated. I'm going to teach you to read, and I'm going to teach you about the ancient world." Cyril looked at Johab wide-eyed and speechless.

Johab's voice rose above the clatter of Sekina's feet and the early morning traffic. "Those pyramids, the ones from the Fourth Dynasty, are called Menkaura, Khafra, and Khufu. They were built thousands of years ago." Johab glanced at Cyril's alert face. "Do you know how many years is in a thousand, Cyril?"

"Oh yes," Cyril responded brightly. "Mustafa told me that he got *baksheesh* worth one thousand in U.S. dollars when he stole that woman's gold watch in the Khan. That was a very good theft."

Johab lifted one eyebrow at Cyril. Telling small lies and spying were what Johab had to do now. Those were small misdeeds for the greater cause of finding his father. Stealing from tourists was wicked.

When Mustafa sent him out to beg, he probably didn't discuss right and wrong with Cyril. Johab decided to change the subject.

"Those pyramids may have been designed as giant observatories. My father says that some people make too much of that. He says the stars and moon and sun were very important to the ancient people because of their religion. I'll tell you about the god Osiris; that will be a good first lesson." Johab put on his best teaching voice, trying to imitate his father.

Cyril urged the donkey ahead as she snatched at scraggly weeds along the highway. "There is a good story about how Osiris' brother Seth killed him. Then, Isis and Nephthys stopped his body from rotting and brought him back to life." Cyril was all ears. Johab had never had such a good audience. Cyril liked the gory parts.

The beans sold quickly with Cyril helping. "We could sell twice as many, Johab. We don't have enough for people on this one street. Your mother is a very good cook. I don't ever remember food that good."

"Cooking the beans is hard work for my mother, Cyril. It's just temporary, a way for us to have a little money for the things we need. My main job," Johab stressed the sound of each word, "is to find my father and get back to our own home."

Cyril looked down. He had already begun to think of Johab's family as his own. The tomb in the City of the Dead was smaller than his aunt's two-room hut, but it was full of kindness and laughter. Now, Johab was talking about leaving it.

Johab could almost read Cyril's mind. His face was transparent when he wasn't guarding it. "Don't worry, Cyril. We won't leave you behind. You are a cousin." He smacked Cyril on the back of his head gently. "Besides, I need your help. I need you to take messages, to scout out things. You are more invisible than I am."

Johab squinted up at the early morning sun. He had two errands—a quick stop by the Khan to get Cyril a robe and a visit to Hetty's apartment. Johab knew her neighborhood well, rows of small apartments with Victorian-style fretwork on every balcony.

When Johab's family visited, Miss Wenkle always put chairs on the balcony for Johab and Jasmine so they could "watch the world go by." Johab shivered even though the hot sun blazed down on him. Mr. Barzoni might be watching Hetty's balcony at this very minute.

"We'll go to the shop in the market where you got the robes for Mother and Jasmine. You need a new galabeya for yourself. Mrs. Radi will be curious if we let you wander around in that thing." Johab gestured toward Cyril's dirty robe. "But, we'll keep your robe for our work in Cairo. It's a great disguise."

Cyril beamed. He didn't need to be embarrassed by his rags. His galabeya had been elevated to a "great disguise." Cyril hustled away and returned in minutes with a fistful of coins and a striped robe. It looked several sizes too large. "It was a bargain. The shopkeeper said that he hadn't been able to sell it to anyone."

Johab wasn't the least bit surprised. He had never seen mustard and brown stripes like that before, but Cyril didn't seem to be fashion conscious. Maybe his mother could hem up the bottom. They had more important things to do than worry about clothes.

The trees lining Hetty's street popped into view before Johab had time to look for danger. Her blue VW was parked on the street in front of her apartment. Dust coated the car. Maybe she wasn't home. Hetty might still be strapped into that hospital bed, forced to smell Mr. Barzoni's lilies. It might be that her English friends hadn't rescued her.

Cyril could go up with a message. No one would notice a ragged boy knocking on her door. Even if Barzoni's men were watching the apartment, they would be looking out for a larger boy. The message must be in code in case someone else snatched it: "Sherlock has a trusted aide. Behind the tent?" That should confuse anyone thinking that he wanted to come up the back stairs.

Cyril looked uneasy. "Those apartment guards . . . they always chase me away. They don't like me begging near nice houses."

Johab felt a twinge of guilt. He had seen the maintenance man at their apartment threaten beggars with his twig broom, even children. Johab had never given street children a second glance.

"It's OK, Cyril. Miss Wenkle is a very nice lady. The guard is down the street smoking with his friend. You'll have time to deliver this message and get back here. I'll poke Sekina and make her bray if the guard starts back across the street."

Cyril dashed toward the front entrance of the apartment building, keeping a wary look over his shoulder. Johab fidgeted for what seemed a very long time before a small figure rounded the apartment from the back and headed in his direction. "Three ladies are there. The one you call Miss Wenkle has a bandage on her head, and the other two told her to stay in bed, but she was very excited to see the note. Here, she gave me one for you."

A crumpled note unfolded from Cyril's dirty hand. It said: "Back of the tent clear. See balcony."

The tall woman called Sarah held a cup of tea and looked up and down the street in a relaxed pose as though she were simply observing the neighborhood before the heat drove her inside. Another clever spy.

"Cyril, I may be in Miss Wenkle's apartment for some time. Go around the block with Sekina, then come back. Keep watching that lady on the balcony. If you see a long, black car or anyone else who looks suspicious, wave in her direction. I'll be down in a flash and meet you at the end of the next block."

Cyril had an uneasy feeling that he wouldn't be able to sort out who looked "suspicious" from anyone else on this street. He avoided these kinds of neighborhoods. The Khan was a better place to beg, because it attracted all kinds of people. Even in rags, he could blend in there. But his job was to watch for anyone suspicious, so that's exactly what he would do. With a sense of dread, he pushed Sekina into a slow walk along this street of fine houses where he didn't belong.

CHAPTER 35

The moment Johab tapped on the back door of Hetty's apartment, the door burst open, and Hetty clutched him in a death-like grip. "Oh, Johab, I have been so worried about you ever since my accident." A frown furrowed her brow. "I should say my 'on purpose'—it was hardly an accident."

She steered Johab toward the couch. The woman named Sarah remained on the balcony. The woman named Ella was working in the kitchen, stacking cans and small bundles into piles.

"Johab, these are my friends, the Misses Hemstead, Sarah—she pointed toward the balcony—and Ella. You've met them before. At the Hotel Semaramis with my note, and, I believe, you helped them at the Khan when they were buying statues." Both women flashed broad smiles at Johab.

"I've told them about the situation, Johab. I hope you don't mind, but they are quite reliable. *Quite.*" She emphasized the latter word and smiled at them. "You should have seen how they stood up to that doctor when he told me I couldn't leave until Mr. Barzoni had signed a release form. Sarah said we were going AMA." Hetty looked very pleased.

"What's AMA?" questioned Johab.

"That's what the doctor asked. Against Medical Advice." Sarah told him it is the law for British citizens to leave a hospital anytime they want." She ducked her head and grinned. "I don't know that there is any such law, but Sarah can come up with rules faster than a grammar book. She told the doctor that Mr. Barzoni has no authority over what I choose to do. She threatened to go to the British Embassy if he tried to stop us."

She smiled fondly in Sarah's direction. "Sarah was my colleague at the British Museum. She works in the Egyptian section reference library there."

"Does she know Ian Parks?" Johab interrupted excitedly.

"Ella, come do balcony duty, dear." Sarah moved inside as Ella stepped onto the balcony and paced anxiously, an uneasy spy. "I know Mr. Parks very well, Johab. When he's not in the field, I work with him every day. He left London at about the same time we did, about a week ago. He was going to the area between the fourth and fifth cataracts of the Nile near Somalia."

Johab tugged Miss Wenkle's sleeve. "We need to find him, Hetty. We need to get him some information that I . . ." his voice trailed off. The woman named Sarah was listening too intently.

Hetty eased herself down on the couch and looked grave. "You can make the decisions about what we share with our friends, Johab, but Sarah and Ella will be spending the rest of their vacation month here with me. Sarah thinks that it is dangerous for me to be here alone."

She bent over and whispered to Johab. "I'm not really afraid, but I enjoy the company." She smoothed Johab's tangled hair back from his face and resumed in a normal voice. "Sarah has an introduction to the Egyptian Museum that will allow her access to the files. Mr. Parks wanted her to check out information on Hatshepsut's Punt Expedition."

Miss Wenkle sighed heavily. "We can use another set of ears and eyes. Mr. El-Hasiim sent word that I am not to return to work for two weeks. I think that is Mr. Barzoni's doing, keeping me away from your father's files."

"Can Sarah . . . I mean . . . Miss Sarah get in touch with Mr. Parks? Can she get him a message about my father? I need to see him. The message has to be coded in case it falls into the wrong hands."

Sarah pulled her chair close to the couch. "Hetty told me that Mr. El-Hasiim and Mr. Barzoni are probably involved in the theft of

New Kingdom antiquities that have recently come into Cairo from an unknown source."

Her expression was grim. "Hetty thinks your father has information that Mr. Barzoni wants. I believe these new artifacts could mean several things. They could mean that someone has found a new tomb, but that's not very likely. Or, things robbers hid are just now coming onto the market. Families that live in the Valley of the Kings have been there for generations. Some of their ancestors robbed tombs. Usually, they get rid of things quickly, but sometimes they hide them, waiting for a better price or a less risky way to sell them."

She paused. "If someone has found a new tomb, everything in it belongs to the government of Egypt. No antiquities can leave this country again." She looked somewhat irritated. "I'm sad to say that the British did their share of damage to these old sites in the past."

Her face brightened. "No one takes better care of antiquities than the British Museum." She lowered her voice. "Hetty, I was shocked to see a little puddle of water in one of the Tutankhamen cases; the humidity monitor wasn't working."

Johab twitched nervously. He wondered how many times Cyril and Sekina had circled the block. He did like this woman, Sarah. He admired her for standing up for him to the shopkeeper in the Khan and the doorman at the Hotel Semaramis.

"OK. Miss Sarah is a partner . . . if she wants to be . . ." his voice faltered. What person visiting a friend in a foreign country would want to be involved in something that had led to murder? The image of Mr. Razik's corpse—so tidily hidden under the shrubbery—flashed before him.

Sarah reached over and touched his knee. "It's Sarah, just like Hetty is Hetty. I want to help your father. I don't know him well, but I did meet him when he visited Ian Parks. They are good friends. That tells me a great deal about your father."

She leaned forward and spoke confidentially: "Your family has been like a real family to Hetty. She has no living relatives; neither do Ella and I—just our friends. They become our family. I can help, Johab. No one will suspect me." The self-assurance in her voice lifted

Johab's spirits. "I'm just a visiting librarian from the British Museum. That's all they need to know," she added.

"Now . . ." she mused "how to get in touch with Ian Parks. I have an idea. I can post a special delivery packet at the airport for my administrator at the British Museum. It should get there in a couple of days, even on Cairo time." She shook her head, thinking about the impossible lines at the airport, the endless forms for entering and leaving the country.

"I'll let him know that the enclosed message must reach Mr. Parks as soon as possible." Sarah looked a little distracted. "That means when the next field shipment goes out, but if the timing is right it might get to him in a week. That also means. . . ." she hesitated. "It means that anyone along the way can read it. The message must be cryptic."

A soft voice piped up from the balcony. "What about writing it as though it is coming from someone not connected to the New Kingdom Project? Someone saying that she saw a story in the Cairo newspaper about his friend, John Bennett, and his family missing. She could say that she had contacted her friend, Hetty Wenkle, who is 'distraught' and 'wants him to come quickly,'" Ella added quietly. "That's no more than anyone who reads the news or works in the Museum could know."

Hetty didn't much like the description of herself as "distraught," but it was a good idea—a simple message, stating publically known facts. Surely, Mr. Parks would sense the urgency behind the words.

Johab wasn't so sure. "Do you have any lemon juice or vinegar, Hetty?"

Odd question, but she nodded.

"We can put a secret message in lemon juice at the bottom of the letter so it can't be seen. If we draw a little oval hieroglyph above it," Johab sketched the pattern with his finger, "Mr. Parks will know that there is something else on this note—this symbol stands for things like 'more than' or 'concerning.' All that he has to do is heat the paper to see the words."

The three women looked at him with curiosity.

"They did this all the time in the War. The spies used all kinds of what they called 'invisible ink' but lemon juice works."

What words would you add, Johab?" Hetty asked.

"Desperate here. Contact Sarah ASAP in Cairo. In person. Urgent."

Ella popped into the room from the balcony. "A big black car has circled the block and is pulling alongside the curb about half a block away."

Johab's fear was mirrored by the expression on Hetty's face.

"Quick, Johab. Down the back way. Sarah, check out the alley to be sure that no one is there. Give Johab those things we packed in the Oxfam bags."

Johab shot her a questioning glance.

"Some things for your family that I thought you might need. Oxfam is a second-hand store all over England. There's even one here in Cairo. They give things away free sometimes. I used those bags so you wouldn't look suspicious carrying things in new packages."

In a tense voice, Ella reported: "There is a well-dressed man with silver hair walking down the sidewalk this way; he has a very large bouquet of what appear to be lilies."

Sarah hissed. "Only the little boy who brought your message is out back. He's there with a donkey going through the trash. Quick, Johab, scoot out now. I'll take care of the message to Mr. Parks. Don't worry. I'm very good at what I do. Take care of yourself and your little friend. I think he said his name was Cyril."

Just as the back door closed, Johab could hear Hetty's voice. "That's a very curious name for an Egyptian boy. My uncle who lived in Cairo for years was named Cyril. You've heard me speak of him and his wife many times. You don'tsuppose . . ." The closed door muffled the rest of her words.

Both Cyril and Sekina were rifling through the garbage. Sekina had found a bunch of wilted lettuce, and her eyes were glazed with ecstasy. Cyril pulled two pieces of wood out of the pile and laid them in Sekina's cart.

Flinging the Oxfam sacks into the cart, Johab muttered, "Mr. Barzoni is up there now. I got out just in time. His men could be anywhere around here."

Cyril grinned slyly. "I saw the car. That's why I'm pretending to be one of the Coptic garbage collectors. Good disguise, huh?"

"It is unless one of those Copts catches you picking up garbage that belongs to him." Johab replied sternly, though, in fact, he thought that Cyril had been very clever. "What are those old pieces of wood doing in the cart?"

"It's very nice wood, off old furniture. I thought that Mr. Feisel would like to have it for his carving."

Johab eyed Cyril. This clever and thoughtful boy gave him a renewed sense of confidence. Mr. Barzoni and his goons might be only steps away, but he had a lieutenant who was bright and kind. Surely the ancient gods would smile on that kind of boy and his friend.

CHAPTER 36

In the spy business, lingering was risky. Mustafa might be on the streets looking for Cyril. Mr. Barzoni and his lilies made Hetty's apartment off limits for now. Johab let out a deep sigh of frustration. He wanted to discuss the photograph of the amulet that Hetty had pirated out of the museum in her jacket pocket. She was amazing. Even with a concussion, she had managed to get a critical photograph to Johab.

Hetty said that someone had snatched her files off the floor when she tumbled down the stairs. Mr. Barzoni, no doubt. He would be interested in what she had been copying. The main clue was in her pocket—photographs of a stolen amulet that the police had returned to the Museum.

The secret compartment in the back of the amulet was empty when his father photographed it. Johab knew without a doubt that it had held those papyrus sheets in the pouch that his father called "dangerous."

Dark thoughts came faster than he could process them. If Mr. Barzoni only *suspected* that his father knew something about the source of the stolen tomb treasures, he might keep trying to find Johab and his family to force his father to give him answers. *But, if Mr. Barzoni saw the photograph of the amulet with an empty secret compartment, he would have proof that Johab's father had removed an ancient secret hidden in the amulet.*

That photograph needed to be destroyed. He would keep the other photograph showing only the front of the amulet. The amulet would be on view at the Museum. Nothing secret about that, but those tiny carvings in the gold around the carnelian stone might mean something.

Johab squinted up at the sun—it wasn't yet noon. His chest inflated with a sense of accomplishment. A letter would soon be on its way to Mr. Parks. Hetty was not badly hurt and had the protection of her friends. With her letter of introduction from the British Museum, Sarah could get access to his father's work.

His father. Those dratted tears welled in his eyes. Nothing he had done brought him any closer to finding his father. Nothing was in the newspapers. For all he knew, the police might be working for Mr. Barzoni. There was a police station near Aunt Rayya's neighborhood. It might be a pointless trip, but as he wiped his eyes so Cyril couldn't see his distress, a sense of optimism came out of nowhere.

In the street across from Aunt Rayya's house, he had seen Uncle Tarek taking a bribe from Mr. Barzoni. Being in the right place at the right time could be chalked up to good detecting. "Just one more stop, Cyril. I need you to help me check out the police station in my aunt's neighborhood."

Cyril froze in his tracks at the word "police." To police and security guards around buildings, boys like him were no more than street garbage—they were unsightly and needed to be disposed of quickly. No. Garbage was more valuable. Some of it could be fed to pigs.

"You did really well this morning, Cyril. I'm proud of you." Cyril colored with praise. The words "proud of you" had gone to the grave with his father. Cyril marched straight ahead, a lieutenant ready for orders, with Sekina clopping briskly alongside him.

Johab yanked rudely on Sekina's halter as they neared the police station.

Sekina considered biting him right then and there. He often smacked her for no reason when she stopped for a small treat along the way.

Cyril reached for her nose, rubbing it gently. She relaxed. This new boy understood donkeys.

Johab would have spotted them a mile away even though they were just down the block from the police station—Mohammed and Aunt Rayya. His aunt had grown almost as wide as Mrs. Zadi. Mohammed's new little brother or sister, what his mother insisted was a surprise that a stork would bring, was due sometime around Christmas. That's why she looked fat.

Mohammed stared directly in Johab's direction. This was not going to work.

Not at all. Johab flipped up his hood, bent to lift Sekina's hoof, and pretended to be picking something out of it. "I can't be seen, Cyril. That's my Aunt Rayya and Cousin Mohammed coming down the sidewalk. They'll recognize me if they get any closer. They're going into the police station. You find out what they're doing here. Listen to what my Aunt Rayya says. Look at the wanted posters on the wall. Pretend you're looking for someone. Be inconspicuous." Johab swung Sekina around and headed in the opposite direction.

Clutching his ragged robe, Cyril planted his bare feet on the hot sidewalk and marched with all the determination he could muster into the police building. His teeth chattered louder than street drummers during Ramadan, but his shoulders were erect.

"I will put this poster of my family up again, and I defy anyone to take it down!" The face of Johab's Aunt Rayya blazed with color as her voice echoed through the lobby. Her poster showed the smiling family of John Bennett, each member carefully labeled with a felt-tipped pen. Cyril stood at the elbow of Johab's aunt, examining the photograph.

Johab looked considerably different, his hair slicked back, his tie askew, his expression one of boredom. Johab's mother, wearing English clothes and holding Jasmine on her lap, looked years younger. Johab's father completed the quartet, a half-smile on his face. It was a family caught in time, safe at that moment.

That family didn't exist today. Cyril looked aside, almost embarrassed by the sudden emotion that he felt. He was glad that Johab was not inside the police station to see his family in a happier time.

Sticking the final thumbtack into the corner of her poster with flair, as though daring anyone to remove it, the voice of Johab's aunt rang out again: "I need to talk with someone in charge. I want to know what the police are doing to find my family."

She stomped her foot. "I've been here half a dozen times and get no answers. Send me someone in charge!" Her voice reached a high, shrill pitch just as she clutched her stomach and staggered.

A sergeant and a private trying to be invisible in a nearby office rushed out to shove a chair underneath her. An emergency birth in the police station would not help their promotions.

The sergeant hiked up his pants and squatted down by her chair, trying to make eye contact with Johab's aunt. "You're getting too excited over something that may not be a crime, just a little error." he said soothingly. "A lady in your state shouldn't get so excited."

Rayya shoved him as she pushed herself up awkwardly. The private braced him from toppling onto the floor.

"Don't you tell me what kind of state I'm in. And don't call my missing sister and her family *a little error*. Hoodlums broke into my sister's house in the middle of the night, and snatched her husband—a noted Egyptologist," she added with pride. "My sister and her two children disappeared from my house that same night."

Aunt Rayya's voice soared. "I don't want to hear any more of this nonsense about how my family is off on a field trip to the desert or how the GDSSI may be looking into this since it could involve the Ministry of the Interior." Her voice rose to the level of a siren.

Cyril watched admiringly from a corner of the room. The policemen seemed paralyzed by her shouts.

The sergeant, who had tried to reason with her, edged further away. "Your photo will stay up here. I promise you that. I did interview your brother-in-law's supervisor at the Museum, Mr. El-Hasiim I think he's called."

Rayya nodded, her face suddenly expectant.

"He told me that John Bennett is a very independent man. He has a grant from an American university and doesn't think he has to report to anyone. Mr. El-Hasiim said it is not at all unusual for this Dr. Bennett to take his family, go off into the desert, and not come back for weeks." The policeman's statement was final and definitive.

Rayya screech stopped the words in his throat. "My *only* sister who has never gone anywhere for any reason without telling me shows up at my house in the middle of the night with her face bloody, telling me her husband has been kidnapped. Then, she and her children disappear in the night. You think they are having a picnic in the desert?" The last few words rolled off her tongue like venom.

Cyril could see the policeman carefully distancing himself behind his metal desk.

"We will check again with Mr. El-Hasiim and some other people at the Museum. I can tell you that some odd things have gone on there. We do have conflicting statements from staff. The American Embassy has been notified." He held his hands out, palms up. "Our hands are tied. We have no evidence of foul play except for your report that your sister's face was bloody."

The sergeant sighed and shook his head. "If you only knew how many women show up here with bloody faces—and they all go back home and show up again the next week." He glanced at Johab's aunt with a sympathetic look. "I know you are worried about your sister and her family. The police are following up on some things. That's all I can tell you."

Cyril watched Johab's aunt grab her son's arm and storm past the policeman out of the door. No one had noticed Cyril. The sergeant turned to the private: "That bloody woman is a nuisance. My hearing is permanently impaired every time she comes through that door." He gave a short cackle and nodded in the direction Johab's aunt had taken down the street. "I have to tell you that I do believe what she's telling us really happened."

The younger policeman rubbing his shoulder against the coat rack reminded Cyril of Sekina who rubbed against any hard surface she could reach. He stopped and eyed his superior skeptically.

The older policeman rubbed his jaw reflectively. "Yes, I do believe her. I talked to that Mr. El-Hasiim when that guard was found dead in the bushes. I wouldn't trust that man in my grandmother's chicken pen. He's a sleazy one. But, word's down from the top that we're off the case."

He spied Cyril. "What are you doing here, boy? Don't you know this building is for police business? See that sign." He pointed toward the door. "No loitering. That means you."

Cyril scooted out the door, full of information for Johab. So that was his Aunt Rayya, a noisy and angry woman. But she held the photograph of Johab's family as gently as she would a little bird. Her anger was that of a person who feels helpless, who has lost something she loves, who is trying desperately to find help. Cyril liked her immediately.

He wasn't so sure about Johab's cousin. That boy Mohammed just stood there with a smirk on his face. He took no more notice of Cyril than if he had been a broom in the corner.

"What went on in there? I saw Aunt Rayya and Mohammed head down the street just now. She looked so angry. I'll bet Mohammed will be on good behavior tonight," Johab said with a slight twitch of his mouth.

Cyril's recall for details astounded Johab. He described the two policemen, the placement of the office furniture, and repeated every word that was said. Had his Aunt Rayya not been so distressed, Johab might have laughed at the description of her with those policemen. No one reacted more strongly against a slight than Aunt Rayya. She went ballistic if anyone crowded in line in front of her.

Johab felt the weight of a sudden, unnamable sadness. His family should be together now, wrapping presents for their two Christmas celebrations. He should be bringing Aunt Rayya sweet tea for her "condition."

A new baby was coming into the family. These days should be happy. They would have a Sebow celebration seven days after the birth of his new cousin, an important event.

Johab looked ahead at Cyril's small neck, bobbing along in unison with Sekina's as they traveled down the busy street. That little boy had not known the meaning of happy days for most of his life.

"Johab, where are we heading?" Cyril's reed-thin voice pierced his thoughts.

"Home, Cyril. We're heading home."

CHAPTER 37

*I can but trust that good shall fall
At last—far off—at last, to all,
And every winter change to spring.*

—Tennyson

As they neared their alley in the City of the Dead, Johab watched the squared-off body of Mrs. Zadi heading in the other direction, waddling like a bottom-heavy goose. She was probably more of a nuisance than a threat. She seemed to believe the story that Johab's mother had purposefully let slip, that she was hiding from an abusive husband. The bruise on her face left by Mr. Barzoni made it a believable story.

Mrs. Zadi loved stories about abusive husbands. She was a widow, "two times," she proudly announced to Johab's mother. "My husbands *only* hit me one time. They weren't able to hit anyone after that," she had muttered.

Johab couldn't imagine anyone hitting Mrs. Zadi even once. She was as wide as she was tall. It would take a considerable blow to knock her off her feet. She had the side-to-side gait of someone who doesn't need to run, someone who can stand her ground.

"Let's get these Oxfam bags inside, Cyril. I have no idea what Hetty put in them," he said hopefully.

Underwear. The first bag was packed with underwear, socks, and bars of floral-scented soap.

"How thoughtful," his mother exclaimed. "Often when I wash your underwear, it's still damp the next morning, Johab. I worry about you catching cold in damp underwear."

Johab ducked his head. He didn't wear damp underwear. He left it under his mat when it wasn't dry. He had on his shorts; underwear wasn't needed under galabeyas. Cyril didn't wear any.

The second sack was more promising. There were boxes of English biscuits, rounds of cheese, Wensleydale, his favorite. There was a heavy fruitcake, not his favorite. The third sack brought a gleam to Cyril's face. It was packed with books, picture books for a child of Jasmine's age, both in English and Arabic. For Johab, there were six Hardy Boy mysteries, new ones, not well-thumbed like his old ones.

Johab knew that Hetty had sent the books for Jasmine and him, but Cyril was so bright-eyed. "Cyril, we can begin your reading lessons this afternoon. I'll read the books to Jasmine and Alice, but you can sit close and memorize the words as I point to them. I'll bet we'll have you reading within a week," Johab reassured him.

There had been no books in the house of Cyril's aunt. He didn't think that Mustafa knew how to read. He had seen some old magazines that his aunt used to look through, but Mustafa threw them into the garbage when his dinner was late.

The look of excitement on Cyril's face over the prospect of "reading" the books didn't change at all when Johab's mother unrolled his new robe.

"Those are the most peculiar colors I've ever seen. Whatever possessed you boys to buy it? It's too big for Cyril. I'll have to cut off the hem and the sleeves." She pulled the fabric through her hands. "Mustard stripes. There is a tribe of Bedouins that wear robes with a wide brown stripe. This must be a reject because the dye was bad. Cheap?"

Both boys nodded affirmatively.

"Good. We'll make it work." She picked up the sewing kit that Hetty had sent in one of the Oxfam bags. "Miss Wenkle, Hetty, is a valuable friend."

Johab gave a vague nod. His mother didn't know how valuable. He didn't want her to know. His mother didn't like conflict. She wasn't like Aunt Rayya. If Mr. Barzoni got hold of his mother, she would tell him anything to protect her family. He couldn't tell her about seeing Aunt Rayya and Mohammed at the police station today. It would make her too sad.

Cyril, Jasmine, and Alice huddled around Johab on the doorstep. He pulled one of the brightly colored books from the stack. *Pinocchio*. That would be a good one for Cyril.

There were lessons to be learned in *Pinocchio*—lessons about being lazy and not wanting to go to school, lessons about trusting someone who offered something for nothing, and—the best lesson of all—that Mohammed lies would make a nose grow. Johab felt his nose. Same size. Amazing. If he had Pinocchio's nose, he would be tripping over it.

Johab settled the children close to him and began reading, pointing out the words to Cyril. Within minutes, Jasmine and Alice were asleep in the late afternoon sun.

Cyril twitched with happiness. Somewhere, a dim memory surfaced. He remembered his father reading to him. He didn't recall the book, but he remembered sitting on his lap, feeling his scratchy shirt, and knowing that he was safe and loved. That feeling had almost disappeared, but he had been remembering it lately. When Johab's mother held his hand, he thought about his father. Even when Johab bossed him around, he didn't mind. Johab seemed to regret it immediately if he were bossy. Mustafa didn't know the meaning of regret.

He glanced up at Johab, trying to imagine the weight of Johab's problems that had taken him so far from the life he once lived.

Cyril had listened carefully, trying to fit the pieces together. He knew about Johab's father being kidnapped by Mr. Barzoni. He knew that Johab's friend Hetty had been pushed down the stairs. He knew that Johab's Aunt Rayya was frantic with worry. He also knew that Johab had a secret that he didn't dare tell anyone.

The job of a good lieutenant would be to watch, listen, and find out about things that Johab wasn't ready to tell him. He needed to know everything so that he could help. Not even Mustafa's big pocket knife could pry information out of him.

"Are you paying attention, Cyril?" Johab's sharp words cut through his thoughts.

"Yes. Yes. I love this story. This Pinocchio is like me," Cyril announced.

"What do you mean?" Johab queried the small boy who had pushed up against him so closely that he was perspiring in the afternoon sun.

"Pinocchio came out of nowhere—from an old block of wood. That's like me," he smiled.

"You're a flesh and blood boy, Cyril. Pinocchio was carved from wood. He came alive because the wood carver wanted a real son. It was a kind of magic that brought him to life." Johab was a firm believer in magic but mostly of the ancient Egyptian kind of magic that allowed rulers to be transformed into gods.

"I was sitting there with my begging bowl like a block of wood, and you found me. Now, I'm someone else and in a new place, just like Pinocchio," Cyril beamed.

Someone else, mused Johab. Cyril was still a skinny boy who didn't know how to read and could only do sums in his head, not on paper. The new, mustard-striped galabeya hung around him like a modified tent. But his eyes were bright with the pleasure of this moment. His hair shone in the sun, thanks to Hetty's soap. He was somewhat like a new boy, not entirely, but somewhat.

"Let's see what words you remember." Johab assumed his schoolmaster's voice and began pointing to the page.

Cyril confused only a few words, but had some difficulty with the words that the fox had spoken. "Foxes don't talk," he said decidedly. He seemed to have stopped focusing on the words to mull over that fact.

Johab stared at him in amazement. Cyril had recalled almost every word in the book. Jasmine remembered some words, but only after they had gone over and over them. She was only four, and Cyril was eight—at least he thought that he was. His aunt and Mustafa did not celebrate birthdays. Maybe eight-year-olds could remember words much faster than four-year-olds, but Johab remembered that learning to read had been a much slower process for him.

He pulled the stub of a pencil and the notebook out of his pocket. "Write them," he directed Cyril.

Cyril seized the pencil stub in his fist, wrinkled his forehead, and dug the pencil into the paper. An ungainly symbol appeared, bearing only a faint resemblance to the word. Cyril's memory for words far exceeded his ability to put them on paper. He looked downcast. He had not met Johab's expectations.

Johab clapped him on his shoulder. "Let's go find some weeds for Sekina. We've had enough lessons for today. You did very well. You can practice writing later."

They ambled down the alley, Cyril beaming at the praise. "Very well."

A military medal pinned to his chest would not have made him happier.

Johab glanced back toward Mr. Feisel's closed door. He might not be the expert on tomb excavations that he claimed to be, but he did say that he knew the land around the Valley of the Kings better than the "Egyptologists digging there today."

Johab flinched at the thought. It was right there in the Valley of the Kings where the bad things started that day near Queen Hatshepsut's temple. His father often thought out loud about his work; Johab didn't always listen.

He did remember an odd thing his father said. *"She's still here—not in the basement."* The words popped out with more assurance than his father usually expressed about things that happened over three thousand years in the past.

Johab knew that the early Egyptologists made errors. "They didn't have our tools," his father had reminded him. "Without the facts, we can be wrong."

Johab walked alongside Cyril, trying to piece things together. *He had very few facts.* It was a fact that his father wouldn't say another word about Queen Hatshepsut that day, as though he had already said too much.

Johab was fascinated by the idea of mummies lying undiscovered in their coffins. He didn't like looking at the "discovered" ones, unwound from yards of linen, their blackened, desiccated skeletons, their teeth smiling up at strangers. The idea of Hatshepsut being unwrapped and alone in the Museum basement, made him sad.

Johab scowled into the afternoon sun, trying to remember everything he could about Queen Hatshepsut. KV20 was the tomb that Hatshepsut had designed for her father, herself—or both—and then deserted.

A thought lit up Johab's face. The tomb she designed was a "bent" tomb, an unusual shape, just like the drawing on the old papyrus sheet in the pouch. That drawing was different from the official sketch of her tomb in his father's papers. *The papyrus drawing showed two additional small boxes angling off the end of the tomb corridor, one adjacent to the other, with some kind of shaft above them.*

Johab knew that the sketch on old papyrus had been hidden in the amulet. And, Hetty had found an identical sketch hidden his father's desk. Hetty told him that the amulet was from the New Kingdom, over three thousand years old. Was it a message from the grave? If so, who had written it?

At that moment, Johab could almost hear his father's voice talking about Senenmut, Hatshepsut's royal steward. Senenmut had been very close to the queen, but some Egyptologists believed that he disappeared or fell out of her favor before she died.

Johab's father had often voiced a different opinion. "Senenmut was the mastermind behind the building of her temple. She gave him the title of high steward. He was important to Hatshepsut. We just don't know enough about their relationship."

As he watched Cyril pulling up weeds along the road, a bright idea struck Johab. If Senenmut could design one of the greatest architectural structures in Egypt, he could also design a tomb that would never be discovered by robbers. Johab sank to the ground, over-whelmed by his own cleverness.

"If you're tired, Johab, why don't you rest. I can get weeds for Sekina." Cyril's concerned voice broke into the thoughts tumbling around in his head.

Johab nodded and waved Cyril on. He needed to concentrate. He was having a major brainwave. What if Queen Hatshepsut's most trusted advisor Senenmut had dreamed up some way to disguise or hide her tomb. It was possible. It had happened only fifty years earlier when Howard Carter found King Tutankhumen's tomb—maybe, with the help of Mr. Feisel.

A clever steward like Senenmut would find a way to protect secret information about his queen. The drawing on the papyrus sheets had been hidden in the amulet for a reason. Amulets were magic. They protected the wearer. Even if they were hung around the neck of a statue, a *usabti*, the amulet would protect the dead king or queen in the underworld.

Cyril nudged Johab. "Ready to go back, Johab? I have enough weeds." Cyril screwed up his eyes, trying to peer inside Johab's thoughts. Johab was a good thinker. His major hadn't moved a muscle since he left him sitting on the ground.

CHAPTER 38

Mr. Feisel was brushing Sekina with a corncob when Johab and Cyril returned with an armload of weeds. "It's what my grandfather used on his horses and donkeys—disposable and good for fuel," he chortled as he tossed it aside. "Let me show you boys how to bundle those weeds." He grabbed a handful, separated a few long strands and knotted them quickly into a small cluster.

Mr. Feisel never failed to amaze Johab. Now, he was an expert on donkey care. Johab gave him a long, penetrating look. If Mr. Feisel really knew something about tombs in the Valley and if he "kept his own counsel" as he had promised, it might be time to take a risk. It might be time to make Mr. Feisel a partner.

The winter sunset, streaked with red and orange, sent a blaze of color across the cloudless sky. Cyril picked up *Pinocchio* and followed Mr. Feisel. Johab could see him nodding as Mr. Feisel went inside his hut. Within minutes, Mr. Feisel returned, carrying a large pad of paper. He sat beside Cyril on the stoop, wrapped Cyril's fingers around a pencil, gripped his fist and began moving the pencil. Curiosity overcame Johab, but he tried to look disinterested as he wandered over toward Mr. Feisel's hut.

"We're working on Cyril's fine motor skills, Johab. He has a good memory for things he hears and sees, but no one has ever helped him do close work with his hands. He thought you were disappointed in him, because he couldn't reproduce the words on paper that you taught him to read. He is desperate for your approval." Mr. Feisel spoke in English.

Watching this old man with a tanned, lined face so gently guiding the hand of this young boy convinced Johab that could trust Mr. Feisel. He sat down on the other side of him.

"What do you know about 'bent tombs,' Mr. Feisel?" Johab blurted out.

"You mean KV20?"

Johab gulped. Mr. Feisel must be a mind reader. He hadn't intended to tell him that he was talking about Queen Hatshepsut's tomb.

Mr. Feisel chuckled. "You copied some notes that someone had made—I assume your father. It didn't take long to figure that one out." He took the pad and pencil from Cyril and drew a little upright basket, a snail and two little hoops—looking something like the croquet hoops at the British club. "That translates to a 'k' and a 'v' in English and two hoops for 20—KV20. If I could figure this out, so could someone else."

He looked gravely at Johab. "You may be wasting valuable time and taking unnecessary risks. I told you earlier what I had guessed about your family. I don't think you wanted to listen. You have new responsibilities after bringing two children home." He touched Cyril's head. "You may want to hear me out."

He rubbed his grizzled chin thoughtfully. "You make trips into the city searching for something—and you don't seem to be having much luck. According to the news story about John Bennett's disappearance, he is a well-known Egyptologist specializing in the New Kingdom era. Those items found in that police raid were from that period. That's quite a coincidence, right?" He looked directly into Johab's face.

Mr. Feisel's expression darkened. "That's a multimillion dollar business, Johab. The people involved in selling antiquities make the Italian mafia look like small-time crooks. If you're too close to their business, getting rid of you wouldn't mean a thing to them." Mr. Feisel drew his finger along the front of his throat.

Johab shuddered, the guard's neatly carved second mouth flashed before him.

Mr. Feisel said warmly. "I'm not trying to frighten you, Johab, but you may be putting everyone you care about at risk."

He shook his head and switched from Arabic to English so that Cyril couldn't understand him. "I don't know how Cyril and Alice fit into the picture. Cyril is from the streets of Cairo. His feet haven't been in a pair of shoes in years, if ever . . ." his voice trailed off. "Alice has been well-fed and doesn't seem to be afraid, but who has been painting her eyes with kohl? Your mother can't remove the stain on her eyelids—it will have to wear off."

Cyril was as alert as a little rabbit, recognizing his and Alice's name, his eyes darting from Johab to Mr. Feisel. Mr. Feisel switched back to Arabic. "If time is important—and it may be more important than you know, Johab—it might be in the best interest of your family if you quit playing games with me and let me know what you're up to, what you know, and what you don't know."

He put a heavy hand on Johab's shoulder. "I said I could help you, and maybe I can. I still have friends working on the tomb projects." He added, ruefully, "Some of them have done a little side business in the antiquity trade. They can find out things. You need help."

Johab fought to keep back the tears. He had believed that he could find where Mr. Barzoni had taken his father—then, he and Hetty would expose Mr. El-Hasiim and Mr. Barzoni as crooks. He had been confident that he could keep his mother and Jasmine safe. At this moment, they *were* safe in a one-room tomb in the Northern Cemetery, dependent on a stray cat to keep out rats and mice.

Being temporarily safe wasn't enough. These days, his usually happy mother rarely laughed. He was using Cyril to spy for him. Mr. Barzoni had tried to kill Hetty for helping him.

A warm little hand snaked around his side and fitted itself around his clenched fist. "Don't be sad, Johab. I'm here to help you. Mr. Feisel is here. We can make him another lieutenant," Cyril announced confidently.

Johab turned toward Mr. Feisel, wiping his welling eyes on his sleeve. He began at the beginning, and the words tumbled like dominos, falling in every direction.

"Father and I were on a field trip at Queen Hatshepsut's temple. She still might be there in a tomb. Then, he got worried. We came home. He gave me a pouch. He made me promise. It can't go to anyone but Ian Parks."

Johab turned a woebegone face toward Mr. Feisel. "That's why I rearranged the hieroglyphs I copied for you. I couldn't completely break my promise."

The next words came out in a torrent. "I met Hetty, I mean Miss Wenkle at the Museum. She's a friend of ours. She helps me look for clues. Mr. Barzoni pushed her down stairs, but her English friends are taking care of her. Cyril had to get away from Mustafa because of what might happen to Alice and . . ."

"Whoa. Stop. Too much information. Too fast. Let's start with the day your father was kidnapped." Mr. Feisel stretched out his legs and put his arm around Johab as though to reassure him that telling the events as they happened could take as long as Johab needed.

During the next half hour, Johab, Cyril, and Mr. Feisel could have been mistaken for carved figures in an ancient tomb, frozen in time, unmoving except for Johab's lips that shaped his story slowly and deliberately. Neither Cyril nor Mr. Feisel muttered a word.

When Johab described the night that he and Cyril rescued Alice from his careless aunt and wicked non-uncle, Cyril vibrated with eagerness to expand the story. After all, Mustafa had been just down the street when Cyril crawled through the window into a hut black as pitch. He could have stumbled over his aunt if she had been there. Cyril held his tongue. Something about the intensity of Johab's expression, the matter-of-fact way that he was giving information to Mr. Feisel, didn't seem to require any enhancements.

It was a frightening account, more so because of the low-key way that Johab was telling it, as though he had somehow become immune to the terror that lurked around the edges of the story. Even his description of crawling against the body of the Museum guard seemed impersonal, as though a dead man had become just one of the ugly facts in a story that shouldn't be real, but it was.

Johab stopped abruptly with his visit to Miss Wenkle's apartment. "Hetty's English friend Sarah is sending a message to Mr. Parks out in the field near Somalia. He's my father's best friend. Maybe he can help us. A hopeless expression settled on Johab's face, as though things that he should be doing to find his father had been delegated to someone far away, maybe someone unreachable.

Mr. Feisel pushed himself up from the steps, grunted and stretched his back. "Arthritis. Damned Greek." He smiled. "Word comes from the Greek. That's a joke, Johab. When you've lifted as many buckets of dirt and rocks as I have clearing out old tombs, your joints never forgive you."

He reached over and rubbed Johab's head. "I'm trying to get you to think about something else for awhile, Johab. You have been carrying a very heavy load for such a young boy. Sekina would have been braying at the top of her lungs if she had a fraction of your burden."

Johab flushed and stared at the ground. Maybe Mr. Feisel didn't understand half of what he said. Maybe his story wasn't believable, no more believable than one of Cousin Mohammed's wild tales. Otherwise, why was he talking about a donkey's burden?

"Here's what I think that we should do. You need to bring me the original papyri sheets and your father's notes." Johab looked disturbed. Mr. Feisel might have seen a photograph of the amulet. He might have guessed that the papyri came out of the back of that recovered treasure. He said his friends still worked in the tombs. Could he really trust Mr. Feisel?

"You can watch me review them. I just want to see the hieroglyphs and script without you turning it upside down and backwards." Mr. Feisel noted the uneasy expression on Johab's face. "You made a promise to give them to Mr. Parks, and when this Miss Sarah's message gets to him, you can do just that. I'll give them back so you can hide them. You don't have to tell me where."

Mr. Feisel gently lifted Johab's downcast face with his calloused thumb. "Johab, your father had no idea what was going to happen when he asked you to make that promise. You told me yourself that your family was having a quiet dinner when Barzoni and his men broke in. Your father could not have imagined that kind of immediate threat to his family," Mr. Feisel added confidentially.

Pointing up to a bright moon, Mr. Feisel said, "The god Osiris is traveling. You boys need to get to bed. You have beans to sell tomorrow. You should probably contact Miss Wenkle and her friend, that British lady, to be sure that the letter was sent to that Parks fellow. I need to sleep on what you've told me. I have a few ideas but must work them out before we discuss them, Johab. We'll talk tomorrow afternoon." He turned and entered his hut. His oil lamp flared up; Johab could see him sitting at his table, writing something on a pad of paper.

Johab steered Cyril back to their hut. Maybe he had made a mistake by telling Mr. Feisel so much. He had told him more than he had told Hetty. What kind of partner was he? He would remedy that tomorrow. He would tell her everything. What if those friends of Mr. Feisel still had connections to the antiquities business? Maybe Johab had made things worse by making him a partner.

Through the open window, Johab could see the large shadow cast by Mr. Feisel against the far wall in his hut. The shadow didn't seem dark and threatening, as shadows often are, but simply a pale facsimile of the shadows cast by the silver moon overhead, as though Mr. Feisel and Osiris were perfectly in alignment and intent on good works.

CHAPTER 39

A secret's safe
Twixt you, me and the gatepost!

—Browning

In Johab's dream, Queen Hatshepsut's bearded chin jutted forward as she strode right out of the limestone cliffs toward him, trying to tell him something important with words that had no sound. He sat up on his mat and rubbed his eyes. He had seen that image of the Queen on her chapel walls many times—but carved and painted figures were flat, showing only one side of her.

He stifled a gasp. In his dream, the Queen had turned her head. Her eyes pleaded with him. Johab shook his head and tossed his blanket onto Cyril's skinny body, coiled up beside him like a snail. He had rescued this little boy and his sister from a man who tried to make Cyril swallow a dead mouse when he didn't bring home enough money from begging on the streets of Cairo.

Dreams didn't mean anything. His mother would blame the rich cheese that his partner Hetty had sent with them yesterday. But, his father would say that dreams should be written down—that they probably had meaning.

Missing his father even more because of that silly dream about Queen Hatshepsut, Johab put his head in his hands and listened to the early morning sounds in the City of the Dead. Except for the distant crowing of a rooster, only soft snores came from a pile of blankets covering Jasmine and Alice.

A rather splendid thought flashed into his mind. A dream was just something imaginary going on in his head. What he had done to save Cyril and Alice from their aunt and that bad Mustafa would make his father proud. He had been clever and brave.

Cyril shuddered in his sleep, humping his back against his own dream of Mustafa's belt striking again and again. Johab patted his head until Cyril relaxed. The fact was that Cyril was braver than he could ever be. Cyril crawled into that dark window of his aunt's hut to rescue his sister. Johab had simply been the lookout, the enabler, but that was brave, too.

"You and Cyril need to get up, wash your faces, eat breakfast and load the cart. We need a few supplies from the Khan. Maybe Cyril can go to that shop that I like there. You might be recognized." His mother spoke of Cyril as though he had always been part of their household.

From the moment he had arrived at night with those two little orphans, his mother had gotten right into the spirit of adding new cousins to their family, making up a good story about why they had arrived so unexpectedly.

Johab watched Cyril eating the breakfast of stale bread and beans with relish. He smiled and nodded and bowed to Johab's mother like a puppet on a string, just like Pinocchio in the book that Johab was teaching him to read.

Pushing back from the table, Johab walked over to the windowsill and dug out the dried clay covering the dangerous pouch he had hidden. He fished into the pocket of his shorts for the photographs of the amulet Hetty had given him. His mother watched him, her eyes alert.

Cyril continued to mop up beans with bread but eyed his major, Johab, who seemed to glitter with new-found authority.

"Mother, I'm taking Mr. Feisel into my confidence. I think it would be OK with Dad." Without another word, Johab gave a brief salute to Cyril, marched across the alley, and rapped on Mr. Feisel's door.

He thrust the pouch and the photos toward him. "It's all I have. It's the secret information Dad gave me that Mr. Barzoni wants. Please help me." The last words ended with a catch in his throat. Johab wouldn't cry in front of Mr. Feisel, but he felt absolutely naked, standing in the doorway, as though he had just given away all of his family's secrets and could no longer protect them.

Mr. Feisel accepted the pouch and photographs silently, as though he knew that Johab had entrusted him with the lives of those he loved best in the world and that nothing he could say would make Johab's decision easier.

As the boys trailed Sekina into the suburbs of Cairo, Cyril encouraged the donkey with soft noises so that she wouldn't be her usual temperamental self. Johab trudged along, deep in thought, making Cyril uncomfortable with his preoccupation over something that he wasn't sharing.

"Johab, will we study again today when we get back home? Teach me to read about that Pinocchio boy some more? So I can be smart like you?" Cyril's voice was thin as a reed pipe.

Johab squinted in the direction of the Giza pyramids. "I will. Later. You need to learn important things if you're going to be my lieutenant and my cousin." A large hawk sailed over their heads, dipped into the roadside grass, and flapped upwards with a mouse struggling in its talons.

"Right there. That's a sign, Cyril, that you need to learn about the ancient gods and goddesses as well as the kings and queens of Egypt. We will start with Horus. He is a god with a hawk's head on a man's body. The ancient Egyptians believed that the eyes of Horus were the sun and the moon and . . ." Johab's voice picked up in volume, competing with the increasing noise of traffic as they neared the city.

Cyril was a good listener. Johab knew that he could repeat, almost word for word, everything that he had told him about Horus. Teaching was fun with someone like Cyril who drank information in great gulps, as though his thirst could not be quenched. Johab liked learning some new things, especially from his father. But Cyril was a little sponge. He danced alongside Sekina's tapping hooves, breathless to hear the stories of Horus and his battles with the evil Seth.

Johab thought about all those mornings when he and Mohammed had dragged themselves to school, desperate to be somewhere else, longing to prowl the alleys—not sit behind a desk in school.

Here was Cyril, who had never had a chance to go to school, eager to learn anything that Johab could tell him. Johab grinned over at Cyril. The learning went both ways. This little beggar knew Cairo. He knew every street, every alley, and every shortcut.

"Keep on your new galabaya, Cyril," Johab cautioned. "People won't buy our beans if we look too ragged. You can change back to your disguise before we get to the Khan. We might need to be undercover there."

Cyril nodded. As long as Johab called it his disguise, he wasn't embarrassed by his old, dirty robe. He hadn't thought about his clothes for a long time. When Mustafa moved in, his aunt no longer mended his clothes or worried about whether he ever had a bath. She did keep Alice clean. Mustafa liked to hold Alice on his lap. "She smells like flowers . . . my little flower," he would say as she struggled to get down. Cyril's face clouded over. He hadn't been able to keep Mustafa away from Alice then.

A smile lit up his face that no bad thoughts could dim. Alice was safe. Johab's mother had taken one look at the pretty beaded dress Alice was wearing that night—a present from Mustafa—and pulled it over Alice's head. The beaded dress sailed into the garbage with the words, "Not for little girls." Cyril had fished it out and tucked it under his striped robe. He could sell it in the market for a few coins.

The marketplace swarmed with tourists. The uniform of the day for male tourists appeared to be Bermuda shorts, brightly patterned shirts, and shoes with black socks. Johab's father wore khaki shorts in the field with boots. He wouldn't dream of wearing them in the city. In the middle of all these tourists, Mr. Barzoni in his black silk suit would stand out like a beacon. Johab felt safe, if only for the moment.

After Cyril repeated the list of food items and shot around the corner, heading for his mother's favorite stall, Johab angled Sekina and her cart so that he could watch in all directions.

"Johab? I recognized your donkey," a voice with a British accent whispered behind him. He turned to see Miss Sarah pointing a camera toward him. "The camera is out of film, but it will be a good disguise—tourists are always taking photos." She moved, angling for a close-up. "I took the letter to the airport. That secret code trick with the lemon juice is great. I experimented with it—when you heat the paper, the writing is as clear as though it had been done in brown ink. I added that little symbol you showed me, so Mr. Parks will know that something else is on the page—even though it isn't visible."

Johab grinned shyly at her. Miss Sarah's animated voice meant that a secret code was her cup of tea. She rubbed Sekina's nose. "That Mr. Barzoni and his lilies. You got out of there just in time. What a slimy man! That spicy cologne he wears." Her voice increased in pitch, causing Johab to look around quickly. No one was paying any attention. She was just an English tourist taking photographs of "the local color."

"I think we're safe here, Johab," she assured him. "Sometimes, you can be hidden in a crowd better than in a quiet place. I'll keep pretending to snap pictures."

She paused. "When he came by yesterday, Mr. Barzoni asked Hetty several questions. Hetty didn't let him know that I will be doing some research at the Museum. She told him that Ella and I were old friends from London, staying with her for a couple of weeks. I eavesdropped from the balcony. He asked Hetty about your family's friends. He kept telling Hetty how shocked he was to see her at the bottom of the stairs and how lucky she was that he called for help so quickly."

A faint smile passed across her face. "I thought that Hetty was going to smack that well-groomed head of his. She was so agitated. Ella told him that Hetty needed to rest, thanked him for the lilies, and practically pushed him out the door. Then, she dumped the lilies."

Sarah bent closer to Johab. "I've been watching the street for strange cars in the neighborhood. There is an old white Volvo with a couple of men in it that is often parked opposite Hetty's apartment. The men try to appear casual, reading the newspaper, but they never let their faces be seen."

Johab moved closer. "I need to tell you some things . . . that Hetty should know. I shared some information with an old man who is our . . ." Johab paused, struggling for words that wouldn't give away the hiding place of his family, "neighbor," he added.

"This man has experience with tombs and can read hieroglyphs. I didn't tell Hetty I had the information. I was afraid I would put her at risk." Johab flushed. Hetty had been injured, and Barzoni's men were watching her apartment. "I need to tell her now."

Sarah looked piercingly down at him. "You are probably right, Johab. Mr. Barzoni suspects that Hetty knows something or he wouldn't be wasting his time bringing her flowers. At present, he knows me only as Hetty's friend. After I take my letter of introduction to the Museum, someone may make the connection, and Mr. Barzoni will be watching more closely."

She angled the camera for a close-up of Johab and Sekina. "Let's decide on a safe place to meet tomorrow. I'm going to the Museum this afternoon to make copies of everything that might be of interest." She moved near Sekina's cart, wrinkling her nose as a wagon with bloody, fly-covered, camel haunches rolled past her.

"I know a perfect place," Johab almost shouted. "The camel market is tomorrow. That's just outside of Cairo. Tourists often go there. Hetty knows the place. My father once took her there with us. There are hundreds of camels with one knee tied up so they can't run away. They still get loose and charge all over the place.

The Nubians bring camels from the desert. Sometimes they have horse races there. All kinds of people gather at the camel market. No one would notice Cyril and me. And you three would look like tourists. Let's meet there early in the morning. Bring your camera, with film this time." Johab added slyly.

Cyril hung back, his arms loaded with packages. Within minutes, Johab and Cyril headed back to the City of the Dead at a fast clip. Johab was eager to talk with Mr. Feisel about the pouch and the photographs of the amulet. Odd how he was beginning to feel a kind of bond with their neighbor.

Their acquaintance started off on the wrong foot when he accused Mr. Feisel of keeping a mummy's hand for black magic. Instead of holding a grudge, Mr. Feisel had helped him bury the mummy's hand. Jasmine immediately made friends with him.

Now, Mr. Feisel was helping Cyril learn to write. If he were a spy, planted by Mr. Barzoni, he had an odd way of spying—carrying heavy buckets of water for Johab's mother and talking to Johab as though he were a grownup. If Mr. Feisel were a spy, he had the best disguise of all—that of undemanding friendship.

CHAPTER 40

The sun shone from high overhead when Johab and Cyril turned off the main road home. The chance meeting with Sarah at the market had eliminated the risk of visiting Hetty's apartment. It would be off limits if Barzoni's men were staking it out in that old Volvo.

Meeting at the camel market tomorrow was an ingenious idea. Just as Sarah had said—a crowded place may be the best place to hide. Johab felt a fine sense of satisfaction settle on him as the donkey pulled the cart to the side of the hut. He was very much in charge of things.

His mother had a different idea about who was in charge. Johab and Cyril sat shivering in thin, cotton undershirts while their galabeyas flapped on a makeshift clothesline. Redolent with Hetty's geranium soap, their skin reddened by a vigorous scrubbing, they didn't cut the dashing figures that Johab thought he often did as he swirled his galabeya about his ankles with strong, manly strides.

The only breathing creature that had escaped a mid-day bath was Bastet; he had streaked down the alley as Johab's mother headed toward him. Even Sekina was dripping with the residue of bath water dumped over her.

"We might as well do your reading lesson, Cyril. We can't be seen out in public like this," muttered Johab. The man of the family—the temporary man of the family—shouldn't submit to the indignity of a public bath, even one conducted in the entryway of their own hut.

Johab's father used to call his mother's sudden bouts of cleaning "purification rites." He would laugh and remind Johab, "It could be worse—she could use natron—that's what the ancient priests used to cleanse the bodies before preparing them for mummification. Just be glad she only uses soap."

Still pouting and huddling against Cyril for warmth, Johab felt the presence of a tall figure that blocked the sun. "You look like a couple of drowned rats," Mr. Feisel chortled. "I've got something that might take away your pain." He motioned them to follow. Once inside his hut, Mr. Feisel reached into a cloth-covered basket and pulled out two large bottles of soda. Orange Crush—Johab's favorite, warm and spewing out as the cap was popped off. "We have some work to do, Johab—can Cyril hear this?" Mr. Feisel queried in English.

Johab nodded. Cyril was at risk like the rest of them. Maybe little boys couldn't be arrested for kidnapping a sister, but biting Mustafa's thumb might be a criminal offense. Johab wasn't sure if children like Cyril—dependent on an aunt who wasn't a blood aunt—had any rights under the law.

Mr. Feisel stretched out his hand toward Johab. The pouch was nestled in his palm. "Very interesting pieces of papyri here, old and damaged on the edges. Just as you thought, they were probably crammed into that amulet. The carvings on the amulet are also interesting. I used a magnifying glass to make out some of them."

He pulled out a large pad and methodically began to go through his notes, his voice no more animated than if he were going through a grocery list. Johab squirmed in anticipation.

"The first line is not unusual. It says, 'May I be received into the presence of Osiris in the land of triumph.' Just what you'd expect the dead to ask." He scratched his head with the tip of his pencil. "This next part gets tricky. As I told you, Johab, I'm an amateur, but your father isn't. His notes are very helpful."

Johab held his breath, waiting for the clues that would unlock the "dangerous" secret that took his father away.

Mr. Feisel frowned. "Those old fellows, those priests, did not intend to make things easy for anyone. Hieroglyphs were the language of the priesthood—but many Egyptians worked as scribes under direction of the priests. If someone wanted to put something in writing that he didn't want the scribe to understand, he would need to do it in a kind of code."

Johab nodded enthusiastically. He knew all about code writing. That's what the lemon juice trick was about—a secret message.

"What that means," said Mr. Feisel, "is that anyone reading the message would have the very devil of a time trying to sort it out. I'll tell you what I've translated—with corrections after reading your father's notes. Then, we can discuss it."

Mr. Feisel had redrawn the images from the papyri. Johab thought that they looked very professional.

"This second line is odd. It speaks of 'unbolting the door of concealed things.' And this third section is very clear. It says, 'I have made the way—the name of its doorkeeper is Senenmut.'" Mr. Feisel beamed. "I never did think that Hatshepsut's favorite steward just disappeared."

He lowered his voice to a near-whisper. "Some think that he was the father of her daughter."

Johab wondered why he was whispering. That wasn't any kind of secret. Many Egyptologists had speculated about Queen Hatshepset and Senenmut. Maybe Mr. Feisel considered it a scandal that they weren't married. Johab's father had explained to him that the Kings and Queens were above scandal. The Kings had harems and more children than they could name. Queen Hatshepsut considered herself a king—she could do whatever she liked.

"Humph." Mr. Feisel grunted when Johab didn't respond. Boys today saw and heard too much. Nothing seemed to shock them. He continued, "This next line is more specific. It says, 'I have gone round the canal, making straight for the middle.' Look here, Johab. This is where your father made the note about the bent tomb, KV20. He made another note about the length of the tunnel."

Mr. Feisel pointed to a series of small marks. "Alongside the hieroglyphs, the scribe has made five ticks. Normally, that means the number five. Your father seems to think the marks stand for something else. In the margin he wrote in English: 'Half the distance of a football field.'"

Johab squirmed excitedly. "I know what that means—it's about 50 meters. I asked Father when he was trying to explain how many football fields could fit alongside of Hatshepsut's temple."

"That's a very clever interpretation." Johab colored with the unexpected praise as Mr. Feisel continued. "If that's true, then these marks by the sketch of KV20 must be your father's measurements. This next cluster of hieroglyphs is confusing. A few symbols are missing. Your father put a question mark in his notes. I think it says '. . . making secret with forms in the presence of the sarcophagus.' I have no idea what that means. The last page is a typical plea for the dead. It says, 'Not shut ye my soul, not fetter ye my shade. Open a way for my soul and for my shade. The god great within the shrine shall have a safe dwelling place.'"

Mr. Feisel pulled out the photograph of the amulet. "The carvings on the amulet are the symbols for 'never perish' and 'not may he suffer destruction of body.' It's a wild guess, but amulets like this were not always left on the mummy. Sometimes amulets were placed on the statues left in the ante-chambers, as special guards for the royal mummy."

Clearing his throat with a loud "haruumph," Mr. Feisel screwed up his face with something that might have been a smile. "If your father thinks that our old girl, Queen Hatshepsut, is still out there, maybe in KV20, then someone may have found this amulet in another location in her tomb."

Johab waited breathlessly while Mr. Feisel continued, "From the newspaper report about the antiquities bust, other items were mentioned—not just an amulet. It is odd that only one small statue has been put on display. Usually, they make quite a fuss about new finds. Drives up the tourist trade."

Mr. Feisel shook his head in frustration and leaned back in his chair. "I made you a copy of my translations—or, I should say mine and your father's. As long as there aren't any references to the KV20 tomb, these notes should be harmless—even if they fell into the wrong hands. But *this*, Johab, is quite another matter." He handed Johab a separate sketch. "Any expert looking at this drawing might recognize KV20. Your father has added the details from the papyrus sheet—the side tunnel and two extra rooms."

"You need to commit this drawing to memory, Johab. Let Cyril do it, too. Then, destroy this piece of paper. Don't wander around with it in your pocket." Mr. Feisel's voice was stern, anxious.

"Your father was right when he said this information was dangerous. I think I know why he wanted to get it to someone outside the country, this friend of his, Mr. Parks. If your father suspected Mr. El-Hasiim of being in the stolen antiquities business with Barzoni, he couldn't share this information with anyone at the Museum."

Mr. Feisel stared out the window, lost for a moment in his thoughts. "Queen Hatshepsut is one of the most elusive of the ancient rulers—first because she ruled as a king, not as the wife of one. Her twenty years of rule were among the most prosperous in Egypt's history. Then, she disappears." Mr. Feisel snapped his fingers. "Her name is removed from monuments—probably by the next ruler who was jealous of her." Johab nodded in agreement.

"Can you imagine what would happen if Hatshepsut were discovered in her tomb, Johab?" Mr. Feisel threw up his hands. "You'd have crews from every county in the world trying to negotiate for rights to dig up KV20 again—if that's where they thought she might be." He chortled loudly. "You'd have Hollywood here again, just like they came for King Tutankhamen's tomb—I'll tell you about that some day, boy."

He lowered his voice to a whisper. "You'd have an army of tomb robbers coming from all the villages near the Valley, not to mention souvenir seekers from Luxor and Karnak." He paused. "Those old families have a *generational memory* of the tombs. They've been going in and out of them for hundreds of years. The government can hang 'Keep Out' signs on the entrances. There are other ways to get inside," he added darkly.

"For now," he squeezed Johab's shoulder, "we need to keep this a secret. As soon as we hear from your father's friend, this Mr. Parks, we can make a plan. Right now, it's just between us fellows."

Johab didn't twitch a muscle. It wasn't "just between us fellows." He had told Sarah that he would meet her, Hetty, and Ella at the camel market in the morning to tell Hetty about secrets he had been keeping from her. Hetty was his first partner. She was his father's friend. She knew both Mr. El-Hasiim and Mr. Barzoni.

Mr. Feisel might know something about tombs and how to read hieroglyphs, but he didn't know the inside workings of a large building, with people who knew his missing father. Johab needed Hetty, as well as Mr. Feisel. This information had to be shared with all the partners.

Later that night, Johab read over and over the pages that Mr. Feisel had translated. He drew the KV20 tomb, measuring off each curve by the meters assigned, trying to visualize distances with his eyes closed. Cyril looked at the tomb sketch and quickly drew it in a puddle of water on the table with his forefinger, exactly as Mr. Feisel had drawn it. When Johab asked Cyril to do it again, he looked bored and repeated the pattern.

Johab's mouth drooped. Why was Cyril's memory so good? Then he remembered something that his father had told him about people who never learned to read. Some of them had exceptional memories. His father said, "When Shakespeare's plays were first seen, some of the people would leave the theater repeating the script almost word for word." Why would anyone want to do that? Word for word of the Hardy Boys, but Shakespeare?

The Hardy Boys were in English. Maybe it was time to teach Cyril English—he knew some words and phrases. "Please, nice lady, I starve without money" would not be something his mother would want to hear. Johab looked around the hut for a better hiding place for the pouch. Finally, he stuck it back under the windowsill. His mother watched him from across the room, her eyes alert, her lips pursed.

Johab looked at her with steely eyes. "What is in here is deadlier than a scorpion if it falls in the wrong hands. It can *only* be given to Mr. Parks—put directly in his hands. That was Dad's last order. You must forget that it is here."

She nodded, so Johab decided to confide one more thing. "Cyril and I are going to the camel market in the morning to meet Hetty and her friends. Her friend from London is helping us locate Mr. Parks. I need to talk to Hetty."

"That's not a good place for you children or for older ladies without a man escorting them," his mother retorted firmly. "There are all kinds of rough things going on there. Pickpockets have a field day with ladies and their purses."

"We have to meet somewhere in a crowd, a place where Cyril and I won't be noticed talking to English ladies," Johab retorted.

His mother turned away. She did not agree, but she would not interfere.

"We're making a plan, Mother—Hetty, Miss Sarah, and Mr. Feisel are helping, it's a plan to find Dad."

His mother's smile was forced. "I just don't want to mislay you, Johab. I couldn't bear it if another member of our family was mislaid."

"Mislaid." An odd description for a missing person, Johab thought. "Mislaying" something suggested a very temporary situation. Maybe *he* should begin thinking of his father as "mislaid." It wouldn't be so painful then. The sound of his voice was fading, like a dream that hangs on the edge of consciousness, then is no more.

Chapter 41

We get the Hump—
Cameelious Hump—
The Hump that is black and blue!

—Kipling

From dun-colored to brown, the ungainly beasts trudged along the roadside toward the camel market. Watching their heads bobbing above the lines of early morning traffic, Johab thought they resembled giant ostriches taking a casual stroll across the desert, curious, alert to the strangeness of the city.

The reality of their journey struck Johab when he saw the camel bodies painted with circles and bars and stripes of red, marks of the owners. It could be worse; they might have been branded like those poor bawling calves, struggling under a red-hot iron in American cowboy movies.

Beat-up pickups, Nubians dark as soot and exotically glamorous in their bright blue robes, herds of camels, and clusters of men, women and children created a scene that was almost unworldly. Johab felt reassured that he and Cyril could disappear into this colorful mob.

"Cyril! Watch out!" Johab shouted, yanking Cyril back from the path of a stampeding camel that had just shaken its knee rope loose. The camel charged in several directions at once, long, gangly legs unfurling as he sailed toward an opening in the crowd. Three Nubians flung themselves against him. The crowd closed around to watch the hobbling of his knee.

It was an efficient way to control a herd of camels with only one or two drivers. One of the camel's front legs was bent into a tight angle. A thick piece of rope was looped around the knee and tied. The camel could make its way, awkwardly, on three legs. Johab thought they looked like someone had entered them into a sack race—hobbled but able to move quickly if they coordinated the other three legs.

Cheering and noise from a nearby horse sale caught their attention. Two short, muscular horses, covered with brightly woven bands of tasseled cloths, had been hitched to carts and set side by side on a line marked on the clay-packed field.

Johab grabbed Cyril's hand and moved closer. Those carts were considerably larger than the one that Sekina pulled, but the horses were bigger than Sekina. Where she had bones, they had muscle. The snap of a whip popped against the horses' backsides, and they lunged. The carts barely moved.

Shocked at their inability to move with the blow of a whip, Johab looked closer. Thick boards had been lodged between the spokes of the cartwheels. These wheels weren't intended to roll at all. The horses were supposed to drag heavy wooden carts under a constant threat of the whip on their backs. The horses' muscles clenched as they lunged a second time, their coats gleaming with sweat as they inched the wooden carts forward.

"I'm going to report you to the Society for Prevention of Cruelty to Animals," screeched a familiar voice.

Johab looked across the crowd to see Sarah with her umbrella clutched like a weapon, forcing her way to the front of the crowd. People were clearing a path, muttering about a "crazy tourist" and eager to get the horse-pulling contest underway.

Sarah wagged her finger in the face of one of the men who looked as though he would like to flatten her with his whip but dared not because of an audience.

Johab pulled Cyril with him. "Quick. We need to get her away from here before she attracts too much attention." We were supposed to disappear in this mob thought Johab as he and Cyril cut through the crowd, intending to block Sarah from getting any closer to the other burly looking man with his whip held high. That fellow looked as though he would happily strike Sarah, crowd or no crowd.

"Sarah! Sarah!" Johab pleaded over the noise of the laughing crowd. "We've got to get out of here." He grabbed her hand, pulling her away.

She stopped, brushed her straggling hair back unto place, tucked her umbrella under her arm, and said, "I've never seen anything so disgusting. We British love our horses. We would never inflict that kind of torture on them. I will go to the British consulate to complain." She drew herself into a queenly pose.

Maybe the camel market hadn't been such a good idea. Just behind them, two men were trying to wedge three camels into the back of a tiny pickup—two camels facing the front and one smashed between them facing backwards. The camels spit and kicked; the men cursed and laughed. It was a good thing that Sarah didn't understand the language.

Butchers moved through the herds, pinching up wads of camel skin between their fingers, checking for fat, selecting the younger camels. Johab shuddered. He had seen those large, skinned carcasses hanging in the butchers' shops in Cairo, often covered with flies—a nasty sight. Johab hated to go near the meat shops, even though his mother never bought camel.

Thinking back to camel rides with his father in the desert, Johab remembered how those grand creatures seem to float above the sand dunes, their large cloven hooves hardly making any impression as they moved rhythmically along. Sitting on top of them was fun. Eating them would be intolerable.

The camel market might appear to be a tourist attraction in Cairo, some colorful ritual left over from the past. But, Johab knew that these animals—camels, goats, lambs, horses—and the people who tended them were essential to the economy of Egypt.

The people in the countryside lived much as they had always lived, bringing their lambs to slaughter for religious festivals, piling their donkeys with loads as tall as the donkeys themselves. It was how they *had* to live to survive.

Animals were also a major part of their entertainment—not those stupid cart-pulling contests. Johab remembered seeing the Bedouins, legs cocked gracefully across their camels' backs, racing like the wind in the North Sinai.

Sarah would simply have to get over the fact that this wasn't England. There was no society for preventing cruelty to animals, only the small donkey hospital managed by the Brits at the edge of Cairo. He would tell Sarah about finding Sekina there. That would make her feel better, knowing that some of her countrymen were rescuing injured animals.

Sarah could sense Johab's agitation. "Sorry. Sorry," she said quietly. "I know that we have important things to do here, but when I saw those poor horses. I had a pony when I was growing up, Johab. I would have taken a whip to anyone abusing my pony like those men were treating their horses today."

She smiled down at Johab. "I'll tell you about my pony. He was a most exceptional animal. Do you know that he . . ." her voice softly continued as they headed over to where Hetty and Ella waited by the parked VW. Sarah stopped abruptly. "That car is too recognizable. Hetty keeps it spotlessly clean."

Sarah pointed to a nearby tent. "You boys go over by that striped tent. They seem to be selling food there. We'll meet you in that small clearing beside the tent."

Balancing plates of *fitiir* (small pancakes topped with tomatoes, peppers and cheese), Sarah and Ella watched Hetty spread a blanket across tufts of dried grass several yards away from the *fitiir* vendor's tent. Beckoning the boys, Hetty said, "Come sit by the food, boys."

Then, with her carefully enunciated Arabic, she motioned toward Cyril. "Here, Cyril, you sit by me. I want to know more about you."

Cyril quivered with suppressed excitement. This nice lady, this Hetty, was interested in him. He couldn't remember anyone wanting to know about him. His aunt mostly ignored him. To Mustafa, he was a nuisance, something to be kicked for no reason.

Johab held up his hand, as he did in school when he wanted permission to speak. "We have to talk, Hetty. I need to tell you something that I haven't told you before." He looked down at the blanket, not daring to look her in the eye. "It was because of a promise. A pouch with old papyri that Dad gave me that day we came back from Queen Hatshepsut's Temple. He said I could only give it to Mr. Parks because it was dangerous."

He now had the complete attention of the three women. Only Cyril continued to eat as though he had never nor might ever have another meal.

Without a single pause, Johab recounted everything he could remember that day and afterwards: his father saying that Queen Hatshepsut was still in her tomb, KV20; hiding the pouch; trying to decipher the papyrus pages; and, finally, giving the pouch to Mr. Feisel.

He handed a fist full of papers to Hetty. "These are my English translations from Mr. Feisel's Arabic of the hieroglyphs on the papyrus and the carvings on the amulet. I didn't write down anything about KV20. That information is too dangerous to put on paper. I did memorize the sketch of the tomb. So did Cyril," he nodded toward his lieutenant who was polishing off the last *fitiir*, seemingly unaware that majors were supposed to eat first.

"I don't want to give you that sketch, Hetty . . . or Sarah. . . ." he included the newest partner, giving a nod to Ella who was staring soberly at him and Cyril. "Mr. Barzoni knows where you live. The information I have about that tomb could put all of us at risk."

"You think your father knows where Queen Hatshepsut is buried? Is that it, Johab?" Hetty's face was red with emotion or toasted by the mid-day sun. "Do you know what that would mean to the Project? People would come out of the woodwork to fund it."

"That's just it, Hetty. We can't let anyone find out what Dad suspected. Mr. Barzoni and Mr. El-Hasiim already know that he was on to something. That's why Barzoni kidnapped him. As long as they don't know what he found out, they probably won't hurt him. I think that's why he told me to give the pouch *only* to Mr. Parks. But, we can't wait to locate him so. . . ." His voice trailed off in frustration.

He took a deep breath and continued. "When you read these translations, you'll see that nothing is clear. If there are clues, someone made them confusing on purpose. Mr. Feisel believes that Senenmut either wrote those hieroglyphs himself—or had a trusted scribe write them."

Johab turned toward Sarah and Ella. "Senenmet was Queen Hatshepsut's steward. He may have been her . . . I mean sort of her husband but secret because he couldn't be a king," Johab assured them, confident that his explanation would make the dubious royal relationship aboveboard.

"That photograph of the amulet was important. I found that." Hetty flushed with pleasure.

"There were actually two photographs, Hetty. Those Poloroids were stuck together. The second photograph showed a hidden compartment in the back of the amulet. We think . . ." he paused to include the other partner who didn't seem to be getting enough credit.

"Mr. Feisel and I think that the papyrus pages that Dad found came from the back of the amulet. They have an oval impression on them. Mr. Feisel did the translation on those pages I gave you." Johab pointed toward the pile of papers in Hetty's lap. "Senenmut's cartouche is carved along the gold sides of the amulet, at least that's what Mr. Feisel says."

"This Mr. Feisel," Sarah said with concern. "This is the first that I've heard of him. Is he someone you work with at the Museum, Hetty?"

Johab twisted his hands together. He didn't want to mention the City of the Dead. Cyril beamed, recognizing a name in all this English gibberish. "Mr. Feisel is nice man," he chirped in English, his face greasy with the rich dough of the *fitiir* despite Hetty's repeated attempts to wipe his face.

"It's a long story, but he is our neighbor . . . next to the place . . . where we are hiding." Johab liked the intrigue suggested by the word "hiding" rather than "living."

He looked around anxiously. The five of them were sitting on a blanket in the middle of the camel market, as though they were simply having a picnic in the country. Johab needed to be sure that they were taking all of this seriously.

"Mr. Feisel is a man with years of experience in digging around tombs. He helped Howard Carter find King Tutankhamen's tomb," Johab added. Hetty raised her eyebrows.

"I didn't believe him either. Not at first," Johab assured her. "But he has a piece of a cylinder seal that he claims Mr. Carter gave him—and he has described what it was like that day when they found the opening. So, I believe him. He also has connections with some of those families that live out near Deir el-Bahari. They are probably descendants of the same people who built and decorated the tombs thousands of years ago."

Hetty couldn't hide her skepticism. "I don't know anything about this Mr. Feisel, Johab. I never heard your father mention him. I'm so worried now that I'm not sure whom we can trust. I'm almost afraid to go back to work. I'll be suspicious of everyone working on the Project."

Sarah interrupted. "That's just it, Hetty. You should be suspicious of people on the Project. When the Project Director, that Mr. El-Hasiim, is involved with someone like this Barzoni fellow, it should make us suspicious of everyone."

She reached over and patted Johab's arm. "I did get many of your father's files copied. Hetty gave me the key to her office. Mr. El-Hasiim was gone yesterday, so no one at the Museum seemed the least bit concerned that I wanted to copy things for Mr. Parks. My letter of introduction worked like a charm."

Johab felt a moment of reassurance. Sarah might get emotional over the treatment of horses, but she seemed to think very critically about the important things, things that might help bring his father home.

She touched her large, brightly colored bag, a favorite purchase of tourists who buy too many souvenirs. "The papers are here, Johab, in my purse. I didn't dare leave them in the apartment. Hetty and I will go through them tonight." She pulled out a rolled-up bundle. "I keep this statue of Hathor right on top so this looks like a stash of souvenirs. No one would imagine that I have important papers here."

Hetty traced her hand along Cyril's bird-like backbone and handed some money to Johab. "Would you buy some more *fitiir* for Cyril? I think he's still hungry. And get some for the rest of us. There don't seem to be any customers around the food tent now."

Johab was hungry. The empty plate of *fitiir* was a greasy smear, and Cyril still looked hungry. The man in the cook tent must have stepped away from his stall. Johab drummed his fingers on the wooden countertop and looked back toward the group on the blanket.

Hetty, Sarah, and Ella in their floral dresses looked like well-tended flowers, as though an English garden had been transported to this loud, colorful marketplace where the noise had increased, along with the heat.

A pad of sickeningly sweet, stinging wetness capped his mouth and nose before he could utter a sound. Iron-like arms embraced him. The small English garden of women seemed to be waving frantically, as though caught up in a sudden desert storm, swirling up and away.

The last sound he heard was the thin scream of Cyril, wailing his name, "Johab," out across the dark night into which he had descended.

CHAPTER 42

Consciousness returned, attacking each of his senses individually, despite Johab's efforts to keep it at bay. The odor of petrol replaced that of chloroform, shooting a dull, aching pain from the base of his jaw to the top of his head. The thump of tires, grinding along the highway, increased the pain. His tongue was fat and leaden, held immobile by a wad of cloth.

A spare tire bounced against his back with every bump in the road, but he couldn't rearrange his body. His hands were tied behind his back, and his ankles were tightly bound. He fingered the rope holding his hands—it was the same prickly hemp rope used to bind the camels' knees.

Gradually, he opened his eyes. The space enclosing him was black and hot.

Occasionally, a glimmer would splinter the darkness. The lid on the trunk angled crookedly, letting in an occasional flash of light from a passing car.

Johab tried to remember why he was in the trunk of a car, speeding down a highway at night. His memory was returning in fragments, just disconnected images. He remembered the high-pitched wail of Cyril calling his name. Then, he remembered the little picnic on the grass, the floral dresses of the English ladies, the *fitiir* disappearing almost as soon as it was placed in front of Cyril.

It came to him in a flash. He had gone back to the food tent to buy more *fitiir*, but the cook was nowhere to be seen. He remembered a nasty, sweet odor, then blackness. That was all. He struggled against the ropes, tried to spit out the gag, and fell back helpless.

A wave of nausea swept over him. He couldn't be sick. The gag would cause him to strangle on his own vomit. He would die in the back of a car on a road to somewhere he didn't want to go.

Wiggling his hands against the scratchy rope relieved the numbness in his fingers. Johab forced himself to relax, to quit thinking about the swaying and bumping motion of the car. He was going to throw up, gag or not, unless he could concentrate on something pleasant, something useful, something calming.

His favorite detective, Sherlock Holmes, popped into his head with a good reminder: "You know my method. It is founded upon the observance of trifles."

He hadn't been observant enough. That's why he had been moved so quickly from the carnival-like world of the camel market to a smelly trunk of a strange car.

Hetty's VW. It would have been easy to follow that car to the camel market. The English women's bright dresses and large hats would be obvious. Johab and Cyril might "blend in," but not the English ladies. That was his first mistake.

Sitting on a blanket as though they were in a park having an afternoon picnic was the second mistake. People at the camel market eat on the run, stuffing food into their mouths as they go about the day's business.

A grim notion swept every other thought aside. Three English women and two native boys in galabayas, chatting companionably around a picnic lunch, had been a perfect target for Barzoni's men— and the camel market had been *his* idea.

He dared not think about what might have happened to Cyril, Hetty, Sarah, and Ella. If Sarah had been prepared to attack one of the Arab horse traders with her umbrella, for mistreating his horse, she wouldn't hesitate to go after Barzoni's men.

He simply couldn't remember anything after going to the deserted food tent. Johab inched back against the spare tire so its pressure would keep him alert. Right now, try as he might, he couldn't even concentrate on his idol Sherlock.

His thoughts were grim as tears streaked his face. Who would look after his mother, Jasmine, Alice, and Cyril? Mr. Feisel. He felt a small, warm spot of comfort. Mr. Feisel would not let them go hungry. And Hetty. If she had not been harmed, she would do her best to take care of them—if she could find them. He had warned Cyril not to tell anyone where they were staying. Not anyone.

The car slowed, came to a stop, and, after a few minutes, proceeded slowly. The road noise was different, almost as though the car were going up some kind of metal ramp. He could hear grinding noises and the voices of men shouting. "Extra pay at this hour and . . ." the voice faded into the screech of metal on metal. The lurching and thumping of the car followed a different pattern, almost as though it were swaying in a strong breeze. The wheels weren't moving, but the car was most certainly traveling. It was on a ferry.

The life-giving Nile flowed beneath him. There could be no other river. Johab knew this ferry. Even gagged, bound, and stuffed within the trunk of a car, he knew this ferry. He and his father had crossed it many times, from the east side of the Nile to the west side, connecting them to the road heading toward the Valley of the Kings.

Johab struggled against sleep. Whatever those men had put over his mouth and nose blotted out memory and made him long for the oblivion of sleep. He gritted his teeth around the gag. He would not sleep. Those "trifles" that Sherlock observed to solve mysteries were the key to the riddle. He needed to stay alert and remember every mile, every turn, every sound. He had been here before and must keep his bearings.

After leaving the ferry and turning onto a bumpy road, Johab estimated the car speed and time, maybe about ten kilometers. The road became smoother, probably clay-packed. His dad drove about 40 kilometers an hour over these roads. Johab began counting the minutes by seconds, ticking off kilometers.

The car skidded to a sudden stop. Doors slammed, a key was fitted into the lock, and the trunk popped open. Johab kept his eyes closed and remained frozen, despite the itching ropes and a desperate need to stretch his cramped legs.

Thick fingers massaged his neck, just under his chin. "Strong pulse. He's OK. We must have given him more chloroform than he needed. He should have been awake by now. The boss warned me that this," he poked Johab, "is a valuable piece of goods." He chortled. "Can't imagine why. Looks just like a little desert rat to me."

Grunting with the effort, he lifted Johab out of the trunk, and flung him over his shoulder. Johab peered out of tiny slits in his eyes. The shadow of another man was inches away. Johab quickly closed his eyes so that they could not lock into the cold eyes of that man. Both of these men had to be convinced that he was still unconscious.

"I'll get those posters from the back seat of the car. We need to put notices on the doors after we lock them. That prissy guy at the Museum made them for the boss, so they'd look official." The man holding Johab swung toward the car. "Wait up. I need to grab that bowl and bottle of water. The boss wants this kid left tied up—he says we can take out the gag so he can get to water."

The man carrying Johab patted his rump. "He'll have to lap it up like a little puppy." They were making their way over rough terrain, avoiding the well-worn paths, breathing hard from the effort, and moving on a narrow path up the side of the cliff face. Johab could see the glint of the sunrise reflecting against the somber cliffs, but it was still dark below.

"The boss paid off the guards so nobody should be here, but you never know who might be prowling around these old tombs."

The tall, gaunt man carrying Johab shifted him to his other shoulder so that his sharp shoulder bones were ground against Johab's ribs. The beefy man picking his way up the trail ahead of them wheezed out a complaint: "I don't know why the boss wouldn't let us use our headquarters up at the wadi. We could have traveled there with the car and used one of the back store rooms for the kid."

The man carrying him responded brusquely, "The boss doesn't want this kid anywhere near his old man. This brat has led us a merry chase all over Cairo." He poked Johab in the ribs again, but Johab forced himself to hang limp.

"We almost had him at the Khan, but that blasted English woman got in the way. This kid will help with what the boss calls 'psychological' torture of his father." The man carrying him nudged the other man aside and moved into the lead along the path, his flashlight casting eerie shadows along the face of the cliff.

The man trailing behind snorted. "I know a better method. Slow removal of fingernails gets more information than any kind of so-called psychological torture."

Johab held his breath, trying not to move a muscle. That was his father they were so casually discussing. And his fingernails.

By appearing lifeless, keeping his eyes shut, Johab had learned something. Mr. Barzoni was not physically torturing his father. And, he was being held near a wadi in the Valley of the Kings. That brought up a wide range of possibilities.

The man carrying Johab skidded as he tried to maneuver down a slope with some flat stones on a path toward what appeared to be a dark, squared-off cavity in the side of the cliff.

As he felt himself being swung up, then dumped on the ground with a thump, Johab felt as buoyant as a balloon. He knew this place. This was KV 20, a tomb that was supposed to have been built for Queen Hatshepsut, the tomb sketched by his father on those notes in the pouch. It was a crumbly tomb, one that Howard Carter had tried to explore; there were no signs that Hatshepsut had been buried there—just signs of robbers and cave-ins.

As the tall man aimed his flashlight beam at the iron bars blocking the entrance, the other man fitted a key into the lock that chained a barred gate. With one kick, the gate screeched open.

Both men shone lights around the large, limestone entrance. The musty, dank air of a tomb that is no longer a secret place of kings and queens struck Johab as sad. This tomb had been of little interest to Egyptologists after Mr. Carter gave up on it.

Just as the man swung Johab back onto his shoulder and moved into the tunnel, he paused. "Quick, flash your light up there, behind that big pile of rocks near the edge of the cliff. I could have sworn I saw something move."

"Probably a fox," the other man said dismissively. "No one would be out at this hour. The tourists are tucked into their beds in those pricey hotels across the river. This tomb has been off limits to tourists for years."

The man leading the way gestured with his flashlight. "I'll put one of those signs on this door. And, we'll put the other one on the next door just in case some tourist is nosing around. That guy at the Museum said he had a new door put on the storeroom where we can dump this brat."

Johab, dangling upside down across the man's shoulder, tried to read the sign being fastened to the metal bars of a door. It was in Arabic and English, a warning that entrance was forbidden due to "dangerous conditions."

The rays of the two flashlights reflected against the rough-hewn limestone tunnel that sloped gently down. Johab tried to estimate the number of feet they had gone before they reached a flight of steps carved into the limestone—about twenty, he thought. Or, maybe forty. It was hard to judge when being carried head down like a bag of potatoes.

"Off to the side now—look for the new door. The boss said it has a sign that says "falling ceiling." He flashed his light upward. This ceiling has been here for thousands of years. I don't believe a tomb robber would be discouraged by one of those signs."

"There's nothing but trash here now." The man holding Johab kicked at a heap of stones. An empty cigarette pack that could have been there for years, but looked as fresh as though it had been left yesterday, spoke to the preservation powers of a tomb underground.

"These old tombs are trash bins. The tourists get sick breathing the stale air and vomit. Watch where you step," he cackled.

After struggling with a stiff lock on a new wooden door, the man carrying Johab eased the door open and checked every corner of the room with his flashlight. Except for piles of rubble, it was empty. He bent over and dumped Johab off his back onto the hard, limestone floor.

"Pour some water for him in the bowl. Set it near enough for him to reach," he ordered the other man. He took out a pocketknife, flipped open the largest blade, and sawed through the cloth holding the gag in Johab's mouth.

Then, he thumped Johab's head with the palm of his hand. "There you go, you little beggar. All the conveniences of home. Water and a roof over your head. Let's get out of here. It will be daylight soon."

As he pulled on the door, the man stumbled on the step as something thumped on the floor. "Damn. That was my flashlight." The tall man flashed his light around the room, over piles of debris, and, into the dark corners.

Johab pretended to be unconscious, but as soon as he had felt the flashlight roll against his body, he shifted his weight and planted his stomach over it.

"Forget it. It must have rolled into one of those big cracks full of debris. We may never find it. We need to get out of here. We have to move the car. The boss doesn't want any evidence of us near this place."

"What about feeding the kid? Is he going to leave him here to starve?" asked the man who had carried the water, his voice sounding almost hopeful, as though he took pleasure in imagining the agonies of Johab starving in an old tomb.

"Don't be stupid. This kid is collateral. The boss just hasn't figured out what he's going to do with him yet. He won't starve until we get back."

The wooden door closed with a resounding thump. The jangling of the chain on the door stopped. The sound of footsteps faded quickly. His hands and feet tied with camel rope, Johab was fettered as tightly as a mummy in the dark underworld of an unknown tomb. He would have screamed. He could have cried. But, not even a ghost would hear him.

CHAPTER 43

Wherever the enemy goes let our troops go also.

—Ulysses S. Grant

The shouts of the spectators at the horse-pulling contest, urging the lunging horses forward, masked the screams of three frantic women and a small boy. Cyril, Hetty, Sarah, and Ella dashed toward the empty space at the food stand where Johab had been standing and shouted out four different versions of what they had seen.

Sobbing with shock, Hetty said over and over: "I'll never forgive myself. I should have known that Johab wasn't safe anywhere, especially not the camel market."

Ella mumbled words of comfort, patting Hetty gently on the back. Sarah fixed a gimlet eye on the man who had just returned to the food stand to bake *fitiir*.

The thin voice of Cyril focused their attention as he struggled to speak English. "Two men Johab in white car. Bad back." He smacked his hand against his arm to simulate a dent in the trunk. Tears coursed down his face. "Big man put thing . . . ." Cyril demonstrated the chloroform pad on Johab's mouth with the sleeve of his galabeya. "That way." Pointing toward the main road, he shifted to Arabic, his sobbing muffling his words.

Hetty's Arabic was marginal, but she understood Cyril's last words. Ella said, "We need to find the police. A little boy has been kidnapped here, in the middle of a large crowd of people. Whoever took him isn't fearful of being caught."

Hetty's sobbing stopped abruptly. She turned toward both Ella and Sarah. "That's just it. They aren't fearful of being caught. Mr. Barzoni has connections with the police. He told me so himself when he asked for information about Johab and his family."

She drew herself upright, her expression grim. "I promised Johab that I would not involve the police, and I intend to keep that promise. Mr. Barzoni took Johab's father, and now his men have taken Johab. They need both of them alive. That much is very clear. They've had opportunities to kill—they could have murdered Johab and his mother the night they broke into the apartment. It's easy to kill someone in this city. It's not easy to avoid criminals."

She cast her eyes downward, her face full of regret. "We just made it very easy. We were far too careless."

Cyril's tear-stained face moved from speaker to speaker, trying to understand what the women were saying. Hetty pulled him close to her and said softly in her broken Arabic. "We're going to find Johab, Cyril, but we're going to need you to be very brave and help us."

Cyril nodded, his face glistening with tears and the grease of *fatiir*.

Sarah had been silent after her first outburst when she realized that Johab had disappeared. She was, first and foremost, a composed person, a logical thinker; and, secondly, a librarian who did not tolerate disruptions. The snatching of a little boy she had sent over for food was an intolerable disruption, somehow making her complicit.

Her steely gaze had not wavered from the man who had returned to cooking. He had not been in his booth when Johab went to buy food. She reached into her purse and brought up a fistful of money.

"Hetty, can you translate to Cyril? Tell him we need to get that man behind the food stand to tell us everything he can about the men who parked their car behind his stand. He left his stand—that gave them the opportunity to grab Johab. The cook was probably bribed." She thrust the money into Hetty's hand. "Have Cyril bribe him again if necessary. We need as much information as we can get."

Hetty knelt by Cyril, trying in broken Arabic to let him know Sarah's plan.

Cyril was a step ahead of her. He wondered why this nice Miss Hetty took so long to say anything. Her "if you could please go over there and talk to that man . . . and if he won't talk, give him this money . . ." was taking far too long.

Cyril had seen the cook leave. If he hadn't been so busy mopping up food crumbs, he would have gone with Johab. The men would have been forced to take both of them. They could not have pried him loose from Johab. He looked at the wad of money that Miss Hetty was forcing into his hand. That low-life cook wasn't going to see a fraction of that. He knew the type. They would sell information for next to nothing.

The three ladies followed him like a small, bright army in flower-patterned uniforms. Cyril looked down at his beautiful, mustard-striped robe. It was good that Johab insisted that he wear it today. These ladies would not want to be seen with a boy in rags. He looked like a lieutenant today. His chin dropped. Lieutenants did not lose their majors.

The cook shifted from foot to foot, unused to facing three British ladies with angry faces and a small native boy wearing an over-sized galabeya. He turned away to lift hot pastries off the brazier.

Cyril's small voice was so authoritative that he surprised himself. "Pay attention to these ladies. Their . . ." he paused, not knowing how to identify their relationship to Johab, and continued with assurance ". . . their cousin was just snatched by two men who parked their car behind your tent. They require you to tell them the names of those men and where they took their cousin."

The man continued lifting *fitiir* from the grill, ignoring Cyril. "They are going to report you to the police immediately for helping those men kidnap their cousin." Cyril added, confidentially, "He's a boy from America, this cousin of theirs. You are going to be in big trouble."

The man leaned over the counter and hissed at Cyril. "Get those women away from here. I don't know anything. I went to get some more tomatoes. I didn't see a thing."

"These ladies are very important people." Cyril gestured to the three women who pulled themselves upright and glared over Cyril's head at the cook. "They can have you arrested and your food stand closed. Forever. Or you can cooperate."

Cyril fingered one bill and pulled it out of the wad that he had concealed in his robe. He showed the edge of it to the man behind the counter.

The man glanced from left to right, increasingly agitated. He had a fleeting sense that the British army, wearing floral dresses, had once again descended on Cairo.

He reached for the bill, the edge of which Cyril continued to hold. "Information first," Cyril muttered between gritted teeth. If he had been wearing his beggar's rags, he could have trashed the inside of this food booth and slipped away before this man could catch him. Maybe he would do it anyhow.

"I never saw those two men before. They are not 'regulars' here at the camel market. They pulled their car behind my stand just after those women bought the *fitiir*. They were watching those women. That's all I know." The man tugged on the bill again.

"Why did you leave? What did they ask you to do?"

Instead of looking like a fat cook, the man looked like a fat weasel, his eyes shifting back and forth from Cyril to the three women. "They asked me to 'disappear' for five minutes."

"Why did you agree?" Cyril asked pointedly.

The man nodded to the bill, still gripped by both him and Cyril.

"*Baksheesh*. Now, give me the money and get those women away from here. They're giving me the creeps."

Cyril smiled up at him in an obsequious way and gently let go of the single bill. He ducked his small head under the overhanging edge of the board that formed the makeshift counter of the booth and gave a mighty, upward push with his skinny body.

The wide board tipped up on one end, swinging the other end toward the cooking counter piled high with tomatoes, peppers, slabs of feta cheese, mounds of flaky *fitiir* dough and two small, glowing braziers. One more push and the entire booth collapsed on itself, the cook screaming and cursing as he danced around, grabbing at tomatoes and dough blackening on hot coals.

Hetty grabbed Cyril's hand, and the four of them pushed through crowds of people to the VW, wedged between two rusty pickups.

Sarah was the first to speak. "I can't believe that you did that, Cyril."

Cyril didn't understand all her words, but he understood the tone. She was smiling from ear to ear, patting his back. He handed the unused wad of bills toward her. "No, Cyril, you've earned it."

They crawled into Hetty's blue Beetle, a good name for a small, never-fail VW. Cyril thought that it looked like a larger version of the scarabs made of blue faience and prized by the tourists as tomb treasures.

"We need to get out of here. We're getting too much attention." Sarah pointed toward a crowd gathering around the *fitiir* booth, or what was left of it. The cook, red-faced, and gesturing wildly, was making more noise than the camels being loaded into the pickup in front of Hetty's VW.

Three Bedouins were trying to wedge a third camel into the impossibly small back of a battered pickup. They had parked too closely to the front of Hetty's car. Another truck blocked her from the rear.

Two kneeling camels, tethered against opposite sides of the pickup bed, grunted loudly and belched streams of slimy mucus. The third camel had braced itself against the front of Hetty's car. She could not inch forward without smashing the camel's legs. The men tugged, shouted, and, finally, held their palms up, with exasperated grins on their faces, embarrassed that they had blocked these English ladies from moving their car.

Cyril leaned from the back seat and whispered to Hetty. "I do it."

Hetty opened the door, pulled the seat forward, and boosted Cyril out. Cyril said. "You start the car. I'll catch up with you." Hetty only understood the Arabic for "start" and turned on the engine.

Inching around the front of the VW, Cyril placed his small hand on the neck of the great, trembling beast that looked as though it might take a flying leap and land on the car at any moment. He spoke quietly to the three men who nodded and backed away. Making soothing noises, Cyril reached down and unknotted the rope holding the camel's knee in a painful position while continuing to hold tightly to its rope halter.

The camel planted all four feet firmly on the ground, shook his body until his skin rippled, then moved placidly along behind Cyril who led him away from the front of the car. One of the Bedouins moved over beside Cyril, took the camel's halter and began talking earnestly to Cyril. Cyril shook his head and pointed back toward the car.

He motioned to Miss Hetty. She inched forward, backed up, turned her wheels sharply and moved down the road. Sarah swung her door open. Cyril hopped into the back seat by Miss Ella. They all looked behind them. The Bedouins had moved the camel back behind the pickup and were, once again, determined to defy the laws of physics and make the camel fit into a space no wider than the width of two hands.

CHAPTER 44

Hetty gunned the engine and sped down the highway leading back toward the city. Her face was tense with anxiety. Pulling over to the side of the busy road, she announced: "We must find Johab's mother immediately and let her know what happened. I know that Johab didn't want anyone to know where she and Jasmine are hiding, but we have no choice. She needs to know what has happened to Johab." Sarah and Ella nodded. Cyril was trying to sort out any English words he knew.

Hetty turned to Cyril scrunched into a far corner of the backseat and said in Arabic. "Johab's mother, Cyril. We need to see her right now."

Cyril understood her Arabic well and her tone even better. At the same time, he remembered that Johab had reminded him many times that no one could know where his mother and Jasmine were hiding. No one. He squirmed uncomfortably.

"She has the right to know, Cyril. She's his mother." Hetty's last words took on a plaintive tone of both guilt and despair.

Cyril's mother had died when Alice was born. He was only five years old at the time, but he could still remember her sweet face leaning over him at night, stroking his hair, singing to him. Mothers have a right to know about their sons.

"City of the Dead. Northern Cemetery." Cyril announced loudly in English.

Two of the women were struck silent. They visited cemeteries in England. They rubbed the lichens off headstones of long-dead relatives. They were often irritated when they saw the homeless sprawled between graves, sleeping off something clutched in a paper sack. To have permanent inhabitants living among the dead seemed unbelievable.

Hetty chuckled. "Johab was very clever. Who would ever imagine that John Bennett's son would think of hiding out in a cemetery?" Then she shook her head. "I would. I wonder that I didn't think of it before. Johab has spent a lot of time around old tombs. A graveyard wouldn't bother him in the least."

She looked back toward Cyril, trying to communicate in faltering Arabic. "When we get there, we must look like tourists. Just visiting the cemetery. We'll park the car some distance from where you are living. You get Johab's mother and bring her to the car. We don't want to draw attention to us. For all we know, Barzoni has spies everywhere."

Cyril pointed to the main road into the cemetery, directing Hetty down tight alleys to a small space between two tombs. He popped out from the seat that she pulled forward, and disappeared. Within minutes, he reappeared at the end of the alley, waving his hands and talking to a woman in a galabeya whose face seemed abnormally strained.

Hetty had never seen Johab's mother wearing a galabeya. She looked exotic, different than in Western clothes. Her troubled face lit up when she saw Hetty. Hetty flung her arms around her, her words a torrent of fears and regret.

Sarah and Ella watched from inside the car. It was odd, but Johab's mother seemed to be comforting Hetty. Although she appeared to be composed, Mrs. Bennett clung to Cyril's hand as though the loss of one little boy was all that she could bear.

Hetty motioned to the open window of the VW. These are my friends, Sarah and Ella. This is Soya, Johab's mother." Her voice was subdued now, hoarse from crying.

Johab's mother responded quietly. "Cyril explained what happened. Johab told me that he was meeting you at the camel market this morning. I was afraid for him . . . for all of you," she said quietly. "But that market is so busy. I thought that being in a crowd would be some kind of protection."

Sarah pushed open the door. The heat was becoming oppressive in the little car.

Johab's mother looked concerned, as though she had suddenly forgotten her manners, leaving her guests in the hot sun. "Come inside. I'll make some tea." She gestured for them to follow Cyril toward a small hut with a donkey in the yard.

Sarah gazed at this woman named Soya—the regal bearing, the self-control, the ability to subdue what must be incredible fear over the loss of her son and husband. Johab's mother reminded her of one of those ancient women on tomb *stelae* in the Museum. Women were always depicted as shorter than the king, sometimes only a smaller version of the king, but regal and correct, doing their duties as time and royal convention demanded. This time the duty was tea for the English visitors.

Johab's mother swung the door to the hut wide and ushered them inside as though this was a home in which she took pride. Two little girls were playing with a single doll on a mat. In the center of the room was a table with four mismatched chairs. She directed the women to the chairs and picked up a heavy, iron kettle, placing it on the grill.

The two little girls jumped up, excited to see company. "Miss Wenkle! Miss Wenkle!" Jasmine dashed over and crawled up on her lap. "Is it Christmas? Is it Christmas?"

Miss Wenkle smoothed the curls back from her face. "Not yet, Jasmine. Soon. It will be Christmas soon." Her voice broke. For this family, Christmas might be very far away. She motioned to her friends. "This is Miss Sarah and Miss Ella. They are visiting me from England. Remember? I brought you that doll from England."

Jasmine wiggled down from Miss Wenkle's lap, sped across the floor and grabbed her doll in one hand and Alice's arm in the other. Alice was shy. Strangers frightened her. "I have my doll and a new friend, Alice. She's only three. Cyril is her brother."

Hetty caught her breath. Cyril was an odd name for an Egyptian boy, but Alice was equally odd for a girl. This was just too much of a coincidence—Egyptian children with the same names as her uncle, Cyril, and his wife, Alice. She needed to . . .

Jasmine's childish voice cut through her thoughts. "Where is Johab? Why isn't he with you?"

No one answered. Johab's mother carefully measured a heaping spoon of loose tea into the simmering kettle. "Jasmine. Take Alice and go knock on Mr. Feisel's door. Ask him to come over here. You and Alice stay outside and play."

Hand in hand, the two little girls trotted out the door and across the alley. A large yellow cat that had been crouching by them on the mat, its eyes never leaving the new intruders, slunk after them. Cyril had not left the side of Johab's mother. He moved when she moved, almost as though he had become her shadow. Soya poured the tea into four slightly chipped cups and took the fourth chair.

"We will need the advice of Mr. Feisel. He was helping Johab with the . . . problem." She searched for the right word and repeated it firmly. ". . . the problem of where my husband has been taken. We need our neighbor's help."

The words were no sooner out of her mouth than a large man filled the entryway. "What has happened to Johab?" He spoke in Arabic, but Hetty understood.

Johab's mother switched to English and nodded toward the three women sitting at the table. "This is Miss Wenkle, a friend of our family. These are her friends. They met Johab and Cyril at the camel market this morning."

Her voice faltered. "Cyril told me that some men in a white car put something over Johab's mouth and locked him in the trunk of their car and . . . took him away." Her voice broke. "Cyril doesn't know which direction they went on the main road . . . He said he couldn't see over the people and camels."

Hetty interrupted. "I know about you, Mr. Feisel. Johab told me that you were helping him interpret the papyri from the amulet. He said you know the tombs in the Valley and you knew Mr. Carter."

Hetty's voice became business-like. "Johab was taken when he went to buy some *fittir*. We were sitting on the ground near the food booth. Cyril said that two men grabbed Johab. Their car was an old white Volvo with a big dent in the trunk. A car like that has recently been parked on the street outside my apartment for several days."

Her voice became agitated, her words less precise. "Sarah gave Cyril money to bribe the cook, but he said he didn't recognize the men—he just left his booth as they requested. They bribed him too." She paused and added, "Cyril got even."

Cyril nodded at the mention of his name. He had moved from the side of Johab's mother to stand at Hetty's knee. She seemed to enjoy stroking his hair.

Sarah and Ella stared at Mr. Feisel. If they had passed him on the street, they would have assumed he'd spent a lifetime in the desert. He sported a quarter inch of gray stubble on his cheeks. His eyes were so deeply set below his lined forehead that they were hard to see, much less read. Yet, he switched to English easily. He remained standing in the doorway, tall and awkward in the midst of these flower-clad women.

Mr. Feisel shifted his gaze from Hetty to Sarah. "You're the woman who sent the message to Mr. Parks—that friend of Johab's father?" His statement ended with a question.

"I did send the message, but I have no idea when it will reach him in the field." She patted the bag in her lap. "I copied all of Dr. Bennett's files from the storage room where the New Kingdom Project files are kept."

Mr. Feisel raised his eyebrows as Sarah explained. "I have a letter of introduction. Mr. El-Hasiim was out for the day; none of the other employees were suspicious. I was looking for information about the voyage to Punt—documented during Queen Hatshepsut's reign. Mr. Parks is trying to find that location, so we don't know exactly where he is."

Mr. Feisel moved over to the brazier and poured himself a cup of tea. He stood by the table, holding the cup in his hand, his eyes moving from one English woman to the other. "Johab trusted you," he announced brusquely. "He trusted all of us. We let him down or those men couldn't have taken him."

Three of the women nodded sadly, each feeling some measure of guilt that a young boy had been so easily removed from their care. Johab's mother stared into space, silent, almost as though she were not part of the conversation.

Mr. Feisel tapped his finger against the cup. "I have an idea. This Barzoni fellow could have any number of hideouts in Cairo, but Johab knows the city well. He'd probably hide him somewhere else."

He paused for a moment. "What Barzoni wants is information about a tomb. Johab and I think it is KV20, the first tomb that Hatshepsut carved into the side of the cliff for herself and her father."

"Johab was telling us what you thought just before he . . ." Hetty's voice stopped with a sob as she lifted Cyril onto her lap and held him too tightly.

"We thought that Johab's father wasn't giving Barzoni the information he wanted as long as his family was safe." Mr. Feisel looked grimly about the room. "Now that Barzoni has Johab, he has the trump card. Or, he probably thinks that he does. Johab is smart. He will pretend that he doesn't know anything."

Mr. Feisel looked directly at Hetty. "I hope he got rid of those translations of the hieroglyphs I made for him—and the photographs of the amulet. He intended to show them to you."

Hetty dug into her purse. "Johab handed these to me just before he went to buy the *fitiir*."

Mr. Feisel paced the small room, grinding one fist inside the other. "We need to move quickly. Barzoni now has the upper hand. He has the son. If the father knows that, he will talk and then. . . ." His voice trailed off, but the three English women stared somberly ahead. They could finish the sentence for him. If Barzoni got the information he wanted, there would be no need to keep the father or the son alive. Vultures in the desert could pick a body clean in hours. The Nile could swallow a body in seconds.

Only the face of Johab's mother was unchanged as she listened to Mr. Feisel. Mr. Feisel swung toward the group. "We need to take your car, Miss Wenkle. We can leave your friends at your apartment; they will create too much attention if they stay here."

"Cyril!" he barked. "Grab that cat and find a box for him." He frowned at Miss Wenkle. "Do you have a galabeya and sandals?" He raised his eyebrows and added. "She can't look like an English woman." Mr. Feisel glanced toward Sarah and Ella whose spines were stiffening against the backs of their chairs. They were women who did not like being ordered around.

Johab's mother would need them—that tall one who could get into the Museum storerooms might be valuable. His voice softened into a confidential tone as he leaned over toward them. "You need to stay in Miss Wenkle's house. You have a telephone?" Miss Wenkle nodded.

"If you have extra money, leave it here with Johab's mother. She can buy food here. You can get a taxi to check on her and the little girls. Tourists come and go by taxi all the time. I don't think that Barzoni will be looking for anyone else in the family."

He looked apologetically at Johab's mother. "I know that you would be more comfortable in your own home or with your sister, but Johab told me about his Uncle. I think he called him Tarek. He might be taking *baksheesh* from Barzoni." The Arabic word *baksheesh* rolled off his tongue with the rasp of a hissing snake.

"Mrs. Bennett and the girls will be fine here. Our neighbors know that things aren't right with this family. They probably don't know what, but they look after their neighbors."

He glanced at Johab's mother who had flushed with embarrassment that Tarek's dishonor had been revealed. "We need to take Jasmine's cat. I'm not sure why, but animals have good instincts. I can hear him howling outside. He won't like a box, but he'd be a terror loose in the car."

Johab's mother stood in the door of the hut, watching three English women in floral dresses, a tall, grizzled Egyptian, and a skinny boy with a yowling cat in a box heading out of sight down the alley.

The late afternoon sun gleamed down on the heads of Jasmine and Alice who were trying to anchor the doll on the donkey's back. Their laughter rang out, echoing against the tombs in the cemetery. It was a sound that can only exist when two children have found a very understanding donkey.

CHAPTER 45

Hast thou come to injure this child?
I will not let thee injure him.
Hast thou come to take him away?
I will not let thee take him away.

—Ancient Egyptian invocation against night demons

Johab's eyes popped open. It was night in the place where he lay, hogtied on a cold, stone floor. He couldn't see a thing, but he could remember: the pungent odor of a dirty rag clamped over his mouth and nose; the bumpy ride in the trunk of a car; and, being carried into this tomb.

It would *always* be night in this place. Only bats could find ways into these tombs once the entrance was sealed. Johab recalled his father telling him that the bat droppings were so thick in some tombs that workers had to wear handkerchiefs over their faces to prevent being overcome by centuries of bat dung.

He was numb and chilled to the bone. His arms had lost all feeling with his hands tied and useless behind his back. He stretched his feet, easing his stiff legs into a different position. They could still move, but something was puncturing his stomach. He turned sideways. The flashlight. It was the only clever thing he had done all day, rolling over to hide the flashlight when that man dropped it.

It had been when the car passed the far edge of Deir el-Bahari, but Johab had recognized the landmarks. Even while dangling upside down from that man's shoulder and keeping his eyes shut most of the time, Johab had his bearings.

Those two men had left him in KV20, Queen Hatshepsut's unfinished tomb. They had dumped him like a sack of garbage. The problem was that no trash collectors, no Copts, would be coming along to discover him here.

KV20 was a tomb of little interest to anyone. Johab's father told him that it had been stripped centuries before Napoleon's troops had arrived in the Valley of the Kings. In the early 1800s, the upper chambers had been explored as far along the passageway as possible, but debris from flooding had blocked further exploration.

When Howard Carter had checked out the tomb, coming down to the mouth of it from the top of the cliff, he had hired workers to clear away piles of rock and dirt that had filled the underground tunnels. By bringing in fresh oxygen with a primitive air pump, Mr. Carter had made the air breathable and found four passages leading to the rectangular burial chamber.

Johab remembered the sad expression on his father's face when he described what was found. Two yellow quartzite sarcophagi, the great stone coffin holders, and one matching Canopic box were all that remained. Through the years, tomb robbers had taken their toll on Hatshepsut's treasures.

Mr. Carter described how the once-magnificent funerary goods had been reduced to rubble, broken shards, fragments of stone vessels, and remains of burned wooden coffins—everything destroyed to peel away the overlays of gold, to gouge out precious stones.

Johab gulped. His throat was so dry. How long had he been asleep? It could have been minutes or maybe days. The darkness hung around him, thick and black.

As he inched forward, Johab's head touched something that rattled softly against the floor. The bowl of water, left so that he could drink from it like a "puppy." He moved carefully, feeling the rim of the bowl with his chin. He was not too proud to lap up water like a puppy. It was simply a skill he didn't have.

He dunked his mouth and nose into the bowl and slurped water—messy but effective. His tongue felt less like a thick leather slab.

"Anyone there?" He whispered. Silence answered.

He rolled onto his other side. One arm was regaining feeling. The one beneath his side felt like a lifeless log. The knots holding his hands were tight, stacked one on top of another.

Mummies must feel like this Johab thought. They would slowly lose sensation as the preservative natron coated their bodies. Then, they would lose all feeling as the strips of linen were bound, tighter and tighter. If the dead have any feeling.

Johab wiggled his nose. The high priests had not gotten to him yet. No hooks had gone up into his nostrils to extract his brain. His nose worked just fine. He could smell the sharp odor of bat poop.

Lying here thinking about mummies and bats wouldn't help. He had no idea how long he had been asleep in the tomb. The men might return at any time. They would make him talk.

He clenched his fists, tucking his fingers into his palms. What did that man say about "removing fingernails" as a way of torture? So far, being brave had meant dashing around Cairo disguised in a galabeya. Being brave had meant trying to get information from Hetty and Mr. Feisel without sharing too much with them. Now, here he was, trussed like a holiday turkey, unable to do anything but wiggle around on a stone floor and wait for those two men to return for his fingernails.

He would not wait helplessly. That's not what brave people did. They planned. They acted. He thought about Cyril. Even though his little friend had lost his major, Cyril was very smart.

By now, Hetty and Cyril would have told his mother that he had been kidnapped. They might have told Mr. Feisel. He just hoped they had not told the police. Alerting the police would mean one of two things: Barzoni would use his "connections" and the police would do nothing; or, Barzoni would take Johab and his father further underground. They would both disappear forever.

He could feel the hump of the flashlight against his leg. He needed to free his hands to use it. Getting light. That was the first order of business. What could be sharp enough to cut this rough, hemp rope binding his hands? He had seen plenty of movies in which the hero sawed ropes against slivers of glass and edges of knives. Glass and knives were in short supply inside this tomb chamber.

Johab pushed himself upright, pulled his knees up to his chest and pushed back. He would explore every inch of this room. He had seen the piles of debris when the men were looking for the missing flashlight. Who knows what might be in those piles of trash?

A tin can on top of a pile of rubble. Johab could feel the lid, still attached, and angled upright. Every mummy is entombed with Canopic jars, a jar for the liver, protected by the god Imsety, a jar for the lungs, protected by Hapi who resembled a baboon, and a jar for the stomach protected by Duamutef. The intestines got the best jar—protected by a hawk's head.

I have a tin can as a Canopic jar in my tomb. Johab smiled to himself. His father would have enjoyed his little joke. There was not even the whisper of a bat, hanging around the ceiling, so it had to remain his private joke.

Johab angled himself backward against the can, turning it awkwardly but carefully, trying to bury the can into the pile of dirt and rocks so that only the lid was exposed. He could feel the rust on the lid and was grateful to the tourist or worker who had left a part of his lunch behind long ago.

Johab offered a short prayer to the jackal-headed god Anubis who watched over the embalming rituals, thanking him for this tin can. A large Canopic jar would not have been useful. Johab scooted backward, inching his tied hands carefully toward the jagged lid. If the lid broke off, the can would be useless. He could feel the chain of knots with his fingers. The knot closest to his wrists was the firmest. Nicking his skin was a risk he would have to take.

It could have been minutes. It could have been an hour. In the dark, time doesn't move. Johab's wrists did. Back and forth, slowly and rhythmically, no sudden movements, no jerking when the edge of the lid slit his skin. He had to be in absolute control.

The rope was beginning to fray. The stinging on his wrist was followed by dampness, a stickiness coating the rope. Luckily, it was the back of his hand that he cut; the thinner skin inside his wrists was protected, bound one on top of the other.

The rope separated so suddenly that Johab jerked in surprise. He flexed his fingers, waiting for feeling to return to his hands and arms. Then, he stuffed the rope into the pocket of his shorts. It might come in handy. The knots of the rope, damp with his blood, would fit nicely as a gag into the big mouth of that man who had dumped him on the floor here. Johab squirmed with the delicious thought of revenge.

The ropes on his ankles unknotted easily. He groped for the flashlight. Revenge could wait. He had to get out of this tomb before the men returned. He flashed the light around the door of the chamber. The door had been recently installed, the wooden frame held tightly with large, metal bolts drilled into the stone wall. He aimed the beam at the top of the chamber. It was only a couple of feet higher than a man's head and appeared to be of solid stone. Piles of debris covered the floor, heaped as high as his knees in the corners of the chamber.

Crawling over to the biggest pile, Johab shone the light on stones, dirt, and an occasional shard of broken pottery. The light flickered so he turned it off. He needed to conserve the batteries in the flashlight. That meant he would have to sift through everything in the dark quickly. He picked up the bottle of water that had been left by the bowl and took a big drink. *What do you think about your little puppy now?*

Digging through piles of rubble was not as easy as he thought it would be. The soil and rocks were thickly packed. He remembered that Mr. Feisel said his digging caused arthritis. If Johab dug quickly with both hands, dust flew up in the air, causing spasms of coughing. He needed to protect his lungs. If he could get out of this chamber into the tunnel, he would have to go away from the strongly barred entrance to find an exit.

There were other ways into tombs. Mr. Feisel told him that some of the villagers were "more like moles than moles when it came to these old tombs." Generations of searching for ancient treasures brought knowledge that passed down through the families. Nature helped sometimes with floods that moved torrents of stone down the cliffs, trenching new routes to explore.

"Iron bars and doors won't keep robbers out," Johab's father had told him. "Mr. Carter gave the guards *baksheesh* to watch his tombs."

Johab would welcome a human mole. Perhaps one of the villagers might decide to explore the KV20 tomb today. Johab flashed the light around the room. Nothing but debris, four stone walls, and a ceiling. Nothing to explore. Nothing to find. Why would anyone bother with this old tomb? Yet, his father had been sure that KV20 held a secret, with its clues hidden in the back of an ancient amulet.

Johab gasped, startled by something he remembered. The tomb sketch on the papyrus showed a connecting tunnel. There was only a single corridor to the burial chamber on other drawings of KV20. *If such a tunnel existed, it had not been discovered. Or*—Johab flinched at the thought—*the tunnel would be so packed with rubble from flooding that it could never be found*. A blocked tunnel couldn't be cleared by a boy with no shovel and no army of workers to dig and carry rubble.

Johab returned to his pile of rubble. Staying busy helped him to focus on one thing—this pile of rocks and dirt. Not his mother. Not his father. Not Jasmine. His mother would take care of his sister, as well as Cyril and Alice.

A smooth, round object moved under his fingers. He probed further into the pile of debris. Something as sharp as a snake's fangs struck his finger. A cobra or a scorpion—these dry tombs attracted them. Johab eased his other hand around the flashlight, and, holding his breath, flipped on the light.

A shaft of splintered wood had pierced his finger. Bright blood dripped steadily downward onto one of the large stones. It reminded him of the story of Hathor going on a rampage. When the god Ra became angry with humans, Hathor took vengeance against them. She was so out of control that Ra distracted her by spreading blood-colored beer on the ground.

That was the sign to have a celebration with lots of beer drinking, his father had told him. It seemed to Johab that the ancient people used almost any excuse to have a celebration with lots of beer drinking.

The drips on the stone were not blood-colored beer; they were his blood. It glistened in the gleam of the flashlight on the head of a hammer with a broken wooden shaft. It had probably been discarded by one of the workers putting in the new door. Johab knew workers often tossed tools aside broken or not, intending to retrieve them later. That's why Johab's father always had a tool count at the end of each day in the field. He said "old habits die hard." Tools were needed for gardening and repairing houses.

Johab was grateful for "old habits." He picked up the broken hammer and hefted it in his hand. It was heavy. The bolts holding the door in place were large, but the stone holding them appeared to be unstable. That's why some Egyptologists thought that Queen Hatshepsut had not finished this tomb. The stone was too brittle for the large wall carvings to tell the story of her birth and powerful reign.

Johab anchored the flashlight between two stones with the beam on the lower bolt. The wooden handle was splintered halfway down. Johab thumped the end on the floor, knocking off vicious splinters. Then he turned toward his work.

The noise ricocheted against the walls. If a human mole from a nearby village were near, he would surely hear this noise. If Barzoni's men were on their way back, they would hear it as well.

Johab had no sense of how many hours had passed since they had left him in the dark chamber, but he knew he was working against time.

One wrist was oozing blood from being cut by the can lid; one finger continued to drip blood, but more slowly. In the past, either one of these wounds would have sent him howling to his mother for a bandage and comfort. No one was here to offer antiseptics or soothing words.

Bleeding in this tomb was a wonder in itself, something for which to be very grateful, thought Johab. Most of the inhabitants of tombs were long past the stage of bleeding. He began to think methodically about the funeral rituals of the ancient Egyptians as he pounded steadily on the lower bolt. Thinking about the purpose for this tomb kept him focused. Remembering his family and friends was too painful.

His father had often reminded him that these tombs were not really graves, not in the sense of modern graves. These were houses for eternity—death was just the gateway to eternity.

The washing and purification of the body, the removal of the brain, and packing of the skull with spices and cloth and mud from the Nile were all part of a ritual to prepare the royal corpse for eternity.

The mummy's tongue was sometimes coated with gold. Johab moved his tongue around inside of his mouth. It still felt swollen from the gag. He needed to hammer harder and think faster—and not about the face of his mother when he and Cyril left that morning for the camel market.

He remembered the large sarcophagus at the Museum that had been found in this very tomb. If it had been used for Queen Hatshepsut, she would have been placed in one gold coffin and that coffin placed in another—like those little wooden Russian dolls that open to reveal another doll inside.

He hoped that she was somewhere safe, inside a gold- plated coffin. The ancient kings and queens were never intended to be seen by anyone after death—not by tourists filing by their unwrapped, blackened bodies, seeing their jaws in perpetual smiles. Johab whacked the bolt harder and remembered his father's descriptions of the ancient ceremony.

The coffin would be sailed across the Nile to the western shore. Perhaps the entire city would have followed, weeping for the loss of the king or queen or other royals. If the people couldn't produce enough tears, professional mourners would be hired to wail with deafening effects. Priests were paid and relatives were sworn to continue remembering the king.

Johab shrugged. It didn't happen. The next king to come along might observe the rituals for a father or mother or grandparents. Once the bloodline was gone, the new ruler often dumped out coffins to make room for *his* sarcophagus. The successors to Queen Hatshepsut did much worse—they chiseled her name off monuments, chipped her figure off *stelae.* They did not name her in the *List of Kings.* That was the worst insult.

Angered by the mistreatment of his favorite ancient queen, Johab popped the head of the hammer harder against the bolt. She showed them. She built the most beautiful temple of all—some called it one of the greatest architectural structures in the world.

Johab remembered that last day with his father when he described how the temple blends into the natural world, into the side of the cliff.

A fierce sense of regret brought tears to Johab's eyes. He should have paid attention. He whacked the bolt in utter frustration. The stone shattered and the bolt fell away. Johab grabbed the bottle of water, the flashlight, and wiggled through an impossibly small space where the bottom of the door hung at a welcoming angle towards a tunnel that might lead to freedom or to nowhere.

CHAPTER 46

Think where man's glory most begins and ends,
And say my glory was I had such friends.

—Yeats

The strange quintet rounded the corner in the City of the Dead and headed toward the VW. Hetty, Sarah, Ella and Cyril seemed lost in their own thoughts. Mr. Feisel mumbled under his breath. Bastet hissed and clawed at the cardboard box.

Mr. Feisel twisted the handle at the front of the VW and, if by magic, produced a shovel, a hammer, a flashlight, and a coil of rope from beneath the folds of his galabeya. The three women and Cyril nodded approvingly. Mr. Feisel seemed prepared for almost anything. Scooting the front seat back as far as it would go, he folded himself into the driver's seat. "I'll drive," he announced.

Hetty's chin jutted out a bit, but she held the other front seat back so that Sarah, Ella, and Cyril could arrange themselves in the back seat. Hetty picked up the box with Bastet and positioned the angry cat on her lap, relieved that cardboard kept them apart.

Cyril chose Miss Ella's lap as the best option. Miss Ella pulled him against her, folding her arms around him. He was secure. It was a good choice.

Mr. Feisel's comments were terse and directed to Sarah and Ella. "We're going to the Valley. That's all you need to know. If Barzoni's men should try to locate Miss Wenkle, they'll only find you at her apartment. The less you know, the better off you will be. If we have not contacted you or returned in a couple of days, you will have to call the police." He snorted derisively. "That will be the last resort—if it comes to that, go up the ladder to the top man."

He glanced at Sarah in the rearview mirror. "A better idea might be to go to the American and the British Embassies. Johab holds American citizenship. I suggest the British Embassy, since you are a British citizen." He glanced over at Miss Wenkle who shuddered every time he shifted gears. "I'm hopeful that Mr. Parks will get the message and come immediately."

Sarah interrupted. "He'll come the minute he gets my letter; he may already be on his way. He and John Bennett are best friends. Johab is his godson. He left on the field expedition just a couple of weeks before Ella and I came to Cairo for a vacation. He wanted me to check out some information for him at the Museum. That's why I had a letter of introduction and was able to copy these files in my bag." She patted her large purse.

She caught Mr. Feisel's eye in the mirror. "If you think that I shouldn't be carrying these files around, you can be assured that I don't have any information that Mr. El-Hasiim can't get. He's probably given all of John Bennett's papers to Mr. Barzoni." She dropped her eyes and muttered. "Maybe I will see something that they didn't."

Following Hetty's directions, Mr. Feisel wheeled the VW against the curb in front of her apartment. Hetty hopped out. "Mr. Feisel, you and Cyril come inside with us. I want to change clothes. "We'll need to take some food and water. Cyril hasn't eaten since the camel market."

A gloomy look passed over Cyril's face. If he hadn't been so greedy, he would have been with Johab at the food stand. He could have fought those men. Now, it might be too late.

A pair of arms reached around him and swung him up. Miss Ella was smiling into his face. She was saying something in English that he didn't understand, but he understood the smile and the hug. He had experienced more smiles and hugs since coming to live with Johab's family than he could remember since his father had died.

His aunt didn't hug. Since Mustafa had come to live with them, she no longer smiled.

The five of them took the stairs, avoiding the tiny, ill-tempered elevator. Both Cyril and Mr. Feisel appeared uneasy. Apartments were not familiar living quarters.

Cyril moved cautiously around the living room, fingering the soft fabric of the sofa and chairs, running his hand along the glass top of the table. It was the loveliest room he could imagine. He trailed Miss Ella into the kitchen where Miss Sarah was slicing a loaf of bread and slathering it with butter and jam.

The wonders of a modern kitchen—he had seen pictures of them in those magazines his aunt sometimes read, but here was a stove and an icebox, white and shiny. When the door of the icebox swung open, Cyril's face was immediately wedged in the door. Just breathing the cold air was a rare experience.

Ella watched him in amazement. This boy appeared to be memorizing every item in the apartment, his fingers dancing lightly over surfaces. He returned to Hetty's photographs on the entry hall table and touched some of them.

There were no framed photographs in his aunt's house. One photograph was of Johab's family, the same picture that his Aunt Rayya had taken to the police station. This next one of a man in a military uniform and a smiling woman beside him looked very familiar. He knew this photograph. He had seen it somewhere before. He reached out to touch it when Mr. Feisel barked. "Time's wasting. We need to be on our way."

As though on command, Miss Hetty appeared wearing a long galabeya, her high heels replaced by thick leather sandals. Cyril stared. Her face had turned a peculiar shade of reddish brown.

"Make-up," she pointed to her cheeks. "I thought it would be a good disguise."

Cyril didn't think so. Her bright blue eyes were even bluer against her darkened skin—he didn't remember ever seeing anyone that color, but perhaps it was some kind of disguise.

Mr. Feisel simply stared at her and grunted. He gathered up the sacks that Sarah and Ella had prepared and headed for the door. Cyril and Hetty followed. Within minutes they were on a main road with Mr. Feisel driving, Hetty beside him, and Cyril in the back seat with his nose pressed against the side window watching everything from a different perspective. Bastet growled softly beside him in his cardboard cage.

For several miles, Mr. Feisel concentrated on shifting gears, moving from lane to lane, pushing the sturdy little car until it reached its speed limit. "Not much horsepower," were the first words he had uttered since they had left the apartment.

"It suits me just fine," retorted Hetty. "It's very reliable." She turned sideways in her seat and stared at Mr. Feisel. He had a classic Bedouin profile, a slightly aquiline nose, a firm chin, a pencil-thin mustache, and eyes so deeply set that they must have been designed purposefully for protection against the desert sun.

Cyril stayed pressed to the glass of the back window, unmoving as though he had become a little bug caught against the glass. Hetty broke the silence, "Where are we going, Mr. Feisel?" He didn't respond immediately, so Hetty filled the gap. "I need to know, Mr. Feisel. I'm part of this . . . this expedition." That was the best descriptor she could produce for this wild outing.

"I'm not trying to be difficult, Miss Wenkle. I haven't driven in years, and never have driven this kind of car. I have the gears right now. I had to concentrate until I got the feel of it." He glanced toward her. The dark makeup was slightly streaked and a peculiar contrast with her blond hair and blue eyes. He pulled a large handkerchief from his galabeya and handed it to her. "I can see you better without that *stuff* on your face." She nodded and applied the cloth, her pale skin glowing now with just a fine glaze of bronze.

Much nicer, thought Mr. Feisel, but he didn't say so. Some Egyptian men thought that women from other countries, those traveling without men, were fair game. Mr. Feisel was from the old school. Respect was due any person unless that person proved undeserving.

Miss Wenkle was clearly a person who was owed respect. She was the first person that Johab had asked to help him find his father. She had risked her own life when Barzoni pushed her down the stairs, and she continued to help Johab. Johab's faith in her was well placed. And, without the odd brown make-up and some decent shoes, she was a very attractive woman.

Mr. Feisel gripped the wheel. Stupid thoughts. He needed to be about the business of finding Johab. "Here's what I think. You may have other ideas, but this is my plan." Mr. Feisel announced.

"We are heading toward the Valley of the Kings with a stop in a small village near Deir el-Bahari. I want to talk to some of the people in that village. They know everything that goes on around the tombs. If strange cars or people they don't recognize have been showing up at the tombs after hours, they might have seen them."

He paused. "It seems unlikely that Barzoni would have taken Johab to a tomb. It is more likely that he has a hideout somewhere near one of the villages close to the Valley. He may have Johab and his father in the same hideout."

"I think that's unlikely." Miss Wenkle's voice countered his statement. He glanced at her quizzically. "Mr. Barzoni is clever. He likes playing games with people. He wants information that he thinks both Johab and his father have. Johab's father has obviously remained silent."

She paused, not daring to let her thoughts carry her down that path. "Otherwise, Mr. Barzoni would not have continued to pester me for information about where Johab and his family might be hiding. Mr. Barzoni was getting desperate. For a well-known and influential man, he has taken some very large risks lately."

Mr. Feisel nodded. Pushing an English woman down a flight of stairs during broad daylight in a place where anyone might have seen him was the act of an overwrought man.

"I think that Barzoni will keep Johab and his father apart and use whatever psychological games he can devise to get both of them to talk." She paused. "I'm not sure how he will convince Johab's father that he is holding Johab. Johab was wearing native clothes, the ones he bought after his father was kidnapped. He doesn't wear a watch. I don't know what Barzoni could take to convince John that he is holding his son."

The frisson of fear shook her so badly that she clutched the edges of the seat. There were pieces of a child that were identifiable by a parent. His little fingers. His stubby toes. An ear. Oh, God, not that. She closed her eyes and began praying to the God of the Anglican Church. She was not a faithful church member, but she was a believer, especially during a crisis.

Mr. Feisel sensed her fear, saw her eyes close and her lips moving silently. Whatever gods she might be praying to might not be the ones to help Johab. It was Hathor, the favorite goddess of Queen Hatshepsut, who might help them now. Hatshepsut built a temple for Hathor. A carving on the wall showed Hatshepsut being suckled by the cow-goddess Hathor.

Maybe the old gods and goddesses were all gone. They probably left when the ancient kingdoms of Egypt fell to that Greek, Alexander. He had brought Roman gods and goddesses to Egypt. The Egyptian gods wouldn't like their company.

Still, it was worth a try. He couldn't close his eyes and drive, but he could mutter a prayer to Hathor. Mr. Feisel thought about a phrase that he had seen on tombs of children that said "beloved of father and mother." That was Johab. No child that age would be so well-schooled in his father's work unless he and his father had an inseparable bond of friendship, beyond the blood tie of a father and son.

Mr. Feisel thought back to his own childhood. He was one of the lucky ones too. His father had not been wealthy, just hard-working, kind, and honest—and burning with the desire to know more about the history of his country. He had learned English and taught his son. He had insured that his son would travel with the clever Howard Carter, a man who seemed to have an uncanny sense of finding his way around the old tombs.

Mr. Feisel's father had given him an unimaginable gift—the day he would remember above all others when he looked into King

Tutankhamen's final resting place. Few people ever experience stepping back in time over three thousand years, into undisturbed time with the sacred rituals preserved for eternity.

He remembered the shouts, the hands clasped in wonder, and then the absolute silence that fell, as though the entire desert had been struck dumb by having to give up its treasure of King Tutankhamen.

Mr. Feisel understood the bond between Johab and his father—it was the same bond he shared with his own father. He would also ask the Goddess Hathor for a blessing for Johab's mother. He recalled how her face had become mask-like with fear every time Johab left with his cart of fulbeans and how her face lit up with relief when he returned.

Mr. Feisel began his silent prayer, "Oh Hathor, watch over this child, Johab, the son beloved by father and mother. See that . . ."

"I need to pee" piped the voice from the back seat. Mr. Feisel's eloquent prayer for Johab was stopped mid-stream so to speak.

He swung the car over to the roadside; Miss Wenkle opened her door for Cyril to climb out. Cyril didn't stand on ceremony. He was a child of the streets and aimed at the nearest scrawny weed.

"Good heavens!" Miss Wenkle's outburst startled Mr. Feisel. "That child isn't wearing any shoes."

"I doubt that he's worn any shoes for years," responded Mr. Feisel. "That man living with Cyril's aunt wanted him to look like a beggar. Beggar children in Cairo rarely wear shoes."

Cyril hopped back into the car. Miss Wenkle passed him the bag of jelly and butter sandwiches. Within minutes, he had eaten the entire bag and was snoring softly in the backseat.

CHAPTER 47

"Mr. Feisel?" Miss Wenkle's voice was soft, taking care not to wake Cyril. "What do you know about Cyril?" She added, "This isn't just idle curiosity. I think my uncle, who is dead now, had some connection to his family. My Uncle Cyril and his wife lived in Cairo. Johab told me that he saved Cyril and his sister from a bad man, but that's all I know about him. He's such a loveable little boy."

"Cyril is an enigma," responded Mr. Feisel. "He's been living with a woman he said is the widow of his uncle—she's not a blood relative. Apparently, his mother died when Alice was born. Shortly after that, both his father and his uncle died of typhoid. I guess the aunt felt obligated to take the children. Cyril said they had no other relatives. Living with her seemed to be tolerable until this man called Mustafa moved in." Mr. Feisel's voice grew harsh.

"He put that child on the street to beg, dressed him in rags, and beat him when he didn't bring home enough money. He apparently took better care of the little girl. He had plans for her too." His voice was harsh with disgust. "Johab's mother told me that when she unwrapped the child from her blanket, Alice had rouge smeared on her cheeks and was wearing a dress that a harlot might wear. This Mustafa is a twisted man—I'd like to put a few more kinks in him."

Mr. Feisel laughed under his breath. "Johab told me that Cyril bit Mustafa's thumb when he tried to make him swallow a mouse. That's when he ran away. The next night, Johab and Cyril took Alice from the house."

When he mentioned "swallowing a mouse," Miss Wenkle gasped aloud, then appeared to be rooted to the passenger seat. Perhaps he shouldn't tell her about the mummified children with mice in their gullets.

He glanced in the rearview mirror at Cyril, propped against the box holding Bastet, fast asleep. "Rescuing Alice must have been a frightening experience for both of the boys. Johab told me that Mustafa was just down the street at a bar, sporting a large bandage on his hand at the very minute they were sneaking away with Alice."

"That child, Miss Wenkle," Mr. Feisel glanced again toward the back seat, "is a rare boy. He has been living a life that neither you nor I could imagine—abject poverty, physical and mental abuse, and not one word of affection from his aunt."

He paused, staring at the road straight ahead. "Most children in such circumstances either take out their frustration on those around them—they turn into bullies or they become withdrawn, secretive, showing their anger in ways that won't be easily discovered."

He glanced at the foreign woman staring intently at him and felt compelled to share his thoughts. "Cyril is different. He is a most optimistic little boy. I think that he has very high intelligence. He is illiterate, but Johab is teaching him to read. His memory is quite incredible. He has a loving spirit." Mr. Feisel paused. "Both these boys do—they risked their lives to take Alice away that night." He turned toward Miss Wenkle. "You might have wondered why I brought Cyril on what might be a dangerous undertaking." She nodded.

"Cyril will be a good disguise for me—a boy and his uncle or grandfather just wandering around these old ruins. Also, Cyril is very insightful. He may see things that we don't notice. He can listen without being observed. No one pays much attention to small boys. And, he is very brave. Hummph." Mr. Feisel's grunt might have disguised the emotion he was feeling had not Miss Wenkle felt the same reaction.

"As for the cat." Mr. Feisel's brow furrowed. "That was just a last-minute thought. That old tomcat watches after Jasmine and Alice—he howls loudly enough to wake the dead when they wander out of the yard. I thought he might have some kind of instinct for locating Johab."

He shook his head. "Stupid idea probably, but we don't have much to go on—just some old papyri, a few notes that Johab's father made, a little boy, and a very angry cat."

Bastet stretched inside the box, twitching his tail. He had initially produced magnificent howls when Cyril stuck him into the cardboard box—sharp yowls, followed by hissing and showing of the teeth. Those noises usually got results. The woman would come outside and get the two little girls, his special charges, when they wandered too far.

Bastet's solitary life had come to an abrupt halt when Jasmine clutched him against her and rubbed his ears. He didn't remember ever allowing a human to rub his ears. But then, come to think of it, none had ever offered. Then the new little girl came. She picked him up roughly, but she was very young. She would learn. Why in the world had that little boy stuffed him in a cardboard box? The piece of jelly sandwich he poked through the lid was not an adequate peace offering. Bastet sat, agitated by the vibrations of the car, his tail flashing back and forth, waiting, just waiting.

Unlike Bastet, who refused to close his eyes, Miss Wenkle, lulled by the heat and road noise, drifted into a troubled sleep. When she woke, the world around them had turned dark. Part of a silver moon shone through a wafer of cloud. Mr. Feisel had located the lights, and they were moving along the highway in the darkness with only faint beams to show the way.

"You've been asleep for hours," Mr. Feisel announced. "Cyril is awake and hungry again. We're near the ferry. They don't like taking anyone over at night, but if you have *baksheesh*, they'll do it. We need to get to the village tonight. The people I know there might talk to us at night, but they won't if they think they might be seen."

Miss Wenkle dug into her purse and produced a wad of money. Mr. Feisel plucked several bills out of her hand. "Keep the rest. We may need it. We're going to avoid the hotels—too many people with questions there. I know a little place where we can get gas amd something to drink. It has a bathroom."

Mr. Feisel whipped the car off the main road, down a bumpy side road, and pulled up to a small square building. A couple of men were smoking on the front steps.

Mr. Feisel unfurled himself gradually, the arthritis in his knees complaining about every minute that he had spent in the cramped space behind the driver's wheel in this toy car. "Keep your hood up and your face down," he said softly. "Watch your feet and walk behind me. This isn't England."

Miffed, Miss Wenkle followed him demurely. Cyril took her hand reassuringly. They had been speaking English, but occasionally he knew a word. He also knew that Miss Hetty did not like Mr. Feisel's authoritative tone but was willing to tolerate it, for now.

Cyril pointed toward the bathroom and stood guard in front of the door. Miss Hetty emerged minutes later with a shocked expression on her face. The bathroom wasn't white and shiny like the one in her house that Cyril didn't dare use.

Mr. Feisel handed her a bottle of water. "I don't think I can eat or drink again for days." She was pale under the sheen of remaining makeup. "You should just see the state of that bathroom."

"A bathroom is a luxury out here. Cleaning them is the last of anyone's concern. Having enough to eat is," Mr. Feisel said in a matter-of-fact way, but Miss Wenkle felt his unspoken reprimand sorely.

He must think that she was just one of those pampered English women who visit the ancient monuments with their guide books and retreat to a hotel when the sun reaches its peak. Perhaps she was, but she was someone else as well. She worked hard. She was skilled in her field. She supported herself. She had never needed a man to support her. Taking orders from Mr. Feisel was a trial, but she would endure it if it meant finding Johab.

Within minutes, they were back in the car, charging down a bumpy road toward a ferry. "Stay in the car," Mr. Feisel barked, as he headed toward a man standing near a metal structure. Miss Wenkle could see hands flying in the air, gestures, heads shaking, and, finally, a swift touching of palms.

Without a word, Mr. Feisel ground the gears, pulled around to the side of the ferry, and inched the car onto the large ramp.

Wide-awake in the back seat, Cyril looked out with eyes big as saucers. "On water, Miss Hetty. In car on water." Miss Wenkle turned toward Cyril and in a mixture of English and Arabic tried to explain the dynamics of a ferry system. Mr. Feisel controlled the twitch of a smile. This woman did know a few things—who would have expected a woman to know anything about mechanical devices? Her Arabic was in a sad state. He'd work on that with her. He could do that for her.

When they reached the west bank of the Nile and rattled off the ramp, Mr. Feisel turned the car away from the main road toward the ruins near Deir el-Bahari and took a road that seemed no more than a goat path. It was rocky and angled upwards in places.

Miss Wenkle feared for the underside of her VW, but remained silent. Finding Johab was the important thing. Cars could be replaced. Boys could not.

Within half an hour, the car lights picked up a cluster of mud brick houses with walled enclosures. Mr. Feisel turned off the lights. "You stay in the car, Miss Wenkle. If anyone asks, I'm saying that you are my . . . uh . . . my sister. Keep your hood up and your face down. If anyone taps on the window, don't look up. Cyril, come with me."

Miss Wenkle stared at the retreating figures of Mr. Feisel and Cyril. Cyril had moved closer to Mr. Feisel. He appeared to be wrapped inside of Mr. Feisel's robe. That image reminded her of something. Yes. The statue of Queen Hatshepsut's daughter, Nefertere, and her royal steward Senenmut. Those statues of Senenmut with the Queen's daughter puzzled the Egyptologists.

Senenmut might have been the tutor of Nefertere and had the statues carved to show his great love for the daughter of a queen.

Miss Wenkle thought differently. To her, they were statues of a man claiming his daughter, wrapping his arms in stone around her so that the two of them would be inseparable for all to see. He couldn't claim his daughter, because Thutmose II was put forth as her father. The bloodlines of kings must be maintained. Bloodlines ended. Stone statues lasted forever. Senenmut, Hatshepsut's architect, would know that.

Two men exited a hut holding a lantern high, approaching Mr. Feisel and Cyril. It was stifling inside the car. Hetty rolled down the window. The sound of men's voices echoed in the night. They disappeared into the side of a wall, and there was nothing to be heard but the sound of Bastet clawing steadily at the cardboard box.

CHAPTER 48

The rabbit-hole went straight on like a tunnel for some way, and then dipped suddenly down, so suddenly that Alice had not a moment to think about stopping herself before she found herself falling down a very deep well.

—Lewis Carroll

Once he crawled through the space at the bottom of the dangling door, Johab stood inside a dark tunnel that might go somewhere or nowhere. If the men had dumped him in KV20, he was in the tomb built for Queen Hatshepsut, but never used for her burial. The sketch of the tomb that Hetty had brought him showed that the first chamber was about sixty meters from the entrance.

When the men carried him into the tomb, he had been partially drugged, bound, and upside down. He might be anywhere in the tomb. Considering the fact that the new door must have been added to the first available chamber as a small storage room, sixty meters was a good guess.

Johab had no idea when the men would come for him, but he was sure that they would return. They complained that Barzoni had made them walk too far to hide his trophy in an out-of-the-way tomb. They would be furious to know that their trophy had sprouted wings and flown the coop. Johab shivered. He remembered the kidnapper's comments about removing fingernails. *That man must not find him.*

Johab stood quietly, trying to suck enough of the stale, damp air into his lungs to last as he went further down into the tomb. He dared not head back toward the main entrance. Barzoni would probably have a guard nearby. Going deeper into the tomb was the only way to proceed. Open space gaped ahead of his flashlight beam with no light at the end of that black tunnel.

Think like an explorer. Johab took slow, calming breaths. He would mark his route with long strides, estimating the meters as he went. He and Mr. Feisel had decided that each of the small ticks on the sketch of the tomb must stand for a distance of ten meters—another trick to confuse who discovered anyone discovering the map in the amulet.

If their guess about the distance was correct, he should stop when he reached the length of an American football field, just over one hundred meters. That would be the place where the old papyrus sheet from the pouch showed another tunnel, one that was not on any other known map of this tomb.

He flashed his light ahead. Except for an occasional heap of gravel, the channel was clear and sloped gently downward. He paused and listened. These tombs made perfect hideouts for bandits. Carved high up on the sides of the cliffs, the tomb entrances provided a perfect vantage point to look down the valley for anyone approaching. In the desert winds, the tomb chambers were more secure than tents.

Johab suddenly felt the chill of the underground space and clutched his robe around him. Furry rodents such as moles were designed to tunnel underground. Humans were not. Johab felt claustrophobic, as though the walls were closing in upon him, becoming narrower as he walked. But he knew that they couldn't be narrowing.

These walls had to be tall enough and wide enough for workers to carry that large stone sarcophagus into the burial chambers where the queen would rest inside her gilt coffin.

Johab shook his head as though to clear it of irrational thoughts. Hunger was making him woozy. He knew that these tunnels were dug as paths to the lower chambers where the queen's treasures and the greatest treasure of all—Queen Hatshepsut—would rest.

His sandals skidded in the gravel as the tunnel curved gradually down. He should be at the peak of the bend where the old map showed a line leading down. That could be a shaft. Or it might have some other meaning. It occurred to him that the information on the papyrus might just be an ancient joke.

Johab stopped and listened to absolute silence. No sound at all was frightening, but he was almost there. If he had counted his steps correctly, he should have traveled far enough to be near the shaft or tunnel—if one really existed. The air was so stale at this level that Johab poured a little of his precious water onto the neck of his robe and pulled it up over his mouth and nose. Taking in air through damp cloth made breathing tolerable.

He flashed his light along the tunnel walls ahead of him, left and then right. There, not two feet off the ground, on the lower part of one of the walls was an unusual shape, not round like a normal entrance to a shaft, but jagged and low, as though the stone had been accidentally chipped.

Johab dropped to his knees, holding the flashlight beam close. He could see the chisel marks. Nothing distinguished them from the other hacked marks on the stones, except that these were angled to make the rock appear fragmented. There were dozens of tiny lines, not made by any natural force, but splayed out like the fronds of a palm tree by a workman's chisel.

Odd. The pattern was odd. When he was standing, it appeared as though the edge of the stone had simply broken away, not fitting tightly against the adjacent stone, like the rest of the walls.

Down here, on his knees, he could see the pattern. He knew exactly what it was: the carving of a branch from an incense tree from the land of Punt. He had seen these carvings many times on the walls of her temple. They were Queen Hatshepsut's favorite plants. She had imported the trees from Punt for their rare perfume, roots and all, to grow in Egypt.

Johab flashed his light along the wall. *Was this a sign left by Senenmut to mark another entrance or just the work of an ancient carver looking for a bare spot on which to practice his art?*

These old tombs were filled with graffiti, both ancient and modern. Johab remembered seeing a wall in a tomb on which someone had painted the top half of a man's face, his eyes tiny gouges, and his large nose hanging over a fence. The word above him was "Kilroy."

His father had tried to explain the "Kilroy was here" mania that swept America. Johab couldn't see the humor. Neither could his father. His father told him that people like the Kilroy painter really didn't do much damage to tombs—"not like that Italian, Belzoni, who went after tombs with a battering ram."

His father had nothing good to say about Belzoni, the Italian circus performer who landed in Egypt in the Nineteenth Century and spent years breaking into tombs. "I don't fault him for being a treasure hunter, Johab. There were lots of those around in his day— just as there are today. He did too much damage. He couldn't leave his circus mentality behind. He wanted to be famous. He wanted to be rich. He did so much harm to the old sites."

Johab remembered his father and Mr. Parks standing with him at a huge statue in the British Museum. "It's Memnon's head. Belzoni sent it over here, but the Museum didn't put his name down as the donor. Belzoni was an embarrassment to museums."

Belzoni—Barzoni. Now, Johab knew why Barzoni's name had seemed familiar. Maybe they were cousins, the same family tree or something.

Or nothing. *That's what he would be if he didn't pay attention to the business of escaping.* He smacked his head using the hand with the injured finger and gasped with pain. Staying focused meant staying alive. He traced the odd carving on the stone one more time. He might return to take another look at it. First, he must reach the end of the tomb and explore the burial chambers for another way out. Robbers might have found a more direct way to the treasures in the burial chambers.

He should mark this place on the wall so he could find it if he returned. Graffiti. That would be the way—but graffiti in the spirit of this tomb. Hatshepsut's beloved Hathor. Johab groped in his pocket for the pencil stub, and on the opposite wall of the tunnel carefully drew a large circle for Hathor's solar disk with the cow's horns supporting the circle. No one but he would pay any attention to those marks if he had to find this part of the tunnel quickly.

The tunnel curved gradually. Johab aimed his flashlight into the large chamber before him. Pillars stood at each end of it. He could see the softer shale where parts of the wall had collapsed. Flooding from somewhere higher in the cliffs had sent piles of dirt and gravel into the tomb.

Now, Johab couldn't restrain violent coughs as clouds of dust billowed with every step. This chamber was bat heaven. That was a good sign. Bats came and went. They left the tomb at dusk to swarm through the skies for their dinner and returned to hang from the ceilings to digest their food. At least that's what Johab thought. Mohammed said that bats left to suck the blood of humans and turn them into vampires. Vampires or not; if the bats found a place to get out, maybe he could find it.

Johab moved into the first of three offset chambers. Nothing there, just centuries of rubble. He flashed his light around the second chamber—more bats. He had just moved toward the third and smallest chamber, when he froze.

He flipped off his flashlight and crouched on the steps separating the burial rooms. The tunnel made a perfect sound chamber. The voices echoed as though from some distance, but the words were clear.

"That brat is somewhere down here. He's not in the tunnel. It's not wide enough to hide. The boss is going to skin us alive if we've lost that kid." Johab shivered as he recognized the voice of the burly man.

"We're supposed to bring him a souvenir of the kid—something his father will recognize as belonging to the boy. He told us to feed that little beggar, to untie him and let him stretch his arms and legs, and tie him up again."

The voice of the second man was louder. They must be getting closer to the burial chamber. Johab couldn't move. He couldn't think. He could only press himself harder against the wall as though disappearing into stone was his only option.

"That kid didn't have anything on him that his father would recognize. He's wearing an old galabeya and cheap sandals. Those weren't the kind of clothes he was wearing when we broke into the house that night." The voices were closer. Johab could hear footsteps and see an occasional flash of light.

"I guess the souvenir will have to be a finger or an ear. That's the kind of souvenir that his father will recognize—-that should make him talk." The man who had seemed fixated on removing fingernails had moved on to something more substantial.

Johab reached up and felt his ears. They stuck out slightly from his head, not nice and flat like Mohammed's. They were just like his father's ears. "We can pick up radar signals with these ears, like bats," his father had laughed when Johab complained that his ears stuck out.

Now, Johab felt very fond of his ears. He'd like to keep them and his fingers. He wanted to scream out, "You can take my shorts. Under my galabaya. Dad will recognize my shorts!" He remained absolutely silent.

Fits of coughing seized both of the men. They must be stirring up more of the bat droppings and rubble. One of them sputtered out: "When I get my hands on that kid, I will take more than a finger or an ear."

Think, Johab, think. Staying alert, focusing on something beyond the terror of the moment—that would be the only way to survive. He thought of the Hardy boys. *They never lose their nerve, because they are hardy.* Two beams of light flashed around the large burial chamber. If the men proceeded logically, they would enter the first offset chamber before they made it into the large outer chamber.

Johab crouched, ready to spring. The minute they entered the small chamber, he would move, swiftly as the wind, softly as a shadow, into the large burial chamber, avoiding the pillars, and head toward the chamber entrance—all of this without turning on his flashlight, tripping on debris, or running into a wall. Having bats' ears would help.

Just as he had hoped, the two men headed, side by side, toward the first chamber on their right. "Let's go inside and check those piles of rubble. That little pest found a hammer in the last place we left him. Who knows what else he has uncovered."

They disappeared into the chamber, their flashlights reflecting only through the open door. It was enough light. The largest pillar was outlined on one side by a faint shine. Johab knew that a diagonal path across the chamber would be the quickest way to the door. Inching his way around the walls of the tomb might be less risky, because he could feel his way. The diagonal path would be in utter darkness.

He chose darkness. With his hands thrust in front of him, he put on a burst of speed, heading for where he thought the opening would be. The frame of the burial chamber's opening scraped his side. He bent over with pain, then plastered his body against the tunnel, just on the other side of the opening.

He would have to travel back along the tunnel until he reached the first bend. There was no other place to go with these men in the tunnel ahead of him. That image of the carving of the incense tree from Punt kept popping into his mind. It was on the wall, just above the floor of the tunnel, exactly the spot where the last tick had been placed on the map next to an odd line leading downward. *It must mean something.*

A shout went up from inside one of the small chambers. "He's been here. The little brat left his bottle of water. He's somewhere in here," the voice boomed triumphantly.

The hunt was on. Johab had to move quickly, but in the dark. He trailed his hand alongside the cool wall of the limestone tunnel, taking big strides, counting the meters as he went. It should be forty to fifty meters from the entrance to the burial chambers. Now, he must take a chance with his flashlight. He had to find the drawing he had made of Hathor's solar disk and horns on the opposite side of the tunnel. That would be the only way to locate that odd-shaped stone with the carving.

Calculating that he was about forty meters from the burial chambers, Johab could hear voices behind him, growing louder. He put the flashlight under his galabeya and flipped on the light. It shone, pale and diffused through the fabric of the robe, virtually worthless for making out the image scratched in stone with his pencil. The carving of the incense tree branch, designed to look like splinters of the soft shale, would be impossible to see in this dim light. He dared not expose the beam. Those men would be on him in a flash.

There. Just shoulder high, a solar disk with cow's horns wavered in the soft light. On the other side of the tunnel, at knee-level, the delicate carving of the incense tree branch seemed to point somewhere. But where?

Johab dropped to his knees and flashed his light around the edges of the carved stone. As he moved his hand over it, little flakes of brownish paint clung to his fingers. He tapped the stone with his fingernails and groped along the ridges of the carving. This stone was not soft shale or even the harder limestone. This stone was something else, like granite or quartzite. It wasn't like the other stones in the tunnel. It had been painted to look like them.

Voices echoed nearer. The men were moving quickly back up the tunnel. He had no more than a few minutes in which to disappear. Johab suddenly remembered the story of *Alice in Wonderland*, a book his father read to him when he was younger. Alice had come upon the rabbit hole quite suddenly. *Please, dear Hathor,* Johab prayed. *Send me a rabbit hole.*

He rolled onto his back, thrust his feet out, placed his heels directly over the carving of Queen Hatshepsut's favorite incense tree, and shoved with all his strength. He could feel his face burning. He was pushing so hard that his breathing became shallow and labored.

Suddenly, as unexpected as the scent of a jasmine bush after a rain shower, a musky odor, sweet—not as sweet as Hetty's rose geranium soap—drifted around him. The stone swung inward against his feet, and he slid quietly into darkness.

CHAPTER 49

And the end of all our exploring
Will be to arrive where we started
And know the place for the first time.

—T.S. Eliot

Miss Wenkle peered into the darkness of the night behind the car window trying to see any movement near the huts. What was taking Mr. Feisel and Cyril so long? Only a few scattered lights, oil lamps from the village houses, dotted the horizon.

Bastet's attempts to claw his way out of the cardboard box had stopped. She began to talk to the cat just to break the boredom of silence. "Do you know that you are named for a very famous goddess, you old tomcat? She was a protector of pregnant women. We'll ask her to protect Johab's Aunt Rayya. Her baby is due around Christmas."

She turned to look at the cardboard box with its jailed cat. Through a crack, she could see Bastet's yellow-green eyes flickering in the palest sliver of moon above. "Do you know that the ancient Egyptians loved their cats so much that they took them to their burial sites? There are dozens of cat mummies in the storerooms. They are probably your ancestors."

Miss Wenkle thought about funeral rites. Her mother had been buried in a London churchyard beneath a stone that said: "Beloved wife and mother." She wasn't sure that was true. Her mother was an awful nag. She thought that her father died prematurely just to escape his wife's constant harping. Then, she became the target of her mother's sharp tongue.

All that was behind her now. Her life in Cairo had been more exciting than anything she could imagine—days and days of sunshine, such a change from fog-bound London. She would choose Cairo over any other city—the Khan, the street markets, the noise, and the color, like an endless carnival. Her face fell. Mr. Barzoni had made Cairo a frightening place.

Her hands ached from constant wringing. She was becoming too angry thinking of what might have happened to Johab and his father. They didn't need negative vibrations on this journey. Bastet was providing enough of those, turning round and round in the box, like a gerbil on a wheel.

Miss Wenkle felt as confined as Bastet in the hot car. She rolled down a window and peered at the village surrounded by mud brick walls. Johab's father had told her that the villages hadn't changed much since the days when the tombs were built. Under these villages lay the ruins of older villages, one on top of the other, stretching back more than three thousand years, maybe even farther in time.

She had read Howard Carter's account of the village family who were famous among archeologists. Unlike their neighbors, the family's trade was not goat tending, but tomb robbing. They had become skilled at finding new ways into the tombs after a flood exposed a crevice in the cliffs. And adept at filching treasures. Sometimes, they hid the treasures for years, until the market was good and the family identity could be protected.

They were wrong. Those treasures belonged to the people of Egypt to be shared with the people of the world in the Museum. The private collectors who bought from the black market were bad—they kept treasures hidden from the public. Those like Barzoni were the worst—middlemen, bargaining with the robbers and the collectors. They had no interest in the treasures beyond what they represented—easy money.

Miss Wenkle squinted toward the cluster of huts with irritation. Mr. Feisel had apparently forgotten her. The flash of a lantern rounding the corner of the wall caught her attention. Mr. Feisel and Cyril meandered along with two strange men. Their voices were subdued. She couldn't understand a word. Before they reached the car, Mr. Feisel turned and grasped each of them, in turn, with a hearty hug and a slap on the back. Obviously, the meeting had been friendly. She ducked her head. Mr. Feisel would not want a blue-eyed, blond woman showing up at this moment.

He pushed back the driver's seat, and Cyril popped into the back, reaching his hand forward to touch Miss Hetty's shoulder. He had not forgotten that she had been waiting so long in the car. He peeped into Bastet's box. The cat glared at him and twitched its tail. Bastet had done considerable damage to the cardboard.

Mr. Feisel turned the key, gunned the engine, fumbled for reverse, and said he had "the hang of this car," but his method of changing gears was brutal. As soon as they had pulled past a low wall enclosing a few goats and a donkey, they headed back down the same steep and bumpy road.

"Here's what I learned," Mr. Feisel turned toward Miss Wenkle as though their previous conversation had simply been interrupted by a short pause, rather than an hour while he visited with his old cronies. She turned an attentive face toward him. She would save her exasperation for later.

"They've seen a strange car here three times—once, a week ago, once yesterday and again in the past hour. It is a white car. They didn't recognize the make of it. One of the small boys in the family said that he had seen it within the hour parked down below the cliff face of KV20. He said there were two men in the car, the same two men every time—and they try to hide the car by parking it behind a small mound."

Mr. Feisel grunted. "They may be hiding it from the main road, but the villagers don't use that road. They roam these cliffs in the old way." He gestured upward, "They can see everything that goes on—a bird's eye view." He whipped out of a rut and skidded back onto the high center of the path.

"My friend said something else that is critical. His son told him that one of the men was carrying something when they came late yesterday. He couldn't see clearly, but he said it was a kind of bundle being carried over the man's back."

Miss Wenkle's sudden intake of breath was sharp. Cyril touched her shoulder again. He did not understand much of the English that Mr. Feisel was speaking to Miss Hetty, but he had understood every word of what went on in that small house where Mr. Feisel had been drinking sweet tea. Cyril knew that Johab was the bundle. He knew that Mr. Feisel was more afraid than he would admit to Miss Hetty. In the house, there had been a lot of discussion about the "black market" and "Hatshepsut's tomb."

Mr. Feisel had asked more questions than the men could or would answer. They did tell him about a suspicious family—one that lived on the edge of the village, new to the village. One of Mr. Feisel's friends said that the family "might be spending too much time at the tombs." Then the man became silent, a worried expression crossing his face, as though he had said too much.

Mr. Feisel turned toward Miss Wenkle. "It may be Johab," he continued, trying to keep his voice even, unemotional, "or, it may just have been tools they are taking into the tomb."

"You know it was Johab," Hetty blurted out, her eyes welling with tears. "The car is the right color. The time is right. No one carries heavy tools on his back like a *bundle*. Hetty's voice took on an acid tone, as though she resented being shielded from the truth.

"You're probably right. It just seems very odd to me that someone would try to hide a little boy in a tomb. They can be very public places. We'll try to get closer to KV20 without anyone seeing the car. Maybe Cyril and I can take one of the side paths to see if the car is still there." He looked at Miss Wenkle apologetically. "You'll need to stay in the car—or near the car."

Mr. Feisel turned the car up a steep trail. The little VW groaned and bounced from side to side but churned upward. "Mr. Feisel?" Miss Wenkle's voice was an interruption as he tried to avoid the larger stones that might take out a wheel. "I timed you. You were with those men for more than an hour. Surely, you got more information, something you're not telling me," Miss Wenkle said firmly, as though she might be a schoolteacher, reprimanding a young boy.

He was silent a moment. "You don't understand our ways, Miss Wenkle. I grew up visiting my grandparents in this village—I spent much of my early boyhood with these men. I haven't seen them in many years. Our way is to proceed slowly."

He swerved to avoid a large boulder that blocked part of the path. "It's a kind of . . ." He searched for the right English word. ". . . a kind of ceremony. We drink tea. We talk about the old times. We talk about what we did as boys. Then, if the moment seems right, I introduce the real reason that I am here."

He stopped talking and frowned. "They have a choice—they can believe me or think that I'm simply someone they used to know who wants information for another reason. The villagers are suspicious of city people," he added sadly. "That's what they think I am—a city person."

He gestured toward the back seat. "Bringing Cyril along was the best idea I've had all day. Cyril's father grew up in one of these villages—not this one but one out by the Farafra Oasis. Cyril's dialect is like that of a villager—when I introduced him as one of my family, he was very believable. He told them that Johab was his cousin and had been stolen away by some men who had also taken his father."

"He didn't say much more. I don't think they have any idea who Johab's father is. They seemed to think that he was a tomb worker who might have come upon some valuable information. Cyril didn't correct that perception. Neither did I," he said firmly. "They'll be more interested in helping us if we are saving one of our own."

"I don't understand," Miss Wenkle said, in a puzzled tone. "How are they helping?"

"Roll down your window and look up toward the right, high on the cliffs. Do you see an occasional flash of light?" Miss Hetty nodded. "My friends are watching us. They will be watching for the white car. They will be there if we need them."

He turned his head away from her for a moment and cleared his throat as though he were experiencing an emotion that a woman shouldn't see. "These old village ties—they are strong. They last for generations. My father grew up with their fathers and our grand-fathers before that. Many of us left the villages, but those kinds of relationships don't disappear."

Miss Wenkle looked down at the floor. She had been lucky enough to have a few of those kinds of relationships after her father had died when she was not much older than Johab. Her Uncle Cyril had tried to fill that gap, but he was in Cairo most of the time—then, when he brought Aunt Alice back to London, she had been so ill. Uncle Cyril was grief-stricken over the loss of his beloved Alice. Within the year, the date of his death was inscribed on the same tombstone. Below Alice's name, Uncle Cyril had a line of ancient Egyptian love poetry engraved: "The love of her protects me."

Hetty's good friends, Sarah and Ella—they were like these vil-lagers. She might not see them for months, but when they met, it was as though they had simply left the room and returned moments later to pick up the thread of a conversation. Those were the kinds of friendships that Mr. Feisel was describing.

Mr. Feisel braked to a stop. Hetty realized that he hadn't told her anything more than that the villagers had seen a white car and a man carrying a bundle toward the tomb entrance. She sniffed with exasperation. He was keeping something from her. Mr. Feisel seemed far too purposeful to sit around recalling old times, especially when he knew that Johab's life was hanging in the balance. He was simply not telling her everything. *We'll see about that.* She flung the car door open, stepped outside, and stretched her cramped arms and legs.

Mr. Feisel pulled his seat forward and maneuvered the cardboard box out of the car. "Cyril, wait here with Miss Wenkle and the cat. I'm going to work my way down this hill to see if I can spot that car." The Arabic was directed to Cyril. Miss Wenkle flushed and watched Mr. Feisel until he rounded the pile of boulders and disappeared, the beam of his flashlight bouncing off rocks.

After a short time, he reappeared and said in English. "Their car is there. They took it as far as they could. They damaged the oil pan—oil has leaked out all over the ground. They won't get very far." He looked over at Cyril and grinned like a conspirator. "Holes in all four tires should slow them down as well." Hetty understood the knife-like motion.

Mr. Feisel yanked open the VW's front trunk, pulled out the coil of rope, then turned toward Miss Wenkle. "I couldn't see any sign of the men, so I went up to the tomb entrance. Someone has posted a sign about the tomb being closed." He shook his head. "It looks official. I think that El-Hasiim fellow made it. It says the tomb is closed because the ceiling is falling." He chuckled. "The ceiling started falling the day this tomb was carved. Too much soft shale in this site," he added.

He turned toward Cyril. "I'll carry the box with the cat, Cyril. You bring the other flashlight and point the way up the trail. We're heading part-way up the cliff above the tomb." As an afterthought, he added, "Miss Wenkle, you stay right here by the car. If anyone approaches, wave your arms. The men on the cliff will see you."

"I'm *not* staying here." Miss Wenkle's voice was low, with the understated power of a cobra uncoiling itself from a basket in the marketplace. "I'm going with you and Cyril. You need an extra pair of hands and eyes. I'm a perfectly strong adult. You need to quit treating me like . . . some kind of . . . uh . . . helpless woman." The line of her lips was as firm as though it had been carved from granite. "I'm going with you."

Mr. Feisel looked at Cyril as if to find another male to support his objections. Cyril was having no part of it. He liked having Miss Hetty along. He understood enough of the English conversation to know that Mr. Feisel had directed her to stay, and she would not.

Mr. Feisel threw up his hands, muttered below his breath in Arabic, and then announced in frustration. "Just don't slow us down. We're not waiting for you."

He took off at a brisk pace, climbing over rocks. Miss Wenkle grinned wryly. Mr. Feisel was somewhat arthritic. She was not. She had noticed his groans when he unwound himself from the VW. She was perfectly spry and able to climb up as many trails and over as many rocks as he could.

The path was torturous, even for a fit woman and especially for a man with complaining joints. Cyril trotted ahead of them, shining his flashlight directly on the path as it wound upward. Mr. Feisel held up one hand. "Here, Cyril. See where the floods have washed these large boulders and rubble into this chasm. My friends told me that those newcomers to the village have been hanging around this area. They said that in the old days, this tomb was used as a hideout. They thought there might be a second way into it."

He turned toward Miss Wenkle. "The villagers are reluctant to tell anyone what they know about these tombs. They are supposed to be off-limits unless the men are working on government-approved projects," he laughed softly. "That's a joke. They consider this land to be theirs, these tombs to belong to their ancestors' kings and queens. The government rules are something to be ignored, but carefully."

Mr. Feisel put the box with Bastet on the ground. He pointed his flashlight toward a large boulder. "There, Cyril—over there beside that big boulder and the smaller one next to it. Do you see a gap? Bat droppings all over the stones—there is some kind of opening there."

At that moment, the soft sound of ripping cardboard stopped the three of them. Mr. Feisel aimed his flashlight at the box. Bastet, like a yellow streak of light, burst out of the box, clawed his way up to the small boulder, angled into the gap between the rocks faster than a weasel, and dropped out of sight.

CHAPTER 50

He eats what the gods eat, he drinks what they drink,
he lives as they live, and he dwells where they dwell;
all the gods give him this food that he may not die.

—Papyrus of Ani

There should be a white rabbit, wearing a checkered jacket and carrying a large pocket watch nearby. But there was not. When she fell into the rabbit hole, Alice landed on a soft mat of leaves and dirt. Johab had landed on a slab of stone. Stretched out full length on the stone, he felt for the back of his head. Spears of sharp pain shot through his skull. He could feel a major lump.

A wave of dizziness swept over him. He might puke. He did not dare open his eyes. When he squinted through them, the pain was worse. He must have a concussion. Mohammed once had one when they played soccer. He ran into a post, popped backwards, and sported a lump as big as a goose egg for a day.

Mohammed's mother had to wake him every two hours just to see if he were sleeping normally, or if he were in a coma. Mohammed had hoped for a coma, because he was sure that would mean extra treats, but he woke up every two hours grumbling.

Johab knew he wasn't in a coma. The agony was too great. Razor-tipped slivers of pain pierced his skull every time he tried to move. He needed to get the pressure off the back of his head. He lifted it gingerly, angled his shoulders forward and inched his body backwards. A comforting wall met his back.

He could touch the flashlight with his foot, but he dared not reach for it. He wanted to burst into tears with the pain, but who might hear him in this tomb? He could think. As bruised as his brain might be, it was still working. He remembered the voices of Barzoni's men coming closer and closer down the tunnel. He had stupidly left the water bottle for them to find in the small chamber.

He remembered pushing his feet against the stone with the incense tree of Punt carved along the lower edge. His last thought had been of the rabbit hole in *Alice in Wonderland*. Then, there had been that marvelous scent. And darkness.

The scent was all around him again, just as though he had wandered into an exotic flower garden. He must be addled. Tombs smelled of bat dung and tourist vomit, not incense. *The soft voice in the tomb chilled him to the bone.*

"My little Horemheb, keep your eyes closed. I have ointment for your injured head."

The touch of fingers on the back of his head was warm and soothing. His lungs ached with the breath he feared to exhale—he could not be detected breathing. He dared not open his eyes or move.

"Do not be afraid. Senenmut intended you to be here, or he would not have shared the secret of my tomb with you." Soft fingers lingered on his forehead and trailed along the side of his face. The touch of the fingers felt almost like the series of small kisses his mother used to place along the side of his face at bedtime—but that was before he was too old for bedtime kisses.

Johab held himself stiff, his eyes squeezed tight, while the melodious voice murmured above his face. "I will tell you why Senenmut had to change the tomb. We had seen the desecration of the early tombs, the glorious kings thrown out of their coffins, their linen coverings stripped from their bodies in the search for gold and jewels—things of this world. They destroyed the sacred bodies to find those trinkets." Her voice quivered with sadness.

"We planned well, my Senenmut and I. Only his most trusted stone cutters could enter the tomb after it had been completed. Where the shale was weak, they carved the shaft and placed a granite slab painted to resemble the limestone, to conceal the passage. Behind that would rest two small chambers, both hidden, but the outer chamber would be filled with some of my treasures. It would be a decoy if anyone ever found a way into the new chambers."

Her voice was low, almost musical. "I will tell you of that day when I came from my palace to this place of everlasting. I was sad to leave my people, but my *ka* longed to leave this body to be with my father, Amun. My funeral procession moved slowly. Not in the years of anyone's memory had there been such sadness. The cries of my people could be heard as far away as the tomb of Khufu down to the second cataract of the Nile. Their tears flooded like the Nile. They piled flowers as high as the palace walls. The people brought fat bulls, gleaming with oil, for the sacred sacrifice. Everything was prepared to please Amun-Ra, Osiris, and Anubis." The voice paused.

"Two of my incense trees from Punt were brought to my tomb so that my *ka* could rest on them. Those who loved me, wept bitter tears—even young Thutmose who would soon forget me. The animals were made to bleed for me; this they did gladly."

"Then, all but the priests and those who crafted the stones left the chamber. Under the watchful eye of the priests, the burial chamber was sealed. My coffins were placed in the great, yellow sarcophagus where I awaited my father, Amun."

Her voice took on a coy tone. "*Or so they thought.* I waited, my *ka* watching from the incense trees. I knew I must stay suspended here until my trusted Senenmut came. He would take me to the secret place he made for me. Only his trusted builders, four of them, knew of these new chambers—not my priests who had become too friendly to Thutmose."

Her voice was regal, exact, as though she were reciting a law. "It was their sacred duty to protect me from human eyes, human hands, from the flooding of the Nile, from the wild beasts of the night. These craftsmen and Senenmut, with my old nurse helping, moved my goods for the other life into these new chambers. With ropes, they pulled my golden coffins up the tunnel and lowered them into this secret shaft. My sarcophagus was too heavy. They had to leave it behind."

Her voice became rich with emotion. "Senenmut wept because he could not trust the priests to say the last words of promise. So he said them. He caressed my coffin with both hands and said those words to comfort my *ka*."

Her fingers trailed along the side of Johab's face, but he kept his eyes squeezed tight. "They sealed the inner tomb with a stela of granite which tells the story of my miraculous birth. The corners are square, not arched. Only a clever eye would know it is a door. They placed the outer mummy coffin in front of the door to hide the scraping of stone on stone. My *ka* watched."

Johab felt hands touching the side of his throat. *This was it.* The ghost of Queen Hatshepsut would strangle him right here in this tomb shaft. Years later, someone might find a dried wisp of a body. Bodies became smaller when they dried in the tombs—no humidity, little decay. Johab shivered and arched his body against the hands on his throat.

"It is a gift, young Horemheb. It is my favorite amulet, a scarab of green jasper. On it are carved the words, 'Not may be made separation from me.'" Her fingers stroked his neck. Some kind of warm metal seemed to burn into his flesh, but the sensation was gentle, not painful.

A face was directly above his. He could feel her soft breath on him. He opened his eyes, unblinking. Even in the darkness, he could see an aura of light around her. Her face might have been carved from granite, so carefully sculpted were the nose, the chin, the cheeks—a proud face, beautiful in a way that Nefertiti's was not.

This was the face of a woman who knew she was a king. Her eyes were brown but with a strange yellow cast to them, as though she could see right past his eyes into the very soul of him.

"Be watchful, my little Horemheb. Senenmut has trusted you with our secret. Use it wisely." She clasped her hands together and said softly, "May the gods give to him life like the sun forever."

Then, like fairy dust, she seemed to evaporate, her pleated linen dress first, the bracelets wrapping her arms next, her face lingering just a moment, and the double crown of Egypt disappearing last.

The pain in his head had gone. His legs and arms were sluggish as though mired in a bath of honey. He seemed to be drifting, drifting back into sleep.

Fighting drowsiness, he remembered the terrible story of the tomb robbers who broke the seal on a very large jar of honey and were feasting on it until they came upon a long, dark strand of hair and discovered that the jar held a small mummy, preserved for all time in the sticky sweet substance.

Johab sank into an untroubled sleep. The scent that lulled him into never land was not honey, but rare incense.

CHAPTER 51

The day is for honest men, the night for thieves.

—Euripides

Mr. Feisel aimed his flashlight at what appeared to be a bottomless pit in the crevasse between two boulders. "That dratted cat. I wanted to use him to help us find Johab. When he's not with Jasmine, he hangs around the boy. Using a cat as a bloodhound. What a stupid idea," he muttered darkly.

"Not stupid at all," Miss Wenkle chimed. "Cats are uncanny creatures. I've read stories about them crossing an entire country to find their families. It was a very good idea."

Mr. Feisel straightened up quickly and put his finger to his mouth as he flipped off his flashlight. "Quiet," he hissed. "I thought I heard something." He craned his neck and stood on his tiptoes. "Someone is coming along that adjoining path. I see lights and hear voices."

He grabbed Miss Wenkle and Cyril, pulling them behind him as he moved quickly back along the path from which they had come. "Hide behind this pile of rocks. They can't see us here." He muttered something in Arabic that sounded like a curse, then said quietly to Miss Wenkle. "I left the cat's box up there. Stay flat on the ground. Don't even breathe."

Three pairs of eyes peered into the darkness through peepholes in a pile of rocks. Cyril angled himself up highest on the pile. In his mustard-striped galabeya, he resembled a crumpled leaf that had blown across the desert and landed on the rock.

Mr. Feisel and Miss Wenkle stretched out side-by-side, low to the ground, sharing a large gap in the rocks, their heads glued together. The twinkling lights of the villagers high on the cliffs could no longer be seen.

The voices reached them before lights appeared. Three men wearing galabeyas, their head cloths wrapped around their necks and chins as though to disguise their faces, appeared on the rocky path, midway up the cliffs, far above the entrance of the tomb. They were talking quietly and angling their flashlights against the ground, shading the lights with the folds of their robes.

They might have been three villagers simply out looking for a lost goat, thought Miss Wenkle. In the middle of the night? That was hardly likely. There was something sinister about the way they crept along the trail, the practiced way they held their flashlights to deflect the light from bouncing off the boulders. These were men of the night. They were very experienced in whatever mischief they were pursuing.

As they neared the crevasse in the side of the cliff where Bastet had recently disappeared, the leader stopped abruptly, almost tripping the man behind him. A flashlight beam lit up Bastet's box. The conversation was in Arabic, but Miss Wenkle sensed the anxiety that the appearance of a cardboard box had created. Just a cat-shredded piece of cardboard, but they were giving it as much attention as though it held explosives.

The tallest of the three, the one who seemed to be in charge, knelt by the box and examined the inside of it, shining his flashlight into the interior. He chuckled and made a comment that brought sounds of relief from the other two men.

Mr. Feisel put his lips against Miss Wenkle's ear and muttered, "He thinks some child from the village caught a fox up here on the cliff and was either taking it home or being sent back to the cliffs to release it. He says those scratches were made by a fox."

Instead of being bothered by the nearness of Mr. Feisel and the soft whisper of his breath against her ear, Miss Wenkle was comforted. After the death of her father, there had been only Uncle Cyril. Her mother had insisted that she go to an all-girls' school. The men in her life were her colleagues at work.

She stared into the night, unblinking, her eyes filling with tears. Johab's father was a colleague who shared his family with her. He made sure that she was not alone during holidays. He was like a . . . a younger brother to her. That's what he was.

A sharp dig in her ribs brought Miss Wenkle back to the present. Mr. Feisel pointed at something. The men moved toward the gap between the rocks where Bastet had disappeared. The smallest of the three was tying a rope around his waist. One of the other two looped a large knot at the end of the rope. The man with the rope around his waist pointed his flashlight toward the gap in the rock, shining his torch all around the edges.

"Scorpions," hissed Mr. Feisel in her ear. "He's checking to be sure there are no scorpions."

"Nahud," barked the tall man, "quit stalling. Get down the hole."

Nahud plopped facedown on the ground, angled his feet toward the hole, and slithered out of sight.

The second man knotted a rope around his waist and tied the other end around a large, narrow outcropping of stone. He picked up an unlit oil lantern and his flashlight, leaned his weight against the rope, spoke sharply to the tall man and disappeared down the hole. The man left behind squatted and tested the strength of the ropes. He was silent, watchful. Then alert.

From down below near the entrance to the tomb, loud voices pierced the silence of the night. The words were in Arabic, and they echoed against the silent, dark cliffs above Deir el-Bahari.

The tall man crept away from the crevasse where the other two men had disappeared and peered over the side of the cliff, trying to determine the source of the racket below.

Mr. Feisel seized the opportunity to whisper in Miss Wenkle's ear. "Those voices below must be Barzoni's men. They've found their car with the damaged oil pan—and the flat tires. One of them seems to be kicking the car. He's banging on something metal and cursing."

"The men here," he paused and moved his lips closer to her ear. "Two of them are brothers. The one they call Nahud is a cousin. I don't think they trust him. That's why one of the brothers followed him down the shaft. My friends said these men come from another village and have been prowling around, looking for another way into this tomb. They are unsettled about the local villagers knowing about their comings and goings. That's why they were so upset when they saw the cat's box."

Moving even closer, his bristly face stubble tickling her cheek, Mr. Feisel whispered: "I just heard one of Barzoni's men say something about 'the brat.' I think they mean Johab. They can't find him. He has disappeared."

Mr. Feisel, Miss Wenkle, and Cyril met the news with three different sets of conflicting emotions.

Mr. Feisel knew these old tombs. They were treacherous, especially those built into the soft shale of these cliffs. Floods dumped piles of rubble along the tunnels, splintering the original tunnels, creating deep cracks in unlikely places. From the comments of Barzoni's men, Johab had escaped from the place where they had left him.

No tomb was that large. If they couldn't find him, something must have happened to him. The face of Johab's mother flashed in front of Mr. Feisel. He couldn't be the one to tell her.

Miss Wenkle's first reaction was one of relief. Her second was a sense of pride. Her little partner had outwitted Barzoni again. He had escaped from the men who left him in the tomb. Fear struck. If he had escaped, could Johab be alone somewhere out here in the desert? She lifted her head to look around. Mr. Feisel's hand shoved her head down.

Cyril twitched with pure joy, clinging to the rocks so that he wouldn't leap into the air. Johab had escaped from those bad men who had thrown him into the trunk of a car and left him in a tomb in the desert. Johab was cleverer than any person he knew and had the best disguises. Cyril thought about the possible disguises inside a tomb. Johab could squeeze into a crack. He could put an old mummy case on his head and be as still as a mummy.

Cyril could hardly wait to hear about Johab's disguises. The cool desert breezes lifted the edges of Cyril's robe, exposing his thin legs to the night air. The little boy's heart was nearly bursting with excitement, thinking about how Johab would tell him of such wonderful adventures.

CHAPTER 52

I Khemi, who comest forth from Shetait (the hidden place),
I have not carried off goods by force.

—Papyrus of Nu

When Johab awoke again, his body felt stiff and cold, as though he had been lying on a hard slab for centuries. He touched the back of his head—a thin layer of some kind of oily substance coated his bump. He groped around on the ground near his feet and felt the comforting cylinder of a flashlight. He flipped it on and beamed it around the space. Above him stretched only darkness. He appeared to be at the bottom of some kind of shaft that had been cut into the limestone cliff.

He was lying in a small enclosure, not much larger than four or five meters square. Aiming the light directly in front of him, Johab could see two elaborately carved wooden doors. At the tops of them were the goddesses Isis and Nepthys, their arms outstretched like wings with the feathers drooping in mourning.

Two ornate handles with the necropolis seal on one side held fragments of what had once been a knotted cord, usually the final act of priests to close the tomb forever.

Johab focused the flashlight on the heavy cord. The cuts on it appeared to be raw and recent.

He knelt in front of the doors, tracing his fingers over the delicate carvings. Here again were the incense trees of Punt and all of the gods and goddesses who participate in the funeral rites. Johab thought that the wood was cedar. It was remarkably preserved in this dry, chilly underground. A noise jolted him.

Johab snatched back his hand as though it had been scalded and looked upward. Was it rain or hail? Tiny pellets of gravel were pouring down on him from above. Faint curses and scraping noises against the limestone were coming from someplace far up in the shaft. Barzoni's men must have found the secret passageway.

He had to hide. Johab grabbed the handle of one wooden door and pulled it open just wide enough to wiggle inside and waved the beam of his flashlight ahead.

The splendors of the tomb were in chaos. Chairs of rare woods with inlaid ivory were piled into the corners. A large, wooden chest came to life in front of the beam of the flashlight. Queen Hatshepsut, standing in her chariot, drove leaping horses into a forest filled with exotic animals. The colors of red, blue, green, sienna, and yellow were bright, as though they had just left the artist's palette.

A wooden bed, with shreds of gold that had been stripped away, lay on its side. The horns of bulls that adorned the corners were splintered against the limestone floor. Two alabaster vases reaching to Johab's waist glowed with an eerie white effervescence in the darkness.

Loud thumps sounded nearer. An occasional shout pierced intervals of silence. Coming down the shaft must not be as easy as it had been for Johab. He had simply tumbled down and awoken with a concussion. Nothing to it.

He needed to find somewhere to hide. Now! The furniture piled into corners and along the walls of the small chamber offered many hiding places. But if someone moved them, he'd be out of luck.

At that moment, he remembered something that Queen Hatshepsut had said. She mentioned that one of her wooden coffins was left as a "decoy." Johab aimed his flashlight along the far wall, the wall opposite the wooden doors leading into the tomb chamber. On the floor was a beautifully painted coffin. It was a large, anthropoid box, one of those kinds of crates designed as the outer coffin, large enough to hold a smaller inner coffin that would house the mummy.

It had been wrenched opened. The lid, encrusted with multi-colored glass decorations, interspersed with gold leaf, set at an angle across the bottom of the coffin. Newly cut chips hacked out of the top marred its beautiful design. Johab moved his flashlight closer. Someone had gouged out the decorations on the top edge of the lid. Only a few turquoise and lapis stones remained in what had been an ornate ring of gold and jewels around the coffin lid.

A loud thump followed by a second thump sounded in the outer chamber. Barzoni's men would burst through the doors any minute. Where to hide?

The wooden casket seemed to beckon him. If they had traced him to this chamber, they could find him easily enough. Maybe, a mummy's house would put them off. He eased himself down on his hands and knees into the length of the coffin and pulled the lid back into place, leaving one corner of it ajar so that he could see through the crack under the lid.

The door creaked open. Johab could see nothing but the blinding sweep of two flashlights. Within a few seconds, a match flared, and a small oil lamp cast strange shadows around the room.

One of the men, the shorter one, lifted the lamp high, illuminating the room and his face. Johab almost gasped aloud. The man's face had been badly burned on one side, the tissue regrouping itself into deep furrows with puckered edges. The eye on the scarred side of the face was a pale oval, trapped inside an eyelid that seemed frozen open.

The unburned side of the face looked angrier than the tortured, damaged side. Barzoni's men looked like ordinary crooks in comparison to these two.

The taller man had a long, cadaverous face. He didn't appear to have been in the tomb before. He picked up the edge of the broken bed, complaining to the shorter man about his destructiveness.

Nahud said, "I have brought up only the smaller things—the carnelian amulet, strings of ivory beads, the collar of gold and lapis, those small chests with ivory spoons, and other things that could be carried up the shaft." The shorter man's explanation sounded flimsy, as though he were fabricating it on the spot.

"Nahud, have you checked the mummy for gold?" the taller one asked. "I've been told that beneath those linen wraps are gold rings and fine jewels, even gold toenail guards."

"There's no mummy here. It's empty." Nahud ducked his damaged face and kicked the wooden coffin brutally.

Johab held his breath, hoping that the hollow sound it made would be convincing. He felt the weight of a hand on the coffin. He couldn't see the man in the wavering light of the oil lamp.

"Where are the gemstones that you dug out of the lid?" the tall one asked acidly.

"I think your brother has them. I'm not sure. Maybe I dropped them on the way up. I've only been down here twice. It's dangerous coming down between that split rock in this loose shale. The whole thing could cave in on us at any minute." Nahud's voice took on a worried tone, his good eye never making contact with the other man's face.

Nahud added breathlessly, "We need to move this big stuff around to be sure that we don't miss any small things that could be valuable. It will be sunrise before long, and we can't be seen around here."

The tall man nodded in agreement: "Something was going on at the village tonight. I don't know what, but I saw lights up high on the cliff. They disappeared before we started the climb up the old path, but we can't take any chances."

He moved his fingers along the top of the casket, drumming them against the gold leaf and glass ornamentation. "Tonight, we'll take what we can carry, but at some point we are going to take all of these chairs, this bed, the large chests. These things are valuable in the market. Collectors will pay for this stuff even if we have to rip them apart to get them out."

Johab watched the pile of treasures mounting in the middle of the room—a small dagger with a gold, incised blade and a jewel-encrusted handle was added. That treasure brought a loud cry from the tall man when he found it tucked under the edge of the chest. The man called Nahud looked even angrier, as though his special hiding place had been revealed.

The men sorted things that were not heavy and put them in cloth sacks. Heavier items were placed onto a pile in the corner. There were wooden oars, crafted beautifully of cedar, tossed aside as though they were of no value. A large statue of Anubis on some kind of sledge was pushed back, but carefully.

Model boats with sails and rigging were examined, the smaller ones stuffed into the sacks, the larger ones set aside. There were piles of baskets, clay pots for baking bread, rolled up piles of reeds. This was not King Tutankamen's treasure trove. Most of the treasures in this chamber were the practical items for the next life, necessities that a king or queen would need for the everlasting journey.

Nahud turned toward the taller man. "Your brother is pulling on my rope. We need to clear out of here now. We may have too many things to carry as it is. You haven't been up that hole before. You don't know how hard it is," he whined.

The other man picked up a small, alabaster statue of a woman, its lips painted bright red, its eyes rimmed with black paint to resemble kohl eye makeup. "This little piece will feed my family for a year." He stared hard at his cousin. "You have some explaining to do when we reach topside. My brother told you not to damage the goods. That coffin lid has been recently damaged. Those stones are worthless compared to what that lid *with* the stones would have been worth."

Johab could hear the man called Nahud protesting his innocence as he tugged his cloth bag along the limestone floor and exited the wooden door. The door was pushed securely shut, then tested again.

Johab could hear scuffling noises, then an eerie quietness. He peeked through the crack at the edge of the lid. A small oil lamp cast long shadows around the room. Queen Hatshepsut's horses trembled among the bright colors of the large chest.

He needed to find a way out of here as soon as he rested a bit. The men might remember that they had left their oil lamp behind and come back for it.

Johab wiggled into a more comfortable position in the wooden coffin and flipped on his flashlight. The inner lid of the coffin lit up with the magnificence of a desert sky. He was encased beneath tiny gold stars set in an indigo night.

Under the lid, he was too close to make out the figures of the gods and goddesses, but he knew they were there, at his feet and at his head as he settled down into a borrowed wooden coffin which seemed as comfortable as a goose down bed.

Johab's neck snapped forward. The top of his head whacked the coffin lid. Had he been asleep? He didn't dare sleep. Strange things happened when he slept. A ghost might visit him again. He carefully pushed the lid of the coffin aside and crawled out of it, clicking off his flashlight. The oil lamp still flickered in the middle of the room.

Behind the wooden coffin—in which he might or might not just have taken a nap—arched a magnificent, granite stela, a stone slab used for funeral carvings and words. Johab thought about the "visitation" or the hallucination caused by his concussion. *The ghost of Queen Hatshepsut had told him something about another room, a second chamber where Senenmut had placed her for eternity.*

The dull ache in his head had returned. He was trying too hard to think. He sat on the top of the coffin. After all, no mummy was in it. This wasn't disrespect. He was very tired and cold and hungry. The food in this chamber meant for the dead queen must be over three thousand years old. He would wait to eat.

He passed the flashlight beam across the stone slabs covering the wall. They appeared to be decorative panels fixed to the limestone wall of the chamber. He recognized some of the hieroglyphs. They were some of the same ones from the papyrus that Mr. Feisel had translated.

Mr. Feisel said that they were confusing and had protested that he was just an amateur, but Johab remembered his translation: "Trees of Punt, anoint my King with your secret everlasting fragrance, concealing her from the defilers."

He stood up and held the flashlight close to the edges of the center slab. No one looking at this ornately carved stone would have imagined that it was anything but one more depiction of Queen Hatshepsut's miraculous birth.

These slabs were attached to the limestone blocks in her temples all over Egypt. Nothing unusual here—except the branches of the incense trees were carved in the same pattern as they had been on the secret panel in the tunnel, the one that hid the shaft into which he had tumbled.

It was at that moment Johab noticed the marks in the limestone floor. Something very heavy had been moved across this floor. A faint, circular pattern had been grooved into the limestone floor just below the central panel. He pushed gently against the wooden coffin. The coffin hadn't been heavy enough to scratch the limestone floor. It was something else.

Johab lifted his head and sniffed. It was that strange fragrance of incense again—not a heavy scent but light and sweet as a spring rain. It was that same odor he had smelled just before he woke up with the bump on his head—or didn't wake up and had a most peculiar dream.

Following the circular pattern on the floor toward the center of it, Johab leaned his shoulder against the edge of the panel and shoved. A fixed granite slab on a stone wall should not have moved at all. It groaned but slid halfway ajar, leaving a space just wide enough for Johab to squeeze through. He thrust the beam of his flashlight into the opening—and crumpled onto the floor in a dead faint.

CHAPTER 53

Not shut ye in my soul, nor fetter ye my shade,
be there open a way for my soul, and for my shade,
may it see the god great within the shrine
on the day of the judgment of souls.

—Papyrus of Ani

Cyril's head bobbed up as noises came from the fissure in the cliff. Mr. Feisel and Miss Hetty were stretched out on the ground below his perch on the pile of rocks. Except for an occasional raised head to peer through their single peephole, they resembled large granite statues, toppled flat onto the desert sands.

"Pull harder. Put your back into it. I have a heavy load." The muffled voice of Nahud echoed from somewhere down inside of the gap as he shouted orders to the lone man at the top who was straining against the rope to bring him to the surface. A large cloth bag sailed up from below and landed with a thud at his feet.

"You damage those goods, Nahud, and you're not long for this world," the tall man said in an even, measured tone. He spoke with absolute authority.

Nahud pulled himself up to the cusp of the fissure between the rocks, turned onto his side, and rolled, nimble as an acrobat, out of the hole.

Using the cylindrical rock as an anchor, Nahud and the tall man heaved against the rope tied to the man down in the hole until a head appeared between the gap in the rocks.

He snarled, "Going down was treacherous; coming up was impossible. I didn't think I would make it out of that hole. It smells as if every bat in this country uses it for a toilet." He hoisted himself up and crawled a couple of feet, dragging his sack. Stretched out on the ground, coughing and wheezing, he moved, snake-like, across the ground to be near his brother.

His voice was icy in the dark desert night. "Our cousin Nahud has some explaining to do. Some of the furniture has been smashed in his eagerness to find jewels and gold. And—unless there are ghosts in the tomb—he's been prying stones and gold from the coffin lid."

Mr. Feisel did not dare translate the Arabic for Miss Wenkle. The easy banter, the low-pitched conversation among the three men earlier in the evening had been replaced by tension, so fierce that he expected to see a fist moving at any moment.

The tall man drew himself up into a rigid position. The voice that cut through the silence of the night was solemn as a judge's, the verdict as final.

Had the small man with the burned face, the cousin called Nahud, not been watching both men, his one good eye flickering from one face to the other, he would have missed the execution.

The curved scimitar moved noiselessly from the folds of the man's robe, flashed briefly in the pale light of the moon, and settled with the faintest of quivers in the throat of his cousin.

Miss Wenkle's muffled scream traveled no farther than Mr. Feisel's hand that clamped over her mouth as soon as he saw the whip-like movement of the man's arm.

Cyril lay as calm and unblinking as a little lizard resting on warm desert rocks. He had watched street fights that were much more brutal and messy. He nodded his head affirmatively. This head man, this leader, was deadly but tidy. He had spun the scimitar through the night with the skill of a knife thrower at a street fair.

Nahud, clutching his sack of treasures, sank to the ground, the glistening blade of a scimitar his only decoration for the next world.

The two brothers stared impassively at their cousin. No prayers from the *Book of the Dead* would be inscribed on his shroud. Each brother picked up a leg and dragged the corpse soundlessly to the gap in the rocks, angling his feet into the void. They moved around to his head and shoved.

The thumps of his body striking protruding rocks seemed to comfort them. "We will leave him down there," snarled the shorter of the brothers. "His own special tomb."

Both men scanned the cliffs for any betraying lights. Only the moon, finishing its journey for the night, shone impassively on the bloodstained desert sand. The men slung the cloth bags up, shielded their flashlights beneath the edges of their robes and picked their way down the path, as sure-footed and confident as goats.

Miss Wenkle sobbed silently into the rough sleeve of her galabeya. Mr. Feisel patted her back awkwardly. He did not deal well with women's tears.

Cyril skittered down from his perch and knelt beside Miss Wenkle, picking up her hand that was clenching and unclenching nervously. He looked at Mr. Feisel and said something in Arabic. Mr. Feisel's response was brusque.

Miss Wenkle looked up at both of them kneeling by her, pushed herself into a sitting position and brushed her arm across her tear-streaked face. "Is Cyril upset by what he saw? I should have been thinking about the effect of that terrible murder on that poor little boy."

"Sure, he's a little upset, but Cyril has seen worse things on the streets of Cairo. He'll be OK. He'll get over it," responded Mr. Feisel.

He lifted his face toward the sky so that neither Cyril nor Miss Wenkle could see it and rolled his eyes. He had taken considerable liberties with his translation of what Cyril had said. Cyril had voiced outspoken admiration for the swift and silent movement of the scimitar and the skill of the man throwing it. He hadn't mentioned the one-eyed man who had been tossed into a hole in the desert.

A faint glow of red and pink stretched the length of the cliffs, warming the chill night air. Mr. Feisel stood and waved his arm to an invisible audience hidden somewhere on the top of the cliffs. The murder of the cousin, Nahud, would have been shielded by the outcropping of rocks. No one could know that the fissure, the gap in the rocks, was there. Had Bastet not dashed into it and disappeared, Mr. Feisel would have thought it was simply an over-hanging rock. These cliffs were covered with similar rock formations.

Mr. Feisel, Miss Wenkle, and Cyril lowered themselves onto flat rocks and sat in a circle like an ancient cabal, silent, unable to plot their next move.

Cyril piped up first, groping for English words so that Mr. Feisel didn't have to repeat him. "I go," he said decisively. "I go down the Bastet hole."

"Oh no you don't," Miss Wenkle encircled his small body with her arm. "One missing boy is enough."

Cyril looked plaintively at Mr. Feisel, then pointed to the pale red Western sky, and spoke quickly in Arabic. "It will be daylight soon. Those men might come back to get more things from wherever they got them underground. We know that Bastet went down there, and Bastet hasn't come back. That could mean he is with Johab. I will go find my friend, my new cousin, Johab."

Mr. Feisel looked directly into Cyril's eyes. They were not the eyes of a young child. They were eyes of someone who has seen too much of this world. Cyril's lips formed a determined line in his small face.

Mr. Feisel shrugged his shoulders and turned toward Miss Wenkle. "Ordinarily, I would say that a child should only be asked to do what a child normally does." He looked down and frowned. "Cyril is not a normal child. He has experienced things that children shouldn't."

He reached across and touched Miss Wenkle's arm, the one clutching Cyril. "Cyril wants to try to save his friend. I'm too fat and too old to get down through that crack between the rocks. You are younger and fit, but neither Cyril nor I will let you go. That leaves Cyril."

Miss Wenkle nodded, squeezed Cyril, and then pushed him to his feet. In faltering Arabic, she said, "Mr. Feisel and I will keep watch here, Cyril. Don't take any chances. Don't stay down there long. Here, take my flashlight."

Within minutes, Mr. Feisel had knotted his rope around Cyril's waist. He stooped down and flashed the beam of his light around the gap in the rocks and said softly in Arabic. "I don't see any scorpions but that doesn't mean they aren't there. They like the cooler places under rocks. Don't put your hand any place without shining the light there first. I can see two small outcroppings of rocks that form a ledge with some tracks in the bat dung. That must be where those men dropped before they descended further down. I can't see past that ledge. If you get into trouble, just pull on the rope. We'll get you up. Go with God."

Cyril nodded, dropped to his knees, angled his feet into the gap, looked up at Mr. Feisel and Miss Wenkle, smiled, winked, and dropped into a black void.

Miss Wenkle clasped her hands together as if in silent prayer. Cyril had looked like the bravest member of a submarine crew—cheering up his shipmates on the shore as he disappeared down the hatch.

Mr. Feisel stared at the plump, blond woman, her face stained with tears and traces of odd, tan makeup. She managed to surprise him a number of times. She was bossy, as were all English women, but she seemed to have a reserve of courage that he wouldn't have imagined. She had risked her life to help Johab. Now, she seemed to have the same affection for Cyril, a street child who could mean nothing to her.

There was more to this woman than met the eye. When she and her two English friends came dashing into the City of the Dead with Cyril several hours earlier, he thought that Miss Wenkle looked exactly like one of those tourist women in their floral dresses who flutter around the marketplaces and then retire to air-conditioned hotel rooms.

Her quiet, barely controlled sobs as she tried to comfort and reassure Johab's mother had been painful to hear. What might be happening to Johab—whatever unimaginable things those might be—were also happening to her.

He touched her on her shoulder and pointed to a large, smooth boulder. "It may be a long wait. Let's work on your Arabic."

CHAPTER 54

The flashlight rolled away from Johab's crumpled form, lighting up an underground tomb that had not been seen by human eyes for over three thousand years. Johab's eyes fluttered open, the hard limestone floor against his backside providing the only touch with reality.

The decay of death could not enter this room. Light and life held sway over death here. In the wavering beam of the flashlight, the objects in the chamber took on a life of their own.

Johab felt the back of his head. A splinter of sharp pain forced him to close his eyes again. He refused to believe that he had fainted like an hysterical girl. He blamed his concussion. He reached for his flashlight and aimed its beam around the room that danced so splendidly with life.

This fairyland, with the finest art of the New Kingdom, suspends life from death. Here, at this very moment, it was now, not back then. The all-conquering Queen, tall and powerful as she reins in her charging horses, is the goddess of this realm. She is subject only to Amun, whose painted image with the double crown of Egypt, holds out welcoming arms to his daughter, Hatshepsut.

Johab's heart pounded. His eyes watered. He stood up slowly, while his breath pumped in and out in shallow, stressed gasps. Nothing in the world made by human hands could be so beautiful. The treasures were indescribable. The glory of this place sang into the very heart of him.

Against the far wall on a small dais rested a coffin of what appeared to be solid gold. The face, marvelously sculpted, sprouted the beard of a king. Otherwise, its features were feminine. The mouth was exactly the shape of the one that had whispered his name, "Horemheb."

The flail and crook, symbols of a king's power, angled across the gold carving of the queen, her white linen robe exquisitely inlaid on the coffin lid by what appeared to be thin slices of alabaster, forming linen-like pleats.

A large gold-plated structure behind the coffin was a perfect model of Queen Hatshepsut's temple at Deir el-Bahari, complete with the cliffs towering behind it. As he aimed his flashlight toward it, the reproduction seemed to capture the morning sunlight, the cliffs casting off the same roseate glow that Johab remembered that last morning when his father had been sketching the actual temple.

Johab moved closer to examine the cliffs carved in miniature. Tiny carnelian bands of jewels angled into the edges of the carving creating shadows and tints of color on the outcroppings of the cliff face.

No sketches or models of Queen Hatshepsut's temple had ever been found. Johab's father claimed that such plans and models must have existed. Here it was, more magnificent than imaginable, and not at all what his father would have expected.

Johab sucked in a deep breath of perfumed air that cleared his head. Nothing in King Tutankhamen's tomb could touch the artistry of objects in this chamber. Howard Carter and Mr. Feisel had been the first humans in over three thousand years to look inside the resting place of a very young king. Now, he was experiencing a greater privilege.

This tomb was different. Queen Hatshepsut's tomb was staving off death, keeping it at bay. Every panel around her coffin seemed to proclaim: "This is my Egypt. These are my people. These are my gods. We are here."

Two gold-embossed statues stood as sentinels on either end of the coffin. Hathor's face was grave, benign, one arm stretched out over the end of the coffin as though daring *anyone* to disturb its contents. The second sentinel, Horus, wore a short kilt of pleated gold. The left arm of the hawk-faced Horus angled in counterpoint to the right arm of Hathor. His right arm hovered above a golden sledge with four Canopic jars of pale alabaster.

Johab dared not venture any closer to the small, angry gods sitting atop the Canopic jars. These were the children of Horus, protecting the vital organs of the Queen. Other small statues ringed the outer edge of the room. Rather than being crafted from wood or stone, these appeared to be of solid gold and were almost a meter in height. Amulets hung around their necks, each fashioned differently, some with giant cabochon carnelians covered with hieroglyphs, others with green jasper, flashed with ribbons of gold, tapering into heavy links.

The walls were a marvel to behold. Johab moved closer to touch them. He knew that Senenmut would not have brought artists into this secret place to plaster and paint the walls of the stone tomb. It had to remain a secret tomb. Johab trailed his fingers along the edge of one panel.

The precious cedar of Lebanon had been cut into slabs about a meter wide, primed with a thin coat of plaster, and then painted with scenes to line the walls of the entire chamber.

Almost dizzy from the bright colors, Johab felt a sudden affection for this architect of Queen Hatshepsut who had insured that his queen would not rest in the afterworld without the color and light and drama of her everyday world.

On one wall, Queen Hatshepsut stood in her golden chariot, urging her horses ahead as they plunged into a jungle of exotic animals, bright birds, and past small wattle huts—the land of Punt. That's where she had journeyed to bring back those incense trees. It was a far-away, unknown place where his father's friend, Ian Parks, might or might not be.

The heady perfume of incense was all around Johab. He touched the lump on the back of his head and sniffed his oily fingers. Same scent. Wonderfully refreshing. Like a lime popsicle on a hot day, with no more school for the rest of the week.

With a feeling of happiness that he couldn't explain, not with all his troubles, Johab moved closer to the panels, wishing he could understand the hieroglyphs etched out in reds and greens and yellows.

On the central panel stood a ring of gods and goddesses, Hathor, Isis, Horus, Hapi, Maat, and Anubis. Kneeling in a simple white robe wearing the double crown of Egypt was Queen Hatshepsut, holding both of her hands open, as if in supplication to these gods.

Something was very different here. The figures were not flat, two-dimensional, as they were in other tomb paintings. These figures seemed to have moved into another dimension, their bodies rounded, more human, more real.

There were lines of soldiers, their spears hoisted high in celebration, and smaller figures of the common people, herding animals, cutting grain, stacking mud bricks, and carpenters working with adzes to carve these very panels from cedar trees.

The panorama of the color and splendor that was Egypt in Queen Hatshepsut's time transported Johab back over three thousand years. He was there. He could see everything. He could hear the noise of marching warriors, the clatter of chariot wheels, and the shouts of the people as their queen passed by, the moments that had been captured in the careful design and brilliant colors of these panels.

The artist had lovingly painted the common people. They were happy and secure, loved by their Queen. The workers on the tombs were the people who most interested his father. That's why he dug around their old villages, trying to find out more about their lives. Johab sniffed back tears. If only his father could see their faces.

Swiping his face with his sleeve, Johab stepped backwards and bumped into a block of stone. He whirled and aimed his flashlight. The deep rich blue of the large block of lapis glowed quietly and alone amidst the glitter of gold and flash of bright stones that seemed to be on every item in the tomb.

Johab had seen a similar statue carved from granite. Surely lapis, a rare stone, could not be found in this size. It was as tall as he was. He traced his fingers over the edges of the block. It was a single block, covered with hieroglyphs, and topped by the somber face of Senenmut, his chin resting against the face of Neferure, the daughter of Queen Hatshepsut. Egyptologists speculated that she might have been the daughter of Senenmut though there was no proof.

Johab had no doubt now. On this lapis stone, one hieroglyph seemed oversized, topping the pictorial text below. It was of a man seated with his hand held against his mouth. Johab knew that symbol. It meant "grief."

At the Museum, Johab had been fascinated by the granite statue of Senenmut and Neferure, the Queen's child he tutored. In that carving, Senenmut's face was impassive, unreadable. This statue was something else entirely.

Senenmut's arms moved like liquid indigo out of the stone and around the figure of the child. His face seemed alive with a contentment that was carved to last for eternity. This was a father protecting his own child, holding her in the tomb of her mother so that both father and child could watch over the Queen forever.

Johab sank to the ground, letting the flashlight roll from his grasp. He searched for a single word to describe how he was feeling. "Overwhelmed" was a word too often used. "Ecstatic" sounded like someone who had just reached the top of a roller coaster, preparing for the downward swoop. "Humble." That was the word.

He dropped his head between his knees and closed his eyes. The feeling of being a small, ordinary boy sitting in the midst of the untouched splendor from the finest artists and craftsmen of Queen Hatshepsut's world was simply too much to bear.

Johab was alone with the mummy and treasures of a Queen who had vanquished the dark powers of death for more than three thousand years.

Johab's feeling of insignificance vanished as fear snapped his head forward. Something was slithering against his leg. Cobras could probably get into tombs such as this. They loved dark places.

This cobra had stopped moving and coiled against Johab's backside. He dared not move, could not risk reaching for his flashlight. Death lay behind him, ready to strike.

A familiar sound came from the snake which was not cold, but warm. It was the sound that Bastet made just as he curled comfortably at the foot of Jasmine's sleeping mat. It was the sound of a cat that had found its home.

Johab snatched up his flashlight, twisted around, and aimed it at the furry lump behind his back. Bastet blinked somberly, yawned, and tucked his head under his front paw, tired, as though he had spent a hard night of mouse hunting.

Johab gathered up the cat and held him close to his chest. Bastet's purring was the first comforting sound he had heard in hours. Or days? How long had he been in this tomb? Time had no meaning here. Only the dull ache of hunger and his dry mouth told him that many hours had passed since he had escaped Barzoni's men.

He sat upright. Bastet hissed at him. What was Jasmine's cat doing here? Cats could travel long distances to find their masters, but why would Bastet leave Jasmine? Could something have happened to his little sister? And his mother? They didn't know anything about this tomb.

Cyril, Hetty, and Mr. Feisel might be another matter. All of them had information of interest to Barzoni. Cyril had seen the tomb sketch on the ancient papyrus—and had memorized it with the metrical marks for distances. Cyril weighed no more than forty pounds, but he could be a fount of information if Barzoni got his hands on him.

Cyril wouldn't talk. Johab had seen the welts on his back and legs. Cyril understood torture, the kind that was regularly inflicted by Mustafa. When Johab asked about the beatings, why he didn't fight back, why he didn't run, Cyril said calmly: "Mustafa can't make me cry. Only Alice can make me cry."

It was the risk to Alice—as well as the skinned mouse rammed into his mouth—that caused Cyril to revolt. Johab smiled to himself when he remembered the bandage on Mustafa's thumb. Cyril's teeth had done considerable damage—a bite that had saved both Cyril and Alice. Or, Johab thought ruefully, a bite that brought the two children into the dangerous circle that Johab was creating around his family and friends.

A muffled thump sounded from somewhere in the outer burial chamber or up in the shaft. Johab's hands went rigid on Bastet's body. The cat squalled and smacked his hand with sharp claws. Johab sat absolutely still. Nothing more could be heard from the outer chambers. Maybe it was a rock tumbling down far up in the shaft. It was only a matter of time before the three thieves from the village returned to get more booty from the outer burial chamber.

Johab eased up and stood, as unmoving as the statue of Senenmut, holding Jasmine's cat, the son of the goddess Bastet in his arms. The tomcat ceased struggling and stared, unblinking, at this world from which generations of his cat ancestors had come.

So many generations had passed that Bastet's little cat memory could not have imagined his family tree. Two cat mummies, their bodies encased in cedar of Lebanon, stared at Bastet from alabaster and lapis eyes. "Silence," they seemed to say. "No tail- lashing in the presence of the gods."

Johab, tense with renewed fear, continued to flash the light around the room, trying to memorize every object, every painting, knowing that this final burial chamber of Queen Hatshepsut *must* live only in his memory. *Her safety from the world depended on his silence.*

Queen Hatshepsut's private world showed her with her daughter, holding out gifts to her servants. Each person's face in these panels was different, individualized, as though these were the people she most loved.

He did not see Thutmose III, her nephew, in any of these scenes. Johab nodded with understanding. She had excluded her nephew from her final resting place. His absence told Johab more than any of the Egyptologists had learned or speculated from the defacing of her temples and the removal of her name from the royal records.

Even if Johab had a drawing pad, he could not have reproduced these panels. His sketches were clumsy and child-like. But, some day he would be able to do that. He would do that for his father.

He clenched his jaw and wrinkled his forehead, forcing images to be etched into his brain, tucking them away into file cabinets and muttering: "Remember, remember. Every scene. Every face. If Cyril can remember, so can I."

Sad as he felt to leave the burial chamber, he knew that he had to get out and never return. Holding the struggling Bastet tightly, he aimed his flashlight on the far wall. The great god Amun-Ra smiled down, holding in one hand a golden ankh, the symbol of eternal life. His other hand stretched protectively over the coffin of his beloved daughter, Queen Hatshepsut.

As he shoved against it, easing his way out, the large granite panel screeched along the limestone floor, then closed with a sudden snap. Johab swept the flashlight's beam along the edges of the slab. The skill of the carvers was incredible. Not even a single line marked where the panel swung out and away from the other slabs. The hieroglyphs linked panel to panel so that no space appeared between them.

Johab looked down and gasped. The floor was another matter. The circular scratches made by the slab swinging open would be a dead give-away to anyone searching for a secret opening to another tomb.

Johab flashed his light around the outer burial chamber where he had watched the thieves from inside the coffin of the Queen. This room looked like the old photographs that Howard Carter had taken of King Tutankhamen's tomb; it had been systematically ransacked, with broken furniture thrown in piles, and baskets and pottery smashed.

Instead of a black and white photograph that starkly depicted the damage in King Tut's outer chamber, these old treasures sparkled with color. Johab felt a chill run down his spine. Those thieves would return. Even a broken basket or a shard of pottery with an inscription from the *Book of the Dead* had value in the market.

Johab dropped Bastet. The cat leaped atop the empty coffin in front of the panel and stared at Johab, its yellow fur blending into fragments of gold leaf clinging to the lid. The cat was rooted to the spot. He might have been part of the surface carvings—except the Goddess Bastet never appeared on coffins. She wasn't part of the underworld.

Johab's throat was so dry that he could hardly whisper. Time was critical. The thieves might return at any moment. They would not ignore a coffin. Many of the stones had been pried out, but some remained. An ancient coffin lid, even damaged, would be worth a great deal of money. Staying in this place wasn't safe for him or the cat.

Johab clicked off his flashlight to conserve his batteries. The oil lamp the men had left behind flickered on the floor of the outer burial chamber. He had to protect the location of Queen Hatshepsut's tomb. That meant finding a way to hide those circular scratches on the floor. When the thieves moved the wooden coffin, as they surely would, the marks would point them directly to the moveable panel.

That tool was an odd item to be in a burial chamber, but there it was, its wooden handle gleaming softly in the light of the lamp—an ancient adze, a carpenter's tool. Johab had seen the fragment of one that his father found around the workers' villages. This one was pristine, the sheen of the blade still glistening with oil. Perhaps Senenmut, the master architect, had left it in this outer chamber as a tribute to the craftsmen who had fashioned some of the treasures for his queen.

Johab pulled the wooden plugs, lowering the blade as close to the end of the wooden frame as possible. He gently pushed the empty coffin aside, knelt with the adze and began scraping the limestone floor.

Perspiration soaked his back. His throat felt so dry that he didn't think he had an ounce of moisture left in his body. This was hard work. The copper blade flexed against the limestone. It had been designed to shave a wooden surface, not a stone floor. Johab pushed the blade down as hard as he could and shoved it away from him. Small slivers of stone flaked off in front of the sharp edge.

This was no ordinary workman's adze. He clutched the two golden lions' heads at the top of the wooden frame and pulled the blade back towards him. The adze worked better when he pushed it forward. He might save himself a nasty cut if he moved the blade away rather than towards himself.

Gently push. Gently push, he repeated to himself, trying to imagine the rhythmical movement of the ancient carpenter who had fashioned this tool. He closed his eyes, his arms and shoulders aching from the effort, working against time, wondering why that thump in the outer shaft had not been followed by gravel and loud voices.

Bastet growled softly, arching his body into a perfect loop atop the wooden coffin. Johab glanced at the cat, and then looked at the floor. The circles had disappeared. Only a freshly scraped surface remained, its lines vertical like chisel marks on the stones of the floor.

Johab spit on his fingers, rubbed them across the lines, and stood up to examine the floor. These stones looked exactly like the rest of the floor, the spittle attracting a fine glaze of dust as it dried. Johab stepped back to admire his work, then he pushed the empty coffin over it.

Faint crunches, like elfin footsteps on gravel, sounded outside the double wooden doors of the outer chamber, the doors that the thieves had closed securely behind themselves.

How could they have returned so silently? Why hadn't he heard them working their way down the shaft as he had earlier? Johab was too terrified to move. He glanced at the wooden coffin. It had hidden him once, but now the lid was firmly fitted in place. If he tried to pry it up, he would alert the thieves to his presence.

Bastet stood upright on the coffin, alert, his tail twitching. The cat's fangs might damage a mouse, but they were hardly fit weapons against the two thieves who had been pillaging this tomb.

Johab snatched up the adze. The copper blade might slice through a man's hand, disabling him. But, there had been that second man, the one who had warned the man with the damaged face. Johab would not be able to fend off two attackers. He had no alterative but to strike first. He held the adze as high as he could and moved quietly behind one of the wooden doors. A direct attack might surprise the thieves long enough for him to get past them.

Small rustling sounds came from outside the door, soft noises as though someone was trying to move a large cloth bundle. That was odd. Then, the wooden door creaked slightly, as though moving against a stubborn force. A flashlight beam shot through the small opening. Johab froze.

The bird-like voice was the sweetest sound that Johab had heard since he had been carried like a trussed turkey into the tomb. "Johab, are you in there?"

Johab dropped the adze, grasped the side of the door and tugged. It moved slightly so that he could see the wide eyes and very dirty face of Cyril. Cyril had grown a foot taller since they had last seen each other. Impossible. Johab shook his head. "Why can't you open the door, Cyril? What are you standing on?"

"A dead man," Cyril responded in a matter-of-fact tone of voice.

CHAPTER 55

In the difficult are the friendly forces,
the hands that work on us.

—Rilke

Far above the underground tomb, holding the end of a rope attached to Cyril who had dropped into a crevasse, Mr. Feisel sat patiently correcting Miss Wenkle's Arabic. She learned quickly, and her accent was really quite good for a foreigner. Mr. Feisel listened to her soft voice repeating again and again, trying hard to mimic the inflections of his voice.

Watching her struggle with a new language, her blue eyes bright with the challenge of learning something new, Mr. Feisel unexpectedly felt protective of this stocky English woman. She was a bit plump, as his wife had been.

The early morning sun cast a soft pink glow along the uppermost edges of the cliffs. At dawn, he often tried to remember his wife. Almost a quarter of a century had passed since her death at sunrise that terrible morning. She was too young to die. He could remember that last day with her, the whites of her eyes yellow from the ravages of malaria. She had clasped his hands and apologized for not giving him children.

Tears sprang to his eyes, not because of her death—those tears had long since passed—but because his wife felt that she had not been a good wife. Her last concerns had been for him. And now, he could no longer remember her face except from old photographs. He could remember her spirit. She had been a bit bossy too, like Miss Wenkle. He shrugged. He must like bossy women.

Miss Wenkle stopped repeating sentences and looked at her watch. "Mr. Feisel, Cyril has been down in that hole for almost an hour. Don't you think we should try to pull him up?"

Mr. Feisel glanced toward the dark gap between the rocks. "Cyril is a very resilient little boy. The floods have washed out sections of these tombs. He's probably exploring every corner. He may have found the tunnel that leads to the front of the tomb. It would take him some time to explore that area."

He squinted into the distance, looking down the path where the two thieves had gone. "I don't think those men will be back during the daylight. By night, they'll be back to take more things from the tomb. Their sacks were bulging with trophies," he added with disgust.

He wrapped the end of the rope around a protruding stone and climbed up on a large shelf of limestone. "I can't see or hear anything coming from below. Barzoni's men must have walked back toward the river. Their car is useless. Let's wait a bit longer for Cyril. We could cause him to lose his balance by pulling on that rope."

He eased himself down next to her, resisting the impulse to push a stray lock of her blond hair back from her face, and said, "Now, you tell me why you are so interested in Cyril."

Miss Wenkle turned an interesting shade of pink. Mr. Feisel's hand against her hair had been gentle, like a breeze skimming it. Johab's friend had initially reminded her of a desert tribesman, one of those haughty men who kept their women veiled and three steps behind them. Out here in the desert, he seemed quite different.

He was a good teacher, patient when she made mistakes, encouraging her to speak faster, to rely on her good instincts for the language. He was someone who invited trust. She spoke rapidly, trying to keep emotion out of her voice. "There are some curious coincidences involving Cyril and Alice—and me. I'll tell you about my uncle, and you tell me what you think."

Mr. Feisel cocked his head and listened. He appreciated the manner in which Miss Wenkle gave information, complete and in a chronological order. "My Uncle Cyril, my father's brother, was an officer in the British military during the war, assigned to Cairo at the end of the war."

Miss Wenkle's voice changed when she talked about her aunt and uncle, who were childless and seemed to have great affection for their only niece. "They brought the excitement of an exotic country into my life. They wrote long, interesting letters about their lives. They came to London to visit me every year . . . and when Aunt Alice became ill . . . they came home."

Miss Wenkle stared at the ground, bent forward, her hand in front of her mouth. Mr. Feisel thought that she resembled the hieroglyphic symbol for grief.

She straightened her back and continued speaking, the tone of her voice even, as though no emotion should intrude: "After Aunt Alice died, Uncle Cyril was gone within a few months. I was left with only my invalid mother."

She flashed him a sly grin. "At least she claimed to be an invalid so that I would never stray too far away from home. I daresay that she could have climbed these hills as quickly as either one of us."

Her smile faded. "She died very suddenly—her heart simply stopped. That's when I decided to come to work in Cairo." She glanced toward the rose-hued cliffs towering over the Valley. "I've never regretted my decision." She turned back toward Mr. Feisel. "That's my history and that of my uncle in a nutshell. But here is the interesting part, the part that might involve the children."

The cool air of the desert night was retreating in the face of the sun. Osiris was beginning his journey across the morning sky back to the underworld. Miss Wenkle pushed the sleeves of her robe back from her arms and stretched. "Cyril is an odd name for an Egyptian boy, as is Alice for a girl. That was the first inkling I had of some kind of connection."

"The letters," she added. "I remembered things in my uncle's letters when I first met Cyril. After Johab sent him up to my apartment to see if the coast was clear, I asked Johab about Cyril. He told me that his little friend's father and mother had both worked for an English major who had been a very good friend to them, such a good friend that Cyril's parents named their only children after this English couple."

She nodded her head affirmatively. "Even in a city the size of Cairo, how many native children are named Cyril and Alice? As soon as Johab left my apartment, I reread those old letters from my aunt and uncle. They both wrote about this special Egyptian couple who worked for them. They were godparents when the couple's little son was born and named Cyril, after my uncle. The next child was expected but had not been born when they had to leave for London."

She looked sadly at Mr. Feisel. "My aunt was so ill. Watching her in pain broke my uncle's heart. He lost interest in anything but relieving her pain. Before he died, he told me two things. He felt guilty that he had deserted his young friends in Egypt." She lowered her head. "That's the word he used, 'deserted.' On his deathbed, he asked me to use the savings that he left in his will to me to find this couple who had not been just employees but good friends. Their names were Yusef and Somia Abbaza. Do you know how many people named Abbaza live in Cairo? And every other one is named Yusef," she added in frustration.

"There was simply no way to find them. I hired a local man through the Embassy, but he just took my money and provided no useful information. He said other people, some Turks, lived in my uncle's old house. No one remembered my uncle. Or the Egyptian couple who lived in the same house. He said he canvassed the neighborhood for blocks. At least that's what the man told me." The frustration she had experienced then reappeared in an angry flush on Miss Wenkle's face.

"It's really not that surprising," Mr. Feisel interrupted. "Cyril told me that his mother died when Alice was born. After that, his father and uncle went to work on the boats down around the temples in Karnak. Apparently, their English was passable, and they thought they could get better jobs as tourist guides. Cyril was only five years old. He remembered that they both returned to Cairo very ill with typhoid. Cyril has some memories of his father and his uncle being taken to a hospital. He was not allowed to see his father again."

Mr. Feisel smacked his fist against his knee. "That's when that aunt took the children to her house. Within a few months of her husband's death, that Mustafa fellow moved in, and Cyril's life became an absolute hell."

Mr. Feisel rarely displayed emotion. Miss Wenkle noted that his jaw was clenched and his hands gripped his knees. She envisioned Mustafa encountering this old man in the desert. He looked quite youthful for his age, certainly very vigorous at this moment.

"The names could just be a coincidence—English names were popular in Cairo after the war. I've never asked Cyril his last name. I don't think any of us have. Cyril flinches every time I've asked him about his family. I think that he is afraid to say too much. He seems to trust us, but he has been a child of the streets for several years. He has lived in a world where no one cares for him; he has been beaten regularly by Mustafa; and, his only relative—not a blood relative, but an aunt by marriage—did not protect him."

Mr. Feisel shook his head and added, sadly, "That boy has come from a dark place. Yet, he is a remarkable child, because he manages to make us all smile just to be around him."

The black hole under the ledge of rock where Cyril had disappeared gaped in silence. Neither of them could say another word.

CHAPTER 56

"What dead man?" Johab asked Cyril, his voice trembling as he peeped at Cyril through the crack in the double doors of the outer burial chamber.

"The one with the bad face. His cousin was angry because he kept some of the loot for himself. You should have seen it, Johab."

Cyril's thin voice went up an octave with excitement. "I didn't see the tall man's hand move. The knife zoomed out of his hand, and the next second it was planted in this man's throat."

Cyril bent over. "Just a minute, Johab. I think I can move him so you can see the hole it made in his throat."

"Don't move him, Cyril." Johab was making every effort to keep his voice low and controlled. Sudden images of the Museum guard with the extra smile carved into his neck flashed before Johab. In movies and television, death was a tidy and bloodless affair. In real life, there was a face attached to it. Johab shuddered and moved the beam of his flashlight toward the crack in the door down toward Cyril's feet.

Like little bird claws, Cyril's bare toes were digging into the soft pile of something that had been the thief Nahud, with Cyril trying to get a firm purchase to enable him to see through the upper crack between the wooden doors. "I'll pull and you push, Johab. If we can move him just a bit more to the side, I can get through the crack in the door." Cyril seemed to be assuming another role. He was the lieutenant, not the major.

Johab whispered, "Keep your voice low, Cyril. There may be two sets of thieves in this tomb. Barzoni's men have the key to the main entrance. The thieves robbing the tomb are coming in from the shaft outside, above this chamber."

Johab stopped abruptly, his voice querulous. "How in the world did you and Bastet get down here?"

Cyril tugged at the crumpled form of Nahud without answering. Squeezing through an impossibly narrow opening between the doors, he hopped down from his perch on the corpse and smiled up at Johab. "We're all here, Miss Hetty, Mr. Feisel, and Bastet." He glanced down at Bastet who was weaving a figure eight pattern between Johab's feet. "There you are, you old yellow cat. We thought you had disappeared."

"What do you mean, Cyril? Where are Hetty and Mr. Feisel?"

Cyril waved his hand over his head. "Somewhere up there on the side of a cliff. Bastet found the hole in the rock. We watched the thieves getting things out of the tomb, so we had to hide. You would have been proud of me, Johab. I was so quiet. A scorpion walked across my hand, and I didn't even jump. I had the best lookout. I had to be quiet." Cyril's little face peered up at Johab, inquisitive, waiting for a word of praise.

Johab realized that Cyril was quite desperate for kindness, starved for it, even though his own family and friends had shown Cyril that they cared about him. Johab reached over and ruffled Cyril's dusty hair. "You are the best lieutenant that I could have, Cyril. You don't know how happy I am to see you."

Cyril's smile split his face. The oil lamp flickering in the middle of the floor paled in comparison to the brightness of that smile. The reality was that Cyril's smile wouldn't be around much longer if they lingered in this tomb. Barzoni's men probably couldn't find the entrance to the shaft, but the thieves had already been in the outside chamber and would return—with one less thief. Johab glanced at the lump of Nahud, blocking the outer wooden doors.

"We'll take small things, Cyril, items to prove to Barzoni that I know where the men got the New Kingdom stuff. He doesn't know about this tomb. I heard those thieves talking about it. Their contact is Mr. El-Hasiim. They haven't told him where they are finding the treasures. I heard them say that El-Hasiim works for a big boss—that's what they called him."

Johab's voice had a ragged quality, as though breathing had become a task for him. "If I can convince Barzoni that I know where the treasures are, maybe I can bargain for my father. Just take things we can carry back up that hole you came down, Cyril."

Cyril looked skeptical. "It was really hard getting down here, Johab. I could see where those men had braced their backs against the wall on one side and their feet on the other. They had knocked off the bat dung in places, but I was too short. I had to crawl like a lizard with both my hands and feet. How can we carry anything?"

Johab reached inside the pocket of his shorts and dangled the piece of hemp rope that had bound his hands. "We can tie up the edge of my galabeya to make a sack. That way, my hands will be free." He plunged both hands into his pockets. "And, my shorts have deep pockets." He glanced at Cyril. "I don't suppose you are wearing shorts under your robe?"

Cyril opened his palms and shrugged his shoulders. Being burdened with extra clothes was an English thing. "Pockets, Cyril. A lieutenant needs pockets. We'll fix that when we get home," Johab said decisively.

The beam of Johab's flashlight danced around the antechamber of the tomb. The thieves had done considerable damage, tossing priceless furniture into corners as carelessly as garbage. The thief with the burned face had hidden a knife under a chest. Johab knelt down and felt underneath for the thief's cache.

"Here." Johab pulled out a small alabaster jar, the lid exquisitely carved as the head of a bird, its tiny feathers crafted of turquoise and lapis. He lifted the lid and tipped the jar toward Cyril. Dark powder fell out. "This was the Queen's pot of kohl, her eye makeup. And this," he held up a small bowl of lapis, holding it under his nose, "held the ointment. The ointment she put on the bump of my head."

"She?" Cyril looked around the room for another person.

"Nothing. I just had a strange dream when I hit my head," Johab answered too quickly. He touched the lump on the back of his head and sniffed his fingers—the same scented ointment in the lapis bowl.

"This box will be a good item. And these," Johab reached for a small pile of cylinder seals. "They belong to the Queen. See her name in a cartouche on this one?" Cyril nodded agreeably. Hieroglyphs were beyond him. He was just learning to read *Pinocchio*, but if Johab said it was the Queen's name, then it was.

Johab stuffed the seals into the pockets of his shorts and placed the other items in a pile at the edge of his robe, gathering it like a sack. "Get that rope, Cyril, and tie a knot really tight."

Cyril picked up the piece of rope. "This is nasty, Johab. It's all coated with something that looks like blood."

"Mine," answered Johab in a surly tone, showing his wrists. "Tie it hard. Make two or three knots." He stood up, the bundle of small treasures bumping securely against his leg. "Let's move the dead man and get out of here. Now, Cyril." Johab had resumed his role as major.

The two boys used their combined weight to push against the door, held partially closed by the stiffening corpse of Nahud. There was just a crack for them to slip through. Cyril stepped on the corpse. Johab stepped over it and was swept by a wave of nausea. Small lights danced in front of his eyes.

"Cyril," Johab's voice was a half-whisper. "I feel sick. I think the bad air in here is getting to me. If I pass out, go back up the hole. Don't stay down here."

Cyril aimed his flashlight at Johab's pale, glistening face. Johab staggered. Cyril steadied him. "Sit down, Johab. Put your head low, between your knees. I sometimes felt dizzy after Mustafa beat me. Keeping your head down helps. I can take care of things here."

Fighting nausea, Johab sank to the ground. Keeping his eyes closed and his head between his knees helped. The pain in the back of his head exploded. Or a door snapped shut. He could hear Cyril grunting and pushing, moving things around. "That should get their attention." Small fingers touched his shoulder. "If you are feeling better, Johab, I think we need to try to get back up through the hole to the top."

Johab opened his eyes and pointed the beam of his flashlight at the double wooden doors. He didn't know whether to laugh or cry.

Nahud sat upright, his back resting against the center of the two doors. His eye stood open, glazed and white as though it had been crafted from alabaster. A wooden spear from the antechamber of the tomb was cradled by Nahud's bent arm. The tall, ebony sentinels guarding the Queen's mummy in the hidden chamber were magnificent. This poor thief with his burned face and newly punctured throat scarcely seemed human—more like some wicked spirit from the underworld.

Johab grinned. It might work. Nahud's cousins would return to see Cyril's artistry. They might have second thoughts about entering the chamber. The corpse of their cousin was a spooky guard. "Good work, Cyril. Let's get out of here." Johab scooped up Bastet. "Let's see if this old tomcat will lead the way up between these rocks."

Bastet balanced like an acrobat, leaping from rock to rock, pausing to check the boys' progress below him. Cyril tied the rope dangling from above around his waist, leaving several lengths of rope, and secured the end of it around Johab's waist.

Cyril was worried. Johab moved unsteadily, groping for footholds. He muffled his coughs behind his sleeve. Every time they stepped on a small ledge, clouds of bat dung exploded, followed by more spasms of coughing.

A powerful flood washing down tons of limestone had cracked open the side of the cliff leaving exposed rocks. The softer shale formed treacherous footholds on the ledges. A faint glimmer of daylight sliced between large outcroppings of limestone that appeared to be very far above them.

The floor below seemed miles beneath them. The sliver of sky above comforted Cyril. He knew that the edge of the hole was not much farther. It just seemed far off, an optical illusion created by the bending of this crooked shaft.

"We're almost there, Johab. This next bend is tricky. Bastet is already up there. He's waiting for us on the ledge just below the top. You'll have to lean way out to dig your hands and feet into these small gaps in the rock. I'm wrapping the rope between us around this rock sticking out. Now lean out and grab the ledge!"

Johab leaned and reached for the ledge. His arms and legs moved as slowly as treacle, but there was no ledge—only a rope, which was slicing him in half, and the darkness of night below.

CHAPTER 57

Unwillingly I left your land, O Queen.

—Virgil

The flash of a yellow tomcat pierced the darkness of the hole. Bastet sprang past the kneeling forms of Mr. Feisel and Miss Wenkle, aimed for the smooth rock where they had been sitting earlier, stretched the length of it, and immediately began grooming himself.

Sharp, frantic screams followed the streaking cat. The rope that Mr. Feisel had tied around his own waist began jerking in concert to the screams. "That's Cyril. He's in trouble."

Mr. Feisel plopped down on the ground in front of the hole under the ledge of rock, positioned both feet on the edge with the gap under them, and leaned backward. He tested the rope. It wasn't tight. "Something isn't right. There's no tension on this rope but it is moving."

Miss Wenkle edged close to the rim of the hole and aimed her flashlight into its depths. She angled dangerously forward, flashing her light around the interior of the gap between the rocks. "I see something." Her voice was tense. "On the ledge. Bat guano is flying everywhere. Can't quite make it out, but something is moving on a ledge. Hold my legs, Mr. Feisel."

Without giving him a moment to protest that upstanding Egyptian men did not grab legs of English women, at least those they barely knew, Miss Wenkle slid almost full length into the hole.

Grabbing Miss Wenkle's legs before she dropped headfirst into the dark hole, Mr. Feisel could feel sweat trickling down his back. The rope tied to Cyril hung slack. Gripping the legs of a woman who was inching headfirst into a pit took all of his strength. He felt only terror at this moment. If he lost both boys, as well as Miss Wenkle, returning home with only a cat would be too much to bear.

"I see them." Her shout was muffled. With that information, a renewed burst of strength coursed through his arthritic joints. He braced his arthritic knees against the overhanging rock and gripped the ankles of Miss Wenkle with the power he remembered as a younger man.

"Cyril is on a small outcropping of rock with his rope anchored to another rock."

She scooted backwards, tucked her knees under her body, and crouched close to Mr. Feisel. "I can't see past the ledge where Cyril is standing. I think that Johab might be hanging on that rope Cyril has looped around a rock."

Mr. Feisel grunted in frustration. "I can't get either one of them up as long as Cyril has the rope around a rock. Do you think you can hang back over the ledge and make Cyril hear you?"

Miss Wenkle nodded, thrust both of her legs behind her, and scooted back to the edge. "Cyril!" Her scream might have awoken the stiffening corpse of Nahud somewhere below. "Unwrap the rope from the rock. So we can drag both of you up. Count to thirty, then release the rope."

Cyril's questioning little face stared up at her from far below. "In Arabic," shouted Mr. Feisel. "He doesn't understand what you are saying . . ." Mr. Feisel shouted words. Frantically, Miss. Wenkle repeated them in a shrill voice down the dark hole below her head.

"Back up quickly! Grab the rope with me! In less than thirty seconds, both of us will be holding two boys at the end of this rope." For once, Miss Wenkle didn't mind that Mr. Feisel's command was brusque.

With Mr. Feisel tugging on her legs, Miss Wenkle wiggled backward and propped her feet alongside Mr. Feisel's knees against the overhanging ledge of rock. She grabbed the rope behind Mr. Feisel's fists. Within seconds, the rope popped like a whip, cinching the loop around his body tightly.

"We need better leverage. With both of these boys hanging in space, I don't know how long the rope will hold. From the weight of this, Cyril must have retied it around his waist and is hanging in mid-air with Johab."

Mr. Feisel's face flushed with his effort to hold the rope away from the sharp edges of the rock. He motioned with his head, "See if you can move your feet across my body to the rope and push on it. If we can get it to swing, maybe one of the boys can get a foothold on the side of the crevasse."

Miss Wenkle nodded, braced her sandals against the rope, and pushed gently.

"That's it. I can feel them swinging. Just a little harder. Not much. We don't want to knock them against the rocks."

Down below them, the terror that Cyril felt had nothing to do with fear for his own safety. Dangling in space with a rope around his middle was not as scary as Mustafa whacking him across his back with a belt. It was Johab, hanging so lifeless at the end of the rope, who terrified him.

"Johab! Johab! Wake up!" Cyril's shouts echoed down the shaft. Johab's head moved slightly but his body hung like a stock-still pendulum. "Mr. Feisel is swinging the rope so we can grab hold of a ledge!" Cyril's voice had reached a near hysterical pitch, but his flashlight beamed unwaveringly down on Johab's head.

Johab's flashlight had disappeared down the shaft. "There, Johab, to your right. See that ledge? There's another one close to me. Move your body with the rope. On the count of three, push off the other side with your feet, and we'll each grab a ledge."

Mr. Feisel could feel added stress on the rope. The smooth swings of an anchored rope holding the two boys now seemed to be doubling back. Either Cyril or Johab or both boys were swinging in tandem with the rope. The tension on the rope stopped. The line went slack.

Mr. Feisel could feel slight movements in the rope but could do nothing but clutch it, waiting for it to tighten.

Miss Wenkle understood the dynamics of leverage as well as Mr. Feisel. It was clear that both the boys had found footholds. Now what? She eased her grip on the rope, moved her feet close to Mr. Feisel, and inched close to the edge of the hole.

"I'm having another look." Aiming her flashlight over the rim, she could see the top of Cyril's head about fifteen to twenty meters below. He was perched on a thin outcropping of rock. Below him, Johab balanced precariously with one foot on a tiny ledge and the other dangling.

Cyril shouted down to Johab. "Wrap the rope between us around that jagged rock sticking up on your ledge. Wrap it very tight. I'm going to wiggle out of the loop around my waist and shinny up the rope to the top. When I get to the top, you unwrap your rope from the rock. We can pull you up. I don't think Mr. Feisel can pull both of us hanging like dead weights."

Cyril beamed his flashlight down so that Johab could see the protruding rock. Johab moved slowly. His foot slipped again and again in the soft shale of the ledge, but he made one loop, two loops around the rock and tested it, and nodded upward toward Cyril's light.

"That's it, Johab. You're safe right there. Now, I'm going to untie the rope from my waist so that I can climb up." The confidence in Cyril's little voice did not reduce the terror that Johab was feeling. Cyril would be climbing up a single, wavering sliver of rope, held by a man whose hands were stiff with arthritis.

His lieutenant took charge. Cyril fumbled with his knots. They were too tight for him to untie. There was an easier way. He sucked in, slipped the rope down his skinny body, and stepped out of it. Gripping his flashlight between his chin and his neck, and using the loop that had cinched his waist as a foothold, Cyril started a long climb upward, hand over hand, his toes gripping the rope, more monkey than boy.

When the rope snapped with tension, Mr. Feisel reared back against it, holding it as taut as possible. Miss Wenkle was of no help.

He waved her back, so she crawled to the edge of the fissure, shining her flashlight down the rope until the beam disappeared into darkness.

"I see his arms. He's climbing up the rope!" Her voice was tense with hushed excitement. Nothing must break the concentration of that small boy. Within minutes, a dusty head popped up at the edge of the hole. Miss Wenkle grabbed both of Cyril's arms, lifted him out of the void, clutched him against herself, and wept softly.

Cyril smiled broadly. No one had shed a tear over him for as long as he could remember—maybe his father did before he went to work at Karnak.

Cyril moved with reluctance out of her arms. "We have to get Johab. Hold the rope tight, Mr. Feisel." Cyril dropped to his knees and crept dangerously close to the edge of the hole. In halting English, he said: "Hold feet, Miss Hetty. I make noise. Johab hear." He plopped down quickly, thrusting his legs backward for Miss Wenkle's grasp.

She dropped beside Cyril, barely catching his ankles before he slid forward, face down. The child trusted her. Another second and she would have missed her hold.

"Johab!" The screech of Cyril's high-pitched voice echoed the length of the shaft.

"Unwind the rope and kick off from the ledge. We'll pull you straight up." Cyril rolled over, sat up, grabbed the rope behind Miss Wenkle's hands and added his small muscles to the job ahead of them.

The rope popped with a twanging sound. Johab could weigh no more than seventy or eighty pounds, but the rope was being taxed. Small hemp curls were breaking away from the rope where it had rubbed against the edge of the surface rock. Frowns across the faces of Miss Wenkle, Mr. Feisel, and Cyril deepened in unison. At any moment, the rope might break with Johab dangling over a shaft that seemed bottomless.

"All together. Pull firmly as hard as you can," Mr. Feisel was beet-colored with effort. "If this rope breaks, he doesn't have a chance. We're working against time."

Time was kind. Johab was dragged from a deep hole where only two thieves, Cyril, and a cat had ever descended. Pulled past the edge of the fissure face down, Johab rolled himself into a tight ball with his eyes squeezed shut.

Bastet was the first to move. He crept over to Johab, lifted one paw, and smacked the side of his head. Johab blinked, raised his head, opened his eyes, and laughed out loud.

Miss Wenkle dropped to her knees beside him, kissing his face, hugging him, examining his scratches. Even his mother didn't kiss him that much anymore. He looked past Miss Wenkle's fluttering hands that couldn't stop massaging his cheeks and saw Mr. Feisel and Cyril. His eyes crinkled at the corners. He gave them a big wink.

"Wait until you see what is inside my pockets and tied up in my robe, Mr. Feisel. Your cylinder seal is nothing compared to what I found." Johab remained on his belly, his arms and legs splayed out as though he were unable to move them.

Going quickly to Johab, Mr. Feisel thrust his hands under Johab's arms and pulled him carefully to his feet. Johab swayed uncertainly, but stared directly into the deeply sunken eyes of his old neighbor who had just pulled him from a dark and terrifying hole but was not saying a word.

He didn't need to speak. The thoughts passing between Johab and Mr. Feisel were too profound, too deeply felt to assume the shape of a syllable, the noise of a sound.

Perhaps the sun's rays flashed across Johab's face at that moment, but Miss Wenkle could have sworn that she saw something tangible move between the eyes of the old man and the little boy—a faint explosion of silver dust, as though they had both been blessed by some invisible hand. Nonsense. Her eyes were playing tricks in the morning sun.

Mr. Feisel broke the silence, his voice in Arabic as solemn as though he were speaking inside a cathedral. "You have seen where she rests for eternity. You have lived the dream. I can see it in your eyes."

The faintest smile twitched at the corners of Johab's mouth. He nodded briefly, then slid to the ground and lay unmoving in the circle of his three friends.

Miss Wenkle dropped to her knees, lifted Johab's head, and looked accusingly up at Mr. Feisel. "What did you say to him? I saw that look on both of your faces. You were sharing some big secret. It stressed Johab. He is barely breathing." She fanned air around his face with frantic hand movements. Cyril stood, chewing his nails, already bitten to the quick.

Mr. Feisel picked up one of Johab's limp hands and held his fingers to his wrist. "His pulse is steady. Look at the boy, Miss Wenkle. He is terribly dehydrated. His lungs must be coated with the debris from that shaft. Only Allah knows what kind of air he has been breathing in that tomb."

He turned Johab's hands over. "He's lost blood from these deep cuts on his wrist and some kind of puncture of his finger. Look at these rope burns on his wrists. Barzoni's men . . . ." His words shifted to Arabic and came in emphatic bursts as he examined Johab's body.

He bent to scoop up Johab, cradling him in his arms as though he were weightless. "We need to go back to the car and get some water into Johab. He'll come around. He's just exhausted."

Cyril scooped up Bastet and nodded toward the cardboard box that had been his cage.

"That cat has earned his freedom. He can choose where he wants to sit in the car. He deserves a place of honor." Mr. Feisel had never kept a cat as a pet and often wondered why the ancient Egyptians prized them so much that they crafted ornate mummy cases to take their cats with them to the next world. He didn't wonder now. He knew.

Mr. Feisel spoke to Cyril in Arabic, and Cyril moved over near the fissure under the rock ledge. He grabbed the cardboard box and moved it back and forth along the desert sand, wiping out every trace of their footprints, then smashed it and tossed it as far away as he could throw it.

Miss Wenkle coiled up the rope, grabbed her purse off the ground, and picked her way down the rocky trail behind the four males—Cyril cradling Bastet and Mr. Feisel holding Johab as gently as if he were the rarest of tomb treasures.

CHAPTER 58

Four men, bristling with guns and shell cases draped over their shoulders, appeared along a small path that ran parallel to the face of the cliff. Miss Wenkle flipped up the hood of her galabeya and lowered her face. *What now?* She asked herself. *What more can happen to us?*

Mr. Feisel didn't break his stride but nodded toward the men and began speaking softly, stopping when they reached a connecting fork in the paths. One of the men held out his arms to take Johab, knelt with him, and swung a small, goatskin pouch over his head, dribbling water on Johab's face and into his mouth. Johab sputtered, coughed, struggled to sit upright and looked around wild-eyed.

"It's all right, boy. These are my friends. They have been watching from the top of the cliffs. They saw us heading back toward the car," Mr. Feisel reassured Johab who seemed dazed, as though he couldn't quite remember where he was.

Cyril, still clutching Bastet, edged up next to Johab and snuggled as close as he could to him. Miss Wenkle stood well back, hiding her face, pretending to be shy but feeling ridiculous. She glanced suspiciously at Mr. Feisel who appeared to be absolutely at ease with these village men who swung guns so casually over their shoulders.

Miss Wenkle edged a bit closer to the men. Johab was standing now, leaning against Cyril, his sturdy shadow. Mr. Feisel, Johab, and the four men were having a rather heated conversation in Arabic, which included a lot of hand gestures. She could understand only part of the conversation.

They were talking about the murder of one of the thieves by his cousin. Cyril's gesture of a whirling dagger toward his throat translated into any language.

The man who had given Johab water reached into his pack and brought out what appeared to be a hard slab of bread. Carefully tearing off a piece for Cyril, Johab waved the remaining piece in Miss Wenkle's direction. She shook her head decidedly. The thing looked moldy, even from this distance. Cyril and Johab chomped away at it.

Within minutes, two of the men nodded, embraced Mr. Feisel, and headed back up the path toward the top of the cliffs. One of the other men swung Johab up on his shoulders, motioned to his friend and Mr. Feisel and moved toward a steeper pathway, almost straight down toward the floor of the valley.

Cyril turned around and grabbed Miss Wenkle's hand, smiling up at her. "I speak English now." He did, but just a few words. Cyril managed to convey that these men were Mr. Feisel's friends. Cyril waved his arm toward the top of the cliffs and pointed back in the direction where he and Johab had crawled out of the fissure. He made circles of his thumbs and fingers and fitted them around his eyes, clutching the struggling Bastet between his knees.

"Binoculars?" queried Miss Wenkle. "They are going to watch from the cliffs with binoculars?" Cyril nodded, smiling. "Bi-nock-cu-laries," he repeated proudly.

"Bi-nock-cu-laries see bad men in car. They wait. Car go." Cyril smiled happily as though he had just communicated a wealth of information.

Miss Wenkle pulled him and the cat next to her. "You are going to learn better English, and I am going to study Arabic. Without Mr. Feisel or Johab as translators, we would be in trouble." She smiled at Cyril as though they had years to learn each other's language and muttered under her breath, "You and me and Alice, Cyril."

The man with Johab on his shoulders took the lead down the steep, stony path, fit only for mountain goats. Mr. Feisel followed, with the second man close behind him. Cyril waited patiently for

Miss Wenkle to pick her way down the steep trail. Her ill-fitting shoes weren't designed for climbing down on soft shale.

The little blue VW, coated with red-brown dust, was just where they had left it behind a small outcropping of rocks, hidden from the road. "We'll have to crowd in, Miss Wenkle. You and the boys get in the back seat. One of my friends will stand on the back bumper. The other will ride in your seat," Mr. Feisel whispered to Miss Wenkle.

"We're going back to my old village first. Then, they'll get their truck and follow us to Cairo. Barzoni's men are still in the area. Your VW will be a dead give-away." Mr. Feisel pulled her closer to him. "Don't look up. Don't speak. I told the men that you are very shy." A smile played across his lips as though he was just about to burst out laughing.

For the first time in her life, Miss Wenkle grunted in response. It was a nasty, rude sound, but she dared not express what she was feeling. *Ladies put in the back seat with mouths shut indeed.*

Three men, two children, and a very testy cat brought the VW to more than full capacity. Miss Wenkle sat on one side of the back seat, Johab on the other, with Cyril in the middle. Bastet stepped disrespectfully across all of their laps, sprang up to the back of the seat, stretched lengthwise and fell asleep in the sun.

Miss Wenkle dared not look behind her at the man plastered against the window, his feet braced along the length of the back bumper, clinging to the bouncing car for dear life.

Mr. Feisel drove too fast, dodging the largest rocks, and always managing to hit most of the holes in the road. This rocky path didn't really qualify as a road though it had two tracks that had accommodated vehicles at some time or other.

She listened to the low drone of conversation in the front seat, trying to sort out words. She recognized some words, such as "museum director," "antiquities," "police," and "London." Obviously, Mr. Feisel was sharing some information about why they were out in the desert with two children and a cat—perhaps he had to do that to get his friends to help him.

She glanced behind her, keeping her face covered. The bearded man clinging to the back of her VW stuck his thumb up in the air and smiled—or perhaps it was a grimace of terror as he clutched the sides of the car. Maybe he liked traveling in this dangerous fashion. It might be less risky than a camel.

Miss Wenkle dared not speak English to Johab, but she had so many questions. She patted her purse. As soon as the car started moving, Johab untied the rope that made a pouch of sorts at the bottom of his robe. He opened her purse and dumped in cylinder seals and exotic jars without a word. Then, Johab stretched his legs as far forward as they would go, cocked his head backwards, and fell into an exhausted sleep.

Cyril sat wide-eyed, looking all around, reaching over and touching Johab's arm occasionally, just to assure himself that Johab was there.

As the morning sun lit up a small village tucked into the hills beyond them, Mr. Feisel whipped the car onto a narrow side road. Miss Wenkle squinted at the road behind them. If Barzoni's men were following, she had no idea what kind of car they would be driving. It wouldn't be a Volvo with a broken oil pan and four flat tires, thanks to Mr. Feisel's handy knife.

She glanced over at Johab's sleeping face. He was too young to take on so many responsibilities. He had cleverly hidden his mother and Jasmine where no one would think of looking for them—in the City of the Dead. He had recruited her to help him. Most boys his age would have gone directly to the police—that might have been a fatal error.

She stared at the back of Mr. Feisel's head, his dark, grizzled hair streaked with gray, his neck brown and tread-marked by the desert sun. Johab had found this man who had learned about tombs from the master himself, Howard Carter.

Johab might not have been found and certainly wouldn't have escaped from the tomb without Mr. Feisel. She remembered the look of fear on his face as he watched the rope shredding before their eyes—and the almost superhuman strength of his sturdy hands on that rope.

A small hand snaked into her hands. Cyril beamed up at her. This little boy and his sister would still be victims of that horrible Mustafa if Johab had not rescued them. She glanced over at Johab. There was a bump on the back of his head and something sticky on it, glistening in the sunlight.

She reached over to touch it. Odd. It appeared to be some kind of ointment. The scent of it wafted toward her as she withdrew her hand. If she didn't know better, she could have sworn that Johab was wearing a dab of rare perfume.

Undisturbed by her touch and snoring softly, Johab needed to rest. This terrible ordeal that began the night his father was kidnapped wasn't over, despite the help of Mr. Feisel's friends. They had guns. They knew the desert, but Mr. Barzoni knew people in high places in the city. He had power, and he had Johab's father.

She had no doubt that Barzoni's men would be searching for Johab with a vengeance. This young boy had outwitted them. They would suffer for their carelessness if they couldn't find him. She recalled the touch of Barzoni's hand on her back just before she tumbled down the stairs. It had been as cold as ice.

CHAPTER 59

The VW bumped to a stop next to a mud brick wall. Two goats and some straggly chickens moved in their direction. Mr. Feisel opened his door, stepped out, and spoke to Cyril in Arabic. Cyril crawled across Miss Wenkle and held down the front seat so that she could extricate herself from the cramped back seat. He tugged on her arm, leading her toward one of the small houses. Johab followed.

A tall, middle-aged woman wearing a bright robe with a matching scarf tied around her head smiled and motioned them toward her. Cyril ran ahead and said something to her. She glanced down as though embarrassed. Johab clamped his hand over his mouth, his shoulders heaving with suppressed giggles. He murmered in a low voice. "Cyril just told that lady you are a deaf-mute, Hetty, and can't talk."

As soon as Johab got himself under control, he moved his fingers as though he might be making invisible Jacob's ladders in the air. "I'm pretending to speak to you in sign language," he muttered under his breath. "Mr. Feisel doesn't want his friends to know you are English. The lady is getting us something to eat."

"A bathroom, Johab," Hetty whispered. "Please ask her."

Johab muttered something in Arabic, and the woman responded. Johab gestured towards a small lean-to. "She'll take you to the outhouse."

Outhouse, thought Miss Wenkle. Surely Johab means "other house," somewhere that is separate from the men's house. She wasn't sure about the protocol of these villages, but she did understand the separation of sexes. Men first. Women last.

A few minutes later, Hetty returned, trailing the other woman. Johab smiled to himself about the priceless expression on Hetty's face. She had been to an outhouse. The English had brought modern plumbing to Cairo—even though it broke out of its traces underground and bubbled up on the pavements with disgusting regularity. The English had not brought plumbing to remote villages.

Miss Wenkle rearranged her face, grinned weakly at the woman, and followed her into a small house. She accepted a plate of bread, goat cheese and black olives. Never had food tasted so good. She could forgive the woman for the state of her outhouse. Johab and Cyril pushed pieces of bread around their plates until they gleamed—oil from small salty olives coated their chins.

When Hetty started to dig into her purse for money to pay the woman for their food, Johab narrowed his eyes and shook his head slowly. She understood. This was hospitality from Mr. Feisel's boyhood friends. Payment would be an insult. She grabbed the woman's hand and pumped it enthusiastically. Some day, when all of this was over, she would send this woman a gift—some nice Wensleydale cheese from the Yorkshire Dales. Sarah could get it for her.

Hetty's thoughts shifted to those left behind in the City of the Dead. What might be happening to Johab's mother and the little girls? She felt a tinge of guilt that she had dumped problems on her two closest friends from London. Sarah and Ella were supposed to be on vacation, and she had given them a family to look after. Well, she thought resignedly, that's what friends are for—to be there when we need them.

The blast of a car horn cut through her reverie. Johab thanked the village lady profusely and backed out the door. Mr. Feisel had just moved a goat off the top of the car and was prying a small bird from between the jaws of Bastet. He motioned to the front seat. Miss Wenkle took the passenger's seat without a word. Cyril and Johab piled in the back with Bastet.

Backing expertly out of the small enclosure, Mr. Feisel nodded in the direction of a rusty pickup, idling nearby. Both of his friends smiled and waved from the front seat. No rifles could be seen, but

Miss Wenkle suspected that knives and pistols were hidden beneath their flowing robes.

"Here's what I found out." Mr. Feisel started the conversation as though there had been no lull in the previous one—no hour-long trek down a perilous mountain path behind villagers armed to the teeth, no outhouse, and no armed guard following them back to Cairo.

Miss Wenkle stared at him, her nostrils flaring in irritation, but silent.

"The two men that left us back on the trail watched from the cliffs all night long. Once they saw the flashlights of the thieves coming along the trail, they could no longer use their lights. But, they could see shapes in the moonlight. They saw us hide behind the rocks, and they saw those three men doing something. They didn't know what."

He glanced at Miss Wenkle's skeptical face, uneasy, as though he might be telling strangers too much. "I had to tell them that the men had found a way into KV20. And, I told them about Barzoni's men putting Johab in the tomb. These are honest men, Miss Wenkle. They don't like tomb thieves. They give all the villagers a bad name. These village men rely on work around the tombs. The French, the English, the Americans, and other foreign museums and universities pay good wages to keep the tombs maintained."

He glanced in the rearview mirror to be sure that the pickup was still in sight. "If the Egyptologists can't trust the villagers to work, if they think they are trying to get into the tombs or into the digs to steal, they'll bring workers from Cairo."

He shifted into third gear, sending shivers down Miss Wenkle's spine as he ground the gears, searching for the right slot. "My friends won't go near the site where we found Johab, but they'll be visible enough to keep those thieves away. I told them that when we decide who should have the information, the right people will protect the site. I also explained that the director of the New Kingdom Project, Mr. El-Hasiim, is a bad man—and other people near him may be involved in thefts."

He clenched his hands on the steering wheel. "My friends recognized the thieves from my description. One of them said he thinks they came from a village near Giza. They like to poke around the old tombs. I told them about the murder. They couldn't see what was happening up on the cliffs, but they did see three men arriving and only two going back. They said the dead man will 'keep' in the tomb. Their plan is to begin herding their goats in that direction, keeping the trails very busy, including at night. They think the thieves will stay away—at least for awhile."

Johab leaned across the front seat. "Are we going to see my mother and Jasmine and Alice, Mr. Feisel? I'm worried about them. If those men weren't able to keep me captive, they might decide that a woman and some little girls are easier to manage."

Mr. Feisel smiled broadly. "Look behind us, Johab. That old pickup looks as though it can barely make it down the road. It has a new V-6 engine. My friends don't like having a pickup that looks too fancy. Thieves leave the rusty heaps alone. My friends will stay on our tail until we get you home."

He chuckled under his breath. "Your mother will be so happy to see you that she might not ask where you've been."

As they pulled onto the ferry, Miss Wenkle rolled down her window. This mighty river seemed angry to her, like a child who has been locked in his room without understanding the reason for punishment. Before the Aswan Dam had been completed, the Nile added drama to the lives of Egyptians—just as it had for thousands of years.

During the flooding season, the river cut off whole sections of villages. People and animals made their way through churning, muddy water to higher ground and safety. She glanced back at Johab and Cyril. Both were sound asleep. Bastet was curled into a knot of golden fur between them.

Miss Wenkle rubbed her eyes. The heat, the rattle of the car on the road, and the stress of almost losing two little boys in an ancient tomb brought on a fierce headache. She reached into her purse and pulled out a small alabaster jar that Johab had taken from the tomb. She popped up the lid and sniffed at its contents. An odd spicy scent wafted out of it. Her headache disappeared.

"Those old ointments worked miracles back then. At least, people thought that they did. That same stuff is on the back of Johab's head. I wonder how it got there?"

Mr. Feisel looked as though he had some inkling. He drove steadily, stopping only for petrol, and shook his head to ward off drowsiness. It seemed as though days had passed since he had slept. They needed to check on Johab's mother and the girls. If Barzoni knew that Johab had escaped, he might go after the wife and daughter to get information from Johab's father.

"I've been asleep for hours, Mr. Feisel. Your turn. You're exhausted." Miss Wenkle's soft voice interrupted his thoughts. "Pull over. I'll drive. I know the way to Cairo and how to get out to the City of the Dead. I'm an expert driver." Mr. Feisel was too sleepy to argue with this bossy woman. She steered carefully back onto the highway. He wouldn't classify her driving as "expert." Cautious was a better description. He waved to the pickup behind them, leaned his head back against the seat and fell into a troubled sleep.

He awoke with a start as streams of traffic flowed around them. Miss Wenkle turned onto a less-traveled road.

Johab and Cyril popped forward, squirming with anticipation. They knew this road by heart and by foot. Miss Wenkle aimed the car in the direction of the Northern Cemetery, taking turns carefully, trying to sort out three sets of directions from Mr. Feisel, Johab, and Cyril.

Under a sky just turning black, the tombs and mosques rose like forbidding shadows ahead of them. Miss Wenkle had an uneasy feeling—cold, like the touch of Barzoni's hand against her back.

They bumped to a stop at the end of the road. Mr. Feisel hopped out and yanked the back seat forward so that Johab and Cyril could be first to announce their arrival.

Sekina brayed a welcome that would rouse the dead. That was the only sound. No oil lamp glimmered through the window. No smoke wafted up the brazier's chimney. Johab pushed against the door, fear overwhelming him, Mr. Feisel's hand against his back as though to brace him for the worst.

The hut was tidy, sleeping mats rolled against the wall, chairs pushed under the table. Mr. Feisel walked to the brazier and held his hand over the ashes. "The fire is cold. They haven't been here for some time." He lifted the oil lamp and struck a match to the wick. The light reflected four frightened faces.

Johab spotted the telltale pile of dried mud under the window ledge. "The pouch is gone, Mr. Feisel. Only Mother and I knew it was there. Something terrible has happened to them!" Johab's voice rang out with despair. Cyril seemed to shrink into himself, so tiny that he made only a faint shadow in the lamplight.

Johab stalked over to his sleeping mat, pulled up the pillow, and rummaged inside the pillow case. Waving his father's gun, he looked defiantly at Mr. Feisel and Hetty, who stood speechless. "I'm going to find Barzoni and shoot him. If he has hurt my mother and sister, I am going to put a bullet through him."

Cyril nodded. He didn't understand Johab's English but he understood the look on his face. It was the same look Johab had the night that the two of them had rescued Alice from right under Mustafa's nose.

Mr. Feisel gently pried the gun from Johab's hand. "I think I need to give you some lessons in how to use this thing before you shoot Miss Wenkle."

"Why are all of you standing around looking as though the world has just come to an end? Where did you get that gun, Mr. Feisel?" The voice was abrasive. The plump form of Mrs. Zadi filled the entire frame of the door. She held a lamp high in one hand and waved an envelope in the other. Bustling over to the table, she pulled back a chair and settled herself into it, like a ruffled hen that had just found a nest.

She smiled cunningly at Johab, her voice sticky as honey. "Johab, your mother has been so worried about you. She wouldn't tell me where you had gone but said you were with Mr. Feisel." Mrs. Zadi looked piercingly at Mr. Feisel. "I told her she should be more careful about the company her son keeps, but she wasn't having any of *my* advice."

Mr. Feisel glared and moved toward her, his arm upraised as though he might smack her with no more concern than he would smash a poisonous spider. Miss Wenkle moved toward the other side of Mrs. Zadi, her hands clenching and unclenching as though she would be only too happy to place them both around Mrs. Zadi's throat.

"Do you know where they have gone, woman? Speak up!" Mr. Feisel's voice thundered within the small room.

Mrs. Zadi ignored him, although her hands shook. She offered a deceitful smile to Johab. "I've been feeding that donkey of yours. Your mother asked me to take care of it, and I have." The tone of her voice was that of someone who had been put upon but was determined to do her duty in spite of the inconvenience.

"That note has Johab's name on it," barked Mr. Feisel. "Hand it over."

"Don't be so touchy. I know it is for Johab. His mother gave it to me for him." She responded in a peevish tone.

Mr. Feisel snatched it from her hand and held it toward the lamp. "Looks as though you steamed it open before resealing it," he said.

"I did not," she retorted frostily. "It's probably in English. I couldn't read it so why would I open something that is private?" Mrs. Zadi stared at them all as though she were some small creature under a microscope, all her flaws magnified. She pushed her chair back, its screeching noise the only sound in the room. "I promised to look after that wretched donkey, and I will. I'm a person who knows how to keep promises." She stood up and flounced out of the room, holding her lantern in front of her like armor.

Johab tore open the envelope and read aloud. "We are safe. Mr. Parks came yesterday with Hetty's friends. He doesn't want us to stay in the City of the Dead. Mr. Parks got the news that John had disappeared from someone who brought supplies to his field station. He rushed to Cairo as soon as he heard."

Johab cleared his scratchy throat and continued. "Mr. Parks is angry that Mr. El-Hasiim did not contact him immediately about your father. Mr. Parks located Miss Wenkle's friends who told him everything. We are at his villa." Johab looked up at his friends, his face bright with relief. "Mother put the directions here on the bottom of the page in English so that the busybody couldn't read it."

Johab showed the note to Hetty, who glanced at the Arabic, turned the page over and handed it back. "Mother says that she has paid Mrs. Zadi to look after the donkey and watch the hut to be sure that no one moves in or takes our things." He smiled broadly and thumped the page. "She gave the pouch to Mr. Parks."

A wave of reassurance swept over Johab. One thing his father asked had been achieved. The pouch that was supposed to be put into Mr. Parks's hands had reached its destination. Johab flexed his battered wrists and grinned into Cyril's dirty face. All in all, things were looking up.

CHAPTER 60

Let us run into a safe harbor.

—Alcaeus

"Quick! Let's go! I've been to Mr. Park's villa. It's out there on the edge of the desert." Johab turned to Cyril. "He has date trees and a pond with ducks. You'll like it there, Cyril." He grabbed Miss Wenkle's hand. Come on, Mr. Feisel. "Let's go *now*."

Mr. Feisel hung back, leaning against the wall, becoming almost at one with the shadows cast by the flickering oil lamp. To Miss Wenkle, he seemed strangely passive, as though he were no longer in charge of leading a strange entourage across the desert to save a young boy.

"I should stay here, Johab, and let you go see your mother and your father's friend. Now that this Parks fellow has arrived, I'm sure that he can take care of your family. This is where I . . . belong." Mr. Feisel hesitated, as though he had become suddenly too exhausted to think past the confines of his old life.

"Certainly not!" The authoritative tone of Miss Wenkle's voice rang out in the still night. "You are responsible for saving Johab's life. You are our partner. You know more about tombs than any one of us in this room. Ian Parks will value your knowledge and experience. You are not staying here."

Her tone was subdued in the face of Mr. Feisel's uneasiness, but her actions were not. She moved toward the shadows where Mr. Feisel seemed to want to hide, grabbed his arm, and pulled him toward the door. "Let's go find those friends of yours. The danger that Mr. Barzoni represents is still very much with us."

The old pickup was parked just down the alley. Mr. Feisel's two friends slouched against the side of it. Mr. Feisel spoke softly to them, pointing first one direction, then another. Then, he obediently followed Miss Wenkle's pointing finger to the driver's seat and ground the little VW into action.

He was relieved that his friends didn't hear Miss Wenkle telling him what he would and wouldn't do. She was very bossy. He smiled to himself. There were bossy women like Mrs. Zadi, the kind that stirred the pot, caused trouble. Then, there were bossy women like Miss Wenkle—a woman who knew her own mind and made good decisions. He could live with that kind of bossy.

Johab studied his mother's directions to Mr. Parks's villa as they wound through the night traffic. Even with the bumpy noise of the road, silence seemed to settle around them with the kind of calm that brings with it a sense of unease, as though something lurks just around the corner.

Bastet purred contentedly. Cyril had snagged him just as they piled into the car. "Jasmine will be lonesome for her cat," he reminded Johab. Mr. Feisel shrugged. Bastet had earned whatever kingdom he chose to inhabit. Following Johab's directions into the countryside, Mr. Feisel turned down a clay-packed road on the edge of the city.

"Your friends are still behind us in their pickup, Mr. Feisel, but . . ." Johab gasped. "I'd recognize that old Volvo any place. I spent too many hours in that trunk not to know it. They've cut in front of the pickup. Speed up, Mr. Feisel! We need to shake them!"

The one thing for which the VW Beetle had not been designed was a high-speed chase. With the gas pedal against its floor, the sturdy little car chugged along at the same speed, reliable, but slow.

Cyril pounded on the back window, waving his arms like windmills. "Your friends cut them off! Their pickup is behind us now. That white car is in the ditch."

Mr. Feisel felt a small surge of pride. His friends from the village—not city men like Barzoni's thugs—had outmaneuvered those men. Goat herders and camel riders. That's how many city people viewed the villagers. with its new V-6 engine, the pickup had swerved and sent the Volvo into a ditch.

Johab leaned forward and whispered to Mr. Feisel. "Barzoni's men had pistols. When they took me out of the trunk, I saw semi-automatic guns in the back seat. I hope your friends don't get hurt."

Mr. Feisel nodded, wondering if he should have accepted help from his friends. They had families—wives, sons, daughters and aging parents—an extended family that relied on them for food and shelter. Nothing much had changed in the way they lived for years. Some of them had pickups for taking animals to market. By and large, they lived in the same way for centuries. It was a good life. Part of what made it good was a sense of loyalty to kinsmen and friends. He glanced in the rear-view mirror. The pickup was the only vehicle in sight. They would have followed to help no matter what he said.

"Next turn to the right and then straight ahead. The villa has two separate houses. One is a kind of office and storage place." Johab smiled, recognizing the familiar road.

Cyril pointed toward a string of lights in the distance. "Those are security lights. They run off a generator," Johab began speaking softly in Arabic to Cyril. Miss Wenkle thought that Johab was probably giving Cyril a crash course on generators. His father used them in the field. She knew at least that much about working in the field. Even back in the early 1920s, Howard Carter had rigged up air pumps and lights for his digs in tombs.

At the end of a bumpy road, a heavy metal gate and fence faced them. Dogs barked in the distance. Bastet hissed and arched his body, ready for the attack.

A bulky man moved out of the shadow of the gatepost with the stealth of a stalking lion and tapped on Miss Wenkle's window. Amused by her startled face, he aimed his flashlight at his own face, resting his arms on her open window. They were the arms of a weight lifter, the veins chiseled out on the surface of the skin as though forming an extra layer of vascular pathways.

"Boris!" shrieked Johab, leaning over Miss Wenkle's seat to grab his outstretched hand.

The man thrust both hands past Miss Wenkle's shoulder and clutched Johab's face. "You little rascal! There will be a celebration tonight. I could see car lights coming down the road and thought I'd check on who might be paying us a visit. I recognized the VW from your mother's description. The boss has been getting some men ready to head to the Valley in the morning to search for you."

The man's voice had a distinct Slavic accent. He was a giant with a shaved head, his bulging muscles gleaming in the glow of his flashlight. Johab hopped up and down in the back seat, clinging to the giant's hand. "This is Boris. He helps Mr. Parks with his field trips." Johab immediately began chattering to Cyril in Arabic. "You should see his exercise room. He has all kinds of weights and rowing machines and everything." Cyril beamed. He had no idea what an exercise room or a rowing machine might be, but if Johab was impressed, then so was he.

"Humph!" Mr. Feisel's guttural sound from the driver's seat spoke more than the most eloquent speech. They needed to be about their business. The gate groaned open, and Boris, in shorts and a muscle shirt, trotted ahead of the VW down a winding path. Miss Wenkle thought he looked like a strong man who had just escaped from a carnival.

The villa appeared to be a traditional box-style desert house with a flat roof and stairs leading up to the roof. As they drove into a circular driveway, Miss Wenkle noted that the house was designed in the ancient Roman style, opening on all sides into a small central courtyard. Shrieking "My son! My son!" Johab's mother dashed across the courtyard with Jasmine and Alice hot on her heels.

Boris grabbed two huge black Dobermans and hauled them back from the car as Bastet hissed from his post in the back window. He did not have the advantage and would stay inside the car for the moment.

Jasmine and Alice flung themselves at Mr. Feisel, each clinging to a leg. "You found my cat, Mr. Feisel. You found Bastet," shouted Jasmine.

Dogs barking, a cat yowling, a woman crying and laughing at the same time, and an old Bedouin fighting back the tears as he swooped up two little girls in his arms made a picture of such emotional force that Miss Wenkle thought she would never see such unbridled happiness and confusion in such a small space ever again.

Order was asserted when a tall, slim, gray-haired man stepped forward and flung his arms around Miss Wenkle, kissing her on both cheeks. "We have been so worried about Johab and you, Hetty. Sarah and Ella are simply beside themselves." He smiled at her gravely. "Now, you are here. You are all safe."

Mr. Parks herded them into a large room with over-stuffed couches and chairs. Brightly colored rugs covered a highly polished tile floor. He motioned toward the couches. "Sit down. Rest." He beckoned toward Boris, who had assumed a post near the door, positioned so that he could see all the way to the front gate. "Boris, would you tell the cook that we need food, whatever she can find quickly?"

Boris pointed toward lights outside the gate. "We have company."

Mr. Feisel moved next to Boris. This man appeared to be some kind of servant to the English man, just as he himself had been for a part of his life. He would stand near him. He had not been introduced to Mr. Parks and felt uncomfortable in this house.

Miss Wenkle touched his arm, sensing his unease. That gesture gave him confidence to speak. "Those may be our friends from the village. They followed to protect us from Barzoni's men. If it's an old pickup, that's them. He muttered in a low voice to Boris. "Barzoni's men were in a white Volvo. They may be near. My friends managed to bump their car into a ditch."

"You must be Mr. Feisel." Mr. Parks strode across the room, clasping Mr. Feisel in a traditional Egyptian man-to-man hug, reserved for best friends and family members. He muttered something in Arabic. Mr. Feisel's face lit up with a brief show of emotion.

Hetty watched them curiously. She would ask Johab later what Mr. Parks had said. At this moment he seemed preoccupied with his growing household. "Boris, will you open the gate for Mr. Feisel's friends and bring them in? We'll have food in a minute. All of you, sit down, rest."

A sharp voice rang out. "Neither one of you boys get anywhere near Mr. Parks's furniture." Johab's mother plucked at the robes of Johab and Cyril. "These are the filthiest clothes that I've ever seen. They are absolutely stiff with dirt and . . ." she wrinkled her nose, "and, bird dung."

Bat dung thought Johab, but he dared not correct her when she had the "cleaning gleam" in her eyes.

"Off with them now." She yanked up Cyril's robe and tossed it into the courtyard. He was completely naked and not the least bit embarrassed. He walked over and plopped down in the softest, over-stuffed chair, smiling all around the room as though he had just discovered the meaning of comfort.

Johab's mother looked grimly at him. "I hope you are wearing underpants. There are ladies in the room." Johab nodded and held his arms over his head.

His mother eased the dirty robe up past his arms and shrieked.

The gold links of the amulet around his neck gleamed warmly under the soft overhead lights in the room. The jasper, huge and rare, which was intricately tucked into coils of gold at the bottom of the amulet, pulsed with an eerie green glow.

Every person in the room turned toward Johab, transfixed by what they were seeing. Nothing so beautiful had been in any museum case. This was the necklace of an ancient and powerful ruler. It jutted out splendidly from Johab's scrawny chest. No one dared to breathe.

CHAPTER 61

"Why are all of you staring at me? Haven't you ever seen a boy in shorts before?" Johab looked from one astonished face to another.

His mother was the first to speak. "My son, where did you get that lovely necklace?"

"Necklace?" Johab reached up to touch his own neck. His fingers traced the circle of reassuring gold. He remembered now. The gift from Queen Hatshepsut, her tender fingers on the sides of his throat, the scent of incense trees from the Land of Punt. Her gift.

In words so soft that only Mr. Parks and Mr. Feisel understood them, Johab repeated the Queen's words: "Not may he be made separation thy from me."

Amazing, thought Mr. Parks. Johab is speaking the ancient Egyptian, but in a dialect that he had only imagined. No one really knows the sounds of the language—linguists and Egyptologists speculate, but the sounds have been lost. Johab's short sentence brought the old language to life, just for the moment in this room.

His mother placed both of her hands on Johab's shoulders and peered intently into his eyes. "Did you find this in a tomb? You must explain to Mr. Parks."

Johab turned slowly, looking into the faces of his mother, Mr. Parks, Hetty, and Mr. Feisel. The gold amulet cast flashes of light as he turned. In a quiet and deliberate voice, he said. "I did not find this. It was a gift from Queen Hatshepsut. It is her favorite amulet. She gave it to me. I did not take it. It belongs to me."

The Egyptian Department of Antiquities won't agree at all, thought Mr. Parks. He had never seen a more spectacular amulet. Johab, his small, shirtless body held erect, looked like a young prince, as though he had been born to wear the gold of ancient Egypt.

There was a breathless hush in the room. The black Dobermans were propped on both sides of the door like modern facsimiles of the jackal-headed Anubis, their ears alert and eyes unmoving.

Johab's mother slid her fingers underneath the golden links of the chain to lift the large amulet from her son's body. Her cry ruptured the silence in the room. "It is leaving a mark, like henna designs! That necklace has been tattooed into his skin." Her voice was rasping, angry, as though her son had somehow been violated.

Mr. Parks moved closer, reluctant to touch the amulet. Johab stared at him, not speaking, as he hesitantly rubbed the reddish brown pattern on Johab's neck. "My first thought was that some kind of poisonous or caustic substance had been placed on the amulet, but Johab's skin is not cut or infected."

"You take it off, Johab." The agitation in his mother's voice brought his circle of friends close to him, their faces registering only astonishment.

Johab moved his fingers under the chain, pulled it over his head, and dangled it from the tips of his fingers towards Mr. Parks. The jasper stone flashed like green lightning.

The pattern left by the amulet could have been the work of a skilled tattoo artist. The curves and swirls of the gold links circled his neck precisely. The place where the green stone had lain against Johab's chest formed a small patch of opalescent skin with faint traces of hieroglyphs.

"Unless a master tattoo artist is hanging about in old tombs waiting to do extensive work on small boys, I'd say that the Queen has put her mark on Johab." Mr. Parks's voice was controlled, matter-of-fact, as though his explanation was completely within the realm of scientific possibility. He moved Johab over to a large wall mirror, all the time rubbing the marks with his fingers. "It's not henna, Johab. Whatever it is seems to be permanent."

Johab stared at his image in the mirror. He looked a bit like a native Hawaiian, one of those fellows with bars of tattoos around their arms and legs. He smiled at his reflection. He really looked rather splendid. Cyril's small face peered up at Johab's reflection. He was impressed. Johab had returned with a medal from the battlefield, one that could never be taken away.

Mr. Parks stared somberly at Johab's mother, Mr. Feisel, and Hetty. "I think that we should all agree not to mention what just happened here. I don't know what any of you think you heard coming out of Johab's mouth or how it relates to this marvelous piece." He swung the amulet from the tips of his fingers. "But, the phrase that Johab quoted is what I believe to be a pure form of the ancient Egyptian language—and it is carved in hieroglyphs on the back of this jewel."

Every pair of eyes in the room settled on Johab.

Johab felt a kind of coldness seeping into him, as though he had become one of those exhibits in the museum, one of those kings with all the linen cloths stripped away so that his old chocolate-colored bones were exposed to every tourist who might casually tromp by his new final resting place. That would not happen to his Queen Hatshepsut, not if he had the power to prevent it.

"It was a concussion!" The small circle of friends and family around him jumped at the loud crack of his voice. "See the bump on the back of my head?" He angled his head toward them and pointed to the offending knot. "I fell into a shaft in the tomb and knocked myself out. I had a strange dream. I don't really know what happened during that time. Maybe I just picked up the amulet off the floor."

A concerned expression on her face, his mother moved over and carefully felt the back of his head. "There is a large bump, but the skin doesn't appear to be broken." She sniffed her fingertips. "What is this greasy stuff on your head, Johab? It smells very nice, like expensive perfume."

Hetty reached into her bag, pulled out the small alabaster jar that Johab had taken from the antechamber of the tomb and waved it in the air. "It is the most expensive perfume—over three thousand years old if I know anything about this jar."

It was a good diversion. Johab grinned appreciatively at Hetty who pulled the other treasures out of her large purse—the other jar with kohl, the cedar box inlaid with turquoise and lapis, and the group of cylinder seals and placed them on a nearby table.

Mr. Parks's eyes widened. "These are New Kingdom things." He peered closely at one of the seals. "This one is marked with Queen Hatshepsut's cartouche."

"And the other with her old friend, Senenmut. Johab and I recognized his hieroglyphs immediately." Mr. Feisel spoke out, moving to the table and pointing, wanting to be sure that this English man, this Mr. Parks, recognized that he had some measure of knowledge when it came to these things from old tombs.

"I purposefully took them from the . . . ante . . . uh . . . I mean the chamber that the thieves had broken into from up on the top of the cliffs." Johab had almost slipped and said "antechamber." He could never use the words "burial chamber" or "antechamber." No one could ever know about a second chamber.

The thieves had partially looted the outer room of treasures. Mr. Feisel, Hetty, Cyril, and those village friends of Mr. Feisel knew that treasures had been brought up from a tomb below that fissure in the rocks. Mr. El-Hasiim and Mr. Barzoni certainly knew that such a place had been discovered, because New Kingdom objects had already been seized by police in the bust of the antiquities ring.

It was the room behind the carved slab that must never be found. That's where Queen Hatshepsut reposed in her coffin forever. Johab knew that he must be careful about any information he shared, even with the people he loved and trusted most in the world. He ducked his head so that no one could see his expression. He rubbed the bump on his head, pretending that it was beginning to ache again.

Keeping secrets had become a kind of art that both he and his cousin, Mohammed, had mastered. Small lies to keep their adventures from their mothers. "Did you go near the Khan when we told you to come straight home after school?" Bowed heads and innocent looks. "No, we played on the swings in the playground after school." What Johab liked to think of as Mohammed White Lies seemed harmless enough.

The lie he was currently telling or not telling seemed overwhelming. It could affect Mr. Parks, standing there, looking so kind and concerned, providing a safe place for his family.

Most importantly of all, this lie could affect his father—a man dedicated to bringing the history of ancient Egypt alive for the world to share. Mr. Parks and his father wouldn't understand how anyone who loved the world of the ancients wouldn't want it shared with the world today.

Johab understood only too well why he had to lie. He remembered reading about how Mr. Carter had put King Tutankhamen's mummy that had fused to its wooden casket out in the hot desert sun to melt the resin so the body could be broken away from the coffin. It hadn't worked. At the end of the day, the workers splintered the elegant coffin away from the King's body with hammers and hatchets because the mummy refused to part company with its resting place.

Johab knew that the British and Egyptian governments and a private foundation in the United States funded the New Kingdom Project. They would claim a share of the trophies. At the end of the day, Egypt would get the lion's share, the Queen, herself. Experts would unwind the long strips of linen, inscribed with prayers from the *Book of the Dead,* to expose her blackened limbs, and, finally, use an x-ray machine to peek into the body of the Queen.

Not while he had a breath in his body. A diversion was required. "Mr. Parks, I took the stuff from the tomb that was being robbed by those men who live near Mr. Feisel's old village. I want to use it to trap Mr. Barzoni."

Mr. Parks looked quizzically at Johab. "Your mother and Hetty's friends told me about this Barzoni fellow." He frowned. "I know something about him. He has a reputation for giving money to help excavations in several countries. He presents himself as a philanthropist dedicated to saving Egypt's treasures."

Hetty moved toward Mr. Parks and said sharply, "Mr. Barzoni's 'philanthropy' put me in the hospital." She held up a crooked finger. "This broken finger is the 'treasure' that I have to remember him by.

He kidnapped Johab's father—Johab saw his face that night in the apartment. It's a face that is hard to forget."

Mr. Parks's arm encircled Hetty's waist, as he pulled her close. "I believe everything you are telling me—and everything that Johab's mother told me about Barzoni. It's just that we need to move carefully and plan every step for damage control. Barzoni has contacts in high places. The Project Director, Mr. El-Hasiim, doesn't have a good reputation in the field, but his uncle heads up the government department that approves excavations—and sometimes helps fund them." He held his hands out, palms up, as though the bureaucracy of governments seemed a hopeless obstacle.

Mr. Feisel narrowed his eyes at Mr. Parks when he saw him touching Miss Wenkle in a manner that seemed entirely too familiar. Egyptian men did not show affection to women in public. And that cheek kissing thing when he greeted Miss Wenkle. Maybe it was as innocent as a handshake. He knew that all Europeans did that kind of thing publicly, but, for once, it seemed to be bothering him more than he wanted to admit.

His two friends appeared with Boris. They stood uneasily beside the door, not understanding a word of English, totally ill at ease. He nodded to them. "We seem to be missing an important point here," Mr. Feisel barked loudly enough to cause the dogs to lurch against Boris's restraining hands.

"Our job is to figure out how to get Barzoni to release Johab's father. Johab took a few things from the tomb to set a trap for Barzoni." Mr. Feisel moved over towards Johab and pulled him close. Hugging children was certainly allowed in Egypt, and this boy looked as though he needed a lot of hugs.

Mr. Feisel could see that Johab was struggling with how much to say and what to say. He had seen this boy's eyes when he emerged from that dark hole below the desert. That little eleven-year-old boy had stars in his eyes then. Now, his face was flushed with guilt.

Mr. Feisel kept his hand on Johab's shoulder. It wasn't fair for children to be weighed down with the "rights and wrongs" of this complicated world of who owned treasures that came from underneath the desert sands. Getting Johab back on the path toward finding his father was the right thing to do.

He pushed Johab forward so he could be seen by everyone in the room. "You had an idea about how these things from the tomb could tempt Barzoni into giving you information about your father. Let's hear it."

Like an unwilling actor who had been unceremoniously pushed in front of footlights on a stage, Johab needed more time to memorize his script. He took a deep breath. These were his friends and family, all of them. He looked around the room at the concerned faces of the people he cared about—even the bearded, swarthy friends of Mr. Feisel fell into that category.

As his father always told him, scientific logic moves from point to point—what you know because of scientific evidence and what you think is possible. Johab cleared his dry throat. He suddenly remembered something else his father had told him. "Before you give a serious speech, Johab, try to make people laugh. That helps them warm up to your ideas."

Assuming a slightly pompous tone of voice, Johab said: "Before I discuss my plan—I should say 'our plan' because Miss Wenkle and Mr. Feisel are my partners, and Cyril is my lieutenant—I need to reveal a great secret that we share."

Miss Wenkle and Mr. Feisel glanced at each other, puzzled by this mention of a "great secret."

Cyril, who had anchored a small rug around his naked body, beamed when he recognized the English word "lieutenant." He was a part of Johab's speech.

"Our secret is . . ." Johab paused for effect. "We are absolutely bloody starving!"

The tension that had been mounting steadily with the disclosure of Queen Hatshepsut's amulet broke with bursts of laughter.

Johab's mother looked stern. She would deal with him later. Guests did not demand food, even if they were starving. And the use of that word "bloody." This boy of hers seemed to be getting out of hand.

As though he had anticipated Johab's announcement, Boris appeared almost instantaneously with trays of bread, goat cheese, olives, and a large dish of yoghurt and cucumbers seasoned with garlic. The room echoed with the noise of a hungry, extended family gathered around a table.

Fragments of English and Arabic wafted past the open court-yard, but the two men cowering in a ditch outside of the perim-eter fence could distinguish only an occasional burst of laughter. Two jackal-headed dogs, their teeth gleaming in the moonlit night stretched unmoving along the fence, waiting patiently for either man to make a move.

Mr. Parks looked around the circle of his dining room table at the odd assortment of guests. The friends of Mr. Feisel ate quickly and moved back toward the door to stand by Boris, who was watching the road leading to the house. Hetty looked exhausted. Both boys nestled against Johab's mother, looking as though they would like to climb up on her lap and sleep for days.

Mr. Parks clapped Mr. Feisel on the shoulder. "I know we need to hear Johab's ideas, but he and his friends are fading. We'll gather here for an early breakfast. We'll all think better after a good night's sleep." He directed the women and children down the hallway toward bedrooms.

Sleep was not what Mr. Parks had in mind for some of the party. Boris had communicated a signal that he knew only too well. Danger lurked outside the fence. The dogs had sped out the door minutes earlier. He motioned Mr. Feisel over to him and away from the others.

"If it's OK, we'll put you and your friends in the bunkhouse. It's comfortable but a bit Spartan. Something or someone is outside the perimeter fence. It could just be a rabbit, but I don't think so. The dogs are too quiet. Boris and I will take first watch. After you and your friends get some sleep, you can take the second watch."

He glanced at Mr. Feisel's impassive face. This man wasn't accus-tomed to taking orders. "I'm sure you have more experience with this kind of thing than I do, Mr. Feisel. And, you've been in the thick of this with Johab. His father is my best friend. I think he is alive because he would be valuable for someone who deals in stolen antiquities. Black market dealers need an expert to know the real from the fake."

Mr. Parks trembled slightly with emotion. "I want to find my friend. I'll throttle Mr. El-Hasiim or anyone who gets in my way." He reached over to take Mr. Feisel's hand in the Arab way. "We need your help. We need the help of your friends. If they can stay for a while, I can pay them to help Boris guard the women and children. You don't think they'd be insulted if I offered to hire them, do you?" This was a sensitive matter. These were Mr. Feisel's friends, risking their lives to protect people who were strangers.

Mr. Feisel returned the grip of Mr. Parks's hand. This English fellow showed sensitivity to the rules of friendship. His friends needed to be working, caring for their animals and crops. They had families. English pounds would be very welcome. Mr. Feisel could broach the subject tactfully, make them understand the importance of helping stand guard. The money would not be *baksheesh,* but payment for dangerous work.

Together, they moved toward the bunkhouse, Mr. Feisel's friends following closely. All were speaking in hushed voices. If Boris had not been wearing black, someone might have seen him with a rifle slung over his shoulder and a pistol in his hand, working his way around a cluster of date palms near the perimeter fence.

CHAPTER 62

The good old rule sufficeth them, the simple plan.

—Wordsworth

Johab awoke to the odor of freshly baked bread. He looked around the room. Cyril slept on the mat next to him, curled into a tight knot. Soft snores came from the bed. Hetty's blond curls were massed against the pillows.

He remembered now. They were guests of Mr. Parks. He and Cyril were sharing a room with Hetty. Jasmine and Alice were with his mother. His mother. She had hugged him tightly at bedtime, but he noted the glimmer of censorship on her face. Children didn't use the expletive "bloody." He braced himself for a morning lecture.

Tiptoeing out of the room, he stepped into the hall leading to the courtyard. Beyond the building that served as a bunk house and storage area, Mr. Feisel, Mr. Parks, and Mr. Feisel's friends stood in a circle, occasionally poking a foot at something lying on the ground.

A dead animal? Something that the dogs had dragged into the yard? As Johab moved closer, he could see a bundle of clothes. A dead person? No. It was writhing on the ground.

Mr. Parks saw Johab and spoke to Mr. Feisel. Mr. Feisel shook his head and beckoned to Johab.

The thing on the ground was a person. He wasn't dead, but he was considerably damaged. A large cut on his head dripped a stream of blood down his nose. Puffy welts stippled his face. One of his hands sported the distinct and bloody mark of a dog bite.

Boris pushed him into a sitting position. "Recognize this bloke, Johab?"

Controlling the chill that shook his body took all of the composure that Johab could muster. He stared at the man's face. The man would not look up. "He's one of the men who put me in the tomb. The other man seemed to be in charge, but this man is the one who planned to cut off my finger or my ear to prove to my father that I was being held captive."

Gasping for breath, the man sputtered, "I didn't hurt him. It was my idea to leave water for him. I was just following orders from the boss."

"And *who* is the boss?" Mr. Parks asked in an icy voice.

The man pursed his lips and shook his head.

"Boris, take him to the storage room. I suspect you need to have a little chat with him." Mr. Parks's voice was quiet, but the tone was deadly.

Johab moved with the others back toward the house. He would have preferred to go with Boris. He didn't dare suggest that possibility. He would just have to speculate about Boris's methods for getting information, probably splinters under the fingernails, something that wouldn't be too obvious. Boris was a subtle man.

His mother, Jasmine, Alice, Cyril, and Hetty sat around the table eating scrambled eggs and English streaky bacon, his favorite. Mr. Feisel's friends stood awkwardly back from the table. Johab thought that they might be Muslims. Pork would be offensive to them.

Mr. Parks called toward the kitchen. A small woman with skin the color of dark chocolate and a Nubian cast to her features came into the dining room carrying a large tray of fresh bread—-the flat kind cooked on a metal slab over a charcoal fire. A platter in her other hand held an assortment of goat cheese and fresh dates. The men moved to the table, pulled out their chairs, and reached for the bread and cheese as though they were bloody starving.

Mr. Parks's voice was low and serious. He spoke in Arabic to Cyril, Jasmine and Alice. "Don't go near the other building today. Boris is working there and cannot be disturbed."

Johab marveled at the business-like tone that Mr. Parks was using to keep the children away from Boris's "office." He had no doubt that the business being conducted would be "disturbing" to Barzoni's man. He had intercepted the look that had passed between Mr. Parks and Boris.

Mr. Parks spoke to Hetty and Johab's mother. "We captured one of Mr. Barzoni's men early this morning. He was outside the fence, lying in a bed of ants. He'd been there most of the night, considering the number of stings. The dogs cornered him and didn't let him move for hours." A look of irritation passed over his face. "There was another one. We saw his footprints and the place where he had been lying. He avoided the ant bed. I suspect that he has hightailed it back to Cairo to report to Barzoni. That's unfortunate. With both of those men in our control, we might have had an element of surprise. Now, Barzoni will be prepared for us."

The fear on the face of Johab's mother replaced any thoughts about lecturing her son for using the word "bloody" last night.

Mr. Parks patted her arm. "It will be okay, Soya. Catching one of these men may bring us closer to finding John. Boris is out there visiting with the man right now."

Johab ducked to conceal a grin. His mother thought that Boris was simply having a social conversation with a man who would quickly see the error of his ways. That was one of the things he loved most about his mother, her belief that evil people were just waiting for a chance to be reformed. Johab had seen the face of the man as Boris hauled him off to the storeroom. He had no desire to be reformed.

He caught Mr. Parks's eyes as they narrowed slightly. They were both on the same page. Some things were best kept from a worried mother. Hetty was another matter. She was absolutely bristling with anger. "Let me talk to that man, Ian. I can tell him a thing or two."

"You'll have to improve your Arabic, Miss Wenkle," interrupted Mr. Feisel. "The man isn't bilingual." He went back to his eggs. Cyril was imitating Mr. Feisel's culinary habits, piling eggs, goat cheese, and dates onto a slab of bread and rolling it into a long tube.

Johab's mother watched him with a pained expression. If she inserted a fork into Cyril's fist, she might offend Mr. Feisel and his friends who were ignoring the silverware. Mr. Parks was making the same kind of roll but without the dates. Johab followed suit—egg, bacon and goat cheese rolled into flatbread with no troublesome fork.

"Let's hear your idea, your plan, Johab." Mr. Parks spoke directly to Johab as though he were an equal partner in some new business venture, one that might involve financial, not physical risk.

Johab knelt in his chair so that his head was at the same level as the adults around the table. "Here are the things we know. The antiquities bust occurred a week before Dad was taken. An inside informer from the police acted as a buyer and caught some of the dealers. Only one photograph of a stolen item, a small *ushabti*, appeared in the newspaper. It's now on display at the Museum."

He cleared his throat. It was still dry from his time in the tomb without water. He would remind Boris not to give that man any water. He had lied. His partner said Barzoni told him to leave water for Johab. He looked back at the circle of attentive faces. "We know the items recovered were taken to the Museum and given to Dad because they were from the New Kingdom period. He wrote descriptions of every item and put those in the files. Then, he returned all the things to Mr. El-Hasiim."

Hetty intruded, "Sarah has copies of John's descriptions of those objects, as well as other New Kingdom artifacts that are supposed to be in storage. She made copies of those files when Mr. El-Hasiim was out of the Museum."

Johab smiled at Hetty, happy that she affirmed his facts, the first steps of a logical path. Dr. Watson sometimes did that for Sherlock. "We also know that my father found something else." His voice took on a hushed tone. "He found a secret compartment in the back of an amulet with old papyrus pages and a sketch of a bent tomb."

Johab smiled at Mr. Feisel. "Mr. Feisel, who is somewhat an expert in hieroglyphs, helped figure out what was on the papyri— and we had my Dad's notes. We think he had already deciphered the hieroglyphs on the papyri but didn't want to make them too clear in case someone found his notes."

Mr. Feisel flushed with embarrassment when Johab described him as an "expert." He was strictly an amateur. He could read some hieroglyphs, but an expert? He blushed again with the thought of Johab's misguided praise.

Mr. Parks seemed unfazed and nodded as though he considered Mr. Feisel an expert. Johab took a deep breath. "We had been in the field, near Queen Hatshepsut's temple. Dad was sketching it as he had done many times." Johab recalled his own boredom that day. Tears welled up in his eyes. He wanted to relive that day, to change it.

His audience waited patiently, turning their heads slightly, acknowledging that Johab's grief was private. "That was when Dad said something about things not being right at the Museum. He didn't exactly put it that way. At the time, I wasn't paying attention, but later . . . after he was . . . taken," Johab faltered, "I know that he was very worried that day."

Johab glanced over at Mr. Parks. "He showed me the pouch with the papyrus and his notes in it and made me promise that I would give it only to you. He said it was dangerous. These are the things we know for certain. We suspect that Mr. Barzoni killed the guard the night he took Dad to his office there."

He had a captive audience now. "Things that happened later have led us to other conclusions." He nodded toward Hetty and Mr. Feisel. "We believe that Mr. Barzoni sent his men back to our apartment to get us that night. It was trashed. But, we had already disappeared." Johab glanced proudly around the room. His hiding place in the City of the Dead had brought fine things, a friendship with Mr. Feisel and two new cousins, Cyril and Alice.

"We know that Mr. Barzoni is desperate enough to take risks." Johab paused. He did not want to reveal that Uncle Tarek had taken a bribe from Barzoni. His mother had been told—and Mr. Feisel and Hetty knew. But, it was an embarrassing truth that needed to stay in the family.

Johab resumed. "He took a risk when he pushed Hetty down the stairs. Hetty and I think that he suspected her of getting information that he didn't want her to have.

She did," Johab nodded toward his partner. "Hetty found the photographs Dad had taken of the secret compartment in the amulet. She managed to keep those in her pocket when they took her to the hospital. The hidden compartment is the same shape and size of folds on those papyrus sheets. That's how we knew they came from that New Kingdom amulet with Senenmut's cartouche carved onto the back of it."

Johab nodded toward Mr. Feisel's friends, thinking that they might not have heard of Senenmut. He switched to Arabic. "Senenmut was Queen Hatshepsut's royal steward. He was also her almost husband and the father of her child, Neferure."

The first expression that crossed Mr. Parks's face could never be reproduced. Incredulity. Senenmut as father to Neferure? Some amateurs, delving into the ancient history, had suggested such a thing. No evidence existed that Senenmut was anything but Neferure's tutor and Hatshepsut's steward. Strong evidence existed that he had fallen out of favor with the Queen and quietly disappeared.

The next expression on Mr. Parks's face was that of acceptance. He had no doubt that this small boy wearing the Queen's mark around his neck was telling only the absolute truth.

Johab frowned. "Here is something else that we believe, but we don't have proof. We believe that Mr. El-Hasiim and Mr. Barzoni were both surprised by the antiquities bust. That means the thieves robbing the tomb are taking their finds to the highest bidder. It also means that Mr. Barzoni doesn't know the location of the tomb that the robbers have found. We believe his men left me at the KV20 tomb because it is closed to visitors. Mr. El-Hasiim made signs for the entrance and put on new locks."

"We also believe," Johab muttered with obvious distress, "that Mr. Barzoni has hidden my father somewhere in the Valley. We think that he kidnapped me as a way to make Dad tell him what he knows about the source of these new treasures."

The face of Mr. Parks remained impassive, as though he were processing information quickly and efficiently. "I read the papyri and John's notes the minute that your mother pulled them out from under the window ledge."

Mr. Parks winked at Johab. "Good hiding place. I would never have found the pouch." He pushed back his chair, stood, and stretched. "I think that what you've said is true. When I arrived in Cairo, I went immediately to the Museum. I questioned Mr. El-Hasiim about the artifacts that were given to him by the police; he showed me the *ushabti* on display and made some flimsy excuse about some other things being cleaned in the lab."

A grim expression pursed Mr. Parks's mouth, as though he'd just bitten into a green persimmon. "I've put out some feelers about Barzoni. No one knows much about him. Supposedly, he gives money to the Museum and has the run of it. He shows up in the storerooms and lab unannounced. Staff on the New Kingdom Project seemed uncomfortable talking about Mr. Barzoni or Mr. El-Hasiim. He's their boss. One word from him and they don't have a job."

Mr. Parks pushed back his chair and smiled. "I have other contacts. People at the Embassy tell me that Barzoni has been under scrutiny for some time. He travels throughout the Middle East and Europe frequently. He seems to have an endless source of money and has been involved in some shady dealings near the Israel-Syria border. He was suspected of bringing a large haul of clay tablets and small bronzes out of Iraq. But no one can pin anything on him. He's an influential man," he added ruefully.

"He has friends in high places. But you, my friends," Mr. Parks looked directly at Johab, Hetty, and Mr. Feisel, "are a step ahead of me."

He pulled the small pouch out of his shirt pocket. "This information would have been very exciting a few days ago. Now, it's second-hand. You made all the right connections—KV20, Queen Hatshepsut's tomb. You found a new shaft to a chamber that has recently been raided, and a bag full of trophies."

He grinned at Johab. "Your queen's amulet is in my safe. I'll give you the combination and show you where it is. I agree that it belongs to you. I'm not sure that the Department of Antiquities would see it that way, but for now, that secret stays in this room."

Mr. Parks looked directly at Johab. "So, tell us how these little alabaster jars and these very fine seals can be used to trap Mr. Barzoni."

Johab slumped down into his chair. He had imagined ways to arrest Mr. Barzoni and torture him. That was a child's fantasy. Mr. Barzoni was an influential man. It would take more than a few theatrics to trap him. Back to logic. Back to his father's methodology.

He perked up. "We have information that Mr. Barzoni doesn't have. We know the location of the tomb chamber. Men from Mr. Feisel's village are guarding that area from up on the cliffs," he added. "I think that I can convince Mr. Barzoni that I know the source of these jars and seals."

"He might think they are fakes," Mr. Parks interrupted. "Seals are easy to copy, and these jars . . ."

"Are like nothing he will have ever seen," Johab interrupted. "Look at the carved head on this one," Johab pointed to the larger jar. "The lapis in the eyes, the carnelian set into the mouth—no jars in the Museum come close to these."

Mr. Parks was reminded of Johab's father in their student days. Johab sounded just like John when he was energized by something he had just discovered.

"Mr. Barzoni might believe you, Johab, but I can't let you take such a chance." He could not be tempted to risk John Bennett's son, even to save his best friend.

"What if I could be protected—say by the police—while I talked to Mr. Barzoni?"

Johab looked directly at Mr. Parks as though such a possibility could be easily managed. He watched Mr. Parks struggling with what was obviously so easy, then said, "It might mean pulling some strings, but you know important people. Dad told me your influence is what got the Project funded. I believe you can arrange for us to meet."

Mr. Parks knew only a few things for sure. He was not as confident as Johab that "beliefs" were so easily translated into actions. Mr. El-Hasiim was well placed in the politics of Egyptian antiquities by a powerful uncle. That was no small obstacle.

He frowned into Johab's confident face. Suppose all of these things that had happened had another explanation? What if the dealers in antiquities, some of those arrested by the police, were behind the kidnapping? Johab's father was well known as an expert in his field. Any dealer in black market antiquities could use his expertise.

This small boy staring at him so soberly and so hopefully must be feeling unbelievable stress after being kidnapped and locked into a tomb. Any child might come up with wild suppositions after that kind of experience.

Mr. Parks glanced over at Hetty. This was a woman who formed strong loyalties with a very select number of people. She did not make rash decisions. She was at heart a librarian and a researcher in whose world facts weighed heavily; supposition did not.

"What do you think, Hetty?" Understanding that she recognized his doubts, Mr. Parks's face flushed with embarrassment.

"My ideas are absolutely in accord with those of Johab," she said decidedly. "But, we can't plan a trap for Barzoni and El-Hasiim if we don't have your whole-hearted cooperation. You must believe in their guilt, as strongly as we do."

Mr. Parks glanced over at Johab, who was wearing one of his old undershirts. The neck opening hung halfway down his chest. The rich bronze of the tattoo, a copy of the chain links of the amulet, looked almost like gold. Mr. Parks shook his head as though to clear his thoughts. Something *had* happened to Johab in that hole in the desert, something so unexplainable that he was getting a headache just thinking about it.

Mr. Feisel held up his hand and repeated in Arabic the same words from *Coming Forth by Day* that Mr. Parks had said to him when they had first met—that decisive moment when Mr. Parks gained the trust of this old Bedouin: "May you give me a path that

I may pass in peace, for I am straightforward and true; I have not willingly told lies; I have not committed a second fault."

Hetty smiled as she watched a change come over Ian Parks's face. He was no longer the skeptical scientist. He was a believer. She recognized what Mr. Feisel said in Arabic. These old Egyptian charms seemed to work magic, thousands of years after they had been written.

"I'll go see some people at the Department of Antiquities, along with a government official I know who might help. I must go over the head of Mr. El-Hasiim's uncle. I won't get anywhere with him. These old family ties are stronger than the law. Hetty, when I return, we need to go to your apartment and get Sarah to help us go through the papers she copied so we can make a case for the missing antiquities—we need proof for the officials. If Mr. El-Hasiim can't produce those treasures, he's in trouble."

Mr. Parks pushed back from the table. "Hetty, you might want to pick up what you need from your apartment. You'll be staying here."

"I'll be fine staying with Sarah and Ella. There's no need to . . ."

"No arguments. You know the entrance to the tomb. Not one of you who rescued Johab from that tomb is safe. I should be back around noon. Will you look after things here, Mr. Feisel? Boris will be here if you need him, but he's busy in the office most of the day," he nodded toward the outer building. Mr. Feisel nodded grimly as though he understood office work perfectly.

Seeing the sullen expression settling on Johab's face, Mr. Parks reached for his hand and pulled him outside into the courtyard. "I have to get through some red tape, Johab, before we can even begin to plan a trap for Barzoni and El-Hasiim. I will share everything with you—just as you've shared with me. We're in this together."

He feigned a punch but lightly touched Johab's chin. "You could help Boris, but I don't think your mother would approve. She needs some time alone with you. She's a bit resentful of the *other* woman." Johab grinned up at him. The "other" woman was over three thousand years old.

CHAPTER 63

They watched a trail of dust blooming behind Mr. Parks's jeep as he headed down the dirt road away from the villa. Miss Wenkle picked up the teapot and two cups, as she moved toward the courtyard. "Let's sit outside, Mr. Feisel. The morning is cool, and we can watch the children while we have another cup of tea."

Cyril and Alice sat side-by-side, poring over the pages of *Pinocchio*. Cyril pointed to each word, and demanded that Alice repeat it. Alice was more interested in the pictures, but Cyril had determined that his sister should learn to read as much as he could read—one book.

The dark hair of both children shone like obsidian in the early morning sun. The night before, Johab's mother had scrubbed both the boys from the top of their heads to the soles of their feet, trying hard to remove the odd tattoo around Johab's neck.

"I believe that Cyril and Alice are the children that your uncle wanted to help." Mr. Feisel kept his voice low. Even though he was speaking in English, he was unsure how much Cyril could understand. He seemed to be picking up English words quickly, as though they stuck to him like burrs.

Mr. Feisel leaned closer. "Last night, I asked Cyril about his father. He told me his father was called Yusef Abbaza and that he was an important man because he was the friend of Major Wenkle. I don't think that Cyril has made any connection between you and your uncle—all English names sound alike to us." He smiled at her, waiting for a retort to his teasing.

Miss Wenkle did not move. She did not inhale or exhale. She might have been one of those small statues at the feet of the colossus at Thebes. When she finally spoke, it was in a brief, declarative sentence. "I want those children."

Mr. Feisel pursed his lips and frowned. "Want them? You mean you want to take them with you?"

"I want to legally adopt them. After my uncle died, I couldn't locate Cyril's father to tell him that my uncle had left a small inheritance for his family. So, I left that money in the bank. Although I was the next to inherit, I could never take the money. While he was ill, my uncle talked about his sadness in losing touch with his young friends, the parents of Cyril and Alice."

Miss Wenkle's hand trembled as she lowered her tea cup. "I thought that I came to Cairo for a job on the New Kingdom Project. Now, I know that the real reason I came to Cairo was to find these children. I want to give them the life their parents wanted them to have. I love them."

Mr. Feisel glanced toward the outer perimeter of the property, shielding his eyes from the morning sun. His village friend stood near the date palms, a rifle hanging across his shoulder. The quiet morning and the chatter of children must not lull them into carelessness. Danger was out there.

"We all love these children, Miss Wenkle. None of us will allow them to be thrown back onto the city streets—Cairo is not kind to orphans." He touched her arm. It was soft and warm in the morning sun.

She needed to hear the truth. "There are three strikes against you if want to adopt these children. First, you are English and of a different religion. Egyptian social services, what few are active, would probably let children starve on the street before they'd give them up to a foreigner. Second, you are an unmarried woman. Government officials probably wouldn't even talk to you. And, third, Cyril and Alice have an aunt out there somewhere who kept them for three years after their father died. She may have legal rights to them."

Mr. Feisel shifted uneasily. These statements didn't sound like truths but excuses. "There is the issue of Johab and Cyril taking Alice without permission. They are just boys. The authorities wouldn't do anything to them. But you, Johab's mother, and I are all complicit in hiding them from their aunt—if she happens to be looking for them."

"Their aunt!" Miss Wenkle spat out the words with a louder hiss than Bastet could produce when one of the Dobermans came too close. "That woman neglected the children. She let Cyril be abused by that man, that Mustafa. I have seen the scars on that child's body. I spent half the night in the bathroom crying when Soya pulled his galabeya off last night."

Her lips formed a grim line. "He is *not* going back to those people even if I have to hire someone to help me get him and Alice out of the country."

Mr. Feisel patted her arm. He liked the spirit of this woman. She had a strong sense of what was right, regardless of the law. Laws protecting children in Egypt—and in most countries in the world—were sadly deficient. Mustafa should have been jailed. Mr. Feisel thought of his old village. Children there were prized. They were part of the continuous chain that made a family secure. The old cared for the young, and the young would care for the old.

"There might be another way." His voice lowered. Cyril appeared to be entirely too interested in their conversation. He had heard his name and was trying to sort out the English words.

"The aunt must have taken the children after her husband, their blood uncle, died, because she felt duty bound to take in his kin. Cyril told me that she was not unkind to them, but that they seemed to be 'in the way.' Those were his words, and I think he was trying to be fair to her. She did feed them."

He stood up and stretched, situating his tall frame so that Cyril couldn't hear him. "If there was any kind of proof, say . . . something left in writing by Cyril's father about who should take care of his children, the authorities would honor that. A father's wishes take precedent over anything else."

Tears welled up in Miss Wenkle's eyes. Mr. Feisel thought that he had never seen sapphires to match her glistening eyes. "After my uncle died, I read his letters over and over, trying to find clues that would help me find his friends. All I have is a letter that describes how he intended to help his friends financially. That letter was written when my Aunt Alice became ill in Cairo. At that time, the main concern of my uncle was to get her back to London so that physicians could help her. They couldn't." She leaned forward, bracing her forehead on her hand so that Mr. Feisel couldn't see her face.

He tentatively reached out his hand, brushing the side of her face. It was wet with tears. He was beginning to think that this European habit of touching women in public wasn't as bad as his culture seemed to think that it was. "We will find a way to help these children, a way to do what your uncle and their father would have wanted for them. You cannot let anyone know that they might inherit money. The aunt and Mustafa would demand to have these children back."

His eyes twinkled. "Some of my countrymen are ingenious when it comes to forging old documents—you'd swear that papyrus they used had been in tombs for thousands of years. Forging a letter from Cyril's father would be child's play."

"Child's play? I know those words. Johab told me. That's what Jasmine and Alice do all day—child's play." Cyril had crept near them, unseen, because Mr. Feisel was blocking Miss Wenkle's view. Cyril looked up at them expectantly. "Can we child's play now?"

CHAPTER 64

I think we are in rats' alley
Where the dead men lost their bones.

—Eliot

In the dark world of Cairo's slums, miles away, inside of a hut made of mud bricks and discarded sheets of tin, another conference about children was taking place.

The aunt of Cyril and Alice, her left eye swollen almost closed, trembled quietly, trying not to antagonize Mustafa. When he woke from drunken bouts, he could be vicious. She carefully placed a plate of bread and honey in front of him. Staring suspiciously at her, he reached for a bottle and uncapped it, ignoring the food.

"Alice was my little princess. I bought her clothes. I made sure that she got the biggest portions of food."

The aunt cast her eyes down, thinking to herself, *and you took those portions from Cyril's share.* She lifted an expressionless face, afraid to reflect her thoughts. She had not dared to share her thoughts with Mustafa since she had been foolish enough to let him move into her house. She had been lonely back then. Her husband had died, leaving her two children—his niece and nephew, not even her own blood kin.

The die had been cast that fateful night that Mustafa talked her into sharing her home, convincing her that he would help with the children, be her companion, earn money. None of those things had come true. She earned money by doing laundry at a hotel in a steamy basement with vats of water reeking of chorine bleach that burned her eyes.

Cyril, that poor little boy who was always eager to help her, had been sent out to beg. No one in her family had ever begged on the streets. What shame. She made a quick sign of the cross. If her husband were watching from the other world, as she was certain he was, he would not forgive her. She needed to avoid death as long as possible. He would be waiting for her. She had betrayed him, for he loved these children more than he loved anything of this world.

Mustafa shoved the plate of bread and honey across the table, dumping it in her lap. "Don't be praying in front of me, woman! If you had been here, Cyril could not have made off with Alice."

He hammered a fist on the table. "I had made a deal with a friend of someone who knows a kind man who takes little girls into this big house he owns. Sort of a school for girls, I think." He glanced slyly at Cyril's aunt who was lifting slices of bread and honey off the front of her robe. Had his face not been so red with anger, she might have noted a faint look of embarrassment.

She eased the honey-soaked bread back on the plate. Food cost money. She knew about this so-called friend of Mustafa's. There was no such "school" for girls. A beautiful little child such as Alice would be doomed once she left her aunt's house—even though that house was not much of a shelter.

She shoved the plate of soggy bread back across the table. She couldn't get Mustafa out of her house. No one would help her. Once a widow took another man under her roof, the roof belonged to him. All of her neighbors would see it that way. They looked at her sympathetically in the mornings. They could hear the noise of the beatings, both of her and Cyril. But, they felt powerless to interfere in another man's business. Mustafa was loud and brash, but the men liked his jokes. They didn't want trouble with him.

She didn't want trouble with him either. Her husband had never hit her. He had been a kind and gentle man. When she met him in the next world, she was sure that he would want to punish her severely—even though she would be dead—just because she had neglected her duties for his kin.

Looking at Mustafa's narrow eyes and cruel mouth made her realize how much she despised this man who was now stuffing the bread into his mouth, the honey dripping down his whiskered chin like a sticky waterfall over brambles. She could not escape from the grasp of this man. The authorities would view her as his common-law wife. They would consider her niece and nephew to be under his power.

There were other ways of having control. In the old wooden crate, standing on its end, in the bedroom—the crate where she kept her clothes—was a small box of photographs. Mustafa had discovered them once when he was searching her things for money. He had thrown the box of photos at the wall. He had not looked again. She gave him every penny she earned. He knew that.

She would keep the photographs safe for Cyril and Alice. If she ever saw them again, they should have the photographs of their parents, young and laughing with that English major and his wife. She didn't like the English, but that man and his wife had been kind to her husband's brother and his wife, treating them like a beloved son and daughter.

The envelope held something quite different. She didn't dare trust Mustafa not to rummage through her photo box again. Since Alice had been taken away that night, his behavior had become even more erratic. The envelope must be well hidden from Mustafa, hidden where a man would never think to look.

She had carefully unstitched the hem of her best galabeya, tucked the envelope into the hem, and put the stitches back in place. She had not worn the robe since Mustafa had moved in. It was her dress for church, but she no longer went. She knew that she had offended God. She had certainly offended her priest. It was better not to face one nor think about the other.

Mustafa grinned self-consciously across the table from her, the honey sweetening his disposition. "Bad eye, old girl. Sorry, the drink gets to me. We could have made a fortune off Alice. I was teaching her some songs. She was a quick learner. She would have done well in that school."

The aunt did not speak. She could not risk what his temper might do to her other eye. Those children were not her blood. She had few regrets that they were gone. She only wished that Mustafa had gone with them. She flinched visibly with the cruelty of her thoughts. She couldn't change what had happened during the past couple of years. She couldn't make herself feel anything for those children except the sense of obligation that her husband had left her on his deathbed.

A deathbed promise. The afterlife would not be kind to those who broke such promises. Her husband's directions had been very clear. Get the letter to the British Embassy if something happens to me. The letter was from Yusef Abbaza to his old friend, Major Wenkle, addressed to the British Embassy in Cairo.

It was a very direct request. It said:

> *"My dear wife died in childbirth, but it was her wish that our daughter be named for your wife, just as we named our son Cyril for you. While my brother and I look for work at Karnak, the children will stay with my brother's wife. If anything should happen to us, she will take this letter to the British Embassy.*
>
> *I make a request to you, who is more to me than a father: if I go too soon to that other world, I ask you to take my children, Cyril and Alice, and care for them and love them in the same spirit that you loved me and my wife. I give you all legal and moral rights to determine what is best for them.*
>
> *I hold you in my prayers. If fate is kind, you will not see this letter. You will see my face greeting you and your wife when you arrive in Cairo. It will be the happiest face you see.*
>
> *Your friend, Yusef Abbaza"*

Cyril's aunt glanced up at Mustafa; he had opened a second bottle. Today would not be much different from yesterday. She needed to find Cyril—an impossible task in this city of millions. Cyril was very bright. Maybe he would find a way to see her. He had obligations too. She was his only living relative, though not blood kin. A donkey brayed in the distance. She took that as a positive sign, not a comment about her.

Back at Mr. Parks's villa, life assumed a kind of tranquility that was misleading. Cyril and Alice, curled like kittens, were sleeping in the shade of a date palm in the courtyard. Mr. Feisel and Hetty were drinking tea and chatting in the manner of old friends.

Johab had spent all morning with his mother, protesting that his "tattoo" could not be scrubbed off despite the purposeful gleam in her eye. He looked toward the adjacent building and spotted Boris. Avoiding his mother's grip, he sped off in the direction of Boris, feeling a delicious curiosity about what kind of torture might be underway.

"Psychological, Johab, psychological. The other kind is too messy. That fellow in there," he pointed his thumb behind him toward the storeroom, "is scared out of his wits about what his boss will do to him. He said his boss's rule is 'don't get caught,' and this fellow broke the rule."

Boris clasped his hands over his head and stretched in the morning sun. His body glistened with the perspiration of his early morning exercise routine, the veins ready to burst through the pale ochre hue of his skin. When Johab had asked Mr. Parks about the unusual coppery color of Boris, Mr. Parks said, "Carrots. Boris eats lots of carrots for the carotene. Body builders like that orangey color."

Johab might consider eating more carrots if he could have a body like that of Boris. Boris seemed to read his thoughts. "When we finish using the storeroom, I'll show you and Cyril some workouts on my equipment. We'll have the two of you sporting huge muscles in no time."

They headed arm and arm back toward the villa. Johab thought that "psychological" torture must mean the removal of one ear or one finger. It would serve that fellow right.

Mr. Feisel and Mr. Parks stood across the courtyard having a tense conversation. Mr. Feisel seemed to be winning the argument, because Mr. Parks held up his palms, nodded, and walked over towards Miss Wenkle.

"Hetty, we need to go into the city to your apartment now. My morning was somewhat successful, but it took far too long. We need those records that Sarah copied, those descriptions of the items from the antiquities bust." He looked toward the perimeter fence. The dogs were pacing back and forth. "If Mr. El-Hasiim cannot account for the items on John's list, he is a very stupid thief."

Mr. Parks nodded toward Mr. Feisel. "Mr. Feisel has business in Cairo. I will drop him off and pick him up after we have finished at your place."

The major was being left home with Cyril, Jasmine, and Alice, just another child. Johab tried to look bored, as though he could care less.

"Johab, will you help, Boris?" Mr. Parks asked.

Help Boris? The muscles on Boris looked like the ridges on a Tyrannosaurus Rex. Boris hardly needed help. Johab turned away. Being treated like a child was one thing. Rubbing it in was quite another.

Mr. Parks put a hand on his shoulder and whispered: "Mr. Feisel's friend, Yuya, is coming with us to watch outside Hetty's apartment while we're going through the papers. The men didn't sleep well last night. The dogs kept them awake. Probably rabbits or foxes, but Barzoni knows where to find you and your family now. If you see or hear anything that seems suspicious, you need to alert the men. We can't let down our guard."

Johab perked up. "Guarding" was a good occupation. It sounded very military. He turned and almost stumbled against his lieutenant who had tiptoed across the courtyard and planted himself against Johab's side. "Time for a reading lesson, Cyril. Let's find another book. You know all the words in *Pinocchio*."

They watched Mr. Parks's jeep pull away. Cyril reached for Johab's hand. "Why did Mr. Feisel ask questions about my aunt this morning?

He wanted to know how to find her house." Cyril's thin voice sounded anxious. "Do you think he is planning to give me back to her?"

Cyril's eyes were the size of saucers in his thin face. His grip was painfully tight.

Johab reflected carefully. "I don't know why Mr. Feisel wants to know about your aunt, but I know he doesn't like what he has heard about her. I wouldn't think he would want to tangle with Mustafa. Maybe he's just curious, Cyril. His business in Cairo today must be about something else."

But what else? And why the sudden interest in where Cyril's aunt lives? Johab had never known Mr. Feisel to leave the Northern Cemetery until he left it to rescue Johab. Cyril's bottom lip quivered. A diversion was needed.

"Hey, Cyril. Look. Those dogs have treed Bastet again. He's in that big date palm. If you can shinny up there and get him down, I'll bet that Mother will make us honey bread with cinnamon."

As Cyril dashed toward the dogs and the yowling cat, a sense of unease crept into Johab's day. Cyril had become a younger cousin, someone important to him. Johab needed to have a chat with Mr. Feisel.

Chapter 65

. . . and they brought relief because
they broke the spell of the dead letter.

—Pasternak

Mr. Feisel motioned Yuya to the front passenger seat and moved beside Miss Wenkle on the back seat. She had seen him talking to Cyril before they left—Cyril looked uncomfortable, almost threatened by the conversation.

It wouldn't do to quiz Mr. Feisel. He provided information when he was ready. She remembered the trip from Cairo to the Valley and her long wait in the car while he visited his village friends. That had worked out all right. Yuya grinned at her from the front seat. He liked riding "shotgun" with Mr. Parks. Their soft conversation in Arabic soothed her.

Once in the city, Mr. Feisel gave directions while Miss Wenkle stared wide-eyed out the window. She had seen poverty in Cairo—legless beggars on makeshift carts, infants dangling from their mothers' arms, their eyelids wearing a rim of flies, not brushed away because of some old myth that the flies protected the eyes.

She had watched the garbage on her own street piled in a way that should offend civic pride. But, the Coptic boys and their donkeys eventually hauled it away. In this neighborhood, the houses and garbage heaps seemed inseparable.

Mr. Parks steered the jeep through narrow streets, past storefronts that were nothing more than sheets of rusty corrugated tin, wired together. Children played atop piles of garbage and wandered down alleys, their bare feet splashing in what appeared to be raw sewage. This neighborhood was not a part of Cairo that Miss Wenkle had seen, nor would she ever want to again.

"Stop here. This must be near the place. I'll wait for you on the corner, over there where that man has a vegetable stand."

Miss Wenkle watched Mr. Feisel unfold himself from the jeep and head down the alley. The clothes he had borrowed from Mr. Parks were too small. The pants struck him two inches above his ankles, yet he cut a fine figure in the ill-fitting English clothes, striding purposefully down the street, as though fashion was the least of his concerns.

Filthy place, thought Mr. Feisel, trying to remember the identifying markers that Cyril had described. The vegetable stand, two more alleys, and then a longer alley with a bar at the end of it. Cyril reminded him that Mustafa spent lots of time at the bar. Mr. Feisel hoped that Mustafa was there now. He wanted to see that aunt of Cyril's alone. Cyril said she worked at the hotel laundry, but she usually didn't leave for work until the middle of the afternoon.

All the makeshift huts along the alley looked alike. Rats scampered unmolested over the piles of garbage. Nasty things. Bastet would make short work of them.

Mr. Feisel stared at the huts piecemealed together, all with the same kinds of junk metal, cardboard, and mud bricks, each different but oddly alike. Finding the right one would be impossible. He didn't want to ask questions, because these neighborhoods could be very resistant to a stranger's presence. He should have worn his galabeya. No one would have noticed him then. These clothes set him apart. Mistake.

An old woman sitting on her front steps, mud bricks stacked high to keep her feet above a stream of muddy refuse, eyed him. Mr. Feisel greeted her, and asked in Arabic, "The Widow Abbaza? She lives near here?"

The old woman's eyes went from his head to his feet. The clothes were English but the sandals were native. "*Baksheesh*?" she smiled coyly, exposing toothless gums.

He thrust a few coins into her hand, and she motioned toward a shack three doors down the alley. "He isn't there now. You might be lucky enough to avoid him."

Mr. Feisel tapped at the old wooden door. Through the crack, he could see a woman sitting with her back toward the door. He tapped louder.

The door opened a crack. A woman who was probably no more than thirty years old but looked much older peered through the slit. "What do you want?" If the dead could speak, that would be the tone they would use—flat, tired, not expecting any answers.

"I need to talk to you about your nephew, about Cyril."

The door swung wide. A large purple and yellow bruise flowered near one eye. The expression on her face was of terror. "Are they safe, Cyril and Alice? Has something bad happened to them?" Mr. Feisel looked at her quizzically.

"My husband made me promise on his deathbed that I would take care of . . ." Her voice faded, and she shrunk back.

Mr. Feisel had the impression that this woman was experiencing a kind of terror that he had never known. Her fear was not related to what might or might not be happening to Cyril and Alice. It was the kind of terror that the ancient Egyptians knew when they faced death—an eternal judgment—the feather of Maat against the jackal-headed Anubis.

The heart would be weighed against truth and justice. If it was found wanting, the heart would plunge into the mouth of a waiting crocodile—and the body and soul would be lost forever.

This woman's soul was already lost. Her face was terror-stricken, but her eyes were dead, dark circles that reflected nothing.

Mr. Feisel could almost feel sorry for her. Almost, but not quite. He remembered the permanent scars from Mustafa's belt on Cyril's thin body. This woman was partially responsible. Those children had been her family. Not protecting them made her guilty. Mr. Feisel had no doubt about how the Goddess Maat's scale would tilt. The crocodile would have a feast when Cyril's aunt left this world.

"Wait here. She pointed toward a chair and hurried into the adjacent room, returning with a galabeya and a small box. She pulled out scissors and began snipping the hem of the robe. She shoved a well-worn envelope across the table. "Take it and these old photos," she hissed. "Get out. You don't want Mustafa to find you here." She pulled the door ajar, looking in both directions. "Now. He's not in sight."

Mr. Feisel stepped out of the door. Her voice, faint as a dying breeze, followed him. "Please tell me that they are safe. Then, I can rest."

Struggling with whether he wanted to give her any assurance or leave her in her present tortured state, Mr. Feisel thought about what Cyril would want. Cyril never spoke badly of this aunt. He simply didn't speak of her at all. Cyril didn't hold grudges.

Mr. Feisel's words were strong and assured. "Cyril and Alice are safe and well-loved." He added, almost as an afterthought. "Some day when enough time has passed so that I can forgive you, I will tell Cyril that you asked after him." He turned and strode briskly down the alley to wait at the vegetable stand and read what was in the envelope, the information that might change the lives of Cyril and Alice.

Chapter 66

At Hetty's apartment, Mr. Parks slid out of the car and motioned Yuya into the driver's seat. "Watch for a white Volvo or a large, black car—or anyone who seems to be hanging about." He motioned to the balcony above. "One of us will be up there watching for a signal if we need to leave quickly. The apartment has a back entrance where we'll be."

The door burst open. Hetty's friend Ella flung her arms around Hetty in a smothering hug. "We were out of our minds with worry when you left with Mr. Feisel and Cyril to look for Johab. We tried to comfort Johab's mother, but she was so withdrawn and kept making us tea. We were beside ourselves to hear Mr. Parks pounding on your door the next morning. He got word to us as soon as you arrived at his villa."

Hetty smiled at her friends and plopped down on the couch. "I've had such adventures. You wouldn't believe what I've seen and done. I watched a man being murdered by his cousin, and I ate delicious goat cheese in a village." Ian Parks nodded solemnly as though the combination of bloodletting and feasting was not unusual.

"And," she announced, hoping that this bit might shock her friends since they seemed to take murder in their stride, "I let Mr. Feisel hold my legs while I dangled down into a hole leading to a tomb in the ground to search for Johab and Cyril."

Sarah smiled brightly as though Hetty were describing a trip to the market to search for fresher produce. Ella blushed for both of the sisters.

"Sarah, we need to see those papers you copied—John's description of the stolen antiquities that the police gave Mr. El-Hasiim."

Mr. Parks glanced at the faintly irritated faces of three women who had a great deal of catching up to do. "Sorry. We need to get any information you've found quickly. The plot has thickened a bit since I sent you the note that everyone was safe. The two men who kidnapped Johab followed us to my villa. My guard Boris caught one of them, but the other one got away. One of Mr. Feisel's friends is outside in my jeep watching the street. Hetty needs to stay at my place for now. You're welcome to come too."

"We're fine, here," Sarah and Ella said in unison. "Sarah still has some work to do, and we can keep a watch on Hetty's apartment," Ella added. Their vacation in Cairo was taking new twists, not particularly comfortable ones. They could hear Hetty muttering to herself in the bedroom as she threw clothes into a bag. She seemed to be extraordinarily pleased about something, as though being chased by thugs and pushed down stairs had energized her.

Ella moved toward the balcony. "I'll watch the street. Mr. Barzoni was here yesterday. He asked why Hetty hadn't returned to work; then, he told us her concussion might make her behave abnormally. He brought another big bouquet of those stinking lilies. We told him we were allergic to flowers and sent him packing." Ella, who rarely said much, and almost never anything negative, surprised Mr. Parks.

Sarah thrust a small cloth bag toward Mr. Parks. "Ian, I went to the Semiramis Hotel yesterday and talked the manager into letting me use the copier. I didn't want to be seen by Mr. El-Hasiim. These are copies of John's descriptions of the missing antiquities, as well as some notes that I find most interesting. It appears that John has been suspicious of Mr. El-Hasiim for several months. He is very careful about what he puts in official reports, but his fieldwork notes, for his private use, have some telling comments."

Her lips were pursed, her eyes narrowed. "In London, you and I questioned why someone like Mr. El-Hasiim, with no qualifications, would be placed in a position of responsibility. The recent antiquities bust may be only the tip of the iceberg. John's notes make reference to other things missing from the storerooms. I've organized everything by item, by description, and with John's comments. I sent another copy to your address at the British Museum." Mr. Parks nodded with understanding. Anything in their possession would be at risk.

"A white Volvo just circled the block and is heading back this way. Your friend is moving the jeep. You need to get out of here," Ella announced in an anxious voice.

Hetty hugged both of her friends. "If you feel unsafe here, get a taxi and come to the villa. Don't take any chances. Ian has armed men out there."

Sarah followed them through the kitchen to the back exit. "I don't think we're in any danger. Mr. El-Hasiim wasn't at the Museum when I made the first copies. The staff doesn't like him. I don't think they would volunteer any information to him. Mr. Barzoni is another matter. He must be threatened by what he thinks Hetty suspects—otherwise, he wouldn't have tried to kill her in a public place like the Museum."

Kill. Hetty shuddered and hurried faster down three tiers of rickety backstairs behind Ian Parks. The words out of Sarah's mouth sounded far worse than her own description of being "pushed" down the stairs. She had never before felt fear for herself.

Her life in Cairo had been such a change from the foggy, disciplined street where she lived in London. In Cairo, camels waltzed down the street as unconcerned about traffic as a London cabbie. From the moment she arrived, Hetty had loved the sun and color and strangeness of this city.

Since John's kidnapping, sadness had unbalanced her. She wept at night for Johab and his family—she had a degree of confidence that Mr. Barzoni would not harm someone as valuable to him as John Bennett. Mostly, she wept for the sadness she saw in the eyes of an eleven-year-old boy who should be reading about intrigue in those mysteries he loved—not experiencing it.

She blinked back tears. All of these bad things that had happened led to one miraculous event. She had found Cyril and Alice. No. Johab had found them and brought her to them. Ian grabbed her hand, pulling her down the alley and around the corner. *She needed to pay attention.* Somewhere down the street an old Volvo smoked and belched—it might look harmless enough with its repaired oil pan and new tires, but it held Barzoni's men and weapons.

Around the corner at the end of the street, Yuya had the motor running and two doors wide open. Pulling into heavy afternoon traffic, he took several different side streets, doubling back toward the slum where they had left Mr. Feisel. He was nowhere in sight.

As if by magic, Mr. Feisel swung into the back seat while the jeep was still moving. Digging into his pocket, he pulled out an envelope and some photographs and handed them to Miss Wenkle.

She glanced at the address and recognized the words for British Embassy. She opened the envelope. "It's in Arabic," she said, frustrated.

"That's why I need to teach you Arabic. You can't even read a letter that is very important to you." Mr. Feisel's voice was low and teasing. In a whisper, he said, "I'll read it to you now but very softly. It is private—something that you may want to decide when and how to share with Cyril. These photographs are of his parents—and, I believe, your Uncle Cyril and Aunt Alice."

As Mr. Parks's jeep headed toward the outskirts of Cairo and safety, Cyril's aunt sat anxiously at the table in her hut, considering her own safety. She fingered the hem of the robe. The bulk of hidden money remained exactly where she had stashed it. Her husband and Cyril's father had kept a small savings "for the children's education." She had hidden it, along with the letter from Cyril's father, in the hem of her best galabeya, the only place that Mustafa would not dream of searching.

The money was intended for the children, but she had hidden it with other intent. Every day when she passed by that old woman a few houses down the alley, begging for money or food, her toothless gums a blatant sign of her poverty, Cyril's aunt became more determined. That small savings meant for Cyril and Alice would be enough to see her into old age. She could return to her village. Life there would be kinder than in Cairo. Now that the children were no longer her responsibility, she could make plans.

The door burst open with the bulk of Mustafa blocking the sunlight. She casually re-rolled the robe and placed her scissors back into the sewing box. Mustafa was naturally suspicious. None of her movements could be unusual. She walked over toward the brazier and poked the charcoal. "You want some tea?"

The color of Mustafa's face made it clear to her that tea was not the beverage of choice. He reeked of beer, but his color was of rage.

"That old biddy down the street told me that a man came to see you, someone dressed in English clothes, but she said he looked like man from the desert, not a foreigner." His fists knotted, and he moved menacingly towards her.

She inched sideways carefully, positioning the table between herself and Mustafa. "It was the man from the hotel laundry. He needs me to work more shifts. They have a lot of tourists coming for the Christmas season. They think they are seeing the place where Mary and Joseph stayed with the baby Jesus."

Her diversion wasn't working. Mustafa's face darkened. "You are lying. I don't think anyone from the hotel knows where you live. When you were sick and stayed home from work, you didn't send Cyril to tell them. They don't care about you. They can find hundreds just like you to do their laundry."

Mustafa's voice was strong, but he staggered and grabbed the table for support, dropping into a chair. He had been drinking since early morning.

Cyril's aunt scraped inside a jar and slathered honey on a piece of bread. "You need something to eat. You'll feel better with something in your stomach."

Mustafa crammed the bread and honey into his mouth.

What had she ever considered appealing about this man? A giant hog would be more appealing. His mean little eyes narrowed at her. He chewed with his mouth open, a wad of masticated bread and honey smeared up to the bottom of his nose and along his upper lip.

He shoved back from the table, knocking over the chair. "You lie! You're hiding something from me. You know something about my little Alice. You are hiding her!" He roared with anger, moving toward her with raised fists.

She bent over, shielding her face, waiting for the rain of blows that always followed Mustafa's outbursts of temper.

A resounding crash echoed in the small space. The table tipped forward. She looked up to see the confused expression on Mustafa's face as he tripped on the overturned chair, grabbed the unbalanced table for support and fell, striking his head against the edge of the table.

She stared at his fallen hulk on the floor and had sudden recollections of seeing a hog butchered on her family's farm. Their neighbors didn't eat pork, but her father said that it was all right for Christians to eat hogs, and her own family came from a long line of Coptic Christians. Just like Mustafa, the hog had lain, belly-up, a line of blood tracing along his throat and oozing down into the mud of the hog pen.

The blood trickling down Mustafa's face came from a large cut across his temple. The corner of the table was sharp. His weight and the force of his fall had made a significant slash in his head.

She did not touch him, did not feel of his carotid for a pulse, and did not get any closer to him. Unlike the slaughtered hog, Mustafa's belly was rising and falling. He was alive, but his face was an odd color and his breathing was sporadic. The gleam of honey on his mouth and nose was the last thing she noticed as she moved to the other room to hide her galabeya before creeping out the door to her job at the hotel laundry.

When Cyril's aunt reached the basement of the hotel, the sharp odor of chlorine rising from the vats assaulted her nostrils. For once, she welcomed the odor—antiseptic, clean, disinfecting. This laundry was a place that she had always despised. Here, she did backbreaking work, lifting sheets and towels, torqueing water from them, and flinging them onto drying racks. Today, she welcomed this world of steaming, clean water and hard work.

She wouldn't think of Cyril and Alice. That man who came out of nowhere this afternoon assured her that they were safe. She believed a man like that from the desert. She dared not think of Mustafa lying in wait for her. That would be a problem she would face in the night when she returned home.

It was well after midnight when Cyril's aunt left the basement of the hotel, clutching her week's earnings. She had never hidden her earnings from Mustafa, only her husband's and his brother's savings. That was life before Mustafa. Her conscience was troubled enough without giving Mustafa money meant for Cyril and Alice. Now, she wished she had saved part of her earnings. Mustafa squandered all of it on beer and cigarettes and sent Cyril to beg for food.

The pale moon lit up the alley, a familiar pathway to her. She avoided the main streets with their lamp-lit paths. She was still a young woman though her youth seemed to have disappeared when Mustafa moved into her house. Women didn't wander around Cairo without companions even though the government punished thieves severely. The alleys were safer. She moved as a shadow.

Her street was quiet; even the bar down the street, Mustafa's favorite hangout, appeared deserted. No oil lamp glimmered through the window of her house. Mustafa must have gone to bed early or, more likely, was off somewhere drinking with his friends. She pushed the door softly and reached for the lamp that sat on a nearby crate.

The flickering wick reflected the chaos that she had left—the upended table, the overturned chair, and Mustafa. Mustafa had not moved. She could see the soft rise and fall of his belly. He was asleep or unconscious.

She lifted the lamp higher, letting out a stifled cry. Mustafa's head was moving, absolutely wiggling.

A sleek, fat rat, its hairless tail, long and repulsive in the wavering light, moved back from Mustafa's face, flashed its black, beady eyes at her and scuttled toward the crack in the door.

Too paralyzed to move, too terrified not to move, Cyril's aunt stepped forward and held the oil lamp above Mustafa's head. The scream that would have awoken the entire neighborhood was smothered by her own fist crammed into her mouth.

Mustafa's upper lip and one side of his nose were no longer coated with honey. They had disappeared. A small, dark pool of coagulated blood rested above his teeth where his upper lip had once resided. A black hole gaped next to his one intact nostril.

He wasn't dead. His breathing was raspy with the changes the rat had made to his mouth and nose. Bile rose into the throat of Cyril's aunt. No time to be sick, no time to linger here.

If Mustafa woke, his rage would be uncontrollable. The rat had finished the job that Cyril had started on his thumb when Mustafa had tried to shove that skinned mouse down that poor little boy's throat.

She smiled grimly. The old gods might be intervening in human affairs after all. The justice of Maat certainly was at work in this little hut. She gathered her few belongings from the other room, blew out the oil lamp, and fled into the shadows of the night.

Chapter 67

The shadows of the night were comforting with Boris and Mr. Feisel's friends patrolling outside. Johab beamed at the faces around the dinner table. His mother had made special treats for them. Small pastries filled with spiced meat and just the slightest hint of cinnamon; bowls of *tahini* were centered on the table. He would avoid the large bowl of chopped cucumber and onions and the platter of *koshari*.

Mr. Parks rapped on his glass with his spoon. "Hetty and I have been busy today—as has Soya, who helped prepare this marvelous meal," he nodded toward Johab's mother. "Thanks to Sarah's work, we believe that we have solid evidence that Mr. El-Hasiim has been stealing the Museum's treasures."

He paused for effect, but none of his listeners seemed surprised. He smiled and nodded at Hetty. "Hetty helped me interpret the codes—she had asked John why he made certain marks like little hieroglyphs by some items and not others, and he told her that he had 'questions' about those items, and that she was to type an asterisk by them. We now know that those were missing artifacts—no longer in the storerooms."

His face lit up with the next piece of news. "Tomorrow, we meet with the head of the Council for Antiquities to discuss the New Kingdom items that are supposed to be in the storerooms. I don't expect that we will find all of them. Boris had a very interesting chat with

Barzoni's man. He has been singing like a nightingale. He admitted to kidnapping Johab and helping to dump him in the tomb."

A grim expression formed on Mr. Parks's face. "He says that he helped take Johab's father, but he doesn't know where he is. Barzoni kept that location a secret. He says Barzoni has lots of secrets. He says he was just doing a job that he was paid to do."

"Did that job include planning to cut off my ear or my finger?" Johab's shrill voice punctuated the quiet room.

Mr. Parks grinned at Johab. "We don't believe this fellow is as innocent as he claims, but he's too stupid to be Barzoni's right-hand man. Boris says our captive contradicts himself. We think that he's just a low-life thug, but Boris will keep questioning him. As long as we have him, we'll make Barzoni nervous." He stood up and pushed back his chair. "Let's move into the other room for coffee and dessert."

As Johab rounded the end of the table, he brushed past Mr. Parks, who leaned over and whispered, "Our friend in the storeroom now has a cauliflower ear, and you should see the odd angle of his little finger. Boris told me that he was leaving the man with a few souvenirs."

Johab knew that he should feel guilty, not this odd sense of pleasure, over another human's pain. Then, he recalled the absolute terror he had felt inside that cold, dank tomb. That thug had gleefully anticipated the pain that he would cause Johab by removing an ear or a finger.

He grinned coyly at Mr. Parks. "Tell Boris to give that fellow plenty of water to drink, in a bowl, so he can lap it up just like a puppy dog."

Johab moved out into the courtyard, watching his friends and family in the dimly lit living room. Hetty and Mr. Feisel were talking together softly. Both of them had been acting odd since they had returned from Cairo, as though they shared some kind of secret between them that wasn't quite resolved.

Hetty kept hugging Cyril and Alice. Cyril didn't seem to mind. At times, Hetty showed a piece of paper to Mr. Feisel. She seemed to be memorizing what was on the page. Maybe they were plotting ways to trap Barzoni.

Trapping Barzoni. That was the major obstacle they faced. With his father's notes on the missing stuff, they could probably snare Mr. El-Hasiim. But, what about Barzoni? He was the mastermind. Maybe Mr. Parks could convince the Chief of the Council that Barzoni was the main criminal. If not, he needed to find a way to ambush Barzoni.

Johab propped himself against the date palm and listened to the night sounds of the desert. Out here, the traffic of Cairo was not even a distant drone. The bark of a lonely fox echoed in the night. Johab thought about Barzoni. He was a vulture, picking through the bones of an ancient world—not because he loved beautiful things—but for money. Sleep came quickly to Johab, and the feather of the Goddess Maat must have touched his eyelids, for he dreamed of a place where justice always prevailed.

When Johab woke, he was on his own mat in Hetty's room. Cyril's mat was rolled into the corner of the room. Hetty's bed was empty. He wandered into the dining room to the noise of plates being cleared.

"Sleepy head," his mother beamed at him. "Mr. Parks left half an hour ago with Hetty for his meeting in Cairo. He said her testimony would be important—he's concerned about Mr. El-Hasiim's connections through his uncle." Her face took on a dreamy look. "I wish your father could be here to see what might happen to Mr. El-Hasiim."

She peered out the window at Jasmine and Alice who were trying to coax Bastet down from the date palm. "I miss your father every day, but I am not frightened here. You children are safe. I never knew what you were doing during those long days you spent in Cairo, Johab. I knew that you were not just selling fulbeans. But that's in the past." She looked at him somberly.

Johab tried not to meet her eyes. *It wasn't in the past—not until his father was found.* Mr. Parks could help, but Mr. Parks didn't have all the information. Neither did Hetty, Mr. Feisel, or Cyril. They all knew about the room in KV20 that had been opened to thieves by the force of nature, a flood that had moved boulders on the side of a cliff.

They had seen the treasures that he and Cyril had brought up. They knew that the antiquities found in the police bust had probably come from that chamber, because they had seen the thieves carrying off other sacks of treasures from the tomb.

Not one of them knew that Queen Hatshepsut slept in a hidden room. Johab couldn't bear to think of her as a linen-wrapped mummy, exposed in her golden casket. Her face and voice were imprinted in his mind, just as she had marked her gift of the amulet on his neck.

By scraping away those telltale marks on the floor of the outer chamber with that ancient adze, he hoped he had helped conceal her burial chamber for eternity. In his heart, he had made a silent promise to the Queen never to reveal her resting place, never to let human eyes see what lay beneath the carefully wrapped and perfumed linen.

Johab clenched his jaw. The evil god, Seth, the destroyer god, could not make him reveal the Queen's secret chamber—much less a common thief like Barzoni. *He would use this secret knowledge to find a way to trick Barzoni and keep his father safe.*

Johab walked outside so his mother couldn't guess what he was thinking. Cyril stood staring into space like a lonely, little statue.

When he moved beside him, Cyril's small hand tucked itself into the crook of his arm, but he remained speechless. That was odd. Cyril usually chattered like a magpie, asking lots of questions. He asked only one: "Johab, what is going to happen to Alice and me?"

Johab stared at him. "What do you mean, Cyril? Nothing is going to happen to you. You are with us. You are safe."

"Then, why did Mr. Parks tell me when he left this morning that I would have a surprise today? And why did Mr. Feisel want to know where my aunt lives?" He ducked his head, and said so softly that Johab could scarcely hear him. "I think the surprise has something to do with my aunt. Maybe they think that Alice and I miss her, or Mustafa, but we don't." His voice soared into a high pitch, just this side of a wail.

"None of us misses Mustafa," a loud voice boomed next to them as Mr. Feisel swept Cyril up in his arms. "If we had Mustafa here, we would put him out in that shed with Boris. I've told Boris about Mustafa. He says he would like to meet him—in the storeroom." He chuckled.

Johab knew that Mr. Feisel was trying to divert Cyril's attention away from the grim thoughts that never left him—even in his sleep. Cyril's nightmares often awoke Johab. When he tried to get Cyril to tell him why he screamed in the night, Cyril would simply say, "Bad things."

"Cyril is worried about some kind of surprise that Mr. Parks promised him this morning." Johab explained.

Mr. Feisel smiled and pointed toward his friends who were strapping boards around the bed of their pickup. "The surprise isn't just for Cyril; it is for all of you children. My friends are helping with the surprise. You don't think they would do anything to harm you, do you Cyril?"

Cyril shook his head. Mr. Feisel's friends had helped them. They had come with their guns to Cairo, a place in which they were not at ease, just to help. Cyril trusted them. He trusted all of his friends here. It was just that those questions about his aunt and where she lived continued to bother him.

Cyril knew how Johab felt about his family. Maybe everyone was supposed to feel that way about family. He looked toward the desert so that no one could see the tears welling into his eyes. His family was Alice, not an aunt who never wanted him or Alice. "You are my burden, not my blood," his aunt had told him many times. Families were not supposed to be burdens. Alice had never been a burden to him. He would risk anything for Alice. Come to think of it, so had Johab.

Mr. Feisel grabbed the arms of both boys. "We may have a long day ahead of us until Mr. Parks and Miss Wenkle return with whatever information they can get from those officials." It was clear from his tone that Mr. Feisel mistrusted all officials.

"Johab, the best thing that you can do for Cyril is to teach him how to read and write in both Arabic and English. He has almost worn out the pages of *Pinocchio*. Mr. Parks has a large library here. Let's check it out until the surprise gets here."

As they moved into the house, Mr. Feisel waved toward his friends in their old pickup that rattled down the road. In the distance, Boris swung the gate wide for them. Johab could not get into the spirit of surprises. There had been far too many of them lately.

CHAPTER 68

In Mr. Parks's large library, Johab stretched out on the floor and listened to Cyril. His questions were endless. Johab found a geography book with colored plates and maps to show Cyril other countries. Cyril didn't even know the world was round. His view of the world was primitive.

Cyril's world was flat and covered a space that stretched from Cairo to Karnak, where Cyril's father got typhoid fever. "From there to there," Cyril, pointed east and then west, "is nothing but sand. If you go out there without a camel or donkey loaded with food and water, you will die or fall off the edge."

"No edges, Cyril. The world is round—like a ball." Johab pointed to the globe, all sectioned nicely, and flat against the page. He shook his head in resignation. That map fit Cyril's worldview—a flat planet.

Maybe a book on astronomy would help. Johab pulled M.V. Berry's *Principles of Cosmology and Gravitation* off the shelf and flipped past thick, dull paragraphs of text to photographs of the solar system.

Knowing that Cyril loved watching the stars, he said: "Our planet is something like one of these stars." Cyril nodded. "Remember when I told you the story of *The Little Prince*?" Cyril beamed. He could imagine a little boy, just like himself, standing in the courtyard of a villa, looking at a star that was his very own planet.

Cyril asked: "Do you think that little Prince was a friend of the sun god Ra? The one you told me about that causes the sun to rise?"

"That was then. This is now, Cyril." Johab snapped Berry's book closed. "Let's work on your reading." Memorizing words was easier for Cyril. Johab found an Arabic-English dictionary that began with "aardvark." He had never seen an aardvark. Neither had Cyril. Somehow, teaching Cyril the Arabic and English words for aardvark seemed much easier than explaining how the earth spins around the sun to a little boy who insisted that the world was flat.

After lunch, Jasmine and Alice disappeared for afternoon naps. Mr. Feisel dozed in the courtyard. Only Cyril sat totally alert, transfixed by the photographs in a book he had found of animals throughout the world. "I would like to hear their voices," Cyril looked up hopefully, pointing to an elephant.

At that instant, a trumpeting bray and the noise of barking dogs split the afternoon silence. Rushing through the door, Johab and Cyril could see a pickup bouncing down the road toward the villa with Sekina trapped in a small, pen-like structure in the back of it. Her front legs were hobbled with a piece of rope. Her back legs had demolished two of the sideboards. Mr. Feisel's friends laughed as they clipped the hobbles, while dodging hooves and yellow teeth.

With a final, loud bray and a mighty kick, Sekina broke the last board, backed down from the pickup bed, and trotted over toward Johab and Cyril. She was home again, a new home, but home, ready to pull the bean cart if she needed to work. Otherwise, she would be happy just to eat sweet grass and let the little girls brush her handsome coat with corncobs.

Mr. Feisel's friend, Yuya, grinned. "Nice surprise, huh? Your mother said that you might be missing your donkey. We almost couldn't get her loaded. She practically stopped traffic in Cairo with her noise."

He scratched Sekina between her ears. "That woman, that Mrs. Zadi, made a big fuss about us taking the donkey. We gave her the note from your mother, but she said we were stealing the donkey—that she had been feeding it and planned to sell it."

Johab flushed with anger. Sekina was thin. Mrs. Zadi had been feeding her very little—his mother had left money with her for the donkey's food and for her trouble.

Yuya patted Johab's shoulder. "We told her that we would be happy to bring her with the donkey—in the back of the pickup—if she wanted a word with your mother." He grinned. "She didn't. I never saw anyone move so quickly."

Sekina was in heaven. A large tub of fresh water had been placed under the shade of date palms. Never before had the donkey experienced such space, so much tempting greenery. Mr. Feisel and his friends were busy constructing a fence to keep her away from the courtyard plants. The small humans would surely sneak a blossom for her once in awhile. This donkey's life would be good here.

It was almost dusk when Mr. Parks's jeep stopped in front of the villa. He and Hetty looked exhausted. They sank into a sofa, gratefully taking tall glasses of lemonade that Johab's mother handed them. "We've had the devil of a day trying to make some officials understand that their little bureaucratic structure has sizeable holes in it. The treasures that are supposed to stay in Egypt are disappearing," Mr. Parks exclaimed with frustration.

"Everything they designed to protect the artifacts—the Council, the Departments, the Committees, the agreements with other participating countries, and universities—these mean nothing when there is a worm in the apple." He sighed. "Today, I think we convinced a couple of people in high places that the worm has grown more sticky fingers than a centipede. Sorry, I mix metaphors when I'm tired."

Hetty looked at Johab's confused face. "We were successful." Hetty's voice rang out with considerably more enthusiasm than Mr. Parks had generated. "Ian is just tired and frustrated. You wouldn't believe the red tape we had to go through just to get someone to listen. Your father's records made them sit up and take notice, Johab." Hetty beamed at him, understanding that Johab was feeling left out of the action, confined at home with the children.

Mr. Parks drank thirstily, put his glass on the table, and took charge. "The Chief of the Council appeared to be most unhappy with his friend, the uncle of Mr. El-Hasiim, for putting him into what he called 'an awkward situation.'"

Mr. Parks grinned. "I suggested it would be even more awkward for him if the newspapers, including the foreign press, got wind of what was happening. These are world treasures—they belong to Egypt; however, people from all over the world flock to this country to see them. I suggested that the Minister of Tourism would have a conniption over this kind of bad press."

Hetty burst out, "Ian made it clear that he was speaking for the Egyptology division of the British Museum would take his concerns to museums throughout the world unless immediate action is taken. It happened faster than I thought. I expected to hear the usual 'God willing, we can put it off,' but that isn't what happened. The police chief responsible for that recent bust of the antiquity thieves met with us. By early this afternoon, government and police officials were sitting at the same table and listening."

Mr. Parks seemed surprised that they had accomplished so much. He had worked with the government's bureaucracy in the past. He didn't think these men would be so alarmed by the loss of some ancient tomb treasures. But they were. He and Hetty had appealed to their national pride with their plea for Egypt's treasures.

"We will meet the Chief of the Council and the police chief at the Museum in the morning at 10 o'clock outside the staff entrance." Mr. Parks turned toward Johab. "This should have been your show, Johab. I didn't bring you today for one reason; these men were willing to talk *only* with me because of my position with the British Museum and my work on the New Kingdom Project. They would see you as a young boy who is missing his father."

He stared directly into Johab's eyes. "They don't know what you know. I don't suspect any of us here do," he added ruefully. "But, tomorrow morning, you will go with Hetty and me to the Museum."

"Mr. Barzoni?" Johab spat out the name.

"We ran against a brick wall there, Johab." Mr. Parks seemed embarrassed, as though he had failed Johab in some large measure. "We spent quite a bit of time today discussing Barzoni. As I told you before, he has a questionable reputation. The officials know that he has contacts in Syria, Iraq, and Iran, as well as in Egypt. He flies regularly to England, France, Japan, and the United States. They are sure that he deals with wealthy collectors in all of these countries.

The hottest items on the market are things purported to come from Egyptian tombs."

Mr. Parks frowned. "Like those of us who work legitimately in this field, Barzoni has a problem. When someone brings something that they claim to have found, many experts can't always determine if it is real or fake—some craftsmen today are just as skilled as they were thousands of years ago. Proving that something actually came from an old tomb increases its value exponentially."

Mr. Parks glanced soberly at Johab and his mother. "This doesn't help us find John, but we do have one of Barzoni's men. We won't release him. Boris is a master at getting information. We'll just have to work on a plan to trap Barzoni. I don't know what that plan might be, but we are not giving up."

The final words of Mr. Parks seemed prophetic to Johab. "Not giving up" had been the words he repeated every morning and every night since his father had been kidnapped. Mr. Parks might not have a plan, but Johab was working out one in his head right now.

The idea had come to him in a flash when Mr. Parks talked about how Barzoni needed proof that something came from an old tomb. Johab knew more about a certain old tomb than anyone but Senenmut, who had designed it to hide the body of his beautiful Queen.

Trapping Mr. Barzoni might prove difficult. Johab looked around the room at his friends and family, mulling over the problem presented by that sleazebag, Barzoni. Johab knew he needed to use his brain—his brawn just didn't measure up. He must be like a spider, small, but crafty, spinning a net that could eventually trap his prey.

He would sleep on it. Everyone else had moved toward the dinner table. Johab grabbed a handful of dates and tiptoed out into the courtyard to concentrate, under his favorite palm tree.

CHAPTER 69

The early morning sun caressed Johab's face, casting a golden glow over everything in the bedroom. Cyril was rolled into his usual knot. When Cyril slept, he never looked relaxed—he slept on his side with his head tucked against his knees as though to protect himself from a sudden blow.

Life with Mustafa must have been frightful. If Cyril could stretch out full-length and fall asleep on his back, it would be a sign that he had reached a safe port. Johab knew in his heart of hearts that Cyril was safe and that Hetty and Mr. Feisel had not been discussing any thing that wasn't in Cyril's best interest. But, they were being cagey about something. Cyril was very intuitive. He knew those discussions involved him.

The faint clatter of dishes from the kitchen sounded down the hallway. Johab pulled his newly washed but well-worn galabeya over his head and sauntered into the kitchen where his mother was poaching eggs. She smiled and popped a gelatinous yellow eye onto his plate. "I saw how quickly you ate the poached egg that morning I fixed them for you and Cyril. I thought I'd make you something you like for breakfast."

Johab eyed the egg that eyed him back. He would need to malinger until Cyril woke. Cyril would make short work of the egg, then Johab, his mother, and Cyril could start the day in good spirits. In the meantime, he hid the offending yellow eye under a piece of flat bread.

"You are *not* wearing that old galabeya to meet with the Chief of the Council this morning, Johab. Whatever are you thinking to get yourself up in that garb? You can wear your shorts and borrow a shirt from Mr. Parks. We need to go by the apartment and get our own clothes." He had, at least, diverted his mother's attention from the egg. Now, she was fixated on the galabeya.

"I'm wearing it for effect, Mother," Johab said decisively. "I need to look less American and more Egyptian for this meeting. I need to look like someone who is at home in the desert and around old tombs. This robe will do the trick."

It was an ugly robe and cheap. She gave Johab a sideways glance. He must think that she had gone blind not to see the lump that the poached egg made under that piece of bread. Johab's little tricks didn't fool her. Still, he had taken on so much responsibility. When she had been hit that night when the kidnappers broke into their apartment, she must have suffered some kind of temporary mental collapse. Days had passed when she had felt only two strong emotions—fear when Johab left the Northern Cemetery and vast relief when he returned.

She could scarcely remember the taxi ride after they left her sister's house in the middle of the night. She remembered walking around like a zombie, so dazed that she actually allowed herself to be questioned by that busybody Mrs. Zadi. At the end of the day, it was Mr. Feisel who brought her around.

Mr. Feisel asked no questions. He simply sat on the stoop in the sunlight talking about his childhood at his grandparents' home in a village—and she began to talk about her life as a child. That's where her idea came for Johab to sell fulbeans. She knew that he was determined to go in search of his father. He needed a better disguise than a galabeya and rubber-soled sandals. She had helped with his disguise—and Johab hadn't even realized it.

She watched him spooning stewed fruit onto his plate. It would be better not to let Johab know that he occasionally needed help. He was very independent, just like his father. "Johab, I imagine that Bastet might enjoy that egg—or perhaps the dogs. It will be cold by the time Cyril wakes." Johab flushed, then smiled at her, and moved with his plate out to the courtyard where Mr. Parks was having his morning coffee.

As she watched them through the kitchen window, she could see that Johab and Mr. Parks were having some kind of disagreement. Mr. Parks was shaking his head in a manner that clearly meant "no." Johab's chin was taking on that fixed position that meant he would not be swayed. Her grandfather's chin. That was the only thing about Johab that reminded her of her family.

John's family said that he was the "spitting image" of John as a boy. "Spitting image." She could never understand why someone would say that. It seemed a rather nasty thing to say about a young child. But then, Americans had some strange expressions.

She gasped aloud. She had forgotten all about John's parents. Who had notified them that John was missing? It was nearing Christmas. They always sent presents to Jasmine and Johab. No one would be at the apartment to receive them. No one would be there to make the Christmas Eve call—on the American Christmas Eve, not the Coptic blessed day. Depression swept over her. After Ian Parks had come to Cairo, her situation had changed; her husband's situation, whatever that might be, had not.

Outside, Johab was in the process of trying to change his father's situation. "That's why I must wear the amulet, Mr. Parks. It gives me confidence. I put on my galabeya because it has a high neck. The amulet can't be *easily* seen." Johab sneaked in the word "easily" because he didn't know at this point what use he might make of Queen Hatshepsut's gift. Part of what he said was absolutely true. He did feel strangely protected by the amulet.

Mr. Parks finally agreed. "You know the combination, Johab. It's in the safe. You need to be sure that the officials at our meeting don't see your amulet. I can't protect it for you if anyone sees it. It's very valuable."

As he reached inside of the dark safe in Mr. Parks's closet, the jasper stone pulsed with an iridescent, green light. Wearing the amulet brought back memories of the soft hands of the Queen placing it around his neck, whispering in a musical voice.

When he had been at the bottom of the tomb shaft, for that brief moment in time, Johab had not felt the hard, limestone blocks of the tomb against his back nor the pain from the bump on his head. He felt as though he had suddenly been immersed in a warm bath of scented flowers—and rare ointments that masked the dry, stale air of the tomb.

Eager to get to the Museum, Mr. Parks, Hetty, and Johab piled into the jeep. His mother, Mr. Feisel, and Yuya waved in the distance until the cloud of dust from the bumpy road obscured them and the villa. The meeting ahead was so important that no one dared speak.

Johab reached into his pocket and rolled two small seals together— these seals, one inscribed with Senenmut's cartouche and one with the Queen's cartouche, clicked like marbles. The sound was reassuring. They were part of Johab's plan. He decided not to bring the alabaster pots. Those might be needed later. He doubted that Barzoni would be anywhere near the Museum this morning. Surely, the thug who escaped had warned him about Mr. Parks. Johab thought glumly that Barzoni would probably make himself scarce.

The meeting this morning was intended to be a surprise to Mr. El-Hasiim. For Johab, it seemed almost anticlimactic, as though catching Mr. El-Hasiim in the act was something his father had done weeks before. Confronting Mr. El-Hasiim was just a technicality.

Confronting Mr. Barzoni might require divine intervention. A clever, influential criminal wouldn't be so naïve as to walk into a trap. Johab stared out the window, watching the early morning traffic streaming into Cairo, maintaining a neutral expression, but spinning a web inside of his head.

Three large buses, packed with Japanese tourists, pulled around the front of the Museum, expelling swarms of chattering visitors. Johab thought that the Japanese tourists all resembled foreign news correspondents in the midst of a battlefield, bristling with cameras, laden with bags full of special lenses and rolls of film. He wondered if they could actually see without a camera's lens.

Mr. Parks pulled into the back entrance. Several police vehicles were parked nearby. Half a dozen policemen were wandering casually around the parking lot, trying to appear as though they had simply dropped by for a morning chat. Johab looked daggers at them. The possibility of surprise just evaporated. Mr. Barzoni wouldn't be coming in the Staff Entrance today.

A short, sturdy man with a dark mustache stepped out of a car and moved toward their jeep. His pale gray suit was so shiny that it dazzled in the morning sun. Two men, carrying official-looking briefcases, trotted beside him. The Council Chief nodded toward Hetty reluctantly, as though he considered this English woman to be a worrisome intrusion into the business of men.

Mr. Parks pulled Johab forward. "This is John Horemheb Bennett, the son of my esteemed colleague, John Bennett. Johab, Mr. Sadiq, the Chief."

Mr. Sadiq flinched slightly with the mention of Johab's full name, wondering about a father, especially an American, who would name a child after an old warrior king. Mohammed or Yusef were good names for a boy—not Horemheb. Imagine being saddled with such a name. He would treat the boy kindly. He glanced again at Johab's galabeya. Maybe they needed to pay their scientists more—this boy's robe was as ragged as a slum child's.

In perfect Arabic, Johab said, "I am so pleased to meet you Mr. Sadiq. Mr. Parks has told me how concerned you are about your country's treasures. I think that it is simply marvelous that a busy man in such a high position would spend his valuable time to work with me and my friends."

Mr. Parks's eyes rolled heavenward. Mr. Sadiq's "valuable time" was being spent because Mr. El-Hasiim had placed him in an "awkward position." That was as specific as their conversation had been the day before.

Hetty appeared to be very preoccupied with a flowering jasmine by the back entrance. She didn't want Mr. Sadiq to see the expression on her face. Johab never failed to surprise her. He had just made a flattering speech to the Council Chief, working on the man's already inflated ego, and managed to align the interests of the Chief with his, hers, and Mr. Parks—all in one tidy greeting.

"Harrumph." A strange, strangled sound came from Mr. Sadiq, whose face turned red, as though he suddenly had choked on something. He recovered quickly and patted Johab on the head. "Let's move on with this business."

The three of them trailed Mr. Sadiq and his aides into the back entrance. He motioned to the Police Chief to remain outside the entrance with his men. The quartet passed down a long hall of offices. The door to the office of Johab's father stood open, as though he had simply left to get a cup of coffee and would be returning any moment.

Hetty's hand on the back of his shoulders assured Johab that she was experiencing the same emotion as he was.

The door to Mr. El-Hasiim's office was closed. Mr. Sadiq rapped sharply on the door. Within seconds, Mr. El-Hasiim barked: "How many times do I have to tell you that I am not to be disturbed when my door is . . ." His voice choked to a sudden stop as Mr. Parks and Mr. Sadiq pushed the door open. Hetty's high-heeled shoe wedged in the door. She intended to participate, despite Mr. Sadiq's reluctance to include her.

Some of the employees clustered at the far end of the hall. They had seen the police cars. Usually, that meant some kind of break-in, but the Museum was open for business as usual. No police guarded the front of the building. This visit by the police and the Council Chief must mean something interesting.

Johab could hear Mr. El-Hasiim protesting and demanding in a loud voice that his uncle be called immediately. "This inquiry is a disgrace. You are not going through the regular channels. My uncle will have something to say about this."

Mr. Sadiq's voice was tense and authoritative, a voice accustomed to commanding. "Lower your voice unless you want every employee in the place to hear you. My aides have lists of items that we believe may have been taken from the storerooms. I am asking my staff to go with Miss Wenkle, Mr. Parks's colleague, to ascertain if these items are in the Museum." He gave a partial nod to Miss Wenkle, as though distancing her from his official business as "Mr. Parks's colleague."

She moved quickly down the hall with his two aides toward the basement. The staff would be only too happy to discover anything that would contribute to Mr. El-Hasiim's downfall. He was arrogant, rude, and ignorant—not a good combination of management attributes if one expected employees to be loyal.

Johab seemed to have been forgotten. He could edge into Mr. El-Hasiim's office and listen to the discussion, but it seemed rather technical—something about "inaccurate documentation" and "misplaced trust."

Mr. El-Hasiim's voice had taken on a distinct whimper. Sharp, little sounds like a rabbit with its foot caught in a snare punctuated the somber voices of Mr. Parks and Mr. Sadiq.

No. His time would be better spent exploring. Even if Barzoni were nowhere on the premises, perhaps he could discover other things. Most of the employees not involved with the business of tourists were clustered in small groups along the hallways, gossiping, wondering what could be happening down in the offices. A small boy in a galabeya wandering the halls was of no interest.

CHAPTER 70

Johab eased toward a nearby staircase and wondered if this staircase was the one where Mr. Barzoni had tried to push Hetty to her death. He backed against the metal railing, testing the floor with the toe of his sandal. Hard as granite. Escaping with a bump on her head and a broken finger had been a miracle. But then, Hetty was much stronger than she appeared.

An image flashed into his mind—Hetty's small hands knotted around the rope with Mr. Feisel's, dragging him out of that tomb in the desert. The Museum hallway before him seemed tomblike this morning, dark, silent, not a breath of air stirring at all. In such dark, cool places in the desert cobras hide, watchful, hoping for a small mouse.

Johab spied the cobra before it saw him. It had a human form, dressed in a black suit. Alert, cautious, its neck seemed to flare as it spotted a cluster of employees crossing at the end of the hall.

The snake's hooded eyes did not see the small boy moving toward it, just out of striking distance. "Mr. Barzoni!" The hiss of Johab's voice might have been the sound made by another cobra, angry that its dark den had been invaded.

Not a muscle twitched beneath the black suit. Only a slight movement of the neck betrayed that Mr. Barzoni had heard his name.

The black eyes, recessed over the beaked nose, widened only slightly, as though he might be trying to process information about why this child in a ragged robe would be standing in the private section of the Museum, calling his name.

Johab expected the careful smile beginning to play along Barzoni's mouth to suddenly gape open to expose giant fangs. He inched back against the iron railing of the stairwell.

The voice was low, cultivated, almost mesmerizing. "Am I supposed to know you, little boy?"

Johab didn't answer but pressed his back against the staircase railing. He needed to be balanced against any sudden attack. He glared at the snake that was disguised as a man. He'd rather think of Barzoni as a vulture, because the cobra was a valued creature in ancient Egypt, a symbol of kingship—and, tasty, people said, like chicken. But this cobra was deadly, one of those that flashed out of dark places with no warning.

Mr. Barzoni's expression changed. "I do believe I know you—John Bennett's son, I presume." He shifted his weight. Johab could see muscles rippling under the silken fabric of his suit, the way a snakeskin does with all that fury coiled into it.

"Do you want to talk to me about something? Is that why you keep staring at me?" The smile spread across his face, but his eyes remained hooded and deadly.

Johab dug into the pocket of his shorts under his galabeya, pulled out the two seals, placed them by his feet, and moved backward. "Those are royal seals, from a tomb in which you have considerable interest—I was your guest there." Johab spat out the words and pushed the seals closer to Mr. Barzoni with the toe of his sandal.

With a swift, unexpected movement, Mr. Barzoni bent over and picked up the two seals. He examined them, then smiled scornfully. "Seals with the cartouches of Senenmut and Hatshepsut. Isn't it wonderful what novelties these modern-day forgers make? Seals are so easy to reproduce."

"Not these. Not without an old seal as a model. The work on these is unique. I guess you don't know as much about Egyptian antiquities as you pretend to know." Johab's voice mimicked the scorn in Mr. Barzoni's voice.

"You need to come with me so that we can have a nice, civilized discussion about what you want—this way, we can go out through the main lobby." He reached for Johab, but Johab shrunk back from his hand. "No need to be nervous. There are lots of tourists there if you are scared of me. I think you are bluffing. If so, you are way in over your head, boy."

"You may be way over your head, Barzoni." Johab almost flinched at his own words. His mother would insist that he use a formal address to an older person, even if he were addressing the devil—which he was at this moment.

Johab pointed toward the end of the corridor. "You see all that commotion at the end of the hallway near Mr. El-Hasiim's office? Important people are here. Your business with him is finished. Everyone knows who you are and what you are. If you let my father go right now, things might not be so bad for you."

Johab's voice quavered with the mention of his father. That was a mistake. Cobras knew the weak spots, the eye of a rabbit, the throat of a fox.

The smile on Mr. Barzoni's face was one of triumph. "You are just a boy who has lost his father. You might have been able to see him if you had stayed put. You've been causing me trouble. I don't like to be inconvenienced." The pitch of his voice changed from a cynical, self-assured tone to an edgy screech.

Johab took a quick, confident breath. Now, he had spotted a weakness in the cobra—a nervous tic quivered just under Barzoni's left eye. Barzoni might be wondering just how much risk Mr. El-Hasiim posed. And his henchman was being questioned by Boris at Mr. Parks's villa.

"Your thug who kidnapped me is our captive." Johab's voice rose an octave, higher than Cyril's. "He's been talking like a trained parrot." *There. That was a good touch.*

Mr. Barzoni rearranged his face to one of mild interest, trying to repress his concerns. His former employee came well recommended for getting a job done quickly, if brutally. If he experienced the same treatment, how much would he reveal? How much did he know?

"The seals. Put them back on the floor. They don't belong to you." Johab's voice was well controlled. He surprised himself that he could be so calm. His calmness might have something to do with the fact that dozens of tourist voices, speaking different languages, wafted up the staircase. People were close if he needed to yell for help.

Johab knew that Barzoni didn't mind taking risks. He had pushed Hetty. He had arranged the kidnapping of Johab in broad daylight at a busy camel market. But things had not been going as planned. Johab had escaped. His man had been caught. And, now his associate, Mr. El-Hasiim, was creating a stir.

"Give me back my seals! Now!" Johab's voice echoed down the dark valley of the stairwell.

"These worthless things? You can buy them anyplace in the market." Holding the seals aloft, Mr. Barzoni might have thrown them at Johab, but he didn't. He placed them carefully on the floor and shoved them gently with the tip of a highly polished shoe toward Johab.

That was a dead give-away. If Barzoni truly believed they were fakes, he would have dropped them on the floor to shatter into a thousand pieces. Johab had spotted another weakness. Barzoni was not quite sure what Johab knew and didn't know. *It was time to strike again.*

"You don't know the source of the New Kingdom antiquities—the stolen ones you have been buying." Johab stared directly into those hooded eyes. He knew that a cobra could immobilize its victim by keeping it paralyzed by fear. That strategy could work both ways.

"If you release my father unharmed today, I might tell you something about where I found these seals." Trying to control his legs, Johab felt them trembling underneath the concealing folds of his robe. The cobra that he was facing was older, larger, and much more experienced in the ways of evil.

The hooded eyes blinked.

"I know you took my father. I saw you that night in our apartment. Your face is unforgettable—and I don't mean that in a nice way." Saying what he had been longing to say to this man ever since the night of his father's kidnapping stunned Johab into silence. *He had been incredibly disrespectful. It felt delicious.*

The angry flush that spread across Mr. Barzoni's face surprised Johab. Hetty and Sarah had described him as "oily," a man who thought he had great powers of persuasion with the ladies. Johab's comment about his face had clearly infuriated him. Johab locked his legs against the stair rail so tightly that the wrought iron cut into his skin. *Time for another strike.*

"If you release my father, I can tell you where I found these seals and many other fine things. I know things you don't know about ancient tombs," Johab's voice was determined, as he watched the greed rising in Barzoni's eyes.

Mr. Barzoni stared, wide-eyed, dumbstruck by this small boy who looked more Arab than American in his ragged galabeya. In the business of antiquities trading, he had never allowed his emotions to surface. Anger? Fright? He never let those feelings intrude into his business dealings. Yet, this small, fierce boy standing before him had managed to anger him—and a certain sense of unease was settling all around him. This was a child. John Bennett's child, but still just a child. Maybe the boy needed some reassurance.

"Did you ever consider that your father might be in business with me, that he went with me willingly that night? That the kidnapping was just a show for you and your mother? To get you out of his business?" The words coming out of Mr. Barzoni's mouth were thick, black as tar—oily, just as Hetty had described the man.

"You lie!" Johab's eyes blazed. He moved closer to Barzoni. The insult to his father had removed caution. He knew that Barzoni listened to what he said about knowing the source of the stolen items, and the seals had caught his attention. But, he needed more convincing. The faintest voice in his head said over and over: "Do it."

Johab planted his feet firmly on the stone floor, grasped both sides of the neck of his robe, and yanked it open.

The massive loops of gold, their intricate designs flashing in the dimly lit hall of the Museum, hung with splendor around Johab's neck. The large green jasper gleamed with an emerald hue, as though an internal fire lit the stone.

Not in all of his years of "trading" in antiquities, in the gold and silver and precious stones pilfered from the ancient worlds of Egypt, Syria, and other countries, had Barzoni seen anything so magnificent.

He took a tentative step toward Johab. This amulet was worth a king's ransom. More than that. Priceless. "Where did you . . ." Mr. Barzoni's voice failed. Emotion was not part of his business. A fortune hanging around a small boy's thin neck was.

Johab stood his ground. "It belongs to me. It is a gift from Queen Hatshepsut."

The look of incredulity that swept over Mr. Barzoni's face did not surprise Johab. Even his close friends and his mother doubted that a queen who had disappeared thousands of years earlier gave small boys expensive gifts.

Barzoni hooked a hand toward the amulet.

"Better not touch it. My Queen doesn't want you to touch her amulet."

Mr. Barzoni chuckled softly. "Your Queen? Where did you find this thing, boy? In what corner of that old tomb where I locked you?"

In an instant, Mr. Barzoni thrust out his hand, clamped it around the amulet, and gave a mighty tug.

Johab could hear the sizzling sound of meat frying before he smelled the odor of burning flesh and saw the expression of horror on Mr. Barzoni's face. The amulet felt strangely cool against Johab's chest.

Mr. Barzoni struggled to open his fist. His entire body writhed, as though thousands of volts of electricity coursed through him.

Those eyes locked into Johab's own eyes registered unimaginable pain.

Johab yanked back. Barzoni's hand fell away from the amulet, his fingertips blackening as shreds of crisp skin drifted off them to land in small, charred heaps of ash on the floor.

Barzoni's scream was one of unparalleled agony, echoing against the stone walls and floors of the Museum. The only answering sound from the tourists in the lobby below might have been a collective and uniform intake of breath from the shock of that unholy sound, the dreadful wail of a beast in torment.

Clutching his hand to his chest, Barzoni staggered toward the staircase, shrinking away from Johab as he rushed down the stairs.

Johab had many more things to say to him, but he didn't think Barzoni could hear them. He wondered if the Cairo hospital had a burn-care unit. He didn't think so. He was glad that he didn't bring the alabaster jar with the magic ointment. The Queen would not want any of her ointments shared with someone like Barzoni. Just look what she did when he touched her amulet without permission.

Johab stooped and picked up his two seals. He rearranged his amulet, pulled his robe high around his neck, and ambled casually back toward Mr. El-Hasiim's office. Two Museum guards thundered past him, in hot pursuit of the screamer.

Still shaky, Johab needed to appear nonchalant. He worked his way back down the hall, past the clusters of employees pointing excitedly down toward the main lobby of the Museum. He should find Mr. Parks and Hetty. He might save his story until he could elaborate on it a bit. Hetty would enjoy hearing about Barzoni's pain. She despised that man. Johab might suggest that she take some lilies to him in the hospital. She would appreciate the humor.

Johab's steps back were not quite as light as he pretended. He had wounded a vulture, but vultures were resilient creatures. They lived off the flesh of the dead. This one still had his father.

Johab tried to keep a sly smile off his face, because he had the magic. Barzoni with his charred and blackened hand would now recognize the power of that magic.

CHAPTER 71

May he come into port in the Sektet boat,
and may he cleave his path among
the never-resting stars in the heavens.

—Papyrus of Ani

On the way back to the villa, Johab sat quietly in the back seat of the jeep and listened to Mr. Parks and Hetty talking about the confrontation with Mr. El-Hasiim. Snippets of their conversation, such as "house arrest," "police guard around the clock," "his uncle's influence" peppered their discussion. It was clear that Mr. El-Hasiim had left the Museum under more than a cloud of suspicion. He was under police supervision.

"Johab, you didn't happen to see Mr. Barzoni around this morning?" Mr. Parks glanced in the rear view mirror at Johab. Johab didn't answer. "One of the guards said that a man who looked like Mr. Barzoni was seen running through the main lobby. He said that it must have been someone else, because the fellow was all bent over, acting weird. That was right after that unholy scream we all heard."

Mr. Parks turned toward Hetty. "The man knocked down three Japanese tourists who apologized for being in his way—and one large German tourist who whacked him over the head with her bag when he bumped into her." He glanced back at Johab. "Odd though. The guard was almost sure that it was Barzoni."

Johab grinned coyly at Mr. Parks in the mirror. He wasn't ready to talk about his meeting with Barzoni until he had a larger audience.

At the moment, Johab was thinking of something else, something he should have remembered when he was envisioning Barzoni as a cobra.

When he was younger, his father had read him a clever story by Mr. Kipling. The main character was a little mongoose named Rikki-Tikki-Tavi, who saved humans in his family by confronting and killing a deadly cobra. Cyril would love that story.

Thinking of the mongoose brought Johab his first sense of comfort in this nerve-wracking day. The mongoose was a member of the *Herpestinae* family—his father had him repeat that word over and over. His father said they made very nice pets. Now that his mother was accustomed to having Bastet in the house, maybe she would be receptive to a mongoose. They could use some protection against cobras.

Back at the villa, lunch was a festive occasion with trays of baklava, dripping with honey and peppered with nuts. Johab's mother didn't say a word as he and Cyril piled their plates with dessert first. They were celebrating the downfall of Mr. El-Hasiim.

Mr. El-Hasiim squealed like a trapped rabbit the minute that the authorities knocked on his door. Barzoni would be tougher. Johab remembered those hooded eyes, that mesmerizing voice. He might have seen Barzoni's throat flaring at the top of his starched collar, fangs descending through that sardonic smile.

"Johab, you look ill. You ate too much baklava." His mother felt of his forehead. "No fever. You've had too much excitement for today. Go lie down. Take Cyril. Tell him one of your stories."

Mr. Parks looked skeptical as Johab pushed back from the table, grabbed Cyril's arm, and disappeared into the library. Since leaving the Museum, Johab seemed disconnected from the morning's events involving Mr. El-Hasiim.

He made a show of being interested in what Mr. El-Hasiim had to say about the missing artifacts, but as though he were watching the actors in some old movie, already familiar with the script. And, Johab had purposefully *not* answered his question about whether he had seen Barzoni in the Museum. This boy was hiding something.

At dinner, he would ask the question again. Secrets were not healthy for little boys.

Everyone in the house seemed to be napping when Johab awoke. By telling Cyril Mr. Kipling's story about the mongoose and the cobra, he had hoped to take his own mind off that grisly expression on Barzoni's face. It hadn't worked. During Johab's nap, cobras writhed in dark places. The odor of burning flesh filled his nostrils.

Cyril's eyes popped open the moment that Johab rolled off the couch in the library. They tiptoed past Johab's mother and Hetty, dozing in chairs in the living room. Mr. Feisel was propped under the palm in the courtyard, maybe sleeping, maybe not.

Johab and Cyril edged close to him. "You boys are disturbing my nap. This better be good." Mr. Feisel growled softly.

"I need to ask you about magic, Mr. Feisel—do you believe in magic?"

"What kind of magic, boy? Pulling coins out of ears and sawing half-naked women apart? That kind of magic?" Mr. Feisel looked up at Johab's troubled face. Then, he pushed himself into an upright position against the palm.

"You mean *genuine* magic, the kind of magic that helped the ancient kings and queens join the gods and goddesses in the other world through the chants and spells."

Johab nodded. "Do you believe that those spells could really do bad things to their enemies?"

Mr. Feisel traced the pattern that had been made by the amulet along Johab's neck. "I believe in things that we cannot see and cannot know. I believe that we found you in that tomb because someone guided us there. A skeptical person might say that my friends from the village gave us the clue for finding the hole under the rock—or that a cat found you, and all we did was to haul you up."

Mr. Feisel pulled Johab against him. "Something else happened at the Museum today. I knew it the minute that you walked into the house—and it didn't have anything to do with Mr. El-Hasiim being arrested. Something happened to Barzoni, didn't it?" Johab's eyes widened, as he nodded.

"It was a terrible thing, Mr. Feisel. I wasn't even sorry to hear him scream. I was afraid, but not sorry." Johab looked distractedly out past the courtyard at Sekina munching her way through a new wafer of hay.

"You tell me, Johab, and your friend, Cyril, here. There is not much that we haven't seen in this world though I'm sorry to say that Cyril has seen the things he has. After we hear your story, we can talk about how much you want to tell the others."

Johab recounted the meeting with Mr. Barzoni, sparing no details. He would have reproduced the scream of pain if he knew how—and the look in those evil, hooded eyes.

Cyril's eyes were as round as saucers. This story was as good as Mr. Kipling's, except that there wasn't a mongoose. The burning of Barzoni's hand was a kind of justice, just what he deserved. Cyril patted Johab's shoulder. His major had done well—except that he had left his lieutenant at home.

"Your Queen was looking after you, Johab. You should feel no guilt. The Barzonis of this world have been robbing the tombs from the minute that the embalmers finished and the doors were sealed thousands of years ago." Mr. Fiesel's face darkened.

"Barzoni may walk through museums as though he owns them and have contacts in high places, but he is no different from the tomb robbers who drugged the ancient guards and tore apart the kings' coffins."

He scowled. "No. He is worse. He has created an organization to plunder treasures on a large scale. I'm surprised that your Queen didn't boil him in oil right there in front of all those tourists."

Johab was feeling vastly relieved, as though he might be able to tell the story to his mother, Hetty, and Mr. Parks. He thought he could even describe how Barzoni's fingers looked after touching the amulet. They resembled the unwrapped fingers of a mummy, dark with resin, the skin pinched tight against the bones. He felt much better.

"Let's go ride Sekina, Cyril. Yuya made her a kind of bridle. I wonder if she has ever been ridden, or just used to pull a cart?"

Mr. Feisel watched the boys slip through the fence and walk hand in hand toward the donkey. Johab's story about Barzoni was just as incredible as his story about Hatshepsut's gift of the amulet.

Mr. Feisel snorted loudly. People who refused to believe in magic, in the power of unseen things, in the old gods and goddesses, simply were not living an interesting life.

He gazed past the boys, struggling with a stubborn donkey, out into the desert far to the west. Thinking about the secrets in those vast spaces made him happy. Just look at this family that had come to his doorstep in the City of the Dead. They had brought many kinds of magic into his lonely life.

Dinner that evening was festive for everyone but the barbequed goat. Mr. Parks brought out a bottle of champagne and poured glasses for everyone, even though Mr. Fiesel swore that he never touched alcohol, and Johab's mother laughingly said only a "thimbleful." Mr. Parks chatted quietly at the end of the table with Mr. Feisel, who seemed a bit uneasy, then smiled broadly.

"We have some things to discuss, so I'll review what was settled at the Museum today." Johab thought that Mr. Parks often talked as though he were behind a podium. He was a commanding figure. People did listen to him.

"As a temporary measure, I have been appointed as Interim Director of the New Kingdom Project." Mr. Parks glanced apologetically at Johab and his mother. "By all rights, that job should be John's—and it will be when he is back with us."

Johab was comforted by that comment, as though his father was away at a conference and would be walking through the door at any moment.

"Mr. Feisel," Mr. Parks touched him lightly on the shoulder, "has agreed to head up the operations in the field to protect KV20. He is the ideal person to recruit villagers to protect the main entrance—and the one that the thieves have been using."

Miss Wenkle looked up, startled at this news. She was accustomed to Mr. Feisel's company. Who was going to teach her Arabic now that she really needed to know the language?

Mr. Parks intercepted her dismayed look. "Mr. Feisel will be spending considerable time in Cairo as well. He will meet at least weekly with other Project members. We are furnishing him a Jeep. He can stay here or we can find him a place in Cairo if he prefers."

A look of frustration passed across Mr. Parks's face. "This won't be as simple as I'm suggesting. The politics will be fierce when news breaks about the finds from KV20, especially since other organizations have been maintaining these old tombs. But, for now, I have the authority from the Chief of the Council to protect the tomb."

Mr. Parks nodded toward Johab's mother. "The most critical issue remaining is the safety of John's family and friends. Johab, your mother and I have decided that it is probably best for your family to stay here for now. We can move you to one wing of the villa so that you have more private space. Mr. Feisel's friends need to go back to their families, but Boris is always here, and I'm hiring two back-up guards. Boris will take you to school, Johab. You can see your cousin there—and your cousin and Rayya can visit your family here."

Johab noticed that Uncle Tarek was not mentioned in these arrangements.

"Barzoni is still at large. He has money and power. We know he has John, so we simply can't take any risks." Mr. Parks looked quizzically at Johab. "Anything you want to add to that?"

Johab took a deep breath, pushed back his chair, and pretended that he was at a lectern, facing a room full of disbelieving students—even though he knew that these faces belonged to his family and friends. "I did have a short . . . uh . . . *encounter* with Mr. Barzoni today. I saw him standing in the hallway, right beside the stairwell, and decided to confront him."

"Confront?" Johab's mother pressed both hands against her mouth. What kind of danger had her son deliberately courted?

Johab smiled, somewhat apologetically. "I needed to let him know that he can't keep Dad. I showed him a couple of things from the tomb to convince him that I knew where it was." He cast his eyes down. "I might have been setting myself up as bait, but I had to let him know that I have more information than my father does. I'm hoping that he'll release him."

"But he might come after you!" His mother's voice was shrill.

"I have Boris." Johab glanced outside at the tall figure, pacing the fence line.

"You have more than Boris. You have the protection of a very powerful Queen." Mr. Feisel bent toward Johab as though the wise councilor had given the prince permission to speak.

Johab drew a deep breath and paced himself through the story of his "encounter" with Barzoni.

Hetty was shaking so hard that she gripped the edge of the table to steady herself. Johab's mother sobbed quietly into her napkin, but her eyes blazed with pride when Johab described the beastly howl that Mr. Barzoni had let loose for the tourists to enjoy.

He modified the description of the blackened hand. Both Cyril and Mr. Feisel had enjoyed the comparison to a mummy's hand, but Mr. Feisel suggested that he "tone it down" for the ladies.

Hardly a person around the table could believe that an ancient, wizened, resin-soaked mummy—even one as mighty in her prime as Queen Hatshepsut—moved her coffins aside like so many stacked Russian dolls and came to the aid of a small boy in this world.

Hardly a person around the table could *not* believe that she came to the aid of Johab. His amulet, worn for this special occasion, flashed with a thousand golden lights. More than two hundred tourists and staff had heard Barzoni's scream of agony. The cleaning crew at the Museum scrubbed hard to get the small piles of ashes off the floor near the stairwell—the charred shapes of fingers remained on the polished stone floor like ancient fossils embedded in the marble.

Mr. Feisel was absolutely convinced. Johab had felt the touch of an ancient Queen, heard her voice, a Queen who trailed Amun-Ra on his journey across the desert sky every day. Would a short visit to a museum during the zenith of the sun be much out of her way?

"That is a very good story, Johab." Cyril's little voice piped up at the end of the table. His English was very careful, very precise. He was bursting with pride to be a lieutenant for someone of Johab's stature, someone who had been helped by an ancient queen. It made perfect sense to Cyril, who better understood the world when the globe was sectioned and flat as it was in Mr. Parks's geography book.

"I have another story." The soft voice of Miss Wenkle punctuated the lull in conversation when Johab finished. "I think that it is almost as miraculous as the story that Johab has told us, but I will need to know what the rest of you think, especially Cyril."

Cyril moved close to her. "I like stories, Miss Hetty. I like story with wood boy, Pinocchio, and mongoose, Rikki-Tikki-Tavi."

"Those are fiction, Cyril. My story is about real people."

Cyril looked confused.

"Johab, will you translate my story for Cyril?"

Johab moved to the other side of Cyril, listening intently to Hetty. Something more interesting than a story was about to happen. Mr. Feisel smiled encouragingly at Hetty.

In a tremulous voice, Hetty began her story, with Johab translating for Cyril. "This story takes place between two countries—my small green and foggy England, and my new home, described by the old kings as our red and black Egypt."

Johab nodded appreciatively. Hetty was setting the tone of the story by creating a sense of place, just as Mr. Kipling did.

"During World War II, the Germans invaded Egypt, and Britain sent many troops to curtail the spread of the German army. A young officer, who had never been outside of England before, was sent to Egypt near the end of the war."

"The war was terrible, but the young officer fell in love with the country." Hetty smiled. "His letters were full of descriptions of the desert at night—the vast oceans of sand and how out of nowhere a small, green oasis might appear. He said that we were spoiled living in such a green world as England—that we didn't know the color of green until we could see an oasis."

She speeded up her story. "This young man came back to England after the war, married his childhood sweetheart, and made a career in the army." Hetty glanced up, a sad expression crossing her face. "By the end of the war, his only living *blood* relative was a niece." She looked over at Cyril, making sure that he understood the word "blood."

Mr. Feisel grinned at her—he knew she was distancing Cyril's aunt from the family as she told her "story."

"A position opened at the British Embassy in Cairo, so this man and his wife moved there. They traveled back to London every year to see the niece, who had her own career but also had to take care of an ailing mother." Hetty reflected momentarily on the "ailing mother," but decided that chapter was not essential to the story.

"Because his wife was frail, this officer hired a young Egyptian couple to work for them and live in a house in their villa." Hetty paused for effect. "This young couple became more than their employees. They became cherished friends. When their first son was born, he was named for this British officer."

Up to this point in the story, Cyril was only half-alert. Stories about a war with no battles and the desert at night were boring compared to stories about a mongoose and a cobra. When Miss Hetty said "named for a British officer," Cyril snapped to attention.

"The Egyptian couple were expecting a second child when the officer's wife became very ill. Her husband took her to London to seek medical care. She lived only a few weeks after their arrival. Her husband grieved. He wanted to lie beside her in her grave."

Hetty looked out the window, blinking back tears. "I guess the fates were kind to him, because his wish was granted—within the year, he had joined her in the little cemetery, beside the church in which they were married."

Johab didn't think that the story was all that dramatic, but his mother had tears in her eyes to match those in Hetty's. Maybe the heartfelt telling of the story was the key. There were some things in it about this British officer and his wife that made Johab stare at Cyril.

Cyril had tucked his head into his chest. He was processing information. Johab used that style of thinking himself.

"Here's the part that might be the most interesting," Hetty announced. All of the faces turned towards her quizzically. "Before the officer died, he asked one thing of his niece—that she do everything in her power to find his Egyptian friends. He only had the address of his former home in Cairo that had been rented to another family when he left. He had received only one letter from his friends—the woman was nearing time for the birth of her second child. Her husband was planning to seek work around Karnak."

Hetty lowered her head, a faint wave of embarrassment passing across her face. "After her uncle's death, his niece hired someone through the Embassy to search for this couple, but the man said that they had left the old address with no trace. His niece has always regretted that she didn't come to Cairo immediately and try to find that young family. It weighs heavily on her conscience today."

Johab held up his hand for a pause while he tried to explain "conscience" in Arabic to Cyril, then nodded to Hetty.

Mr. Parks widened his eyes. For the first time, since the telling of this rather odd little story, he wondered why he hadn't made connections to Hetty. He had thought only of Cyril and Alice as children that Johab had rescued from the slums. That information had come from Johab's mother when they showed up at the City of the Dead one night with Johab.

Soya had taken them in without questioning why they both had English names. They were bright and polite children—but, a bit fearful around adults. They were no trouble out here at the villa, but Ian Parks wondered how his friend John would react to a family that had doubled in his absence.

As Hetty talked, a number of emotions crossed Mr. Feisel's face. Here was this English woman feeling an enormous weight of guilt because she had not been able to find her uncle's friends and their children. His lips pursed into a grim line. It should be the Egyptian people themselves who should feel guilt for not protecting their children. This woman—this Miss Wenkle, for all her bossy ways and those idiotic shoes she insisted upon wearing—was a very fine human being.

"Now, the miracles begin." Miss Wenkle had the attention of all around the table. "The niece had an opportunity to work in Cairo. Because her uncle had filled her imagination with the splendors of Egypt, she had the courage to leave her home and begin life in a new country."

She stared intently at Johab. "The story gets frightful here. An evil man kidnapped a boy's father. This boy and his family were good friends of this woman from London. The boy came to this woman and asked her to help him find his father—and he asked a small boy that he saw begging on a corner by the Khan to hold his donkey."

Both Cyril and Johab nodded enthusiastically. They knew these characters. This story was about them.

"We all know what happened from that day to the present in the search for this boy's father. What we couldn't be certain about was the identity of the small boy and his sister."

Cyril frowned at Miss Hetty as she used this odd word, "identity," that Johab was trying to translate. He knew exactly who he was and who Alice was. A glum expression passed over his face. He wasn't sure where they belonged.

"Mr. Feisel solved the problem of their identities." Hetty smiled appreciatively across the table. "He courageously went to the house of their aunt, not a *blood* aunt, to get valuable information. We owe a great deal to him."

Mr. Feisel flushed. Miss Wenkle was making too much of his involvement in solving this puzzle. Of course, that Mustafa might have come home while he was there with the aunt. That would have thickened the plot.

"And, the identities?" Mr. Parks thought the story was dragging on, and he didn't seem to have any role in it.

"Cyril and Alice are Cyril and Alice Abbaza, the children of my Uncle Cyril's friends," Hetty announced loudly.

Cyril looked at her with a strange expression on his face. If Miss Hetty had asked him, he could have told her their last name—and he could have told her that his father had worked for a kind English officer and his wife, and that Alice and he had been named for them. He wondered why Miss Hetty didn't ask if she were so interested.

"The first miracle was of Johab's doing—he found Cyril near the marketplace and recognized how helpful Cyril could be to him. Then, he helped Cyril rescue Alice from a very wicked man named Mustafa."

Cyril cringed visibly at the mention of Mustafa's name. Mustafa with his bloody thumb might be looking for him at this very moment. He glanced out the window to assure himself that Boris and the dogs were prowling the grounds.

"The second miracle is this letter." Miss Hetty took a carefully folded sheet of paper out of her pocket, smoothed out the folds, and handed it to Johab. "I am asking you to do the honors, Johab, to read this letter to Cyril and translate it so that everyone will know what this miracle means."

Not a dry eye appeared around the table as Johab read the letter. Even Boris who had crept through the open courtyard door sniffled quietly in the corner.

"But what does this mean for the children, for Cyril and Alice, since their father is no longer here?" Johab's mother was careful not to use a permanent word such as "dead." Those kinds of words were not allowed when talking about fathers.

Mr. Feisel interrupted before Miss Wenkle could respond. "I think that it means Miss Wenkle's uncle was given charge of the children if anything happened to their father. Her uncle left explicit directions in his will and on his deathbed for Miss Wenkle to take over that charge. I suspect any official in this country will observe the last wishes of these children's father."

Cyril had not taken his eyes off Miss Hetty's face while Johab read the letter. She seemed to have memorized it and was repeating the Arabic words softly as Johab read them. A gleam of recognition passed into his eyes. He announced in faltering English, but loudly, as though he wanted all of the world to know. "I be the boy in this story and Alice, the girl. Miss Hetty be that niece person." Cyril beamed around the room, happy that he had revealed the plot.

Mixed emotions followed Cyril's announcement. Johab's mother wondered what an unmarried woman, a spinster such as Hetty, would do with these children—besides, they had become like members of her own family.

Mr. Feisel simply emptied his mind of all concerns. The smile on Cyril's face contented him for the moment.

Mr. Parks folded his hands together, making "the little church, the little steeple," then stopped himself, wondering why that silly little child's game had intruded at this rather dramatic moment. It was a game that his own father had shown him so long ago—maybe even the most self-contained adults are reassured by good childhood memories. He stared at Cyril's thin face, his bony shoulders. Perhaps this small boy still had time for good memories.

Johab sat quietly, staring at the words on the letter in front of him. He had taken ownership of Cyril, after a fashion. He had enlisted him. And, he had helped rescue Alice. Didn't he have some say about what would happen to them? There was still that aunt and Mustafa out there.

Hetty watched the emotions register on Johab's face. This boy might be very good at facing down Barzoni, but his face was an open book of concern about his friend, Cyril.

"I would like to adopt Cyril and Alice, to have them live with me here in Cairo. That is my desire, and I think that my uncle would be in absolute agreement. But, at the end of the day, Cyril has to make that decision." Hetty looked directly at Johab, not at Cyril. "I don't think he will be able to decide without your help, Johab."

Johab whispered Hetty's words to Cyril. Cyril responded with a brief comment, so soft that no one but Johab could hear. Johab struggled with his emotions. Through all their adventures, Cyril had actually become a cousin, not just a word thrown out to Mrs. Zadi that morning in the City of the Dead to stop her questions. He felt closer to Cyril than he did to his real cousin, Mohammed. He trusted Cyril. He had trusted Cyril with his life.

The table was waiting for Johab to speak, their faces fearful that whatever came out of his mouth would shape the lives of everyone in ways that they could not as yet imagine.

The slyest of smiles crept around the corner of Johab's mouth. He looked sternly at Hetty and said in a booming voice. "Since Cyril is my cousin, I guess I will need to call you Aunt Hetty now!"

The desert sun cast its eerie night shadows over the land, with purple and rose streaks so beautiful that Queen Hatshepsut paused with Amun-Ra to observe her beloved land before returning to her small jeweled chamber in the tomb of everlasting.

The shouts and laughter and happy tears of her subjects in this little villa on the outskirts of this mighty city called Cairo might have brought a tear to her own eye, but kings never weep. Maat's feather of justice swept by her cheek like a fleeting kiss. John Horemheb Bennett would sleep safely tonight.

The End

MORE ADVENTURES OF JOHAB
COMING SOON

In *The Saint's Arm,* Johab continues to search for his kidnapped father in England.

Johab and his friend Cyril discover that the magic and miracles they found in Egypt surround them in the Tower of London and in an ancient Saxon church in the English countryside..

The missing "non-putrefying" arm of King Oswald that was wrapped in gold and stolen from Peterborough Cathedral holds the clue to a missing fortune in Egyptian antiquities that once belonged to Queen Hatshepsut.

Made in the USA
Monee, IL
02 January 2023